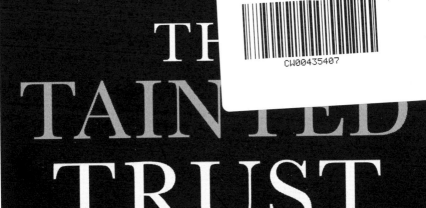

THE TAINTED TRUST

VOLUME TWO OF THE KING TRILOGY

A DOUGLASS CRIME AND ROMANCE THRILLER SERIES

STEPHEN DOUGLASS

1

THE TAINTED TRUST

VOLUME TWO
OF THE
KING TRILOGY

STEPHEN DOUGLASS

To Ann. A love that a man experiences only once in a lifetime.

CHAPTER 1

New York. April 23, 1980.

Louis Visconti was a happy man. Alone at his massive glass topped desk on the fifty-sixth floor of the south tower of The World Trade Center, he stared pensively in the direction of the windows, refusing to allow his steely grey eyes to focus on anything. He reflected on his considerable achievements. Thirty-three years of age, ten years out of Harvard Business School, and already a multimillionaire, he figured his income for the year would be between two and three million, his lofty projection based on annualizing outstanding results of the first half of the year.

His personal spending had increased in proportion to his considerable investment successes. With every reason to believe the cash flow would continue forever, there was no need to save. The cost of most anything he wanted was irrelevant. Image and profile were everything. When he threw a party, his only concern was how lavish he could make it. No expense was spared to make certain it was more ostentatious than any he had attended. There were women in his life, but only one of his relationships had ever reached critical mass, the price of love and commitment refusing to allow that threshold to be breached. Money was his real lover, possessions and power his consuming passions.

Finally realizing his dream of becoming one of the most important figures in New York's financial community, his picture had not only appeared in the Wall Street Journal and Barron's, but also in the financial sections of most important newspapers in the industrialized world. His brilliant and phenomenal investment record had become legendary. He was the man, in demand. Movers and shakers stumbled over one another to be and seen in his company. His schedule had become so tight that he was compelled to turn down numerous invitations to speak at luncheons, dinners and conventions in North America, Europe and Asia.

His brief experience with marriage was an unmitigated disaster, fortunately ending before wealth and children. He was strikingly handsome and extremely eligible, the only child of near penniless Italian immigrants who had fled to the United States in late 1946. He frequently boasted about the source of his survival instincts by claiming that both he and his mother had narrowly escaped death when she gave birth to him within minutes of her arrival at Ellis Island.

Blessed with a brilliant mind and fanatical ambition, he had scratched and clawed his way through public and high schools in Queens. Hustling, working and studying hard eventually earned him a near full ticket scholarship at Harvard Business School. His lucky break was to have been offered a full partnership with his two friends and former classmates, Jerry Mara and Allen Griesdorf. Seven years earlier, the three had taken an enormous gamble when they quit the relative security of their jobs as account executives with Green, Waltrum, a large and extremely prestigious Wall Street investment banking firm. With the horsepower of youthful courage and a boatload of borrowed money, they boldly formed their own company.

Mara, Griesdorf and Visconti grew quickly. The partners took a pass on ordinary money. They romanced and managed only wealthy money in a single investment fund. From the very beginning they had set an unrelenting minimum per account of five hundred thousand dollars. By investing the bulk of the fat portfolios in tangible assets during the highly inflationary seventies, they had enriched their clients and achieved personal success beyond their wildest dreams.

As word of the company's brilliant investment techniques and incredible track record spread, more clients came, anxious to receive the twenty-plus percent annual return others had enjoyed for five consecutive years. Now that the partners were managing over a billion dollars, the fund had become unwieldy. Closing it and refusing further entry was now well within the partners' contemplation.

Visconti displayed a lecherous smirk as he watched Susan, his secretary, a shapely twenty-eight year old brunette, enter his office.

"I have a call for you on line eight," she announced with a fetching smile, then placed a black coffee mug on Visconti's desk.

"Who is it?" Visconti asked, refusing to shift his grey eyes from Susan's tantalizing breasts.

"Alfred Schnieder. He's calling again from Caracas... You know him?"

Visconti nodded. "One of the old-time banking farts. Been around since Methuselah was a teen-ager."

"Want me to tell him you're busy?"

Visconti took a micro sip of his coffee, then shook his head. "Nope. I'll take it. Thanks for the coffee." He lifted his receiver, then forced a smile. "Alfred, thanks for calling. What's shaking?"

"I have clients for you."

Visconti tightened his lips and rolled his eyes skyward. "Don't do me any favors. I need more clients like I need another wife."

"But these are not ordinary clients."

"What makes them different?"

"Over three hundred million reasons."

Visconti bolted upright and immediately began to salivate. "How much?" he shouted.

"I believe you heard me the first time."

"Who are they? You said clients."

"I had the distinct impression you had no interest."

"Well suddenly I do. Who are they?"

"The ownership is quite complex. I'm compelled to tell you it's hot money."

"If it's In God We Trust, I don't give a shit what the temperature is."

Schnieder chuckled. "Am I to assume you're interested?"

8

"That's a gigantic understatement! Jesus, Alfred, who the hell are these people?"

"Shortly, you will receive a telephone call from a man named Mike King. He will arrange a meeting with you to determine your qualifications to manage that vast sum of money."

"Is he one of the clients?"

"Yes. His wife was married to the man who accumulated the money. Currently, it's under my care and control, but the wretched calendar never lies. Soon I will be too old to continue the responsibility. That is the primary reason I have referred you to Mike King. If he approves of you, I will make the necessary arrangements to transfer the responsibility to you."

"What's your fee?"

"One percent on the capital, and ten percent of real annual gains in excess of ten percent."

"Visconti completed a quick mental calculation and salivated more. He wondered however, why Schnieder had chosen him. "Why me, Alfred?" he asked.

"Elementary, my friend. You are the most qualified," Schnieder conceded, well aware of Visconti's larcenous tendencies.

"Cut the bullshit! What's in it for you? I know you're not doing this for the good of your health."

"As perceptive as ever, Louis... I want my retirement to be as comfortable as possible. If King gives you the job, I plan to give you the number of my bank account in Geneva. Then before we complete the transfer of responsibility, I will expect to see the balance increased by five million."

"I'm sure you will. Maybe you can tell me where the hell I'm going to get five big ones."

"From the trust, my friend. Your first assignment will be to arrange five million of transitional slippage. Of course it will have to be replaced with first proceeds... Do you understand what I'm saying?"

9

"Exquisite," Visconti declared, chuckling at the irony of Schnieder's proposition. Five million dollars would be removed from the trust during the transfer, wired to Schnieder's Swiss account, then replaced with future income in the trust. Subsequently, the accounting would be cooked to hide the removal. "You need me to help you to steal five million dollars of stolen money."

"Precisely, my friend. I prefer to think of it as an interest free loan, to be used for the balance of my useful life... I expect King will call you very soon. When he does, you must be prepared to romance him."

"I'll be ready. You can bank on it."

"Good pun... One final word of advice. Beware of interest rates. They are heading north."

"When and how far north?"

"Soon. Bankers are living in fear of Paul Volcker's intentions. They're convinced he's serious about killing inflation. They think he'll raise Prime to twenty percent, perhaps higher. With twelve percent inflation in the United States, you can draw your own conclusions. Real rates must climb well above historic norms to break inflationary psychology. You know that."

"Thanks again, Alfred. I'm gonna start liquidating. I'll talk to you soon."

CHAPTER 2

John Hill, head of the Criminal Investigation Division of the I.R.S., relaxed uncomfortably in his Washington, D.C. office on Constitution Avenue, his mind struggling with a multitude of trivial problems. The silence was rudely shattered by the shrill sound of his telephone. He lifted the receiver. "Hill," he barked.

The call was from Alex McDowell, Head of Canada's Security Intelligence Services in Ottawa. He and Hill had met as students at Dartmouth College in the early fifties, Hill at the outset of his career and McDowell, a retired R.A.F. pilot, as a mature student.

"To what do I owe the pleasure of your call?" Hill asked.

"Would you believe Jim Servito is dead?"

"You're kidding!"

"I kid you not. I just received a call from one of our External Affairs people. She told me he was killed in Venezuela. Evidently he kidnapped his son in Toronto and flew him to Caracas. King and Servito's wife followed them there to try to get the boy back. There was a messy confrontation and Servito ended up with the short stick."

"King killed him?"

"Nope. Servito's wife did. She messed up his face with a tire-iron and then pushed him over a railing into a three hundred foot canyon."

"Wow! Sounds like she really wanted him dead. How the hell did she and King get out of the country? I thought you had them locked up."

"They shocked us by posting a million dollar bail, then they disappeared. Both have refused to disclose how they did it, but we're amazed they were able to pull it off."

"Where are they now? You got someone on them?"

"Nope. We had to drop the charges. The Toronto Police got a full confession out of Jerrold Allison, one of Servito's slaves. He was involved in a nasty automobile accident in Toronto about two weeks ago. He told the police everything they wanted to know before he died in the hospital. His statement cleared our friends and implicated Servito in everything we thought we had on them."

"That's just fucking wonderful!" Hill bristled. "Everybody lives happily ever after and we get the shaft. Dammit, Alex! Servito stiffed us for hundreds of millions. Now tell me how the hell we're going to get it back."

"I can't, but we have a pretty good idea where it is."

"Where?"

"The Cayman Island branch of The Banco International Venezolano."

"Why am I not surprised? Have any of your people talked to anyone there?"

"Exercise in futility. Short of torture there's no way we can get tax haven bankers to tell us anything about client activities."

"So where do we go from here?"

"Several options. One is to put pressure on the Venezuelan government, and the other is to talk to King and Servito's wife. We think they know where Servito hid our money."

"You must be joking. They won't give you the time of day. In fact, I'll be shocked if they don't sue our asses."

"I wouldn't blame them if they did, but the Minister of Finance is breathing fire. He's ordered me to put a full-court press on this thing, and not to stop until we get every dime of that money back."

CHAPTER 3

Toronto. April 24, 1980. Ten A.M.

Mike King lifted a silver canister from the shiny surface of the large oval mahogany table in front of him. "Coffee?" he asked.

"Please," Karen Servito replied with muted disinterest, pushing her gold rimmed cup and saucer in Mike's direction.

The heavy oak twin doors to the ornate boardroom burst open and Dan Turner, nattily dressed in his usual grey pin striped legal uniform, appeared. "Welcome back," he bellowed with a warm smile, then hurried to kiss Karen's cheek and shake Mike's hand. He moved to the opposite side of the table, placed his black briefcase on the surface and took a seat. "Sorry I'm late. It's the telephone. It's become an appendage of my ear."

He leaned backward and clasped both hands behind his head. "I'm so happy for both of you. I had pretty well written you off when you left the country. I had recurring nightmares of your horrible demise in Venezuela."

"It nearly happened, Dan. If it hadn't been for a hell of a lot of luck, we wouldn't be here," Karen confirmed, then took her first sip of coffee.

"How does it feel to be free?" Turner asked.

"Wonderful," Mike replied with an enormous smile, "You start, Dan. My curiosity's killing me."

"I'll give you the highlights, then I want your story. I can't wait."

Mike nodded.

"Two days after you and Karen left for Venezuela, I received a call from a man named Alex McDowell, the head of Security Intelligence Services for the Feds. He advised that they've dropped all of the charges against you. After I climbed back onto my chair, I asked him for an explanation. He told me Jerry Allison lived long enough to confess everything. He confirmed everything you were trying to tell me."

"Incredible!" Mike exclaimed. "I was convinced he was dead when I left him in Servito's limousine."

"The police managed to pull him out and transport him to the hospital in one piece. His neck was broken and both of his legs were crushed. Miraculously he kept breathing long enough to give them a pretty good statement."

"Did McDowell ever apologize?" Karen asked.

Turner nodded. "He asked me to convey a sincere apology to both of you, and to express his deep regret any inconvenience the Fed's actions may have caused."

Mike gritted his teeth and pounded his fist on the table, his deep blue eyes exuding outrage and contempt. "Inconvenience!" he shouted. "Those actions nearly cost us our goddamned lives, Dan!"

"When an elephant walks, he's totally unaware of the insects he tramples."

"Do the insects have remedies?" Karen asked.

Turner spread his hands and turned his palms skyward. "You could sue, but I would strongly advise against it. You'd be locked into a protracted and expensive pissing contest. The Feds would defend themselves vigorously. They would insist that they acted entirely within the law, that they had probable cause, and that Jim Servito was entirely responsible for the damages you sustained. At best, you'd get a settlement, but it would be a Pyrrhic victory."

Mike turned to Karen and winked. Turner's assessment of the situation had vindicated his decision. He waited for her nod, then turned again to face Turner. "We've already settled with the Feds."

Turner glared at Mike. "You've done what! How?"

"I want it clearly understood that Karen and I continue to enjoy lawyer-client privilege," Mike insisted. "If there's any question about that..."

14

"Understood."

"Phillip led us to his father's money after I was released from the hospital in Caracas. Before he died, his father introduced him to Alfred Schnieder, a bank manager in Caracas, and instructed Schnieder to make Phillip his beneficiary. Phillip had Schnieder's business card in his wallet."

Turner leaned as far forward as he could, his deep set grey eyes fixed on Mike. "How much is it?" he asked.

"Somewhere north of three hundred million," Mike replied.

"Incredible!" Turner declared, his eyes bulging. "Does anyone else know this?"

"Alfred Schnieder, Karen, me... and now you. We told Phillip that we're returning it to the Feds. We don't want the money to corrupt him."

Turner squinted. "Surely you're not planning to keep it."

Mike nodded, his tightened lips displaying deep resolve. "An eye for an eye."

"Absolute insanity!" Turner protested. "As your attorney, I'm compelled to advise you in the strongest possible language. You must abandon this madness and return the money to its rightful owners. You can't imagine the trouble you'll be in if the Feds ever discover what you've done. They'll lock both of you up and throw away the key. No bail this time. You're both flight risks."

Mike shook his head and pointed a defiant finger at Turner. "All the king's horses and all the king's men aren't going to convince me to change my mind. What the Feds did was nothing short of atrocity. You can't imagine the anguish they've caused Karen and me. The money stays where it is. No negotiation."

Sensing Mike's determination, Turner re-directed his protest to Karen. "Can you knock some sense into this man's head?"

Even though Mike had displayed an uncharacteristic larcenous trait in making the decision to keep the money, Karen still had difficulty faulting

15

his logic or his motive. She too had suffered greatly at the hands of the Feds. "Sorry, Dan," she said, shaking her head. "I agree with Mike."

Turner shrugged his shoulders and raised both hands in surrender. "At least I tried. You can't say I didn't warn you." He smirked. "Off the record... I might be inclined to do the same thing if... That's not legal advice, just a private thought."

"I appreciate your candor, Dan," Mike said. "Karen and I want to thank you for sticking with us."

"My pleasure. You're the most exciting clients I've ever had... You have any plans for the money?"

Mike shook his head. "Only to make sure the Feds never see it again," he said.

Karen stood, walked around the table and kissed Turner on his forehead. "Mike and I are finally getting married."

Turner chuckled, his face reddened. "Congratulations. Where and when?"

"We'll send you a formal invitation as soon as we know."

"Wherever it is, I'll be there."

Turner stood and accompanied his clients to the elevator. "Good luck to both of you," he said. "I hope we never have to meet again under such unfavorable circumstances."

Karen waited until the elevator door had closed, then wrapped her arms around Mike's waist. Pressing her head against his chest she felt a sense of closure. At last she was completely free to be with the man she had never stopped loving. She lifted her head and kissed him hard. "I love you, Mike King. I love you from the bottom of my heart... Do you think we could ever make up for all the years we missed?" she asked, her lips barely grazing his.

Mike grinned. "We could have a hell of a lot of fun trying... When and where do you want to get hitched? Have you considered that?"

"You bet your cute butt I have! It's all I've done for the last eighteen years."

"Then let's do it, soon."

The two lovers proceeded toward the heavy glass doors leading to Bay Street, then Karen squeezed Mike's hand to get his attention. "I'm really worried," she said. "What the hell are we going to do with over three hundred million dollars of stolen money? What's going to happen to us if we're caught?"

Mike frowned. He was not sure what to do with Servito's millions. His only certainty was that he would rather die than turn it over to the Feds. "We won't get caught if it stays out of sight long enough. Schnieder will continue to manage it, we'll forget we even have it and let time take care of the details."

"Do you trust him?"

"I do, but I worry about his age. He's getting a little long in the tooth. He's sixty-four. He told me he was twenty-eight when he left Germany in nineteen forty-four."

"What if he dies?"

"He's covered that. He's picked a successor. His name is Louis Visconti. Alfred told me he's in his early thirties, brilliant, extremely capable, and very discrete. He lives in Connecticut, works in New York. With our permission, Alfred's prepared to bring him up to speed on the trust."

"Then five people will know about it."

"It has to happen eventually, Babe. Even if Schnieder lives, someone will have to replace him when he retires."

"Did he tell you anything more about Visconti?"

"Yup. He gave him a heavy duty testimonial and said he would trust him with his life."

"I think we should meet him first, and I don't think we should give Schnieder permission to tell him anything until we do."

17

"Definitely. I'm going to call Visconti and set up a meeting."

"Are you going to include me?"

Mike grinned and nodded. "Unless we both agree, without reservation, Visconti's out. Okay?"

"Deal," Karen replied, feeling only slightly more comfortable.

CHAPTER 4

Caracas. Friday, April 25, 1980.

A brilliant financier, Alfred Schnieder fled war torn Germany in early 1945, leaving behind all of his wealth, almost all of his teeth, and a dubious past. Arriving in Caracas, Venezuela without a cent to his name, he committed his remaining years to the banking business. He was acutely aware that by keeping his mouth shut and remaining religiously discrete with clients' money, he could live like a king in South America. And he did.

A gentle knock on his office door caused him to turn his bald head and raise his graying eyebrows. "Hold for a minute. Someone's at my door," he said into his gold plated telephone receiver, then placed it on his desk and hurried to the door. He opened it to see a very excited Manuel Blanco, his diminutive administrative assistant, about to knock again.

"Mister Schnieder, two people from the United States Internal Revenue Service are in my office," Blanco announced. "They have been very rude and have demanded to see you immediately. They have refused to tell me why they are here."

"Stall them for a minute, then show them in," Schnieder ordered, then returned to his desk to pick up the receiver. "Forgive the delay. I have visitors. I'll call you later."

Thirty seconds later, Blanco appeared at his door with the two I.R.S. agents. He politely ushered them in. "Mister Schnieder, these are the people from the Internal Revenue Service who want to see you."

Schnieder stood and nodded to Blanco. "Thank you, Manuel. You may leave now," he said, then turned to face his visitors with a confident smile displaying a glittering array of gold capped teeth.

One of the two I.R.S. agents, a short fat man with a white brush cut, removed his standard issue sunglasses, took several steps toward Schnieder's desk and removed a badge from his sweat-stained beige summer suit. He held it out for Schnieder to see while he introduced himself. "It was kind of you to see us, Mister Schnieder. My name is Charles Anderson." With a pompous sweep of his right arm, Anderson introduced his partner, a very attractive Mexican in her thirties, wearing dark sunglasses, a white blouse, beige cotton skirt and navy blue jacket. "This is Mary Sanchez. We're with the Criminal Investigations Division of the I.R.S., in Washington, D.C. We have a few questions."

In no way intimidated by his visitors, Schnieder had been subjected to similar interrogations numerous times in his long career. "I'm at your service... I must remind you however, if your questions relate to the activities of any of our clients, I am by no means obliged to answer." He winked at Anderson. "Besides, it would appear that you are considerably beyond the limits of your jurisdiction."

Shaken by Schnieder's response, Anderson took a deep breath. "We're very much aware of your banking laws, sir. And you're quite correct about our jurisdictional limits. It would be appreciated however, if you would try to cooperate with us. The government of the United States is attempting to recover a very large amount of money and Miss Sanchez and I have been directed to find it."

"What money?" Schnieder asked, aware his bank was home to the fruits of crime and flight capital of many clients. "Perhaps you could be more specific."

"Hundreds of millions of stolen gasoline tax dollars. We have reason to believe they've found their way into your bank... Several years ago, it came to our attention that a Canadian citizen by the name of James Servito might be involved in gasoline tax evasion. In addition to other things we did, we followed him all the way to your branch in Grand Cayman." Anderson riveted his green eyes on Schnieder's. "We did that too many times not to conclude that he was making very large deposits in your bank. Would you care to comment on that?"

"You know I can't do that," Schnieder replied.

"Let's cut to the chase, Mister Schnieder." Anderson said. "Our people have photographed Servito's wife and Mike King enter this building on several occasions. Did they visit you?"

"Yes."

"Why?"

"That's privileged information."

"Have they ever deposited any money in your bank?"

"None," Schnieder replied, aware that he had provided a truthful answer, in spite of the fact that he was not obliged to do so.

"Then if they didn't put money in your bank, what the hell were they doing here?"

Even though Schnieder knew he was not required to answer Anderson's question, he decided to deflect suspicion. "You appear to be an intelligent man, Mister Anderson. Did it ever occur to you that they too might be looking for Jim Servito's money?"

"Are you saying they are?"

"I'm not saying that. I merely asked you a question."

"Do you know where they are now?"

"No, but I will tell you that Mike King and the former Karen Servito are now husband and wife, and I believe they've gone somewhere to enjoy a honeymoon."

Obviously frustrated, Anderson pursed his lips, turned to Sanchez and shook his head. "Let's go. We're wasting our time," he hissed.

Schnieder stood and followed them to the door. "I'm very sorry I could not be of more help. If you care to leave a card, I'll call you if I learn anything which might help."

Anderson gave his card to Schnieder, then left with his partner.

Mary Sanchez stopped several feet outside the bank's front doors. "Hey Charlie," she said, then lit a cigarette. "Stay in the shade. Let's talk."

Anderson leaned against the building beside Sanchez.

"What did you think of our friendly banker?" Sanchez asked.

Anderson turned and spit on the pavement. "Fucking ice man. We could put that son of a bitch on a rack and still get nothing out of him."

"I think he knows a hell of a lot more than he's telling us, don't you?"

"No question. I bet my pension he knows exactly where Servito's money is, and he's giving it his personal attention."

CHAPTER 5

Mike's return to his office in North Toronto was a defining moment in his unique career. At last he was free to resume his duties as the president and owner of an extremely successful company. His staff stood and gave him a long, standing and loud ovation when he hobbled into the reception area on crutches. After spending more than an hour drinking champagne and telling them the details of his life-threatening excursion to Caracas, he proceeded to his office and immediately placed a call to Paul Conrad, the president of Golden National Oil Inc. Conrad liked Mike from the day they met. He saw a lot of himself in Mike. He had taken a chance on Mike years earlier by giving him a sweetheart gasoline contract. The generous credit terms gave him the financial horsepower to launch his business. The price escalation clause had later rewarded him beyond his wildest imagination. He waited patiently for Conrad's secretary to connect them.

"Congratulations, Mike," Conrad said. "I'm delighted to have you back in the saddle."

"How did you know?"

"Dan Turner called me this morning and told me the whole story. He's maintained close contact with me ever since you left the country... So what are you going to do for excitement now?"

Mike chuckled. "Watch the grass grow. I've had all the excitement I need for a long time."

"You might have that opportunity. You might even enjoy the luxury of boredom now that the business has settled down to a dull roar."

"In that connection, I want to thank you and Golden National for supplying my company in my absence. I appreciate that more than you could possibly know."

"It was nothing. We had the extra gasoline available. More importantly, we need people like you in the business."

"Thanks to you I'm still in it, and thanks to a fortunate break, I'm about to get married."

"Congratulations. Who's the lucky girl?"

"Her name is Karen. You don't know her but her former husband stole a hell of a lot of your company's gasoline."

"Well I'll be damned! Where did you meet her?"

"Long story. Karen and I go back a lot further than her husband and the gasoline business. For one reason and another it took us a lot longer to get together than it should have."

"Put me on the list. I wouldn't miss it. Will it be in Toronto?"

"I'm not sure, but we'll send you an invitation as soon as we pick a time and a place."

"I'll be there, wherever and whenever... By the way, did you ever find out what Servito did with all his money?"

Mike privately scolded himself for being unprepared for Conrad's question. Again he had cause to question his motives for keeping the fruit of Servito's crimes. Until now, his worst transgressions had been nothing more than white lies. Now he was a co-conspirator in a three hundred million dollar scam. The excitement of it intoxicated him. His compulsion to continue it worried him. He adjusted with a measured and oblique statement. "Sure we did. We also discovered the streets of Caracas are paved with gold."

"Please let me know if you hear anything. A chunk of that money belongs to Golden National."

"I will and I'll talk to you again soon," Mike said, then hung up. He lowered his head and pushed his fingers through his wavy blond hair. "I can't believe I'm doing this," he said aloud.

CHAPTER 6

New York. Friday, July 18, 1980.

Standing beside their bags and wearing faded jeans, T-shirts, and well worn sneakers, Mike and Karen King had just emerged from a cab near the entrance to the Plaza Hotel. Mike, tired and unshaven for twenty-four hours, paid the driver and hurried to the front door. He approached the portly doorman who was dressed neatly in an olive colored suit, long-coat, and matching top hat. "Excuse me. I'm looking for a man named Louis Visconti. Would you..."

"Are you Mister King?" the doorman interrupted with a broad smile.

Mike nodded.

"Mister Visconti's been expecting you. He's right in there," the doorman said, pointing to a man standing just inside the glass front doors. "He's the good looking young man in the beige suit. Will you be staying at the hotel this evening?" he asked, his arm raised to summon a bellboy.

Mike stuffed a ten dollar bill into the doorman's shirt pocket. "No. We'll be leaving after we have lunch with Mister Visconti. I would appreciate if you'd store our bags until then."

The doorman winked, smiled and nodded, then Mike and Karen proceeded to the lobby.

Visconti flashed his irresistible white smile and extended his right hand to Mike. "Hi. I'm Louis Visconti. I saw the doorman pointing to me and knew you had to be Mike King." He shifted his focus to Karen and was instantly captivated by her beauty. "Hello," he sang, his grey eyes penetrating her clothing.

"Louis, please meet my wife, Karen," Mike said with a disapproving scowl.

Visconti grasped Karen's hand with both of his own. "Pleasure to meet you, Karen," he said, then motioned toward the lobby with his left arm, his eyes still riveted on Karen. "I took the liberty of making reservations. Would you like to follow me?"

Mike and Karen followed Visconti through the lobby and into the ornate dining room. They stopped at a beautifully decorated and windowed alcove.

"I hope you like this. We can dine in comfort here," Visconti said, then pulled out a chair for Karen. "From what little information Alfred gave me about you, I assumed you would appreciate the privacy."

Karen liked Visconti's appearance and demeanor, but had difficulty determining why. Strangely, she felt attracted to him. The complete big city package, Visconti was slick, clean, sharp, and super suave. He exuded confidence.

A waiter materialized carrying menus. "Would you like to order lunch now, Mister Visconti? Or perhaps you would like to relax for a while with a beverage?"

Visconti turned to face his guests. "What's your pleasure?"

"White wine, please," Karen ordered.

Mike placed his hand on the waiter's forearm. "Bring us the whole bottle. We're celebrating."

"What are we celebrating?" Visconti asked, puzzled.

"Karen and I were married yesterday."

Visconti flashed another of his irresistible smiles. "Congratulations," he declared, then turned again to face the waiter. "Peter, bring us the best in the house, chilled."

The waiter nodded. "Just give me a few minutes, Mister Visconti," he said, then hurried from the table.

"So, you were married yesterday. Any plans for a honeymoon?" Visconti asked, then eased himself into the chair next to Karen's.

"When we're finished here, we're going to get lost in Europe for a while," Mike answered.

Visconti glanced at Mike, then at Karen. "I envy you guys," he said, displaying a perceptible expression of sadness. "I see happiness and anticipation in your eyes."

"Are you married, Louis?" Karen asked, unable to contain her curiosity.

Visconti frowned and shook his head. "Marriage and I didn't get along too well. I experimented with one and paid the price in misery. She was a wonderful girl, but couldn't cope with my life style."

"The fast lane in New York?" Karen asked.

"Not really. I wasn't born with a silver spoon in my mouth. We were practically broke when we were married. Most of the time we were living from hand to mouth. I hated that existence, and was so determined to dig us out of it, I worked ridiculous hours." Visconti shook his head and stared at the ceiling. "Unfortunately, she wanted a nine to five husband and it didn't take her long to realize she had the wrong guy."

"Any children?" Karen asked.

"No. Fortunately, we split soon enough."

"Would you consider marrying again?"

Visconti exhaled, then gave a delayed and barely perceptible nod. "Maybe later. Right now I don't think I could afford the time to devote to a marriage, or children."

"How old are you now?"

"Thirty-three."

"If you're thinking of ever having kids, you might want to get started sooner rather than later." As she spoke, Karen thought of her own plan to have Mike's child, at thirty-eight years of age.

Visconti accepted Karen's advice with diplomacy. "I understand what you're saying, Karen. By normal standards you're right. But what's normal these days?"

27

Mike, anxious to discuss more substantive issues, changed the subject. "Louis, in referring us to you, Alfred spoke very highly of you and your abilities. I respect his opinion, but I would still appreciate if you would explain to Karen and me why you think you're qualified to manage the trust."

Visconti was about to reply when the waiter returned. He remained silent while the waiter opened a bottle of Le Montrachet and filled three glasses. The waiter quickly replaced the cork, placed the bottle in a sterling silver ice bucket, then left.

Visconti smiled broadly and lifted his glass from the table. "Before I answer your question, I would like very much to propose a toast to both of you, your happiness, and the success of your marriage."

"Thank you, Louis," Mike responded, then all three clinked their glasses, one to the other.

"Now I'll answer your question... I'm qualified because, with a modicum of humility, I'm one of the best in the business. The statistics verify it. For the past five years, the people whose money I've managed have enjoyed better than twenty percent annual returns. Very few managers on the street can match that record. If it was just one or two years, one could suggest it was a fluke. But five consecutive years, no fluke."

"What assurances can you give us that those returns will continue?" Mike asked, unimpressed by the boastful and cocky tone of Visconti's response.

"None. I can't guarantee any returns. All I can guarantee is honesty, integrity, privacy, and a conservative prudent investment strategy. If you honor me with the responsibility of managing your money, I'll invest it as if it were my own."

"Where?' Mike asked.

"You mean where would I invest it?"

Mike nodded.

28

Visconti flashed a condescending smirk. "I could waste the rest of your day answering that one. The first thing we have to do is determine your objectives. Then I can give you a more definitive and satisfactory answer. Our analysts have identified a broad range of attractive investment vehicles, but I could narrow the range considerably if I had an understanding of your investment objectives and risk threshold."

"Preservation of the purchasing power of the funds must be the primary objective," Mike said.

"Am I correct in assuming the funds are inherited?" Visconti asked.

"We'd prefer not to disclose the source of the funds," Mike answered, a clear signal to Visconti to back off.

Mike's curt response jolted Visconti, but his youthful ambition refused to allow him to let the opportunity slip through his fingers. The implications of attracting a client with more than three hundred million dollars to Mara, Griesdorf and Visconti, were enormous. He parried. "Then if preservation of the purchasing power of the capital is your one and only objective, the job should be relatively easy. If I'm selected to do it, I promise I'll pursue that objective vigorously. The first question is whether I manage the trust, not what I do with it."

"I agree... We'll let you know after we talk to Alfred," Mike said, refusing to concede even the slightest measure of security to Visconti.

Disappointed, Visconti tried to smile. "What time did you say your flight is?"

"I didn't. It's four o'clock. Panam, out of Kennedy."

"Then let's order? I'll drive you out there after lunch."

CHAPTER 7

New York. Kennedy Airport.

Mike complied with the request of the cute Panam stewardess to fasten his seatbelt, then turned to Karen. "What did you think of Visconti?" he asked.

"I liked him. I think he'd do a good job, but something tells me you don't agree."

"I have reservations."

"That was obvious."

"I'm not sure what it was that bothered me. I just couldn't get comfortable with him. Maybe he was too smooth. Maybe it was just my paranoia."

"It must have been something he said or did that made you uncomfortable. Can you think of what it was?"

Mike tightened his lips and shook his head. "It's not that simple. I kept seeing a flashing red light, but I'm not sure why. It's been bugging me since we left the hotel... Okay, give me Karen's take on him."

"No reservations. He's smart, obviously very capable, and he has a very impressive track record."

"Wow! Did we have lunch with the same guy, or were you just blinded by his charm and good looks?"

Karen postponed her response to turn and stare out the window. She then directed an angry glare at Mike. "That's bullshit and you know it! Something's bothering you and I want to know what it is, right now," she demanded.

"I'm sorry. You didn't deserve that... I think Visconti's young and impulsive. He might do something stupid."

"Like what?"

"Like telling someone about us."

"He never has to know. All he knows is that the money was inherited, and that the trust is in place for the future. Why can't we just leave it at that?"

"That would be great but I don't know how much Alfred's told him. If he's told him more, we've got a problem. That's one of the reasons I didn't want to give him a commitment at lunch. Also, I wanted to talk to you first."

Karen's frown melted to a broad grin. "I love you, King. I can't begin to tell you how refreshing it is to hear that from my husband. The previous one never consulted with me on anything."

Mike reached into the right pocket of his jeans and removed a gold ring adorned with a cluster of seven diamonds, the two in the center dwarfing the others. "This is a little late, but it's from the heart, and it's forever," he declared, then lifted Karen's left hand and placed the ring beside her wedding band on her third finger.

Ritz Carlton. Paris, France.

Reminded of the first time he and Karen had showered together in Santo Domingo, Mike applied soap to every square inch of her body, then methodically removed it with the spray from the shower head and his hand. When Karen returned the favor, Mike once again found it impossible to wait until they got to bed. Shower sex was imperative.

Afterwards, Karen stared lovingly into his deep blue eyes. "There's a wild steak in me that tells me we should never go back," she said, still panting.

31

"Where's that coming from?" Mike asked, surprised by Karen's declaration.

"I don't know. I just want to disappear into obscurity, and stay there."

"Do you have any idea where obscurity is?"

"Buying a villa in Monte Carlo and living happily ever after. Phillip could finish his education in a private school in Switzerland."

Mike exhaled, then rested his chin on Karen's shoulder and closed his eyes. "I would be lying to you if I told you that kind of obscurity isn't appealing, but I don't think we would live happily ever after."

"Why?"

"We're still in the Feds' crosshairs. A ton of their money is still missing and you know they suspect we know where it is. If we did what you're suggesting, they'd be all over us like a tent."

"They can suspect all they want," Karen scoffed. "As long as we keep our mouths shut, what can they do?"

"Harass the hell out of us... They're missing over three hundred million dollars!"

"Screw the Feds, King! Will you at least think about living happily ever after?"

Mike frowned and shook his head. "This isn't you, Babe. It's so uncharacteristic of you to talk this way. What happened to that responsible girl I once knew?"

"You're such a great lover, you make me lose my head," Karen teased with an impish grin. "Now tell me why you still want to keep the money. I'm amazed. I still can't believe you would do such a thing. It isn't you."

"I'm amazed too," Mike conceded. "I guess I'm more larcenous than either of us ever imagined."

"That's my point. You've really confused me. It would be far easier to understand if you intended to keep the money for yourself, but by just hiding it in a trust you're taking all the risk while you don't stand to gain a thing."

"You would understand if you knew how pissed I am. The Feds really messed with my head. If I live forever I'll never forget when those bastards marched into my office like Nazis and ruined my life without an ounce of remorse. They didn't give a shit about us. They were covering their over-paid political asses. Then when they realized they couldn't touch your husband, they arrested us and put us in jail without any consideration for the damage it would do to our lives, and to the lives of people who depend on us."

"I understand that, but does the money mean anything to you?"

"Not really. I have no intention of ever spending it."

"Then why did you... ?"

"It's a statement," Mike interrupted. "Keeping it helped to even the score. It gave me closure. Maybe we'll use it to some real good in this world, anonymously. It wouldn't be too difficult to find a charity that beats the hell out of paying bloated salaries to too many civil servants and politicians who waste too much money on too many useless programs... It's also a hell of an exciting caper."

Karen placed her hands firmly against Mike's buttocks and pressed him against her body. "You're exciting, King," she said, grazing his lips with hers. "You're body gives me a far bigger rush than the caper."

CHAPTER 8

Almost an hour later, Mike telephoned Alfred Schnieder from his hotel room.

"And what did you and Karen think of Louis Visconti?" Schnieder asked, struggling to mask his anxiety.

"We were impressed. It's not hard to understand why you recommended him."

Relieved, Schnieder leaned backward and flashed a golden smile. "Any negatives?"

"How much did you tell him, Alfred? How much information did you give him about the trust, its history and its current owner?"

Schnieder spun the stem of his glass between his index finger and thumb, staring at his swirling brandy. "I must remind you that many years ago, when I came to Venezuela from Germany, I learned very quickly that secrecy is of paramount importance in the banking business. I learned that if one wants to survive in the business, one must be discrete with his clients and their holdings."

"Never mind the crap, Alfred. What did you tell him?"

"I merely told Louis that you would be contacting him to arrange a meeting, and that the purpose of the meeting was to determine his suitability to manage the trust. I swear to you, Mike. I will go to my grave with your secret. Please rest assured that unless and until I am instructed to disclose any further information, my lips will remain sealed."

"I was afraid you'd told him more, and I needed to be certain. I want the memory of that money to die a natural death, Alfred. Only time and absolute secrecy are going to kill it."

34

"Mike, I must remind you that it is my intention to retire in August. On the fifteenth of that particular month, I will have completed my sixty-fifth year on this planet. Have you made a decision with respect to Louis Visconti? I must insist on an answer."

"Karen made her decision in New York, but I needed to talk to you before I made mine. It's absolutely crucial to me to know that our secret stays with you... Visconti's our man."

"Splendid!" Schnieder shouted, again flashing most of his gold teeth, thrilled that his net worth had suddenly escalated by five million dollars. "Would you like me to tell Louis the good news, or would you prefer the pleasure?"

"You do it, Alfred. Karen and I have officially started our honeymoon... Exactly how much money is in the trust?"

"It's quite difficult to give you a precise answer to that question at any specific point. The value is constantly fluctuating. Conservatively, however, I estimate it's current value to be close to its value when you left Caracas: three hundred and twenty-five million," Schnieder said, deliberately shorting the actual value by five million.

"Thank you for everything, Alfred. Your personal attention to our little secret is very much appreciated."

"The pleasure is all mine. I wish you, Karen and Phillip much happiness."

CHAPTER 9

New York. Saturday, July 19, 1980.

"Good of you to call, Alfred. What's happening?" Visconti asked, close to bursting with anticipation.

"Congratulations, I just received a telephone call from your new clients."

"Are you telling me what I think you're telling me?"

"As soon as the paperwork is completed, you will assume the management of the King's trust. I assume it will have an appreciable impact on your bottom line. It is conservatively valued at three hundred and thirty million."

"Fantastic! Alfred, you're incredible!" Visconti shouted.

"Competent perhaps, but never incredible. Allow me to remind you that before the transfer is completed, five million must find its way into my account in Geneva. My lawyer will call you this afternoon to give you the details."

"Why can't you just do it yourself? You have..."

Schnieder interrupted. "Too much of a risk at this late stage in my career. Banks are terribly bureaucratic organizations, my young friend. An internal audit of the transaction would quickly reveal my indiscretion. Furthermore, while brandy helps me to make it through my days and nights, I don't believe they serve brandy in prison."

"No problem," Visconti conceded, now on his feet and pacing back and forth, pondering the implications of managing the gigantic trust and calculating the huge increase in his income it would bring. "We'll bury the shrink here in no time," he promised.

"There are several things of which you should be aware, Louis. They are crucial to the success of your relationship with the Kings."

"Shoot."

"The fact that they have anything to do with the money must remain a tightly guarded secret. They assume I have told you very little about them, the trust, and the source of the money. They assume all you know is that the money was inherited. I strongly suggest you do everything necessary to preserve that assumption."

"That shouldn't be difficult. Where did it really come from?"

"It actually was inherited. Jim Servito, a long time client of mine and former husband of Karen, accumulated most of it by forgetting to pay taxes on a very large quantity of gasoline. You can be certain that the governments of both Canada and the United States would dearly love to recover it."

"Incredible! I thought we had some pretty heavy tax evaders here in the Big Apple. Servito makes them all look like penny-ante pikers."

"That may be so, but with one major difference... It is very likely that those penny-ante pikers are still alive."

"Good point. Do you have any idea what possessed the Kings to keep the money?"

"I can only speculate. I understand the Feds treated them very shabbily. Personally, I don't blame them for keeping it. In similar circumstances, I would be inclined to do the same thing."

"To keep three hundred large? That's a no brainer. It would take me a microsecond to make the decision. I would keep it and spend the rest of my life swinging from the trees... How did Servito die?"

"His wife killed him. She pushed him over a cliff."

"Nasty lady. I'd better be careful with her."

"You had better be careful with both. They are extremely shrewd."

37

CHAPTER 10

August 14, 1980.

Louis Visconti had a banner day. All of the documentation was now properly executed, the blue cornered indentures safely in place in his firm's fire-proof safe, and he was now officially responsible for the management of the funds in the King's trust. The implications for Visconti's firm were enormous. Annual management fees would increase by orders of magnitude. If the funds were invested to yield a return anywhere close to those generated by the firm in the past five years, the fees would be stratospheric.

He worried about the intentions of Paul Volcker, Chairman of the Federal Reserve. Schnieder had told him that interest rates were going up, soon. If Schnieder's prediction was correct, the immediate future of investments in stocks and tangible assets was extremely bleak. He had to move fast. He commenced a program of liquidating stocks, investments in real estate, and other tangible assets. He planned to short bonds and ride the interest rate wave to the top. He would wait for the inevitable crash, then plunge again into stocks.

The plan gave Visconti an uneasy feeling, however. In March of that year, interest rates had peaked at sixteen percent and had been dropping ever since. Conventional wisdom continued to suggest the Fed was stimulating the economy and that interest rates would continue to drop, but his respect for Schnieder's opinion allowed him to overcome his concerns. Schnieder had been correct too many times for Visconti to ignore his counsel. With prime rates at eleven percent and fear and trepidation in his heart, he pressed ahead with his plan. To him, preserving the trust's purchasing power as Mike had requested was a joke. Maximizing his fees was the name of the game.

38

CHAPTER 11

Toronto. August 15, 1980.

Rain drenched Mike and Karen's plane as it touched down at Toronto's Pearson International Airport at two in the afternoon. Following the usual agonizing and prolonged delay, the result of too many travellers and too few officers, they cleared customs and took a taxi to Karen's penthouse apartment on Avenue Road.

Martha Perkins, Phillip's aging and overweight nanny, rushed to greet them when she heard the front doors open and the sound of their happy voices. Her gray work dress complemented her swept back gray hair which ended in a tight bun. "Welcome back, you two," she said with a gigantic and wrinkled smile. "How was the honeymoon?"

Karen, happy to be home and to see the woman who had stayed with her through extremely difficult times, dropped her bags and hugged her. "Fabulous! Just fabulous! How are you, Martha?"

Martha closed her eyes and exhaled. "A bit frazzled, but I survived."

Karen frowned and took a step backward. "Is everything okay?"

"Everything except Phillip... He's been a big problem. Ever since you brought him home from Venezuela, he's been different. He's not the same happy boy I remembered. He's become very difficult to control. He used to do everything I asked without question. Now he refuses do just about everything."

Mike turned to Karen. "Have you ever been away from him for this length of time?" he asked.

Karen shook her head. "This is the first."

"It could be that he misses the attention you've been giving him," Mike suggested.

Karen hoped Mike was right, but deep in her heart she knew the problem was probably much more complex. "I feel guilty about leaving him, but I'm worried that it's related to Venezuela. I think the whole thing has finally caught up with him. I can't imagine what damage that experience must have done to him."

Mike turned to Martha. "Is there anything else we should know?"

Martha stared at Mike with a pained expression. "He's been stealing, taking money from my purse. I haven't confronted him about it yet, because I thought it would be better if I waited to talk to you first."

Karen reached for Mike's hand. "We've got to talk to him. This is serious."

Martha picked up Phillip at Royal Canada College, less than a mile away, and returned to the apartment forty-five minutes later. His face, still rounded by baby fat, showed hints of the chiseled features of his late father. Instead of smiling and running to hug his mother as he had done so many times in the past, he stood and glared at Mike and Karen with what appeared to be anger in his large gray eyes.

Karen ran to hug him. "I missed you so much," she said.

Phillip remained motionless, his arms passively limp.

Karen pulled backward to probe his eyes. "Did you miss me?"

Phillip gave his mother a vapid stare, then looked away. "I guess," he said.

"Something's bothering you," Karen accused. "What is it?"

"Nothing's bothering me," Phillip hissed, then bolted from her arms and ran in the direction of his room.

Karen began to follow, but Mike stopped her. "Don't go. He expects you to do that. Give him some time to cool."

"But I missed him so much," Karen protested.

"If you rush in there right now, you'll just reinforce his negative demand for attention. Wait for ten or fifteen minutes. Give him some time to think about it."

Karen waited for ten anxious minutes, then hurried to Phillip's room. She found him lying on his bed, pretending to read a Superman comic book. "Let's talk," she said, slowly removing the book from his hands. "It's pretty difficult to do it through a book."

His eyes, unblinking and appearing mesmerized, continued to stare at the space previously occupied by the book. His expression displayed unconsolable depression, one Karen had never seen.

"Something's bothering you, son. I want to know what it is," Karen demanded.

Phillip wiped his eyes with the back of his right hand then slowly focused on his mother. "Why did you tell the newspapers about dad?" he asked.

"I didn't tell the newspapers anything," Karen replied, shocked by his question. "What ever gave you the idea I did?"

"Now all my friends know about dad and everything he did."

Karen's worst fears had suddenly been realized. She kissed his forehead. "I'm sorry the newspapers published the story. If I could have stopped them, I would. You must understand that we wanted more than anything to keep the whole story a secret."

"If you didn't tell them, who did?"

"I have no idea... What have your friends said about it."

Phillip's eyes resumed their unblinking stare. "They keep saying my father was a crook. I hate them."

Karen wrapped her arms behind her son's back and hugged him. She closed her eyes and prayed he would soon forget his father and the ugliness of the incident in Caracas, but worried that the experience had engraved a permanent psychological scar in his memory. She hoped the theft of Martha's money was merely a manifestation of his frustration. "You have to be stronger than them. They're just silly little boys who don't have enough sense to understand that you should never be punished for the sins of your father." She remained with him for more than an hour in an effort to give him the feeling of security and assurance she knew he needed.

She returned to the living room and found Mike reading a newspaper on the couch. "I know what's bothering him," she said, then waited until Mike put the newspaper down. "We have a major problem and it isn't going to go away soon. The story of his father appeared in the newspapers. He assumed we leaked it."

Mike frowned and shook his head. "We should have anticipated it. I don't blame the kid a bit."

"I haven't the slightest idea how to handle it. What are we going to do?"

"I have a suggestion."

"What?"

"If you and I are going to have a family, Phillip should be part it. I would like to adopt him."

"That's a wonderful suggestion," Karen declared with a grateful smile. "I can't imagine a better one." She sat beside him and hugged. "Each day I know you, the more I love you."

"I'm not finished."

"Then keep going, King. You're on a roll."

"A whole new environment might improve his attitude. I think we should send him to a boarding school."

CHAPTER 12

New York. October 24, 1980.

In accordance with Alfred Schnieder's prediction, and to the enormous relief of Louis Visconti, interest rates began to tick northward. Until that point, conflicting newspaper articles and numerous mixed signals had constantly plagued Visconti's mind and caused him to sweat his decision to liquidate investments in stocks. Newspapers and financial publications had been filled with stories about Paul Volcker, the second most powerful man in the United States. Volumes had been written about his preoccupation with inflationary psychology and his failure to break it. Throughout the summer, optimists and bond bulls had confidently predicted a rapid decline in rates and a return to better times. Visconti had stayed the course and now had more than fifty percent of King's trust committed to short sales of corporate and government bonds. He stood to lose a fortune if Schnieder was wrong.

Toronto. October 31, 1980.

Mike shook his head as he stared at Karen's dinner plate. "Babe, you haven't touched your filet. Aren't you hungry?"

Karen grinned as she stared at the uneaten meat. "I can't eat another molecule. I stuffed myself at lunch today." She changed the subject. "Tell me about your daughter. You never talk about her."

"What do you want to know?"

"Everything. The only thing I know is that you have one. Where is she now? Have you communicated with her since you and Barbara split?"

"Often, particularly after Barbara moved to San Diego. Aside from the distance and time involved in continuing my visitation privileges, Barbara began to make things difficult for me."

"How?"

"Whenever I phoned and told her I wanted to see Kerri, she invented an excuse. It didn't matter what I said, the visit was always inconvenient for her. I think she wanted me to cease and desist, and her new husband to become a surrogate father to Kerri."

"Did you continue to write?"

"Every week, until my letters started to be returned, unopened." Again Mike shook his head, tears flooding his eyes. He looked away. "That broke my heart. She was nine years old when I last saw her. I considered hiring a lawyer, but didn't. I reasoned that it didn't matter what I did, there was absolutely no way I could ever be a father to her. I saw myself as a meddling sentimental fool who moved in and out of her life. So I decided to stay out of it. It was the hardest thing I've ever done. It hurt, and it's still hurting."

"She'll find you," Karen predicted. "Her need to know you will eventually consume her."

Mike displayed a worried frown and looked away. "I wish I could share your optimism," he said, then changed the subject. "Would you like some wine?"

"No thanks."

With bottle in hand, Mike dropped his lower jaw. "I don't believe it. I can't remember the last time you refused red wine. Are you ill?"

Karen's face and smile glowed in the soft candlelight. "We're pregnant, King. No more booze for the duration."

"That's incredible news!" Mike said with gigantic smile and beaming with pride. He placed the bottle on the table, then hurried to her side. He leaned and kissed her, long and passionately. After the kiss he stared into her dark brown eyes. "A toast. Join me with a glass of milk."

"Milk makes me sick, but I'll join you with water and extreme pleasure."

Mike filled Karen's wine glass with water, then raised his glass. "To the newest member of the King family," he said as they clinked their glasses. "How long have you known?"

"I've suspected it for three weeks. The doctor confirmed it today. She said we're both very healthy, and there's no reason to believe we can't have a normal healthy baby, sometime next August... She strongly recommended amniocentesis."

"What's that?"

"It's a test, particularly for women over thirty-five. They stick a long needle into the womb and draw out a sample of amniotic fluid. They test the fluid for Down's Syndrome and other genetic abnormalities. While they're at it, they determine the sex of the child."

Mike smiled, attempting to hide his worry. "So we're going to know?"

"If you're referring to the sex of the child, they won't tell you unless you ask. Any preference?"

"I think I would like to have a boy or a girl," Mike said, privately hoping it would be a girl.

"I   like   your   chances,   King."

CHAPTER 13

Toronto. December 12, 1980. Ten A.M.

Mike jerked the telephone receiver to his ear.

"It's William Dare, Mr. King. I'm sure you remember me."

"What can I do for you?" Mike snarled. Even though he was in no mood to talk to Dare, he was curious to know why he had called. Pangs of anger, paranoia and anxiety coursed through his blood stream.

"I would like to arrange to meet with you and your wife as soon as possible. Of course it would be at a time and place convenient to both of you. I'd like to ask some questions about Karen's former husband and his financial affairs. I'm hoping you might be able to help us to recover the considerable amount of money he stole from our government."

A powerful rage invaded Mike's mind as he vividly recalled the search and seizure operation conducted by Dare and his C.S.I.S. agents in his office. "I think a meeting would be wasting your time and ours. Under the circumstances, I think you should direct your questions to our attorney. Would you like his number?"

"Is Dan Turner still your lawyer?"

"Yes."

"We have his number on file. Thank you very much."

CHAPTER 14

New York. Friday, August, 21, 1981.

Gerry Mara, Visconti's partner, was genetically structured for Wall Street, and he dressed for the roll. He wore a svelte black pin striped suit, neatly pressed blue shirt, yellow silk tie and suspenders, and black Gucci loafers. His long black hair was slicked straight back, exposing his cerebral temples. He butted his cigarette, popped two champagne corks, then displayed a proud smile as he mounted an elevated wooden platform erected for the occasion. He raised both bottles above his head. "May I have your attention, please?" he shouted.

The loud conversations of staff members and account executives ended. A hushed silence ensued.

"A little over a year ago, Louis Visconti succeeded in landing the biggest account in the history of our firm. With courage and steadfast conviction, he defied popular market opinion by liquidating most of the stock positions of the portfolios he managed, then shorted government and corporate bonds. Those brilliant moves have generated astounding returns, and made us all absurdly rich... A toast is in order." He smirked at Visconti. "To the Crown Prince of Wall Street... May his brilliance and clairvoyance live on, and continue to keep us all in the style to which we have become accustomed."

Mara's toast was followed by the clinking of glasses, loud cheers, whistles, and warm applause from the entire office staff. "Speak to us, Louis," he demanded.

The cheering, whistles and hoots intensified as Visconti slowly mounted the platform. He sipped his champagne, flashed a triumphant smile, then took a deep bow. When he moved his lips close to the microphone, his audience hushed, anxious to listen to anything he had to say. "Thank you very much for your kind words, Gerry. Coming from you, it is indeed an honor. I also want to thank all of you for your support and capable assistance during these trying times. I deeply appreciate it... I'm really not sure if what I accomplished in the past year was the result of brilliance, clairvoyance, or just plain luck. Whatever it was, I hope it continues forever. In any event, I will try to wear the crown with pride and humility."

Again a loud applause erupted.

Allan Griesdorf, the genius of the three partners, overweight, bald and a PhD in math from M.I.T., stood. "Predictions, Louis?" he shouted.

As if in deep thought, Visconti gazed at the ceiling, then surveyed the crowd. He was where he wanted to be, admired, respected, on top. For him, the feeling was better than sex. He was surfing the crest of a huge wave of good fortune, one he fully believed was entirely the result of his divine intelligence, unique talent and insight only few possessed. "It's time to cover the bond shorts," he pontificated. "Interest rates have peaked, but the stock market's still going south." He smiled and waved regally as he stepped from the stage. He was on a high. The buzz of numerous hushed conversations fed his ego, excited him to know that each was diagnosing his advice.

Visconti followed his own advice by covering his bond shorts and going long. As interest rates plummeted, the value of the bonds increased enormously. So too did Visconti's income, the fortunes of his firm, and the value   of   the   King's   trust.

CHAPTER 15

Toronto. Saturday, August 26, 1981.

Joy and happiness was the mood in a private room on the fourth floor of Toronto's North York General Hospital. Almost twenty years after their first fateful meeting, Mike and Karen had consolidated their marriage with a love child. A smiling nurse delivered Kevin King, an eight pound seven ounce baby boy, to his proud parents.

"He's absolutely beautiful," Karen said with a broad but strained smile. "Almost as beautiful as his father."

"He doesn't look like me at all," Mike protested.

"Bullshit, King! Maybe he doesn't have your beautiful thatch of blond hair or as many straight teeth, but he's a dead ringer for you."

With tears of joy in his eyes, Mike sat on the bed beside his wife. The birth had filled a void. For a very long time the loss of Kerri from his life had been an unhealed wound. "Thanks, Babe," he said, then kissed her lips. "Thank you from the bottom of my heart. This is the happiest day of my life."

New York. Thursday, December 31, 1981.

Pride urging him to boast about the extraordinary success of his investments, Visconti dialed Mike King's office number in Toronto. "I'm sorry to bother you Mike but I couldn't resist calling. I have fantastic news."

"What is it?"

"The value of your trust now exceeds four hundred and fifteen million."

"That's wonderful. This is the last time I'm going to tell you this. If you ever call me again and mention one word about the trust, you're fired. Is that understood?" Mike barked, then quickly hung up.

Humiliated, Visconti swallowed his pride and had the annual report on the trust mailed to Mike's postal box in Toronto.

CHAPTER 16

Toronto. Wednesday, June 30, 1982.

Now fourteen, Phillip's cheeks and chin sported peach fuzz and pimples, trophies of the transition into manhood. To give him spending money and to keep him out of shopping malls, Mike had given him a summer job with his company, XG Petroleums. His responsibility was to pump gasoline at one of XG's serviced retail outlets in Scarborough, a Toronto suburb.

Three days after Phillip started to work, Mike received a telephone call from his very excited manager. "Mister King, it's Terry Morgan. Sorry to bother you. I just had to call. Your son was supposed to be here at seven this morning. He's still not here. I'm going to have to call someone else."

Mike glanced at his watch. It was nine fifteen. "I'm glad you called, Terry. Go ahead and get a replacement, but call me if Phillip shows up."

"I hope you weren't talking about Phillip," Karen said as she entered the room.

"Unfortunately we were," Mike replied with a disappointed frown. "He was a no-show this morning. The second he shows up here, we're going to have a nice little chat, and this time I'll take the gloves off. I'm going to get through to that kid, one way or another."

Mike approached Phillip when he returned to the apartment at six P. M. "Hard day at work?" he asked.

Using his foot to remove his shoes while they were still tied, Phillip nodded. "Yup," he said, deliberately avoiding eye contact.

Mike placed his hands on his hips and glared at Phillip. "What did you work at? Terry Morgan called at nine-fifteen this morning. He said you weren't there."

51

"I was late."

"I asked him to call me when you showed up. He didn't call. Now don't lie to me again. Where were you today?"

Phillip hung his head. "Hangin' out with my friends," he admitted.

"Where?"

"At the mall, mostly."

Mike struggled to restrain his anger. He knew venting it would help him, but not Phillip. "Put your shoes back on," he demanded. "You and I are going for a walk."

Annoyed, Phillip wiggled both feet into his shoes, then reluctantly followed Mike to the sidewalk.

"Let's go," Mike said, then turned and began to walk at a brisk pace. Phillip was forced to trot to keep up. When he did catch up, Mike began to run and continued to run until Phillip stumbled and fell to the pavement, exhausted and unable to run further. "What's the problem, son?" Mike chided. "Can't keep up with an old man?"

Phillip's face was beet red and contorted with anger and frustration as he jumped to his feet and continued to run. Mike quickly outdistanced him, but when he noticed Phillip had quit the race, he turned and hurried back. "I wanted you to run this little race for a reason," he said, placing his hands on Phillip's shoulders. "I want you to understand that you're living in a very competitive world. If you don't prepare yourself to compete in it, you'll never make it. I have to assume you want to be more than a shiftless mall-rat." Mike turned and walked away.

"I promise I'll work," Phillip shouted when Mike had distanced himself by fifty feet.

"Talk's cheep, son. Show me," Mike said, continuing his walk.

Phillip nodded. "But I really don't like school."

Mike stopped and turned to face Phillip, encouraged that he might be making some progress. "I didn't like it either, until I discovered the more I put into it, the more I got out of it. So far you've put very little into it. It's no wonder you don't like it."

CHAPTER 17

Aurora, Ontario. Six months later.

Mike sat at one end of the long mahogany table in the center of the St. Edwards School staff-room, adjacent to the headmaster's office. He had arranged through the school's secretary to have Phillip excused from class and sent to the staff room. The door opened and Phillip entered. Sloppily dressed in a navy blue blazer, white shirt, blue and yellow school tie, and gray flannel trousers, he shuffled to the far end of the table, then slumped in a chair, his face contorted to express his annoyance. He said nothing.

"I bet you're wondering why I'm here," Mike said, leaning forward and glaring at his adopted son.

Phillip looked away and slumped further in his chair. "I know why you're here," he muttered, as if bored. "The secretary told me. It's because my marks aren't very good."

"That's only one of the reasons. I want to know why you're misbehaving. Is it because you're unhappy here?"

Phillip reached for the heavy cut-glass ashtray in front of him and began to twirl it on the surface of the table with his index finger. He said nothing, avoided eye contact.

Mike waited patiently for an answer, then stood. "I guess you're too important for this school. I'm going to make arrangements to have you removed. Then you can decide what you're going to do with the rest of your life."

"I'll try to do better," Phillip said, his voice barely audible.

"That's not good enough!" Mike shouted. "You will do better and there will be no more meetings like this! Is that understood?"

Phillip nodded in silence.

54

"Dammit, Phillip! Give me more than a casual nod. Convince me you're serious. I'm at the end of my rope with you, son. If I don't see positive results, and soon, I'm going to pull you out of this school so fast it'll make your head spin."

Phillip sat erect and stared directly at Mike, his eyes glazed with contempt. "Okay, I promise I'll work harder."

CHAPTER 18

New York. Friday, April 17, 1987.

The flashing green light on Visconti's telephone console indicated his secretary was calling. He pressed the speaker-button. "Yes, Sue."

"Mister Raza's here. Would you like me to show him in?"

"Give me sixty seconds," he requested, then terminated the call. He was about to entertain Assif Raza, an extremely wealthy investor from Kuwait City. Visconti hurried to the full length mirror behind the door to his lavish private washroom, anxious to ensure that every aspect of his appearance was perfect. He stared at perfection: the three thousand dollar dark blue suit, the yellow silk tie, the custom made black Italian leather shoes, the fifty dollar haircut, the complete package.

A gentle knock on Visconti's office door was a signal for him to return to his office and stand in the center of the expensive multicolored Persian rug adorning the floor. "Come," he commanded.

Sue entered with Visconti's visitor. Smiling and with graceful and professional hand movements, she performed the introduction. "Mister Raza, please meet Louis Visconti."

Visconti displayed his triple-A commercial smile, then stepped forward and used both hands to clasp the extended hand of his visitor. "Very pleased to meet you, Assif. Welcome to New York and to my office."

"A pleasure to be here and to meet you, Louis," Raza replied, stone faced. Raza, a fine featured but plump Kuwaiti wearing a black suit and tie, appeared to be in his mid-forties. His skin was light brown, his black hair thinning on top and graying slightly on the sides of his head. His brown eyes were beady, his nose hawkish.

Visconti gave a barely perceptible nod to Sue, giving her the cue to leave.

"I'll leave you two alone, now," Sue said. "Please call if you need anything." She turned and left the office, closing the door behind her.

Visconti pointed to two large green leather covered couches near the windowed corner of his office. They faced each other and were separated by an elegant glass topped coffee-table. "Assif, please join me over there. We can talk in comfort."

When they had moved to the couches and were seated facing each other, Visconti leaned forward. "Would you like something to drink, Assif? Coffee maybe?"

Raza crossed his legs and relaxed against the back of the couch. "No thank you. I've just finished a rather large breakfast."

"Then perhaps we can discuss business. I'm sure you're a very busy man and would rather not waste time with small talk."

Raza nodded.

"You mentioned a large amount of money in our telephone conversation." Visconti prompted, then stared at his guest, anxiously anticipating a positive response, hoping his approach would not be considered too bold.

Raza smirked. "I like that," he said, holding his hands in front of his chin and placing the tips of his fingers against one another. "You Americans don't beat around the bush."

Relieved, Visconti leaned backward and relaxed. "Thank you. That's exactly what I wanted to hear. Maybe you could begin by telling me what I can do for you."

"Certainly. I represent a group of wealthy Kuwaiti investors. I am one of them. Having my own skin in the game creates a higher level of comfort among the members. The group has given me a mandate to diversify, both in terms of investment vehicles and geographic allocation."

"Is there a specific reason for the decision to diversify in that fashion?"

Raza nodded. "There's growing concern among my clients over the level of unrest in the Middle East. Consequently, they would like to move as much money as possible out of the area and place it in safer, more politically hospitable havens. As you know, the United States falls nicely into that category."

"I'm curious to know why you called me."

"The news of your investment success is well known, Mister Visconti. In addition, a mutual friend has recommended you."

"And who might that be?"

"Alfred Schnieder."

Visconti grinned. "So once again I'm indebted to Alfred. How is he?"

"Alive and well and living in Zurich. He sends his very best wishes."

"Please convey mine to him... Assif, you mentioned unrest in the Middle East. What, specifically is concerning your clients?"

"It's no secret the area is a tinderbox. A match could be lit at the wrong time or in the wrong place, and start a fire which would burn for a long time and prove very difficult to extinguish. Additionally, we worry that oil may not continue to be the goose which lays golden eggs."

"That sounds absurd. Everyone knows that Kuwait is virtually floating on an ocean of oil."

"That's precisely the problem. Too much oil is chasing too few customers. Everyone is overproducing in an effort to capture incremental revenue. Most of the producing countries are desperate for cash, and are pushing as much oil into the market as they can. Much more than it will accept. The consequences of that are painfully obvious to us. With the conservation ethic taking hold throughout the world, we can no longer count on the phenomenal growth in demand we once considered our birthright."

"If the consequences are obvious to you, why aren't they obvious to the whole world?"

"Good question. Most people overestimate the strength of OPEC. Believe it or not, even the most successful cartel in the history of the world has vulnerabilities. Its greatest is weakness of demand, or stupid greed. I'm not sure which."

"Then what consequences are obvious to you?" Visconti asked, thoroughly fascinated by Raza's story, thrilled to be entertaining an insider in one of the largest and most lucrative trading markets in the world.

"The price of oil is too high. It must come down. We fully expect it will drop a long way, soon."

"How far?"

"To five dollars a barrel. Perhaps further."

"That's absolutely incredible! It's over twenty-two right now."

"Correct. Perhaps now you can see why I'm here, and why my clients would like to diversify their investments. Even though they are perfectly aware the world will continue to use oil for generations to come, they would like to ensure that there is life beyond it. They wish to preserve their wealth and incomes by investing in areas and assets which are less sensitive to oil prices."

"If you're so sure the price of oil's going to crash, why don't you short it?"

"Some of my partners have already done so, however anything they've done in that connection is on a small and very discrete scale. Shorting the price of a commodity which has been their lifeblood for generations, is totally alien to them, tantamount to treason. More importantly, they're prudent and very conservative people. They're not looking for, nor interested in high risk, fast dollar schemes."

Visconti sensed the time was right. He sat upright and locked his deep set gray eyes on those of his visitor. "How may I help you?" he asked.

"I would like you to handle our investments in the United States. If you agree, we'll start on a small scale. As time and circumstances permit, we'll increase our commitment."

59

"How small?" Visconti asked, struggling to hide his disappointment. Small was not the word he had expected Raza to use.

Raza gave Visconti a barely perceptible smirk. "Would a hundred million be too small?'

"No sir," Visconti answered, stunned by Raza's overture. "I think we can work with that," he said, sensing a mild erection.

"Fine. Then let's discuss your fees and the other arrangements."

While they talked about fees, investment criteria, banking and reporting procedures, Visconti had difficulty containing his excitement. In addition to the acquisition of another extremely large client, once again he had been privy to inside information. Raza had told him the price of crude oil was about to drop to five dollars a barrel, soon. He remembered the last time he had been given inside information, and how much he had profited from it. Seven years earlier, Alfred Schnieder's warning about the direction of interest rates had proven to be correct. He mentally calculated the enormous profits involved in a sizable crude oil short sale. If the price dropped from twenty-two dollars a barrel to five, the reward would be gigantic.

CHAPTER 19

Within seconds of Raza's departure, Visconti telephoned Miles Dennis, a friend and senior account executive with Iacardi & Sons, Commodity Brokers.

Dennis, a fifty-three year old high school dropout, had defied the odds in the financial world. He had not only succeeded beyond his wildest dreams, he had been instrumental to the continued success of Iacardi & Sons. Hired in 1947 as an office boy, he began to study the commodities business by night and any free moment he could steal. He was promoted to floor trader in 1951. In 1960, he became an account executive. With street smarts, an infectious personality and a wonderful sales ability, he had established himself as the number one producer in the company. "Why would the Crown Prince of Wall Street be calling a peasant like me?" Dennis asked. "Is he seeking new worlds to conquer?"

"Cut the bull-shit, Miles," Visconti retorted. "This is a business call. I need to know what your research people think of the price of crude oil. Where's it going?"

"Probably nowhere exciting. Why are you asking?"

"I just had a meeting with a big hitter from Kuwait. He told me crude oil was about to go south, big time. His name is Assif Raza. You ever heard of him?"

"I certainly have. He's one of the founding fathers of Q8."

"What's Q8?"

"The Kuwaiti national oil company."

"So he's for real?"

"That's putting it mildly... How far south?"

"He thinks it's going to five bucks. Maybe lower. He's prepared to put a ton of money where his mouth is."

"He's shorting crude?"

"No. He's diversifying out of it."

"So why are you calling me?"

"I want to short crude."

"Why does that not surprise me? How high do you want to fly?"

"A thousand July contracts."

"At the market?"

"Sure. Let's not quibble over nickels and dimes."

July 31, 1987.

Primarily as a result of Visconti's astute stock picks, the value of the King's trust had grown by astounding proportions, now exceeding eight hundred million dollars. Save and except for the money used for the margin deposit on the crude oil short, every nickel of the trust was committed to the purchase of stocks.

Visconti was once again a big winner when the spot price of West Texas Intermediate crude oil dropped to seventeen dollars and ten cents a barrel. The thousand July contracts he had shorted at twenty-two dollars and fifteen cents, now showed a paper profit of slightly over four million. The most spectacular aspect of the transaction was the return on his original investment. He had come close to doubling the margin deposit in the space of three months. As an encore, Visconti promptly shorted a thousand October contracts at seventeen dollars and twenty-five cents a barrel.

CHAPTER 20

A large and persistent low pressure cell over the Atlantic Ocean continued to pump cold damp air into the city. Dense gray clouds had enveloped the area and an on and off drizzle had enhanced the atmosphere for five consecutive days.

Visconti shifted his position to stare at the now cold coffee on his desk. Depressed, and tired of the relentless constancy of his life and his business, he needed a change, to be out of touch, unavailable, to go away. It didn't matter where, his only stipulation was that the destination had to be devoid of telephones and any other modern communication device.

That evening he left his office without advising anyone of his destination, or the identity of his companion. He merely told his partners of his desperate need for a break, and that he would return on Tuesday of the following week.

He and Marilyn Daring, a young and well painted blond bimbette he had recently charmed and romanced at a chic Manhattan piano bar, boarded a chartered executive Lear at La Guardia Airport. "She's short on gray matter but she has a body that never stops," he had recently said, bragging about his conquest to Jerry Mara.

Visconti smirked as he buckled his seat belt, satisfied that he was about to disappear, and at long last experience freedom from the merciless invasion of telephones, television and newspapers.

The jet whisked the two to Puerto Rico. From there, a yellow twin-Otter carried them to Anegada Island in the British Virgins, where they planned to spend four relaxing days at an expensive, yet primitive hotel.

The timing of Visconti's brief sabbatical could not have been worse.

CHAPTER 21

New York. Friday, October 16, 1987.

The following day's record plunge of 108.35 points in the Dow Jones industrial average on the New York Exchange served as a clear warning to investors. Something was terribly wrong. The stock market dive could have been compared to a loud tremor in advance of a violent financial earthquake.

Panic swept financial markets on the following Monday. Stock trading activity was frantic and emotional. The swiftness and magnitude of the decline was staggering. Widespread panic selling steadily gained momentum with each passing hour. The activity tested the technical capacity of the New York Exchange. The ticker was more than one hundred points behind actual trading activity for much of the day. Traders were ordered to remain on the floor of the exchange until transactions were completed.

The capital implosion was far worse than that recorded during the massive stock market crash of 1929 that ushered in the Great Depression. Fortunes were lost in a matter of hours as the New York Stock Exchange suffered a gut-wrenching collapse.

The sudden financial meltdown resurrected fears that the global economy was about to slide into recession. It more than wiped out the gains made on the New York Exchange, the financial heartbeat of the United States, since April 7, 1986. In percentage terms, it was an incredible disaster, almost double the mark of twelve point nine percent, recorded on October 29, 1929.

The Dow Jones industrial average, the most widely watched measure of share values on Wall Street, lost over five hundred points, a precipitous drop of over twenty-two percent. It closed at 1,738.41. By the end of the day, more than six hundred and four million shares had changed hands. The previous record daily volume of three hundred and thirty-eight million shares, achieved the previous Friday, was smashed by midday, as investors liquidated their holdings and fled the market.

The scene at the posh and lavishly decorated offices of Mara, Griesdorf and Visconti was a recreation of an ugly image from October 29, 1929. Wealthy investors clustered around in stunned silence, staring in disbelief at the electronic ticker tape giving the latest bad news from the floor of the New York Exchange, blocks away.

From the moment the market had started its plunge on Friday, Mara's staff had been frantically trying to reach Visconti, or someone who knew where he was, without success. Visconti's partners worried that he was enjoying his holiday, unaware of the unfolding financial nightmare. He alone had the power to deal with and trade the stocks in the fat portfolios he managed. Without Visconti, all of them were naked to the ravages of the market. They desperately needed attention. With each passing hour his portfolios were losing enormous amounts of money.

Jerry Mara, a tense and excitable individual, took a long and deep drag of his Marlboro while staring at the moving electronic tape with glazed eyes. "Where the hell are you, Louis?" he muttered, deeply worried, not only about the failure of Visconti to liquidate stocks, but also the implications of that failure for the reputation of the partnership.

The King's trust, by far the largest and most exposed, was poised to take the largest hit. With divine premeditation, and in flagrant violation of Mike King's directive, Visconti had maxed the trust's risk, loading it with numerous highly volatile stocks of small to medium sized companies. Unless he returned to liquidate those investments, the losses and consequent fallout would be horrendous.

CHAPTER 22

Black Monday, October 19, 1987. 7:30 P.M.

Shortly after Visconti's chartered Lear 55C landed at La Guardia, he deposited Marylin Daring in a taxi, prepaid the driver and sent her home. He climbed into a black airport limousine and told the driver to take him to his Fifth Avenue apartment. Heavy traffic brought the limousine to a complete stop when the driver attempted to cross the East River on the Queensboro Bridge.

After a painful wait of more than ten minutes, the driver smiled at Visconti and broke a prolonged silence. "Guess the bridges of New York will be gettin' a pretty good workout tonight, sir."

Confused by the statement, Visconti faked a smile. "I'm sorry. I don't understand."

"A whole lotta people will be using the bridges to end it all. That's for sure."

Visconti's smile evaporated. "Why?" he asked, nerves twanging.

"You haven't heard?" the driver asked, wide eyed. "The market. It took a big hit today. Real big."

"How big?"

"Over five hundred points."

Visconti's heart pounded wildly. "No!" he groaned.

"Yah, they're talkin' about this thing makin' twenty-nine look like a small correction... Were you in the market?"

"You could say that," Visconti muttered, beads of sweat bathing his forehead. "Take me to the World Trade Center, South Tower, as fast as you can get there?" he ordered, then turned to stare at the water below.

Shocked and stunned by the news he had just heard, he trembled involuntarily and pondered the implications.

Entering his office ninety minutes later, Visconti switched on the lights, then hurried to his computer.

His worst fears unfolded before his eyes as he scrolled through the day's closing market data on his monitor. He wondered how the Crown Prince of Wall Street could possibly explain his incompetence. He was fully invested in high risk volatile stocks, totally exposed and completely out of touch when the disaster struck. The only conclusion anyone could reach was that he had been careless, stupid and irresponsible.

His first priority was to quantify the damage. He began with the King's trust, by far the most exposed. When the figures appeared on his screen, they exceeded his worst expectations. Even though he knew the computer never lied, he checked and rechecked the data. The computer continued to give him the same horrifying results. While he was recklessly cavorting with a meaningless bimbo in the Bahamas, the King's trust had sustained a paper loss of almost a half a billion dollars.

At the close of business on Monday, October 19, 1987, the value of the trust had dropped to three hundred and thirty-two million dollars, very close to its value on July 12, 1980, the day Visconti assumed its management. So, after more than seven years of management of the trust, The Crown Prince of Wall Street had managed zero growth.

He stood and walked to his window. While he stared blankly at his pale reflection, the horrible reality of the disaster attacked him. The coincidence was outrageous. The first time in years he had chosen a weekend sanctuary from the constancy of stress, the market had simultaneously taken a dive of historic proportions.

When he shifted his focus to the lights of the city below, his thoughts were of the following day, and what further horrors it would bring. The optimism with which he had viewed the financial world had been abruptly crushed. Suddenly he had been reduced to a mere mortal, vulnerable to

67

loss. The great Louis Visconti had experienced his first failure, his self-esteem mortally wounded.

Shaken and trembling, he returned to his computer to review the remainder of the funds he managed. Fortunately, none had been so exposed as the King's trust. As he reached to key in the access code of another portfolio, he glanced at his monitor. One particular item caught his attention. In sharp contrast to all other items in the King's trust, the October crude oil short position miraculously showed a profit.

Visconti keyed in the closing commodity prices on the Nymex. The spot price of West Texas Intermediate had dropped to sixteen dollars and fifty-five cents a barrel. Again he was reminded of his conversation with Assif Raza. He rubbed his face and covered his eyes with his hands. "Were you right about that, Assif?" he asked aloud. There had to be a reason for the market to have sustained such a terrible loss. Maybe the economy was heading into a deep recession, or depression. If it was, demand for commodities would slow and demand for crude oil would collapse. The price would go through the floor.

After a brief and troubled sleep in his Manhattan apartment, Visconti returned to his office at nine-thirty the following morning. The atmosphere resembled a funeral home when he entered and traversed the open office area. No one spoke or smiled. He marched directly to his office while remaining stiff-lipped and scrupulously avoiding eye contact with anyone.

Jerry Mara knocked softly, then entered. "... Sorry, Louis... You have no idea how hard we tried to reach you. We even..."

"It's not your fault, Jerry," Visconti interrupted. "I'm the idiot who disappeared at the most important time in the history of the market."

"Is there anything we can do?"

"Just give me some time alone. I'm going to need it."

"Shout if there's anything," Mara said, then left.

CHAPTER 23

Now desperate, Visconti telephoned Miles Dennis. "Miles, it's Louis. I need to see you immediately. It's extremely important."

"What's the problem?" Dennis asked, sensing the anxiety in Visconti's voice. "You don't sound happy."

"I'll tell you when I see you. I'll be there in fifteen minutes."

Visconti emerged from the South Tower elevator, marched directly across the hallway and entered the no frills, bare bones offices of Iacardi & Sons, Commodity Brokers. He crossed the linoleum covered floor of the small and cramped reception area to sit in one of two dark brown wooden chairs, the only furniture available.

Dennis appeared from the inner office. Tall, thin and sharp featured, his thinning hair was gray, his teeth slightly crooked, but his smile somehow enhanced his appearance. He wore a well tailored gray suit with a dark blue silk tie. "Good to see you again, Louis," he said, extending his hand.

"How did you know I was here?" Visconti asked.

"I saw you on the monitor," Dennis replied, pointing at the camera mounted on the wall above and to Visconti's right.

Visconti turned to glance at the camera, then shook his head and grinned. "If there's a way to save a buck, you guys are going to think of it. Maybe we should all take a page out of your book."

"Strictly contrarian, Louis. When everyone else spends, we cut... What can I do for you?"

"Can we talk in private?"

"Sure. Let's go to my office." Dennis led Visconti to his tiny glass-enclosed cubicle, then closed the door. He chuckled as he pointed to a metal folding chair on the opposite side of his desk. "Sit on that, Louis. I'm sure you'll find it uncomfortable."

Visconti pulled the metal chair away from the desk and sat erect. He faced Dennis with reddened eyes. "I need your help, Miles. My requirements are simple. I need a miracle."

Dennis laughed. "I don't do miracles, Louis. Maybe you could scale your expectations down a notch."

"I need to make a very large amount of money in a very short time." Visconti's face flushed red. "I took a hit. A big one."

"So did the whole world. How big?"

Visconti looked at the ceiling. "I'm managing a trust that just went south by a half a billion."

"Did you say million, or billion?"

"With a B."

Astounded, Dennis jerked forward. "You've got to be kidding!"

"Unfortunately I'm not."

"How the hell did it happen?"

"I picked last weekend to disappear with a barfly, incommunicado. She's no mental giant, but she's got all the right body parts. Honestly, I had no idea what was happening until I got back last night."

Dennis shook his head. "Probably the most expensive piece of ass you ever had," he said with a sympathetic smirk.

"I just reached the point where the telephone was growing roots in my ear. I couldn't stand the sight of it any more. If I had any idea how much the trip was going to cost me, I would have stayed in New York and screwed her in a telephone booth."

"So how do you propose to make a half a billion in a hurry?" Dennis asked, restraining a chuckle. "Please forgive me if I sound the slightest bit skeptical."

"Where do you think the price of crude oil's going?"

Dennis rolled his eyes skyward. "Not this again. You can't expect..."

Visconti interrupted. "Never mind. Just answer the question."

"We've got a hung jury on that one. Our research guru thinks it's going south, but some of us aren't so sure. It's an extremely important complex and there are a lot of powerful forces affecting it. If those forces weren't there, the price of crude would go into free fall."

"Enlighten me."

"Most of the oil producers in the lower forty-eight can't survive on ten dollar crude, and the government of this country is well aware of that reality. They know that if the price goes below ten dollars, domestic production gets cut and is replaced with imports. If that happens, our already sick balance of payments gets pneumonia, consumption increases, and eventually we have another energy crisis. Probably worse than the one in seventy-nine."

Dennis's answer was not what Visconti wanted to hear. "Suppose the price did go into free fall. How far would it go?"

"Eight bucks. Maybe further."

The answer was consistent with Raza's prediction. "What would you say if I told you I wanted to take a very large short position in crude oil?"

"How large?"

"Thirty or forty thousand contracts."

"I'd say you're out of your mind."

"Why?"

"The powerful forces, Louis. They're keeping upward pressure on prices."

71

Visconti was blinded by pride and his insatiable need to make more money than anyone else on the planet. "So maybe I'm crazy, or maybe I'm sitting on the opportunity of a lifetime."

"And maybe you're about to blow your financial brains out."

"I've already done that," Visconti admitted. "I don't have much to lose."

"Okay, if you really want to let it all hang out on a roll of the dice, I can't stop you. Give me twenty-four hours to talk to some people and check this thing out. Will you do that?"

Visconti struggled with his impulses. "Not one second longer," he warned. "There's no way I'm going to call my client and try to explain to him how I lost a half a billion of his money this weekend. If I do, my ass is fired and I lose the largest portfolio the company's ever had."

Dennis called Visconti at noon the following day. "Your timing's bad, Louis," he said. "I strongly advise you not to take a short position in crude at this time, not even with pocket change."

"Why?"

"A number of extremely well informed people in this country and in Europe think the price is going to strengthen before it weakens."

"Where's it going?"

"Twenty bucks. Then it's probably going to drop like a stone. I'll give you a list of reasons if you want them."

"I want them."

"Saudi Arabia's the biggie. They're still prepared to act as the swing producer. As long as they are, the price won't drop. They'll continue to cut production to keep supply and demand in balance. We think there are limits to their patience, however."

"What limits?"

"Money. Believe it or not, the Saudis are running out of it. They've cut their production so far, their cash flows aren't even enough to cover their purchases of war planes. Our advisors think it's only a matter of time before they capitulate. When they do, it might be time for you to jump in. I'll call you when I think the time is right."

"I'll have your ass if we miss the boat on this," Visconti warned. Privately, however, he respected Dennis's opinion. Dennis was renowned for having made millions for too many clients.

"Trust me, Louis. If there's a boat, you won't miss it."

Visconti hung up, now more desperate than ever.

CHAPTER 24

New York. Thursday, December 24, 1987.

The final days of 1987 were nightmarish for Visconti. Shortly following the last day of December, the annual report for the King's trust was due, and would have to be mailed to Mike King. In it, Visconti would be compelled to reveal that by virtually any standard, he had failed miserably. For weeks he had struggled with the possibility of including a covering letter with the report. It would be carefully crafted to cushion the blow, but in the end it was brutally obvious that words were totally inadequate. A letter, irrespective of how well written, could not possibly obscure the enormity of the disaster.

When King cast his eyes on the report, he would be furious. In addition to showing no increase in the trust's value after seven years of Visconti's management, the report would reveal Visconti's failure to do the minimum he had promised: to preserve the purchasing power of the trust's original capital.

Clearly, Visconti had run out of options. To salvage the respect he had once enjoyed, there was only one solution. King would have to read a fraudulent report. Instead of sending a document containing the potential to ruin him, Visconti elected to falsify it, merely by adding an extra line indicating a cash reserve of two hundred and fifty million in the trust. In addition to satisfying King, the fictitious amount would buy the time Visconti needed to recover the money lost in the stock market. No one would ever have to know. He was always the last to see the report before it left the office, and the Kings would be the only humans reading it.

Fully aware of the risk he was taking, Visconti took it willingly. Even though the action was patently fraudulent and flagrantly illegal, it was by far his best option.

Mike received the contrived report in early January. He studied it carefully, as he did all of Visconti's quarterly reports. "I'm surprised it's done so well," he said, then handed it to Karen. "I expected the October crash would have hit it harder. I guess Visconti was smart enough to have a lot of cash at the time it hit."

Karen briefly scanned the report, then frowned. "Where are we going with this? What are we doing with this money?"

For some time Mike had asked himself the same questions, but pride had prevented him from talking about it, and memories of the harsh treatment the Feds had given both of them had prevented him from doing anything about it. "I'm torn, Babe," he admitted. "Half of me wants to keep it forever, and the other half wants to get rid of it. All my life I've been an honest man. I can't even tell a lie without breaking out into hives, but this one's different. As long as I live I'll remember how those sons of bitches treated us like numbers. I'll never spend a dime of that money, but I'd rather die than give it back to them."

The stock market continued its gradual recovery in 1988. Capital gains were slow and difficult to achieve, however. Even worse, the price of crude oil had continued to sag, never once coming close to twenty dollars a barrel. Each time it showed any sign of strength, Visconti called Dennis, anxious to get his blessings to proceed with his planned short sale. Each time Dennis advised him to wait, his advice driving Visconti to unchartered levels of desperation.

The spot price of West Texas Intermediate had dropped to fifteen dollars a barrel by the end of May, and Visconti's hopes had plunged with it. Convinced he had missed his seat on the boat intended to deliver him from his nightmare, it was apparent that he would have to falsify a third consecutive quarterly report to Mike King. Deeply discouraged, he telephoned Assif Raza in Kuwait City. After an agonizing delay of more than twenty minutes, Raza finally answered, "Sorry to keep you waiting, Louis. To what do I owe the pleasure of your call?"

"I need some information, Assif. It's extremely important... When we first met over a year ago, you told me that you and your fellow investors expected the price of crude oil to drop a long way. Do you still think it will?"

"Nothing has happened to change our opinion. There is no factor, with the exception of the Saudis, which we think is capable of providing sustained support to the price of crude oil."

"If that's true, what's keeping it up?"

Raza chuckled. "Forgive me, Louis. I have difficulty understanding your question. We haven't seen the price as low as fifteen dollars for a long time."

"That's true," Visconti conceded. "But you said it would drop to five, didn't you?"

"Yes, and we still believe it will, because we don't think the Saudis can continue to carry the full weight of world crude prices on their shoulders for ever."

"How soon? Can you give me an informed opinion?"

"I can only assure you that we believe in the inevitability of a crash. The longer the price of crude oil defies gravity, the further and faster it will drop."

Raza's words were sweet music to Visconti's ears, nourishment for his obsession.

CHAPTER 25

Toronto. Friday, June 24, 1988.

Phillip received his high school diploma in late June, a bittersweet experience for Mike and Karen. His marks were abysmal, barely high enough to pass. His teachers spoke of their enormous frustration with the boy. Tests had confirmed his extremely high intelligence level, yet consistently low marks had revealed a low level of motivation. His teachers agreed that his poor academic performance would make it nearly impossible for him to be accepted at any reputable university, and strongly recommended a repeat of his final year.

Armed with that information and Phillip's final marks, Mike and Karen confronted him. Karen was stricken with the embarrassment most mothers feel when one of their children does poorly in school. Mike felt a strong sense of failure and frustration. In spite of all his efforts and attention, he had been unable to motivate Phillip to realize his potential.

Instead of eating alone in front of the television set in the den, as Phillip normally did, he joined his parents for dinner in the dining room, planning to remind them of the car they had promised to commemorate his high-school graduation. He dressed for the occasion; baggy blue jeans, a heavy multicolored T-shirt, and scruffy sneakers.

While Karen stared at her son, she was brutally reminded of her former husband. His baby fat had given way to muscle, forming a firm body structure very similar to that of his father. She was horrified by his unshaven face and the tiny gold earring in his left earlobe. She winced as he jerked a chair from beneath the table, then allowed himself to flop onto it. "Phillip, how many times have I told you to sit gently?" she scolded.

"Sorry," Phillip said, smirking as if he took pleasure in annoying her. "I forgot."

"It's apparent that isn't all you forgot," Mike barked.

Phillip flashed a defiant stare. "What do you mean by that?"

"Your marks clearly indicate that you forgot to work hard in school. Your mother and I were so concerned that we arranged interviews with each of your teachers. They all confirmed that you achieved far below your ability. When we asked them for specifics, they said you frequently failed to turn in assignments and to complete your homework. In addition, they suggested that you repeat your final year, to have another chance to elevate your marks to a level consistent with your ability, and that required for acceptance at university... What do you think of that?"

Phillip hung his head. Clearly, it was the wrong time to ask for a car. "The only thing I can say is that I hate school," he said, attempting to feign as much regret as possible.

"If you hate it so much, why waste any more time at it?" Mike asked, assuming he had successfully challenged Phillip's bluff. "You should get out and do something you don't hate."

Mike had said exactly what Phillip wanted to hear. The statement had actually sanctioned his most fervent desire. "You really think I should?" he asked, struggling to conceal his joy.

"It's your call. You have to decide what's more important. You're almost eighteen. You should be making your own career decisions. Do you have any plans?"

"Nope."

"Then I suggest you take at least a year out of school and get a real job. Maybe you'll hate work so much, you'll want go back to school."

Phillip seized the opportunity. "But how can I get a job if I don't have a car to get me there?"

"Take a bus," Mike retorted, amused by Phillip's infantile attempt at manipulation. "If you work hard enough and long enough, maybe you'll make enough money to buy your own car."

It was impossible for Phillip to hide his disappointment. Time to protest. "But you promised I could have a car when I graduated from high school."

Mike relented. "Tell you what I'll do. If you promise to work, and work hard, I'll give you a job with the company. If you're interested, I'll teach you everything I know about the business... Who knows? Maybe some day you'll want to run it."

"Can I drive a company car?"

"We can arrange that."

Phillip tried to appear excited and grateful, but was neither.

New York. Friday, July 29, 1988.

After a brief flirtation with the seventeen dollars a barrel level in July of 1988, the spot price of crude oil resumed its descent. As it knifed through the fifteen dollar resistance level, there was joy among the world's consumers of oil, even speculation that O.P.E.C. had finally failed as a cartel and lost its pricing power, perhaps forever. The price continued to decline through the summer of 1988. In October it hit thirteen dollars.

Enraged and convinced he had lost the opportunity of a lifetime, Visconti called Miles Dennis. "You son of a bitch!" he shouted. "Crude's at thirteen dollars! Do you have any idea how much money you've cost me? I don't know who the idiots are that give you advice. Obviously they don't know a goddamned thing about what's happening in the real world."

Dennis's response was cool and professional. "Relax, Louis. I'm still confident those idiots are right. I still think you should wait for twenty dollar crude before you jump in. Patience is crucial in this game."

His comments failed to placate Visconti. "That's unmitigated bull-shit! You gave me that same crap a year ago. If I had done the short then, I'd be sitting on a paper profit of over a hundred million."

"That's probably correct," Dennis conceded. "If you had done the short, would you take your hundred million and run, or wait for still lower prices?"

"I'd hang in there," Visconti replied without hesitation. "A hundred million is peanuts compared to what I could make when crude really crashes."

"If you're patient, you might still do it."

"Do what? Die with the bat on my shoulder?" Visconti countered.

Dennis chuckled, then changed the subject. "Do you know where I could find a good secretary? I'm looking for one that's young, beautiful, intelligent and eager to learn?"

"If   I   did,   I   sure   as   hell   wouldn't   tell   you."

CHAPTER 26

New York. Monday, October 24, 1988.

North winds howled and the temperature was plummeting when twenty-one year old Kerri Pyper left her two bedroom Manhasset apartment and climbed into a yellow cab. Rain droplets splattered against her window, blurring everything in her field of vision as her taxi inched its way through heavy Manhattan traffic. The inclement weather compounded the emptiness and loneliness she had confessed to Brian.

Kerri was alone in a city of millions of people, none of whom knew her or cared she existed. With the exception of her marriage to Brian, her job search was the only brightness in her life. In spite of being frustrated and offered nothing but rejection, she thrived on it. The challenge of finding a job kept her busy and helped her to forget her loneliness. Instead of tolerating each day by making tedious boring domestic jobs last, she now found herself hurrying. She had a focus and liked it.

In an attempt to broaden her resume and to fill some of her empty evenings, she had enrolled in a course on commodities at Long Island Community College, near Smith Town. The forty hour course was to be given in two hour segments, every Tuesday and Thursday evening. Kerri's business courses at university had given her an elementary exposure to the world of commodities. She discovered an intense fascination for the subject. In her final year of university she won a prize for her brilliant essay on the subject of the supply and demand equation for soybeans.

She arrived for her first session at one minute after eight and ran as fast as she could to Lecture Room Four. She took a seat in the back row near the door, then looked around the room, an amphitheater with seating capacity for one hundred. Almost all seats were occupied, by men. Including herself, she counted only three women.

The lecturer entered the room through a door to the right of the blackboards. He was tall, thin and sharp featured, with thinning gray hair. He wore a dark blue suit, matching tie, a buttoned-down pale blue shirt, and tasseled black loafers. He marched to the middle of the podium and stood behind a maple wood lectern. He reached into the inside pocket of his jacket and removed his notes, then looked up and scanned the audience. "Good evening, ladies and gentlemen," he said with a warm smile. "I had to scan the audience to confirm that I could include ladies in my salutation. I'm pleased that I can. Welcome to the Long Island Community College, and to the fabulous world of commodities."

The speaker paused to take drink of water, then smiled again. "I'm happy to see a few of my clients here tonight. For them, I need no introduction. For those of you who don't know me, my name is Miles Dennis. I'm a broker with Iacardi & Sons, in New York. For those of you who are unfamiliar with the company, it's small, very well respected, has offices in the World Trade Center, has been operating successfully for over fifty years, and specializes in brokering commodities." Dennis grinned, then blushed. "One of the perks of this job is to have the privilege of plugging my company, whenever I want."

While the audience laughed politely, Kerri continued to stare at Dennis. She liked him and was delighted to have enrolled in his course.

Dennis continued, "My job is to deliver the course to you and to try to make the subject interesting and fascinating to you. I urge you to ask questions, as many as you like, but please save them until the end of the class. Believe it or not, your questions might not be of any interest to others. They might also waste time... Any questions?" he asked, smiling again.

Silence.

"If any of you could determine the future, you would certainly have the means to become wealthy beyond your wildest dreams. It's evident, however, that none of you is so blessed. If you were, you wouldn't be here. Please dream with me for a moment. Suppose all of you were blessed with the ability to predict the future, and that you wanted to apply this ability to commodities. Your only limitation is that you could forecast only changes in prices, not the times of their occurrences... Can anyone tell me what problem that limitation presents?" Dennis searched the audience for a raised hand.

After a very long fifteen seconds, one hand was raised. It was Kerri's.

Dennis pointed to her. "At last we have an answer. Please go ahead."

"With that limitation, we would have to live with an element of risk," Kerri offered.

"Bravo!" Dennis declared. "Good answer. I couldn't have said it better... Now, suppose we mortals decided to try to improve our chances of determining the future by graphing a series of events over time. If we graphed the series long enough, it would run off the end of the page. Eventually we would notice that a portion of the line we are producing looks like another portion of the same line. Can anyone tell me the significance of that?"

Kerri raised her hand once again.

"I'm pleased we have one alert person in this class," Dennis acknowledged. "Go ahead, please."

"The similarity would suggest history is repeating itself."

"Exactly. Take a bow for that answer." Dennis picked up a piece of chalk and proceeded to draw a crooked continuous line across the full length of the five sections of blackboard. He turned to face the class when he ran out of blackboard. "Now, assume the line I've just drawn is our graph of a particular series of events. If we were to spend enough time graphing it, eventually we would be reasonably certain which direction the line would go next... Can anyone tell me why?"

Kerri glanced around the amphitheater to see that once again, no hand was raised. Her modesty refused to allow her to raise hers for the third time.

"Time's up," Dennis declared. "I'm going to ask you all to return to the Thursday session fully prepared to answer that question. The answer is absolutely crucial to your success in this business. You must learn how to follow a line and react to it. If you do, the future will belong to you. The line is the only thing that really counts in this game. Discarding the vast majority of lines and selecting the ones that have the potential to make you money are the most important things you will ever learn about the commodities game. A line on a chart is the historical price record. There can be no argument, no mystery. It's a fundamental fact."

Dennis continued without interruption until ten, then concluded the first session. "Thank you for your kind attention. I look forward to seeing all of you again on Thursday evening."

Kerri was thrilled. At last she was doing something useful. She was involved, growing again. Commodities fascinated her, and so did Miles Dennis. She had identified him as a learned confident man, a professional. She looked forward to the Thursday session and resolved to arrive early enough   to   get   a   front   row   seat.

CHAPTER 27

After racing through another two days of her frustrating job search, Kerri returned to the Long Island Community College, this time early enough to have a choice of all the front row seats.

Dennis, reviewing his notes on a chair behind the lectern, looked up and recognized Kerri immediately. It was difficult for him not to recognize her. Dressed in a tight pink skirt and breast enhancing red cashmere sweater, she was drop dead gorgeous. Her long blonde hair, large blue eyes and infectious white smile reached out and captivated him. "I'm glad to see my star pupil has returned," he said with a big smile. "It's like a breath of fresh air to see a woman showing such interest in my class."

Kerri smiled, nodded politely, then took a seat in the front row.

"I'm curious to know why you have an interest in commodities. Would you mind telling me?" Dennis asked, continuing to stare at Kerri, almost intoxicated by her beauty.

Embarrassed by his stare and nervous about answering the personal question, Kerri blushed. "I was involved in a business case study in my last year of university. The more involved I got, the more the subject interested me."

"What university was that?"

"The University of British Columbia."

"You're Canadian?"

Kerri smiled and nodded.

"What brought you to New York?"

"I married a football player. He brought me here."

"Really. Who does he play for?"

"The Jets. He's their quarterback."

"Brian Pyper?"

Once again Kerri nodded, displaying a proud smile.

"You sure know how to pick 'em. I think he's an extremely talented quarterback, even better than Nameth. Maybe they'll win another Super Bowl with him."

"That's his fondest dream."

"Oh no," Dennis said, suddenly realizing his oversight. "I rudely asked your husband's name without first asking yours. Can you ever forgive me?"

"Certainly. I'm Kerri."

Dennis stood and approached her. "Delighted to meet you, Kerri Pyper," he said, reaching for her hand, and practically drooling over her good looks. "I have some great books on commodities. Would you be interested in reading them?"

"I certainly would. Thank you for offering."

"Fine. I'll bring them here next Tuesday... Or maybe you could pick them up at my office. Do you ever get to Manhattan?"

"My job search has taken me there many times, regrettably all in vain."

"That sounds like fun. What type of work are you looking for? I mean, do you have something specific in mind?"

"I'm really not qualified to do anything specific, but I would really like to find a job that would give me some business experience. Eventually I want to return to university and get an MBA."

Dennis reached into the inside pocket of his jacket and removed a card. "Here's my business card," he said, handing it to Kerri. "Please drop by my office anytime. I'll have the books waiting for you. If you don't make it, I'll bring them with me on Tuesday."

Now that Kerri had talked to Dennis on a personal level, she liked him even more. Maybe it was his sincerity, or the self-confidence he exuded without appearing arrogant. Both reminded her of so many self-effacing but competent professors she had known. Uncertain why she wanted to see him again, or even impress him, she just did it instinctively. She reached the front door of Iacardi & Sons at eleven-fifteen the following morning. She opened it timidly and entered the sparsely decorated reception area.

Dennis appeared seconds later. "Hi," he said, delighted to see her. "Sorry we don't have a receptionist here. We replaced her with a video monitor. Welcome to my kingdom."

Kerri's face flushed red and she lied, "I had a job interview down here this morning, so I thought I would drop by and pick up the books you offered to me last night."

Dennis gave her an understanding smile. "Would you like to come in? I'll show you our operation."

Kerri nodded, thrilled and excited. She had expected Dennis to give her the books and show her the door. Instead, she found herself in the financial center of the world and about to be introduced to a fascinating business by a man she barely knew.

At one o'clock, Dennis lifted three books from the table behind his desk and handed them to Kerri. "Take these and spend as much time as you want with them. If you enjoy them half as much as I did, your time will be well spent. Feel free to call me if you have any questions."

Kerri smiled. "Thank you, Miles. Thank you for your time and for the books. I wish there was some way I could express my appreciation."

"There is," Dennis said with a large grin. "You could come to Iacardi & Sons and work for me."

"I could?" Kerri asked, shocked, thrilled and surprised by the offer.

"Sure. If you agree, I'd like you to be my assistant. I can't pay you much, but I guarantee you'll never be bored. You'll have a wonderful opportunity to learn the business from the inside... You interested?"

"Interested! I'd be delighted!"

"Then I'll see you sharp at eight tomorrow morning. I've been looking for an assistant for quite a while," Dennis said as he shook Kerri's hand. "I was about to hire one until you came along. She has all the secretarial skills I could want, but there's no way she has the keen interest in the business that you do. To me, what you have is far more important. My instinct tells me you'll do very well at the job, and that you'll like it. I promise I'll do my best to keep it interesting."

"I'll do my best to justify your choice," Kerri promised, thrust into a state of euphoria. She had a job. At last her meaningless empty days were about to come to an end. Now she could contribute, start to grow again. Not only would she be working in a business which fascinated her, she would be working for Miles Dennis. Tomorrow could not come soon enough. She wished Brian was with her to share her incredible news.

Dennis found Kerri waiting on one of the two wooden chairs in the reception area of Iacardi & Sons at seven-thirty the following morning. She had dressed neatly in white silk blouse, navy blue jacket and light gray skirt.

"You're going to be very successful here, young lady. Come on in. I'll introduce you to all the crazies who work here." He led her to the inner office and took the time to introduce her to each of the office staff and account executives. The final introductions were to Charles and Mario Iacardi, the two sons and only progeny of Armando Iacardi, the firm's founder. Together, they held eighty-five percent of the company's stock. The remaining fifteen percent was employee owned. With the formalities completed, Dennis spent much of the remainder of the day familiarizing Kerri with the investment portfolios of his clients, including the one held by the King's trust.

Thrilled with her new status, Kerri wanted to tell two people: Brian, her beloved husband, and Mike King, the father she had not seen since she was nine years of age.

CHAPTER 28

New York. Sunday, November 5, 1988.

Kerri stood alone in the Arrivals Lounge at La Guardia Airport, the tip of her nose no more than an inch from a thick plate glass window. She stared anxiously at the spot where she had expected Brian's airplane to come to rest over thirty minutes earlier. The swirling streamers of beaded snow whipping across the concrete below were evidence that the forecast of strong winds and snow had been accurate. She scanned an angry gray sky, then turned and walked in the direction of a nearby coffee-shop. Another unwanted coffee would help to waste time.

She was thrilled and relieved when she returned to the same window fifteen minutes later. The familiar Jet's chartered aircraft was parked at the gantry, its black nose pointed directly at her. Her heart raced in anticipation of being in her husband's arms again. She hurried to Gate thirty-eight and stood on her toes, eagerly trying to see above the people in front of her, hoping to get a glimpse of Brian's handsome face. When she saw his black brush-cut, then his imposing athletic figure, she squeezed through the crowd and darted down the hallway.

Brian, dressed in faded jeans, green sweater and Jets jacket, standing on the tips of his toes, his brown eyes opened wide, smiled when he heard the hoots and whistles of his teammates. He dropped his carry on bag barely in time to accept Kerri into his arms.

"God, I missed you!" Kerri cried.

"Me too you," Brian replied, squeezing Kerri's buttocks with both hands and lifting her from the floor. "The flight was delayed for an hour in Chicago. They had to de-ice the plane. That's the bad news... Wanna hear the good news?"

"I watched the game. You won," Kerri said, continuing to kiss the love of her life. "And you were fantastic, as usual... I have more good news," she said.

"What?"

"I got a job."

Brian's smile evaporated. He released Kerri and lowered her to the floor. He looked straight into her eyes, struggling to appear interested. "That's fantastic! Where?"

"Let's get out of here," Kerri demanded, tugging Brian's arm. "I'll tell you all about it on the way home."

Toronto. Saturday, November 11, 1988.

As a harsh reminder of the approaching winter, a late autumn storm pounded Toronto for four hours and left a seven inch blanket of snow in its wake. The storm had forced Phillip to work deep into overtime. Most of Mike's gasoline outlets in the city and surrounding area had run out of windshield washer fluid and it was Phillip's job to re-stock them. To complete his assignment, it was virtually certain he would have to relinquish the freedom of his beloved Saturday night.

Heavy slush in the streets had slowed traffic to a crawl. Phillip waited impatiently for a traffic light at the intersection of Bayview and Sheppard Avenues. He pounded his fist on the dashboard. "Shit I hate this!" he shouted.

New York. Friday, November 17, 1988.

In sharp contrast to the wealth and happiness Visconti envisioned when he reached forty, reality had presented a different picture. Now forty-two years of age, he was unmarried, alone, and extremely unhappy. Gone were the excitement of making brilliant financial maneuvers, making a seven-figure income, and one-night stands with nameless girls. A large part of

90

him wanted to be free of it all, unencumbered by responsibility, to start again at something entirely new. A larger part, however, would not let go. A series of less than spectacular investments had conspired to make him feel as if he had painted himself into a corner. He felt hopelessly trapped, not only by his inertia, but by his stupidity.

Almost a year had passed since he dared to falsify his annual report to Mike King. Facing no alternative but to repeat the procedure, he vowed that 1989 would be the year he made his move. It would be bold and decisive. Never again would he find himself in such an untenable position.

The 1988 playoff hopes of the New York Jets ended substantially sooner than the management, coaching staff and players had expected. With near perfect hindsight, sports writers offered a bewildering list of reasons. None of them however, criticized the performance of Brian Pyper. Instead, they gave him glowing reviews. One writer summarized, "Pyper has clearly established himself as the number one quarterback in the league. It was a shame to waste his talents on the Jets."

CHAPTER 29

New York. Friday, December 23, 1988.

Kerri and Brian began a long anticipated one week vacation when they boarded a plane scheduled to fly from New York to Seattle. From there, they planned to rent a car and drive to Vancouver, spend Christmas with their parents, take a brief skiing honeymoon at Whistler, then return to Vancouver to attend a New Years Eve party at the Capilano Golf and Country Club.

When the 747 had climbed to its planned altitude, high above the thick cloud layer covering most of north eastern U.S., Brian turned to Kerri and reached for her hand. "Do you remember when you complained about being so lonely whenever I was away?" he asked.

Kerri nodded. "Sure. Why?"

"Guess you never thought our roles would be reversed."

"You poor baby," Kerri said, then smiled and stretched to kiss Brian's cheek. "Why is it so difficult for me to believe the great Brian Pyper could ever be lonely?"

Kerri's sarcasm failed to amuse Brian. "It shouldn't be any more difficult for you than it was for me," he countered.

"It certainly should. We're talking about two entirely different situations. When you go to work, you don't come home every night. I do. Besides, you have your friends and teammates in New York. You're a celebrity. All you have to do is walk out the door and everyone recognizes you. I was a nobody before I got a job. Now I have one and I'm still a nobody."

"You're not a nobody. You're the love of my life. You're the most beautiful woman I've ever seen. When you walk out the door, I notice."

"Thanks for the compliment, but it's obvious you see the difference."

Brian nodded and looked away. "I guess I'm just feeling sorry for myself. I assumed we would live in Vancouver in the off-season. Now that you have that job, we can't."

"Brian, I love Vancouver. I miss being there for a lot of reasons, but I absolutely had to do something in New York. That job saved my sanity."

"Is it just a job, or something more?"

"At first it was just a job, but now it's more than that. Aside from meeting you, it's the most exciting thing that's ever happened to me. I actually look forward to going to work. Can you understand that?"

"I understand, but I have difficulty accepting it."

"You'll get used to it."

"Tell me about your boss. What's he like?"

"He's wonderful. He's considerate and incredibly patient. I still can't believe he picked me to work for him."

"Is he happily married?"

"He certainly is. Why?"

"I don't want any competition."

"Oh, God!" Kerri swore, annoyed by Brian's infantile jealousy. "You don't have any and you know it."

"I think you're underrating yourself. I've seen how men look at you."

"You have absolutely nothing to worry about. Miles is all business. He hired me because he saw I was genuinely interested in the commodities business, and prepared to commit myself to learn it."

Brian smirked. "Maybe when I'm retired from football you can keep me in the style to which I've always wanted to be accustomed."

"Maybe   I   will."

93

CHAPTER 30

New York. Thursday, February 23, 1989.

Visconti paced back and forth in front of his desk, his telephone receiver pressed tightly to his ear. His lips were compressed as he waited for Miles Dennis to answer his telephone. His trigger finger and wallet were at the ready.

"What's happening Louis?" Dennis asked.

"Crude just went north of twenty. It's time to roll the dice."

Dennis recalled the advice he had given Visconti in October of the previous year. He had implored him to wait until crude rose above twenty dollars a barrel. "I thought you had forgotten all about that insane plan. I hope you're not telling me you're still interested in a big short?"

"Damn right I am! I want to do it now, and don't give me any reasons why I shouldn't."

"Give me one hour. Then come to my office."

"I'll be there," Visconti promised.

Forty-five minutes later, Visconti entered the office of Iacardi & Sons. Inside the reception area, he smiled and waved at the camera mounted on the wall.

Dennis saw Visconti on the video monitor in his office and buzzed Kerri. "That's Louis Visconti, Kerri. Would you show him in? Be nice to him. He's about to be a very important client."

Kerri, conservatively dressed in a gray knee-length skirt and pink silk blouse, hurried to the reception area. "Good morning, Mister Visconti," she said, then exposed her irresistible smile. "Mister Dennis has asked me to show you in."

Visconti, instantly captivated by Kerri's stunning beauty, stared shamelessly at her young body. "You could show me anywhere," he said with a wink and a lecherous smirk. "What's your name?"

"Kerri," she replied, her smile gone. "Would you follow me, please?"

"With pleasure," Visconti said, then followed Kerri to Dennis's office, never once taking his eyes from her perfect body.

As they entered Dennis's cramped and cluttered office, Dennis stood and extended his hand to Visconti. "Hi, Louis. How are you?"

"Fine and ready to roll," Visconti declared, his gray eyes unblinking.

"Good... I trust you've met Kerri?"

Visconti turned to face Kerri with another lecherous smirk. "I certainly have. You have excellent taste, Miles."

Dennis frowned as he watched Kerri turn and head for the door. "Don't go Kerri. Stay for this meeting. You'll find it interesting." He turned to Visconti. "You mind?"

Visconti shook his head. "Hell no," he said, continuing to stare at Kerri. "I'd be disappointed if she left."

Kerri wheeled her chair into the office and closed the door, thrilled to be asked to attend.

"Louis, I made some calls," Dennis said. "I had to scope the crude market. I wanted..."

Visconti interrupted. "Miles, please. I don't want to hear it. It doesn't matter what you or anyone else says. I'm not going to change my mind."

Dennis raised his hands in surrender. "That isn't what I was going to say. I was merely..."

Visconti interrupted again. "You couldn't find a bull anywhere. Right?"

Dennis nodded. "The consensus is that O.P.E.C.'s production ceilings will hold for the winter. But by spring or summer the complex is expected to get extremely weak."

"I hope you're not telling me to keep my hands in my pockets again," Visconti protested.

"No. I was merely attempting to advise you to go out four or five months. In fact, you should probably do both."

"Why do I need to get fancy? Either I get in or I don't."

"Timing, Louis. It's everything. At this point you have every reason to believe the price of crude is going south, and it most likely will. But you don't know exactly when. If you anticipate and believe in price weakness by the spring or summer, you should take those positions. If you spread your contracts over several months, you reduce the risk of being forced to liquidate your entire position in one particular month."

"How the hell could that happen?" Obsessed with tunnel vision, Visconti could see the price of crude oil going in only one direction.

"How many contracts do you have in mind?"

"At least thirty thousand," Visconti announced. No delay. No apparent emotion.

Kerri completed a mental calculation and was stunned to realize Visconti had proposed a commitment of over six hundred million dollars.

Dennis leaned backward and placed his feet on his desk, his eyes riveted on Visconti's. "Suppose you shorted all thirty thousand in the July contract month. And suppose instead of going down, as you fully expected, the price went up and kept on rising until July. In addition to being forced to put up the cash required to cover margin calls, your entire position would be closed out in that month. That would be a disaster, Louis... If, on the other hand, you had allocated ten thousand contracts to each of July, August and September, only a third of your position would be liquidated in July. You would still have a chance of making money on the remaining two thirds."

"Okay. Let's do August and September," Visconti said.

"Fifteen thousand each?"

Visconti nodded.

"You have a price in mind?"

"At the market. Anywhere above twenty dollars."

Dennis raised his eyebrows. "You want a trailing stop-loss?"

Visconti shook his head, annoyed by Dennis's relentless attention to detail. This was his big chance, his opportunity to vindicate himself, to free himself from the self-imposed vice he had created as a result of his mismanagement of the King's trust. He had tunnel vision, and almost nothing to lose. "Let's just forget the bells and whistles and get it on. I have absolutely no intention of liquidating until the price hits single digits."

Dennis shrugged his shoulders and turned both palms face up. "I wouldn't want you to accuse me of not warning you."

"I appreciate that. So what's next?"

"I presume you remember our margin requirements."

"Still ten percent?"

"Dennis nodded, then lowered his feet and leaned forward. He completed a calculation on the back of a brown envelope on his desk. "At twenty bucks, the deposit is sixty million. You got the cash?"

Visconti nodded with tightened lips.

"Who, or what organization will be making the investment?"

"The same trust that took the short position in crude over a year ago."

Again Dennis raised his eyebrows. "I presume it's good for the money?"

Visconti smirked. "In anticipation of that question, I brought a copy of that trust's most recent financial statement. It's for the year ended, December thirty-first, nineteen eighty-eight." He reached into the inner pocket of his jacket and removed a copy of the fraudulently amended report, then handed it to Dennis. "Please understand that the information contained in this statement must be kept strictly confidential. I'm giving it to you only to confirm the trust's credit worthiness."

Dennis opened the report and smiled as he glanced at the bottom line. "I don't think we'll have any problems with this... Would you like a coffee?"

Normally, Visconti would have declined the offer. Wasting time in idle chatter over coffee was alien to him. The opportunity to spend more time with Kerri, however, was too tempting. "That's a wonderful suggestion," he said, fighting a inflexible urge to stare at her. "Black."

Dennis turned to Kerri. "Would you look after it, Kerri? I'll have black, too. Get one for yourself."

Kerri nodded, then stood and left the office.

Visconti waited until Kerri was out of sight, then leaned forward. "You sly old dog!" he declared. "Where the hell did you find her? She's a goddess, absolutely the most beautiful female I've ever seen. I'm lusting. I can't help myself. "

Dennis leaned back and once again placed his feet on the desk. "Out of bounds, Louis. She's happily married."

"So what? I was happily married too."

"She's married to a football player."

"You're kidding! Who?"

"None other than the great Brian Pyper."

"The Jet's quarterback?"

"Yup."

"What the hell is she doing working for you?" Visconti asked, questioning why the wife of the Jets quarterback had to work at all.

"A damned good job. In addition to being beautiful, she's smart, and a terrific employee."

"Where did you find her?"

"She's enrolled in my commodities class on the island."

"I'm jealous as hell. Maybe I should start teaching," Visconti said, shaking his head. "Do me a favor. Let me know if she ever leaves Pyper."

"Don't hold your breath. I'm sure they're very happy."

"Sure they are," Visconti scoffed. "I was happy once, myself."

Kerri returned with three coffees. She distributed two, then sat to drink hers.

Visconti took a sip, then turned to face Kerri. "This is very good coffee. Thanks, Kerri. Miles tells me you're new here. How do you like the commodities business, and how do you like working for Miles?"

"I love the business, and Miles is the best boss I've ever had," Kerri replied, aware that Miles was her first and only boss.

Visconti pointed to Dennis and grinned. "I should tell you he's a real tyrant. He goes through secretaries like the seasons. If he ever gives you a rough time, come to my office. The second you walk through my door, you're hired. I'll pay you twice as much as you're getting from this old tightwad."

Kerri had already concluded she would not want to work for Visconti, no matter how much he paid her. "Thank you. That's a very generous offer but I'm very happy at Iacardi."

"You've broken my heart," Visconti said, symbolically clutching his heart with both hands. He finished his coffee, then stood and faced Kerri. The relentless stare of his cold gray eyes seemed capable of penetrating her clothing. "Time changes a lot of things. I'm sure we'll meet again."

Dennis also stood. "I'll need some time to assemble this deal," he said, extending his hand to Visconti. "Will you be in your office?"

"Until six or seven," Visconti replied. He shook Dennis's hand, smirked at Kerri, then quickly left.

"Wow!" Kerri said.

Dennis chuckled. "Breathtaking, isn't he?"

"Do you know him well?"

"Not on a personal level. We've known of each other through our respective businesses for a long time."

"What business is he in?"

"He's a partner in a company called Mara, Griesdorf and Visconti. It specializes in money management. As you already know, his office is also in this building."

"I can't believe what he just did."

"He's a world class plunger. He made his mark in the early eighties, had a track record of amazingly high investment returns, and a reputation for almost always being right. His predictions were so accurate, it was scary. They called him The Crown Prince of Wall Street, until his house of cards came crashing down."

"What happened?"

"The stock market crashed in October of eighty-seven and the trust we were just talking about went with it. I was shocked when he told me it lost a half a billion dollars. Ever since then he's been desperate to make it all back, fast."

"Is that why he just made that investment?"

Dennis nodded. "He's wanted to do it ever since the crash. Until this point, I've been able to persuade him to wait. I advised him to stay out of the market until spot crude broke through twenty dollars a barrel on the upside. I had hoped he would find a less risky alternative and forget the crude short. Obviously he didn't."

"Is the investment really that risky?"

"Enormously. If he's right, he'll make an incredible amount of money. God help him if he's wrong."

"Do you think he's right?"

Dennis shrugged his shoulders. "He could be right at the wrong time. It's a gigantic investment, fully leveraged. It's the stuff of which financial legends are made, both negative and positive. He could go to the moon or lose the farm on this one."

"How much is the trust worth?"

Dennis handed her the falsified report Visconti had given him. "Take a look at this," he said.

She read the report, then looked up at her boss, amazed. The experience was a learning explosion for Kerri. She had never conceived of anyone possessing such a large amount of money. To wager so much on one single investment was unimaginable.

CHAPTER 31

New York. Wednesday, June 14, 1989.

The price for July delivery suddenly nose-dived to eighteen dollars and ten cents a barrel. When news of the price decline reached Visconti, he was ecstatic. His investment showed a paper gain of over sixty million dollars. He was certain he was witnessing the beginning of long awaited crash in crude oil pricing. His incredible risk was on the threshold of reward. He telephoned Assif Raza, anxious for reinforcement.

"Good morning, Louis," Raza said, lifting his feet above the tepid bath water in the bathroom of his lavish Manhattan apartment. "How are you?"

"Struggling, but maybe not much longer. I think your prediction of lower crude prices is finally about to become a reality. Would you care to comment on that?"

Raza chuckled. "I think the universe is unfolding as it should."

"Can you be more specific? It's extremely important."

"Would I be correct in assuming that you now have a tangible interest in crude oil?"

"That's putting it mildly," Visconti said, rolling his eyes skyward. "I'm short, big time."

"You have chosen wisely. For all of the reasons I have stated in our previous conversations, my associates and I still think crude is substantially overpriced."

"When does the plug get pulled? You must have some idea."

"Only God has the answer to that. As mortals, we continue to be limited to mere speculation."

"Would you be kind enough to speculate?"

"It would appear that the central bankers of the seven leading industrial nations are acting in consort to dampen inflation. Moreover, we believe they will soon succeed. One of the consequences of their efforts will be a slowdown in economic activity and substantially reduced demand for oil. I'll leave the rest to your imagination."

Raza's words bolstered Visconti's confidence. "Thank you, Assif. You've been most helpful." He put the receiver in its cradle and pounded his desk with both fists. "Yes!" he shouted, his eyes closed and teeth bared.

As the summer of 1989 wore on, Visconti's euphoria and his sixty million dollar paper gain evaporated. The liquidation of his August contracts realized only a twelve million dollar gain. By mid September, he was out of the crude oil complex and virtually no further ahead than when he started, seven months earlier. He glanced at a graph of spot oil prices and shook his head. Instead of crashing as Raza had predicted, the price had fluctuated very little. It was almost exactly where it was when he shorted thirty thousand contracts.

Frustrated and wary of the capricious crude oil market, Visconti was inclined to abandon it. Making a lot of money by virtue of a quick windfall was elusive, but the effort and aggravation involved in making it slowly was totally unpalatable to him. If he chose the slow route, he would have to continue to falsify King's report for what seemed like an eternity. The pain of inaction seemed far worse than the risk of once again shorting crude oil. Finding an investment vehicle as potentially rewarding would require elaborate and time-consuming research. He decided to give crude oil one final shot.

He arranged a meeting with Miles Dennis and placed orders to short fifteen thousand crude contracts in each of the months of August and September, 1990. The average price of the transactions was just north of twenty dollars a barrel.

His   timing   could   not   have   been   worse.

CHAPTER 32

New York. Sunday, November 26, 1989.

"May I speak to Kerri Pyper, please?"

"Speaking," Kerri replied.

"It's Doctor David Hanley, Kerri. I'm calling from Buffalo General hospital. I'm told that you're already aware that your husband was injured this afternoon."

"Yes. How is he?" her heart racing.

"He's under sedation and resting right now... He has badly torn ligaments in his right knee. The good news is that he'll probably play football again. The bad news is that it won't be until next season, at the earliest."

Kerri was relieved, but heartbroken. "Please tell him I'm flying to Buffalo as soon as I can get a flight," Kerri said, aware of how much Brian had worried about being injured and unable to play.

"Not a good idea. Stay where you are. The team has made arrangements to fly him to New York early tomorrow morning. They'll send him home in a limousine from the airport. I'll have the team physician call you with the details."

"Will he be able to walk?"

"With difficulty. We put a cast on the knee and loaned him a pair of crutches... I should warn you that he'll need at least one operation to repair the torn ligaments, as soon as the swelling subsides... Even though I'm a Bills fan, I want you to know how much respect I have for your husband's ability, and how truly sorry I am that this has happened."

"Thank you for saying that," Kerri said, then hung up and immediately phoned Miles Dennis. "It's Kerri," she said, tears gushing. "I just called to tell you that I won't be..."

"Don't even think about it," Dennis interrupted. "I watched the game. I don't want to see you in this office until you're ready to return. Brian's going to need you more than me."

A dark blue airport limousine glided to a stop at the curb in front of Kerri's apartment building at ten forty-five the following morning. Seconds later, a rear door was opened by Gary Smith, one of the Jets' trainers.

Kerri raced to help. When she reached the limousine, Brian was already on the sidewalk with crutches in his left hand and his right arm around Smith's shoulders. Kerri grabbed the crutches and placed Brian's left arm around her shoulders. "I'm so glad you're home," she said, squeezing him with her right arm. "I can't tell you how much I worried about you."

"What a piss-off!" Brian muttered. "It was a cheap shot. I'm already down and some animal piles on. The Bills got fifteen yards and I'm out for the season. Anyway you cut it, that's a piss-off."

"Fortunately you're not out for life," Kerri replied in a vain attempt to console Brian. "The doctor told me you'll be back next season."

"Terrific!" Brian hissed. "I'm going to be a fucking vegetable for months."

CHAPTER 33

Kerri returned to work after Brian's knee was successfully subjected to corrective surgery. His doctor predicted confidently that by the time he reported to the Jets' training camp for the 1990 season, his knee would be "as good as new." The doctor warned however, that healing would be slow. He further cautioned Brian to avoid stressing the knee with all possible care. Finally, he suggested that physical therapy should begin in six to eight weeks.

Brian's injury was not limited to his knee. He lacked the psychological maturity to accept the setback to his career. He had been extremely lucky throughout his football career, miraculously managing to escape major injuries. He had sustained numerous cuts and bruises, but never anything serious enough to slow him down. Suddenly he had been stopped, removed from the limelight, and brutally introduced to the vulnerability of a professional athlete. Instead of using his free time to do productive things, he wasted it by brooding and feeling sorry for himself. Each morning following breakfast, he parked his body in front of the television set and consumed endless hours with less than stimulating programs. To enrich his evenings, he began to drink, lightly at first, then heavily. His behavior took an entirely predictable toll on his relationship with Kerri. The thrill and excitement with which they had once greeted each other was soon replaced by hostility and anger.

It was no accident that Visconti arrived at the office of Iacardi & Sons, just in time to share in the festivity of the company's annual Christmas party. His excuse for being there was to deliver the check for the margin call on his crude oil short. His real reason was to see Kerri Pyper again. He had been unable to forget her. Her youthful beauty had intoxicated him, touched him like no other female had. The fact that she was married to a famous athlete made her even more alluring, the challenge of possessing her even more exciting.

Visconti heard the sound of loud conversation, music and laughter when he entered the reception area. He continued to the inner office through a wide open door.

"Merry Christmas, Louis. Have a drink with us," Dennis offered, smiling and extending his hand.

Visconti forced a smile, in no mood for Christmas festivities. "Humbug," he muttered. He removed a white envelope from the inner pocket of his jacket, then handed it to Dennis, never once casting his eyes on it.

"What's this?" Dennis asked, staring at the blank envelope with a puzzled expression.

"Eight and a half big ones," Visconti replied, still looking away.

Dennis grinned. "Thanks. Hopefully it'll be your last."

"It will be," Visconti promised with tightened lips.

Dennis placed his right hand on Visconti's back. "What can I pour for you?"

"Scotch. Rocks."

Dennis turned and headed in the direction of the bar, the top of a desk in the center of the office.

While waiting for Dennis to return, Visconti scanned the office until his eyes fixed on Kerri. She stood alone in the doorway to Dennis's office, nursing a clear plastic glass filled with white wine. She had dressed for the occasion in a red skirt and a green blouse.

Dennis returned with Visconti's drink. "Drown your sorrows, Louis. It's the least I can give you for eight and a half million."

Visconti took a sip, placed the glass on the desk beside him, then shifted his focus to Kerri. "Miles, is it my imagination or is the love of my life unhappy?"

107

Dennis glanced at Kerri, then at Visconti. "You're as perceptive as ever, Louis. It's not your imagination. There's trouble in paradise. She's been miserable ever since her husband injured his knee in that game in Buffalo.

"Wonderful!" Visconti said, flashing a contented smile. "Are you sure? I mean have you asked her about it?"

Dennis nodded. "Kerri's an open book. She wears her heart on her sleeve. She told me her husband really took the injury hard. He gets pissed on the couch every day, watching television and wallowing in self-pity."

"Would you mind if I talked to her?"

Dennis frowned. "Be careful. She's very tender." He lifted Visconti's drink from the desk. "Take this. You'll need it to wash down the rejection."

Visconti accepted his drink. "You might be surprised," he said with a confident wink, then turned and headed straight for Kerri. "Merry Christmas," he said, stopping in front of her and touching her glass with his.

"Same to you," Kerri replied in a bored monotone, then looked away.

"Why do I get the feeling you don't really care if I have a Merry Christmas?"

Visconti's question encouraged a wry grin from Kerri. "What brings you here?" she asked.

"I just dropped in to deliver a check for eight and a half million dollars to your boss... When I saw you looking very depressed, I decided to try to cheer you up. How am I doing?"

Kerri showed a hint of a smile, but refused to answer.

"How's your job? Are you still enjoying the commodities business?"

She nodded. "Thanks for asking."

"Miles still treating you well?"

"Yes. He's been wonderful."

"Sorry to hear that. I was hoping you were going to tell me he beats you and works you like a slave. I was hoping you would tell me you wanted to quit your job and come to work for me. Have you forgotten that I offered to double your salary? I was serious you know."

"No, I haven't forgotten," Kerri replied, the corners of her mouth suggesting a smile.

"Well?"

"Well, what?"

"Are you interested?"

Kerri decided to call Visconti's bluff. "Did Miles tell you he's paying me two hundred and fifty thousand a year?"

Visconti accepted the call. "Is that all? Then I'll triple it."

Kerri smiled, then laughed. "You really are serious."

"Very serious about cheering you up... I did a pretty good job, didn't I?"

Kerri was compelled to concede. Visconti had made her laugh when it was the last thing she wanted to do. "Yes, you did. Thank you."

"My pleasure. Any time you need to laugh or just talk, you know where to find me." Visconti kissed Kerri's forehead. "Merry Christmas," he whispered, then turned and walked away.

Visconti's kiss and sudden departure both startled and fascinated Kerri. "Merry Christmas to you, too," she said, her expression tinged with a strange combination of curiosity and melancholy.

Visconti, pausing without turning, raised his hand in acknowledgment, then continued his march back to the bar. He placed his right hand on Dennis's shoulder. "Two predictions for nineteen-ninety, Miles," he declared. "I'm going to win big in crude oil, and Kerri Pyper will be mine." To punctuate his statement, he finished his scotch in one gulp, then left before Dennis could respond.

CHAPTER 34

New York. January 12, 1990.

Brian's right knee had healed to the point where he could begin physical therapy. While the pain of the injury and the subsequent operations continued to prevent him from running or subjecting his knee to sustained pressure, he was finally able to walk a short distance.

In addition to the pain and suffering the injury had caused him, it had taken a severe toll on his relationship with Kerri. Their infrequent conversations usually erupted into arguments. Affectionate touching, once a large component of their marriage, had all but disappeared. Their sexual relationship had also changed. The tender, sharing lovemaking of their past had been replaced by sporadic and selfish intercourse, initiated solely by Brian whenever he felt the need for release. He no longer had the patience to ensure that Kerri was satisfied. Whenever she expressed or demonstrated the need to be loved, he rejected her, or demeaned her, usually fomenting another argument.

Brian's drinking also increased. His renewed mobility enabled him to do it away from the apartment and to use therapy as an excuse. At first Kerri believed his only destination was the team's training center. Only when he began to return with the unmistakable smell of alcohol on his breath did she suspect that he had been detouring. Rather than confront him with her suspicion, she chose instead to welcome him and ask him about the progress of his knee. Her heart told her that once the knee was completely healed, he would discontinue his excessive drinking and become the caring sensitive man she had once loved so dearly. Her mind told her the problem was much more serious, and that the marriage was in deep trouble.

Believing he could help, she decided to confide in Miles Dennis. She waited until he was alone in his office and not on the telephone, then entered and closed the door behind her. She took a seat and faced him.

"Problems?" Dennis asked, smiling but continuing to read.

"Yes, but not what you think... Are you any good at marriage counseling?"

Dennis pushed aside his file, leaned backward and relaxed. "Not bad. Why?"

"It's Brian," Kerri said, her voice cracking, tears flooding her eyes and rolling down her cheeks.

Dennis bolted upright, sensing Kerri was deeply troubled. "Tell me the whole story," he demanded. "Don't leave anything out. Get it all out of your system."

Kerri lowered her head and wiped her eyes with the back of her hands. "I don't know him any more, Miles," she whimpered, desperation obvious. "Ever since he came home from the hospital in Buffalo, he's changed. He's drinking, heavily. I can't even have a civilized conversation with him."

"Has he ever hit you?"

"No. I don't think he's a violent person. I'm more worried about what he might do to himself."

"What do you think he might do to himself?"

"Aside from ruining his health and career, I don't know."

"Has he threatened to leave you?"

"No."

"Is there another woman?"

Tears reappeared. "I don't think so."

"Then the problem seems relatively simple... Before the game in Buffalo, the two of you were happy. Everything was wonderful. Right?"

Kerri nodded.

"Then everything went to hell, in a hurry."

"That's all true but..."

"Then it's simple. What's the most important thing that's missing from his life?"

"Football?"

Dennis shook his head. "Something more important than that."

Suddenly Kerri realized what she had overlooked for so long. "Recognition."

"Exactly. I knew you were a bright girl. Brian's a celebrity. He's been living on a steady diet of adoring fans and media attention. Suddenly he's injured and goes off the diet, cold turkey. At first he feels sorry for himself. Then he supplements his diet with booze."

"But how do I help him?"

"Somewhere in the back of his mind he knows he's screwing up his life and his marriage, but self-pity is still the overriding consideration, and booze is still the higher priority. You should give him all the love and attention you can. Avoid criticizing him. You should also talk to his teammates. Tell them exactly what you've told me. They might be able to reach Brian in ways unavailable to you. Peer pressure is a very powerful force. It might work."

Discussing her problem openly, and without reservation was enormously therapeutic to Kerri. "You're wonderful, Miles," she said, feeling an injection of relief and renewed strength.

"Don't you ever forget it. I invested in you because I think you're a winner. However I'm aware that even winners have to be happy to perform to their potential. Don't keep me in the dark, Kerri. I want to know everything that happens. If you have further problems, I want to know about them immediately. Is that understood?"

"Understood.   Thanks   again,   Miles."

CHAPTER 35

Long Island. Wednesday, February 15, 1990.

It was sunny and extremely cold. Breath turned to ice crystals.

Brian, dressed in jeans, heavy white sweatshirt and Jets' jacket, left the Jets' training center shortly after two P.M. and took a taxi to Runway Thirty-eight, an upscale strip joint several blocks from La Guardia. The crowd acknowledged him with a standing ovation. Waiters rushed to deliver free drinks to him. Girls danced for him, gave him special attention, while and after they removed their clothing.

He loved it. Runway Thirty-eight and its strippers had allowed him to recapture the rapture of a steady diet of attention so long missing from his life.

Twenty-two year old Tina DeSouza, a tall slender raven haired Cuban beauty, centered her entire routine directly in front of Brian. The climax of her performance was as close possible to him, with his line of sight directly between her legs. She smiled and winked as she briefly pulled aside the business end of her G-string.

"Wow!" Brian shouted, aroused and excited by her antics. He stuffed a ten dollar bill inside her G-string and asked her to sit at his table.

Tina accepted willingly. Clad only in her red silk track suit and still panting, she took a chair beside him.

He leaned toward her and placed his right arm around her shoulders. "Hi, I'm Brian," he said with a big lecherous smile, his dark brown eyes riveted on the tops of her perfect breasts.

Tina flashed a coy smile. "I know who you are. Doesn't everybody?"

"Would you like a drink?"

"Sure. Gin and tonic."

Brian turned and waved at his waitress, a six foot and change peroxide blonde with blue lipstick and astounding measurements.

She approached the table and leaned toward him, dangling her bare breasts close to his face. "More of the same, Brian?" she asked.

"Yup, and a gin and tonic for Tina."

Tina unzipped the top of her track suit to expose more of her breasts, then reached under the table and placed her hand on his thigh, inducing an almost immediate erection. "I enjoy dancing for you. I feel appreciated."

The waitress returned with the drinks and placed them on the table. "They're on the house, Brian," she said, then left.

Brian raised his glass and took a huge gulp, then returned his gaze to Tina's breasts. "How long have you been doing this?" he asked.

"This is my third year."

"Does it pay well?"

"I make at least fifteen hundred a week, almost all tax free."

"Amazing. I had no idea. You married?"

Tina shook her head. "I live alone with my kitten, but I'm going to quit this business as soon as I have saved enough money. Then I'm going to get married and have a whole bunch of kids."

"Then you really don't enjoy stripping?"

She winked, placed her hand between his legs, and stroked his erect penis. "I do when you're here... I have to get ready for my next show," she said, then leaned close to Brian's ear. "I'm free after that. If you take me home, I'll give you the best dance you've ever seen."

Brian stayed, drank more rum and thought of his wife as he watched Tina's last performance. He was troubled. To this point in his life he had never made love to any other woman. "You can't do this!" he admonished himself.

By the time Tina was once again naked and lying on the stage floor with her legs straddling his line of vision, his decision was made. Her private performance offer was impossible to refuse. "Why not?" he said aloud.

Tina led Brian into her apartment, a small but neat one-bedroom flat, less than a mile from Runway Thirty-eight. She poured a large rum and coke, handed it to him then pointed to the couch. "Sit over there and relax. I'm going to ring your bell." she promised.

She turned on her cassette player, then gave Brian a super seductive performance, no longer constrained by the stringent rule of her employer, free to make physical contact with Brian in very sensual and provocative ways.

Long before the music was completed, they had frantically assisted each other in the removal of clothing, the event culminating in a desperate love making crescendo in the center of the living room rug. Brian closed his eyes, exhilarated, but guilty. He had cheated, broken his marriage vows to Kerri   for   the   first   time.

CHAPTER 36

Kerri telephoned Billy Ray Vincent, an aging black linebacker and one of Brian's teammates. In happier times, Brian had introduced Vincent to her as his closest friend on the team. Vincent, a giant of a man, deeply religious and nondrinker, was happily married. He lived with his wife and four children in nearby Port Washington. "It's Kerri, Kerri Pyper," she announced, agonizing over making the call and revealing the details of a very personal and sensitive problem to an individual she barely knew.

"Hi, Kerri. How you doin'?" Vincent asked.

"I'm fine, but Brian isn't... That's why I called... I was hoping you would help him."

"Did that old dog hurt himself again?"

"No... It's much more serious than that... He's drinking heavily and if he doesn't stop, he's going to ruin his health and his career."

"I'm very sorry to hear that, Kerri. That must be hell for you. How can I help?"

"I would be grateful if you would try to get him to understand what he's doing to himself. He has an enormous amount of respect for you, and if anyone can do it, you can."

Brian rested the back of his head against the rim of the whirlpool, then closed his eyes and allowed the jets of hot water to massage and stimulate the circulation in his injured knee. Thoughts of Tina DeSouza and soon returning to Runway Thirty-eight danced in his brain.

"You sleeping it off?" Vincent asked, then placed his strong black hand on the top of Brian's head and pushed downward, completely submerging his head.

Hot water splashed in all directions as Brian hoisted himself to an upright position. He glared at Vincent. "What the hell was that for?"

"I'll tell you what the hell, Pyper. You're blowin' it. You're pissing away a once in a lifetime opportunity."

"What kind of bullshit is this? I don't know what you're talking about."

"I know you do, Pyper, and that's what I'm talkin' about. I've known a whole hell of a lot of guys with less than half your talent. They made it in this league because they were motivated and focused. They made it because they looked after their bodies and their minds. You know the history of this league is replete with the sad endings of super talented washed up drunks?"

"Where the hell do you get off, Vincent? What I choose to do with my mind and body is my business, not yours."

Vincent frowned and glared at Brian. "I'll tell you where I get off. Someone who loves you very much cared enough to call me last night. She was real upset, Pyper. She told me you're drinkin' your way into oblivion. You better smarten up or you're goin' to find yourself out on the street with all those other washed up million dollar hotshots who thought they were indestructible."

Vincent's confrontation succeeded only in alienating Brian, clouding his mind with contempt for another individual who had dared to invade his privacy. "You have no fucking right to tell me how to live my life! It's none of your business!" He jumped from the bath and headed for his locker.

Brian slurped a large and very dry martini as he paced his kitchen floor. "I'll put an end to this crap once and for all!" he vowed.

Kerri entered her apartment at seven fifteen, shivering from the cold and tired from a long work day. Her fatigue was forgotten when she saw Brian moving toward her as fast as he could hobble. She saw anger in his eyes. Before she could remove her coat, he seized her right shoulder with his left hand and slapped her face as hard as he could with his right. "That's

117

for Billy Ray!" he shouted. "Next time you decide to tell someone how you think I should live my life, tell me first."

The stinging pain of the blow caused Kerri's knees to buckle. The shock and surprise of being hit by her husband for the first time brought tears to her her eyes. She trembled in fear of being hit again.

"Why?" Brian bellowed, his face contorted with rage.

The smell of alcohol turned Kerri's stomach. "You're hurting my arm," she screamed.

The moment Brian released her, she fell backward against the wall, then slowly sank to a fetal position. She buried her face in her hands. "All I wanted to do was help you," she sobbed, fighting an urge to criticize.

"Don't do me any more favors," Brian said, then opened the closet door beside Kerri. He removed his winter coat and left the apartment, slamming the door behind him.

Devastated and more alone than ever, Kerri remained on the floor for a long time, pondering her marriage and worrying about its future.

CHAPTER 37

March, 1990.

For Louis Visconti, every one dollar decline in the price of crude oil represented a paper profit of thirty million dollars. For Saddam Hussein, the president of Iraq, a similar price decline represented huge losses. In view of the dire financial plight into which his country had fallen, oil prices meant everything. With annual oil production of three million barrels per day, every one dollar drop in the price of crude oil meant an annual loss more than one billion dollars.

Since the end of its costly war with Iran in 1988, Iraq's economic condition had been deteriorating. Saddam resented the fact that his country had borne the full weight of resisting Iran. He complained bitterly that Iraq's sacrifices had not been fully appreciated by its Arab neighbors, particularly Kuwait. His resentment, festering for a long time, was approaching the boiling point.

By contrast, Kuwait, the world's sixth largest oil producer, was flush with cash. It's assets abroad exceeded one hundred billion dollars. The ruling family and other wealthy Kuwaiti investors held an additional fifty billion dollars privately. Kuwait's income from diversified investments actually exceeded that from oil sales. Consequently, they had little incentive to increase oil prices in 1990. Such increases would slow the world economy and depress the value of their investments, the main source of their income. Kuwait's intransigence on crude oil pricing further enraged Saddam.

Another extremely contentious issue between Iraq and Kuwait was the huge banana-shaped Rumaila oil field. The pool, just over ten thousand feet below the desert surface, straddled the border between the two countries. With reserves of more than thirty billion barrels, it was one of

119

the world's largest reservoirs, more than three times the size of Alaska's Prudhoe Bay field. More than ninety percent of the fifty mile long formation was inside Iraq, yet most of the oil pumped from it was by Kuwaitis. Aware that Kuwaiti pumps could theoretically drain the pool, Saddam claimed full ownership and accused them of stealing Iraq's oil. Storm   clouds   were   building.

CHAPTER 38

Long Island. Friday, March 16, 1990.

Brian parked his black Eldorado, then hurried inside Runway Thirty-eight. He was hurt and angry. No, betrayed. His pain and suffering had never been fully appreciated by Kerri. Worse, she had the audacity to enlist the support of that prick, Vincent. Pushed beyond the limits of tolerance, he had once again escaped to his refuge. There he was appreciated, adored, free from interference.

Pausing only to watch Tina DeSouza's performances, he spent the evening drinking excessively and re-living glory days with adoring fans who paid for his drinks. Shortly after one A.M. he folded his forearms on the table, lowered his head and fell into a deep sleep.

He opened his eyes the following morning to see Tina's smiling face. "What happened?" he groaned, closing his eyes to shield them from sunlight.

Tina moved closer, pressing her naked body against Brian's. "We poured you into a cab last night. How do you feel?"

He kept his eyes shut and swallowed, tasting foul saliva. "Like I've been hit by a freight train... What time is it?"

"It's ten thirty and I want you," Tina whispered, nibbling at his ear.

Unable and unwilling to respond, Brian lay motionless, trying to remember the events of the previous day. Guilt invaded his mind and caused him to bolt upright. He covered his face with his hands and rubbed his eyes with his fingers. "Do you have any tooth paste?" he asked.

"On the sink in the bathroom," she replied, staring at his naked athletic body.

Brian felt filthy and ashamed as he looked at the bathroom mirror. Once again he had wasted the purity of his marriage. Remorse obsessed him as squeezed a half inch of toothpaste onto his index finger, then used it as a toothbrush. After urinating, he marched directly to the chair beside Tina's bed, gathered his clothes and started to dress.

"What are you doing?" Tina asked.

"Gotta go," Brian replied, focusing on his task.

"Back to your wife?"

Brian shook his head. "I'm already late for my physical therapy. It's part of my contract."

He had told the truth about his destination, but not about his reason for leaving.

"Will I see you later?"

"I'll call," Brian promised, then left.

Miles Dennis approached Kerri's desk, staring at the swelling and bruising on her left cheek. "What happened to you?" he asked.

Kerri covered her cheek with her hand. "It's really bad, Miles. I followed your advice and asked one of Brian's teammates to talk to him."

"So he resented the interference and hit you?"

Kerri nodded, tears flowing. "He was drinking again. After he hit me, he left and stayed out all night."

Dennis shook his head in disgust. "So our football hero hits his wife. If there's one ounce of decency in his body, he'll come home and beg for your forgiveness... If he doesn't, will you hang in there?"

"I don't think I have any alternative," Kerri replied, wiping the tears with her fingers. She was well aware that she did, but that choice was still totally unpalatable.

Dennis changed the subject. He handed Kerri a large manilla envelope. "I have an errand for you. I would like you to deliver this to Louis Visconti. I told him I would get it to him this morning."

CHAPTER 39

Visconti, as usual looking like a Wall Street fashion statement, smiled when he saw Kerri. He lusted immediately, staring at her tight black skirt and form fitting white blouse. Then he saw her cheek. "You have a fight with your husband?" he asked, hoping.

"No, just a stupid accident."

"How stupid?"

"I'm too embarrassed to say."

"Then don't. Would you like a coffee? I just ordered one for myself."

Strangely, Kerri felt comfortable. She tried to smile. "Sure. Black."

Visconti lifted his receiver, ordered the extra coffee, then pointed to two black leather couches near the windows. "Let's sit over there. Coffee will be here shortly." Every fiber of his body ached to sit as close as possible to her, but discretion convinced him to occupy the opposite couch. "You any happier than you were when I saw you at Christmas?" he asked, leaning back and crossing his legs.

"Why would you think I was unhappy then?"

"Intuition, and it tells me you're still unhappy." He focused on her eyes, probing for a reaction.

"Miles told me you you were once married."

Visconti nodded.

"Did you ever have an argument with your wife?"

Visconti displayed a microscopic smirk. "Is the Pope Catholic?"

"Then you understand."

"Yup. You want to talk about it?"

Kerri's face reddened as she shook her head.

"Let me know if you ever do. I'm the best listener you'll ever know."

The conversation continued until Kerri realized she had finished her coffee. The interval with Visconti was a pleasant diversion from the strain of her situation. Strangely, she had enjoyed his company and wished she could stay. She stood after glancing at her watch. "I really should go. Miles is going to wonder what happened to me. Thanks for the coffee and the hospitality."

Visconti displayed a disappointed frown. "The pleasure was mine. Sorry you have to go... Would you consider having lunch with me sometime soon? I'd love to continue the conversation."

"Sure." Kerri said, delighted he had asked.

CHAPTER 40

"Kerri!" Dennis shouted as he raised his arm above the crowd behind him, about to enter the elevator adjacent to the one from which Kerri had emerged. He turned and squirmed free. "Brian called you an hour ago."

The news triggered an explosion of conflicting emotions in Kerri. Part of her wanted to rush to the telephone. A larger part wanted to do whatever was necessary to avoid any further conversation with her husband. "Did he leave a message?" she asked with a frown.

"No, he just asked me to tell you he called. Gotta go. I'm late. See you after lunch."

Kerri returned to her desk, still confused and hurt by the events of the previous evening. She slumped in her chair, totally disinterested in her work. Curiosity usurping control of her pride, she lifted the receiver and dialed her apartment number.

Brian answered after three rings.

"... Hi. It's me... I understand you called."

"I just had to talk to you, Kerri. I would have gone out of my mind if I had to sit here all day without apologizing for what I did last night. I'm really sorry. I..."

"Let's talk about it later," Kerri interrupted, disappointed that Brian had chosen to apologize rather than ask about her cheek. She concluded that he was more interested in massaging his guilt than in her health. "See you tonight," she said, then hung up, still feeling pain and anger, yet mildly relieved to have resumed communication.

Nick Parker, the rotund and neatly bearded owner of Runway Thirty-eight, carefully straightened his flaming red bow tie, then brushed lint and hair from his wrinkled and well worn tuxedo. Gripping his portable microphone he hurried to center stage, stopping in the area where the beams from six spotlights converged. "Good evening, gentlemen!" he shouted with an enormous commercial smile, then paused to scan the audience. "And yes, ladies! It's show time, and it is with extreme pleasure that we present the pride of Runway Thirty-eight. The Cuban bombshell. From Miami, Florida... Misssssss, Tina DeSouza!"

Tina took her cue from Parker's introduction, a generous ovation and very loud bump and grind music. Wearing a tight fire engine red, well zippered track suit, she leaped to the stage and commenced her performance with a dynamic cartwheel. She landed with a spectacular splits and faced the table Brian usually occupied. The zest and vitality with which she had begun her show quickly dissipated when she saw four strange men occupying the table. Her heart sank when she scanned the audience. No Brian.

Brian was plagued by a terrible hangover and relentless guilt. The enormous quantity of alcohol he had consumed the previous day and evening had been processed by his body and expelled by early evening. He was sick and nauseated. A vile taste plagued his mouth. His stomach had violently rejected the dinner of toast and scrambled eggs he had prepared. He awoke from a brief nap and experienced a burning thirst. Dehydration had caused his blood vessels to contract and his hands to shake involuntarily.

He chose beer. The soothing effect of sleep and the reintroduction of alcohol to his bloodstream relaxed him. Delirium tremens disappeared.

His quest for a second beer was interrupted by the loud ring of the telephone on the kitchen wall. "Shit!" he shouted, slamming the refrigerator door and fumbling with the receiver.

"... Brian?"

"Who's this?"

"Tina... You okay?"

"No. I'm sick as hell," Brian groaned.

"I missed you today."

"How did you get my number?"

"You left your wallet in my apartment. It was on the floor under the chair where I put your clothes."

Brian placed his right hand against his rear pants pocket. "Thanks for letting me know. I didn't realize it was missing."

"Do you want me to bring it to you?"

"No. Just bring it to Runway Thirty-eight tomorrow. I'll pick it up there."

"Why not tonight?" Tina asked, disappointed.

Brian had begun to experience an axiomatic truth of an extramarital affair: the better it gets, the worse it gets. By now, his system had normalized to the point where he could respond to her body. He ached to be in Tina's bed again, but still tormented by guilt, he felt compelled to pass on the opportunity. "I would love to, but you wouldn't enjoy the company. I'm still sick as a dog."

"Will I see you tomorrow for sure?"

"Yup."

"For sure?"

"For   sure."

CHAPTER 41

Kerri returned to the apartment at six-thirty. Before she could close the door, Brian was in front of her, displaying a sheepish grin and blocking her entry with outstretched arms. He was unshaven and wore a wrinkled white T-shirt and red and white striped boxer shorts.

She tried to duck under his right arm and pass him, but he lowered it and held her.

The smell of beer filled her with revulsion. She tried in vain to squirm free, then snapped her head backward and glared at him in anger. "We need to talk," she hissed.

Brian rested his head on her shoulder and strengthened his grip. "Kerri, I'm so sorry. I have to know you forgive me."

"It's not that simple, Brian. We can't just sweep this thing under the rug," Kerri argued, turning her head away.

"Sweep what under the rug? What are you talking about?"

In spite of Dennis's advice not to confront her husband about his drinking, Kerri concluded there was no alternative. "Booze! It's killing both you and our marriage!"

Brian's balance was disrupted. Kerri had never before mentioned his drinking. Denial was his first impulse. "Booze! What the hell has that got to do with it?"

"You're incredible!" she shouted. "How can you possibly stand there and suggest that your drinking has no bearing on what's happening to us?"

"Maybe I drink a bit," he conceded. "But I can't see how you can stand there and suggest it's changed anything."

"Brian, do you agree there's a problem in our marriage?" Kerri asked.

"Sure. It's pretty obvious we're not as happy as we used to be."

"But why? Can't you see it?"

"I see it very clearly. You've changed. You're different. You've become a condescending bitch from the day you got that goddamned job. I think you love it more than you ever loved me."

"I give up," Kerri declared, stunned by Brian's intransigence and confused by how to respond to it. She wriggled free of his arms and removed her coat. She hung it in the closet, then turned and headed in the direction of the kitchen.

Brian caught up with her and turned her with a violent jerk of her right arm. "You said we needed to talk," he said, anger in his bloodshot brown eyes belying the calmness of his voice. "So let's talk."

Tears drenched Kerri's eyes. Her body trembled in fear of being hit again. "I was wrong. I really don't think we have anything to talk about."

Brian clenched his teeth and strengthened his grip on Kerri's arm. "You can't handle the truth!" he shouted. "That's why you don't think we have anything to talk about! The truth is that you're married to your job. You can't wait to get out of here in the morning and stay there until they turn the lights off."

"We don't have anything to talk about until you're prepared to admit you have a serious drinking problem."

Brian's body stiffened. His wife's declaration had ignited an uncontrolled rage. Even worse, she had dared to interfere by disclosing the problem to Billy Ray Vincent. "That's absolute bull-shit!" he screamed, then struck the side of her face with the back of his left hand.

Kerri winced in pain, but glared defiantly into Brian's eyes.

"You're the only problem in this marriage!" he shouted. "I waited for you all day. All I could think of was apologizing to you. Now all you want to do is give me attitude! You're no different than that tea-totaling prick, Vincent!" He hurled Kerri to the floor with a violent jerk. "You never appreciated what I did for you, and you probably never will!" he yelled, then stepped over her body and marched to the kitchen.

Dazed and bleeding, Kerri remained face down and motionless on the floor. She heard the refrigerator door open and close, then the sound of a beer can opening. Seconds later, she heard Brian lift the telephone receiver, then order a taxi. She lifted her head to watch him leave the kitchen and walk to the bedroom.

Minutes later, he reappeared, fully dressed and carrying his sports-bag slung over his shoulder. On his way out the door, he stopped and half turned. "See you around," he snorted, then left, slamming the door.

Kerri stood and struggled up the stairs to the bathroom mirror. Blood oozed from the wound on her cheekbone where Brian's wedding ring had broken the skin. She cleaned the blood with a wash cloth soaked in warm water. While rinsing the cloth, she noticed Brian's toothbrush was missing. The terrifying specter of an end to her marriage hit her hard. Desperate and alone, she wept.

Hours later, Kerri dialed her mother's Vancouver number. "Please answer," she pleaded after listening to consecutive rings. She was relieved to hear the familiar voice of her mother.

"Hi, mom," Kerri said.

"Kerri!" Barbara shrieked. "I'm so glad you called. You must be psychic. I was just about to call you tonight. I have wonderful news... I'm going to be married again."

"Who's the lucky man?"

"His name is David Harmon. I met him at the Gas Light Restaurant a week after Christmas. I'm sure it wouldn't surprise you that I wasn't the slightest bit interested in him at first. But he persisted, and I finally agreed to have dinner with him. It was fantastic. It's absolutely amazing how much we have in common."

"Who is he?" Kerri asked, suppressing a strong desire to discuss her own problem.

"You'll love him. He's quite a bit older than me. He's a writer, born and raised in Vancouver. He has a beautiful house on Hornby Island and want's us to live there after we're married."

"When's the wedding?"

"The minute you can get here. I asked David to wait until you get here. Is there any way you can?"

Kerri made a quick decision. "I'll try to get a flight tomorrow. It might end up in Seattle. If it does, could you..."

"Don't even think about it. Just call as soon as you have a flight. We'll arrange to pick you up wherever you land. I don't care if it's Calgary."

"I'm happy for you, mom."

"Me too... What about you? Is everything okay?"

"Yes. I'll call as soon as I get a flight."

Kerri hung up and phoned Miles Dennis. "Miles, it's Kerri. I'm sorry to bother you, but I need to ask you if I can take a couple of days off."

"No problem. What's happening?"

"Same problem, only much worse... It really blew up tonight."

"Tell me about it."

"I know you told me not to confront Brian about his drinking, but I did it... He's gone. It might be forever."

"Did he hurt you?"

"Physically, I'm okay. Emotionally, I need help. I need to spend some time with my mother. She lives in Vancouver."

"Take all the time you need, and please tell me if there's anything else I can do. I'll miss you."

Brian slumped in the back seat of a taxi and rested his head on Tina DeSouza's shoulder. "The whole world's hassling me, Tina," he slurred, his eyes glazed and his mind groggy. "You're the only person who doesn't hassle me." He rolled his eyes skyward. "You won't ever hassle me, will you?"

Tina kissed Brian's forehead. "Never," she promised.

CHAPTER 42

Newark Airport. Saturday, March 17, 1990.

Kerri boarded an Eastern Airlines DC-9 at nine-twenty, A.M. After switching planes in Toronto, she took a direct flight on an Air Canada 747 to Vancouver.

Time had been unkind to Barbara. Her once tall and slender frame now sported considerable excess weight. Her beautiful blue eyes were now surrounded by wrinkles and pronounced crow's feet. Her long flowing blond hair had grayed. Her elegant single chin had doubled. Thrilled to see her daughter again, she ran to her and hugged her. "I can't tell you how happy I am to see you again," she said with tears of joy. "You mean so much to me," she said, constantly plagued by the memory of the daughter she had given up for adoption. She touched Kerri's swollen cheek with her index finger. "What happened?" she asked.

"... It's a long story," Kerri said, shifting her focus to a tall well dressed man standing beside her mother. He wore a brown tweed sport coat, gray flannel pants, and well buffed brown shoes. A brown bow tie adorned his pale blue buttoned down shirt. His hair was shoulder length, thick and white. He looked like a hippy who had morphed into a college professor.

"Oh, I'm so sorry," Barbara said, embarrassed by her oversight. "I should have introduced you two right away." She turned to her elderly companion. "David, I want you to meet my daughter... Kerri, this is David Harmon, the man I'm going to marry."

Harmon offered a warm smile, then took a step in Kerri's direction and extended his hand. "I'm very happy to meet you, Kerri. Your mother's told me nothing but good things about you."

In spite of Harmon's age, Kerri immediately understood why her mother was attracted to him. His smile and deep brown eyes exuded kindness and a knowing awareness. She held his hand and grinned. "I'm happy to meet you too, David," she said, struggling to suppress her sadness.

"I'm sure you girls have a lot to talk about," Harmon said. He pointed to the exit. "I'll get the car and meet you just outside the Arrivals door."

Barbara smiled and blew a kiss to Harmon. "Thanks, darling," she sang, then turned to Kerri. "Now, tell your mother all," she demanded.

As if a dam had burst, Kerri released her caged emotions. Tears streamed from her eyes as she hugged her mother and wept.

Barbara elected to postpone insist on an explanation. "No matter how bad it is, please remember I'm here for you. I always will be." She kept her arm around Kerri's shoulder and led her toward the door.

The shrill horn of Harmon's car caught Barbara's attention. "There he is," she said, pointing to Harmon's steel-gray Jaguar, splattered by heavy rain and parked more than fifty yards away. "Let's run," she said, reaching for Kerri's hand.

Kerri remained silent in the back seat of Harmon's car while it inched northward on Granville Street toward downtown Vancouver. She was in no mood for small talk and unwilling to discuss her situation in the presence of a man she barely knew.

"Did I tell you David's a writer?" Barbara asked, loud enough for Harmon to hear.

Kerri interrupted her constant stare out her window to glance at Harmon. She forced a pleasant smile. "What do you write, David?" she asked.

Harmon focused on Kerri's face in his rear view mirror. "Most of the material I've written lately is..."

Barbara interrupted. "David's far too modest. He has a doctorate in biochemistry and he's written five books on genetic codes. The last one's been published in thirteen different languages."

Kerri was both interested and fascinated. "Congratulations. Would it be possible for me to get a copy of the last one? Even if I don't understand it, it would be an honor to read a book written by my stepfather."

Harmon smiled at Kerri via the rear view mirror. "It would be an honor to have my stepdaughter read it, but I'm afraid it would bore you."

Thirty minutes later, Harmon maneuvered his car into a parking space very close to the front door to Barbara's apartment building, an aging but clean ten story structure facing English Bay. He turned to face his passengers. "I doubt it will disappoint either of you to learn that I'm going to have to leave you here for a couple of hours. Some rather urgent business requires my attention."

Barbara commenced her interrogation when they entered the elevator. "Okay, start from the beginning... No. First tell me what happened to your cheek. Was it Brian? Did he hit you?"

Kerri nodded. "Everything was fine until Brian's knee was hit last November. That was the beginning of the end."

"Why?" Barbara asked, then leaned against the mirrored elevator wall.

Kerri exhaled and shook her head. "I wish I knew for sure. I can only guess... He replaced center stage with booze. I had no idea it was a problem. We laughed about it at first, but eventually it stopped being funny."

"Did you ever confront him about it?" she asked.

"Miles Dennis suggested I get one of his teammates to do it instead, so I did. That was a big mistake. Brian really resented the interference. He hit me for the first time ever. Then he left and stayed out all night... He came home yesterday. Foolishly, I decided to confront him. That turned out to be the coup de grace."

"What did he do?"

Kerri burst into tears and covered her face with her hands. "He went ballistic and hit me again. Then he packed a bag and left."

"He'll be back. I know he will," Barbara promised, then wrapped her arms around Kerri.

"I don't care what he does any more. He's ruined the marriage, mom. It can never be the same."

Barbara lifted Kerri's chin with her fingers. "I can't believe it!" she said, shaking her head. "You two were so much in love."

"I really tried, mom. The man I loved got lost in a bottle."

"Is there another woman?"

"I don't know."

Barbara, exuding empathy for her daughter's emotional turmoil, kissed her forehead. "I've got a great idea. Take a hot bath. I know you'll feel a lot better."

Kerri entered the room where she had spent so many nights as a teen. She frowned as she stared at her one and only window and saw the same narrow view of English Bay, wedged between the same two ugly apartment buildings she had grown to hate. Minutes later, she lowered her head to one of the numerous pillows on her bed and fell into a deep sleep.

CHAPTER 43

She was awakened by a stabbing pain caused by the pressure of her left cheek against her pillow. After a moment of disorientation her thoughts returned to her New York job and to her marriage, both of which she was certain were terminal. Even though a large part of her wanted to return, she knew it would be impossible to survive alone in that expensive city on her salary. Her expenses would easily eclipse her income from the job which had given her a measure of independence she had never before experienced.

A gentle knock interrupted her thoughts.

Barbara opened the door barely enough to look in. "Good. You're awake. How are you?"

"Fine."

"Want to talk?" Barbara asked, then sat on the bed beside Kerri.

Kerri shook her head. "It hurts too much."

Barbara reached for Kerri's hand. "I understand... Do you want to be alone?"

"No. Please stay."

"Guess what," Barbara said, almost bursting with excitement, her face radiating happiness and anticipation. "The wedding's tomorrow afternoon. That urgent business David said he had to complete was really to set the whole thing up. Nigel Bennett, a minister in Victoria and a dear friend of David's, will be taking the ferry to Vancouver tomorrow morning. David and Nigel are going to take us to lunch at my favorite restaurant in the whole world. Then we're going to come back here and get dressed. At four, I'm going to marry that man and spend the rest of my life with him."

"Where's the ceremony going to be?"

"On top of Grouse Mountain."

"Fabulous! Have you planned a honeymoon?" Kerri asked, dying inside yet prodding herself to share her mother's joy.

Barbara frowned, shook her head and squeezed Kerri's hand.. "We can't go anywhere under the circumstances... I can't leave you now."

"Yes you can," Kerri insisted. "I won't let you to miss one day of happiness because of me. I won't let you do it, mom. It wouldn't be fair to you or David."

"Then come with us. David wants to go up to Whistler for a couple of days, then to Hawaii for two weeks."

"That wouldn't work and you know it. I'd be a terrible drag. Don't worry about me. I'll be fine. I've learned how to survive on my own. Be happy, mom. If you don't go on that honeymoon, I'm going to tell David to kidnap you."

"What will you do? Have you made any decisions?"

Kerri shook her head.

"Will you join us for dinner at the Bayshore tonight? David really wants to get to know you."

Kerri smiled. "I'd like that very much."

New York. Saturday, March

Tina DeSouza placed a quarter in the pay telephone inside the entrance to Runway Thirty-eight. She dialed the number of The Times.

A woman answered. "The Times. How may I help you?" she asked.

"May I speak to the sports editor, please?"

"One moment."

Seconds later, a man answered, "Hi. Mark Duncan speaking. What can I do for you?"

"Are you the sports editor?"

"Ah, no. I'm his assistant. May I help you?"

"Maybe you can... Have you ever heard of Brian Pyper?"

"If you're talking about the Jets' quarterback, I sure have. Why?"

"You interested in a big scoop?"

"I like scoops of all sizes. What have you got?"

"Pyper's spending a lot of time with a stripper at Runway Thirty-eight, near La Guardia. Her name is Tina DeSouza."

"Sounds interesting. Who am I talking to?"

"That's not important. If you're interested in the story, just send a reporter to Runway Thirty-eight, tonight. Make sure he has a camera."

"They don't allow cameras inside strip-joints. Just tell me what a reporter's going to see."

"Tell him to use his imagination," Tina said, then hung up.

CHAPTER 44

Miraculously, the thick gray layer of clouds which had blanketed Vancouver had dissipated, allowing the wedding to begin under an almost cloudless sky. The late afternoon sun blessed the wedding of Barbara Larkin to David Harmon. Warm air made it possible to have the ceremony on the outer deck of The Observatory, a magnificent steel, glass and wood restaurant perched at the summit of Grouse Mountain, six thousand feet above the City of Vancouver.

To the extreme delight of David Harmon, Peter, his handsome forty-two year old son from his first marriage, had flown all the way from Hong Kong to be his father's best man.

Nigel Bennett, a graying giant of a man, wearing a black suit and clerical collar, stood facing the four in the wedding party. "Let us begin," he commanded with ministerial authority, his hazel eyes focused on Barbara.

Kerri stared beyond Bennett, her eyes focused on the silhouette of Vancouver Island, fifty miles to the west. The minister's words seemed distant and muffled to her as she allowed her mind to wander. She managed to focus when Bennett asked for vows.

"Do you, Barbara, take David to be your lawfully wedded husband, for better or worse, for richer or poorer, in sickness and in health, until death do you part?"

"I do," Barbara declared.

Bennett turned to David and smiled. "Do you, David, take Barbara to be your lawfully wedded wife, for better or worse, in sickness and health, until death do you part?"

Kerri repeated the vows in her mind and in unison with the minister. She remembered her own vows and recalled how important they were to her when she married Brian. "How could he forget?" she asked herself. "The commitment was forever, without reservation. No matter how..." She glanced upward and smiled. "No matter how sick he was."

An elbow bumped Kerri's arm and interrupted her thoughts. She turned to see her mother glaring at her. "The ring," Barbara mouthed with an annoyed and anxious expression.

Kerri had been carrying David's wedding ring in the palm of her left hand. The white knitted wool dress she was wearing had no pockets. Sporting a reddened face and sheepish grin, she handed the ring to her mother.

Barbara turned and placed the gold band on the third finger of David's left hand.

Clasping the left hands of both Barbara and David, Bennett continued, "With the exchange of rings and the declaration of your vows, one to the other, and by the power vested in me by the Province of British Columbia, I hereby pronounce you husband and wife." He grinned. "It's okay now, David. You may kiss your bride."

After a lengthy and passionate kiss, David held Barbara's hand high in front of him and pretended to address a large congregation. "Ladies and gentlemen of the City of Vancouver and the world, it gives me great pleasure to present the new, Misses David Harmon." He faced Barbara and winked. "The whole world won't stop clapping until I kiss you again... May I?"

With an adoring smile, Barbara did the honors.

David took a deep breath after the kiss, then turned to face the small wedding party. "In the spirit of the occasion, I've made reservations for cocktails and dinner for the five of us aboard The Islander. At this moment she's docked at the foot of Burrard Street, and will be casting off at five-thirty. If we leave immediately, I think we'll make it."

As the members of the wedding party headed for the cable-car, Barbara reached for Kerri's arm and drew her closer. "Where were you during the ceremony?" she asked with a muffled whisper and a scowl.

"New York."

"I'm sure you were."

"Your vows helped me make a decision. I'm going back, mom."

"What did our vows have to do with it?"

"I promised to have and to hold him in sickness and in health. Brian's sick, mom. His injury and the alcohol made him sick. I can't just walk away from that vow. I can't."

"I think you're being overly sentimental. That son of a bitch hit you and left you."

"There's no way he would have done either if he was well. I wasn't there for him. I chickened out and left him."

"But to go back to him! That's got be the ultimate in masochism! I hope you realize you could be hurt again," Barbara warned.

Kerri nodded. "I have to go, mom. Brian needs me and I'm going to do whatever it takes to help him."

CHAPTER 45

Vancouver International Airport. Monday, March 19, 1990.

A torrential downpour drenched Kerri's gigantic red and white Air Canada 747 as it thundered skyward. Seated behind the starboard wing, she stared unfocused at the hundreds of droplets on the outer surface of her window. Trepidation plagued her, yet she looked forward to returning to her job and to Miles Dennis, the one and only person in New York City who would be happy to see her.

The captain's baritone voice broke the silence on the airplane four hours later. "This is your captain speaking. We should be landing in the next ten or fifteen minutes. The weather in New York isn't all that bad, for March. It's clear and cool, about forty-five degrees."

It was six-fifteen, New York time, when Kerri's plane touched down at Kennedy International Airport. After clearing customs and picking up her bags, she took a taxi to her apartment.

Her heart pounded when the cab rounded the final corner and moved to within sight of her apartment. She strained to see the living room and bedroom windows facing the street, but saw no lights. Her hands shook when she unlocked the front door. She kicked three unopened newspapers inside, then entered and closed the door. She turned on the lights and scanned the apartment for evidence of Brian's return. None.

She telephoned Miles Dennis. After three rings, she heard the familiar message on his answering machine.

"Miles, it's Kerri. I just called to tell you I'm back in New York. I'll see you at work tomorrow morning."

Kerri was awakened at ten forty-five by the loud ring of the telephone beside her bed. She managed to turn on the night table lamp with her eyes tightly shut. With one eye barely open, she lifted the receiver, answered, then pulled the covers over her head to preserve darkness.

"It's Miles... Did I wake you up?"

"No. I'm still asleep."

"Sorry. I just assumed you'd still be awake. How are you?"

"Fine, under the circumstances. How are you?"

"Tired. I've been working my fingers to the bone. I didn't realize how valuable you had become until I had to work without you. I can't tell you how glad I am to have you back... Is Brian there?"

"No. I'm alone."

"No notes, flowers?"

"Nothing."

"Do you subscribe to The Times?"

"Yes. Why?"

"... If you've got today's edition, you'll find a picture of your husband in the sports section... I should warn you. It's not pretty."

"Why? What am I going to see?"

"He's with a woman... A stripper."

"It's probably just a publicity thing," Kerri said, unwilling to accept any notion of her husband's infidelity.

"Unfortunately, it doesn't look like it's got anything to do with publicity... Maybe I should come over there. I don't want you to be alone when you see it."

Kerri's heart pounded as she wiped tears from her eyes. "Thanks for offering, but I can handle it. I'm over twenty-one."

"Don't hesitate to call me if you change your mind."

"I won't," Kerri promised. She hung up, then leaped from the bed and raced to the front door. She descended to her knees and ripped the Wednesday edition of The Times from its clear polyethylene cover. She removed the sports section and dropped it on the floor in front of her. In the center of the front page was an eight inch square photograph of Brian and another woman. Brian, obviously unwilling to be photographed, was attempting to shield his face with the palm of his left hand. His right arm was wrapped around the woman's shoulder.

Kerri's eyes shifted to the caption at the bottom of the photo. Her blood turned cold as she read, "QUARTERBACK SNEAK??? New York Jets' star quarterback, Brian Pyper, was seen leaving Runway Thirty-eight early this morning. Accompanying him was super-stripper, Tina DeSouza. Pyper's wife was unavailable for comment."

The photograph spoke volumes. Kerri's focus darted back and forth between her husband and the stripper. Disappointment and rage exploded inside her. She was heartbroken. The equation of her marriage had been altered, permanently. Never again would she experience the purity of their relationship. She thumped the photograph with her fist. "You bastard!" she screamed, tears blurring her vision. "How could you do this? How could you   destroy   such   a   beautiful   thing?"

CHAPTER 46

Visconti telephoned Nick Benedetti, an unscrupulous private detective who had been enormously helpful to him in the resolution of a number of his previous and unfortunate affairs. Benedetti received the call in his Staten Island office. "Louis, baby! Good to hear from you. What's shaking?" he sang, resting his feet on his cluttered desk and flicking cigar ashes to the floor.

"I've got a job for you. You busy?"

"Never too busy for you, Louis. You know that. What've you got?"

"You know the Jets' quarterback, Brian Pyper?"

"Who the hell doesn't? I saw his picture in The Times today. Looks like he's running with a Cuban squeeze."

"I want you to follow him. Stick to him like wet underwear. I want the whole book on this dude, Nick. I want pictures. Real good ones. None of that kissy face crap. Give me skin, enough to nail him to the wall."

"This guy got something on you?"

"No. His wife does."

"You care to tell me what?"

"I'm in love with her."

"That's a lot to have on a man. I'll give it my undivided attention, Louis. Count on it."

Kerri raced through a breakfast of toast and coffee, frequently glancing at her watch. With less than enough time to avoid being late for work, she hurried from the kitchen. To her surprise and horror, she saw Brian removing his jacket in the foyer. He appeared to have recently awakened, his face unshaven, his hair ruffled, and large puffy circles sagging below his bloodshot eyes.

Brian dropped his empty night bag on the floor. "What are you doing here?" he asked with a raspy voice.

"In case you've forgotten, I live here," Kerri challenged.

"I thought you left... I phoned here at least five times and there was no answer."

"Did you phone my office?"

Brian nodded. "All they would tell me was that you were out of town."

"... I went to Vancouver for two days."

"How did you pay for the flight?" Brian asked with an antagonistic scowl.

"I put it on the credit card." Kerri anticipated a confrontation, but almost welcomed it, hoping it would clear the air.

"How much was it?" he asked, raising the decibel level of his voice.

"A little over six hundred."

Brian placed his hands on his hips and tightened his lips. "Six hundred! Where do you plan to get six hundred dollars? I'm sure as shit not going to pay for it."

"Brian, maybe instead of telling me what you aren't going to do, you should tell me what you are going to do. Maybe you could start by telling me if you're coming or going." Anger prodded her to be more specific, but instinct inhibited her.

"You really care?"

"Sure I do, and I think we should talk about what's going to happen to our marriage."

Brian smirked. "Aren't you the same girl who told me we have nothing to talk about unless I'm prepared to admit I have a drinking problem?"

"Yes, but when I said it, I assumed it was the only problem we had."

"So now you're saying it's okay for us to talk because we have more than one problem. Is that it?"

Brian's belligerent and deliberate attempts to provoke Kerri had come very close to succeeding. She struggled with an almost overwhelming urge to scream. "Don't you find it difficult to live with uncertainty?" she asked.

"What do you mean by uncertainty?"

"Let's start with the obvious. If you're planning to live somewhere else, I've got to make other arrangements."

"That's completely up to you. There's no way I'm coming back here if you're going to hassle me about the way I live my life."

"You still don't see it," Kerri said, exasperated. "I'm trying to help you and save our marriage, but I need a little cooperation."

"Well that's the problem right there. It isn't about drinking, or uncertainty. It's all about you trying to get me to live my life according to your standards. Forget it!" Brian shouted. "It isn't going to happen!" He stormed past Kerri and climbed the stairs behind her.

Confused, angered and frustrated, Kerri left the apartment and headed for the bus stop, a block and a half away.

CHAPTER 47

It was almost nine when Kerri entered the office of Iacardi & Sons. She marched directly to her boss's office and closed the door behind her. Dennis smiled and jumped to his feet. "Welcome back. You can't know how glad I am to see you. You had me worried."

Kerri left her overcoat on and sat on the metal chair in front of his desk. "Sorry I'm late. I was on the way out the door when Brian arrived. I should have kept going, but I couldn't."

"I bet you're going to tell me it wasn't a happy reunion."

"That's an understatement. We can't even communicate any more."

"You bring up the subject of his picture in the Times?"

Kerri shook her head. "I knew it would make things worse. I just asked him if he planned to come home. He said he wouldn't if I continued to hassle him about the way he lives his life. Then he refused to continue the conversation and went to the kitchen. I presume he was going to pick up some of his things and leave again, but I didn't stay long enough to find out."

Dennis looked away and shook his head. "I feel so sorry for you. I wish there was a simple solution to it."

"So do I, but there isn't... I'm such a fool, Miles. I was absolutely determined to save our marriage. I was prepared to do whatever it took. I was even convinced the split was my fault."

"You may be guilty of being naive, but you're no fool."

Kerri blinked, vainly trying to suppress tears. "If I'm not a fool, maybe you can tell me what I'm doing here."

"At the risk of sounding trite, I'll tell you what you're doing here. You're working for me, and you're doing a damn good job."

"Thank you. It's the one good thing to come out of this whole mess. Unfortunately I'm going to have to end it. I would give anything to stay here with you, but it's impossible. I can't afford to stay in New York on my salary."

"It's not impossible. You know that regardless of whether you reconcile with Brian or not, he's going to have to maintain your life-style."

"No way!" Kerri argued, shaking her head. "Accepting money from Brian would be worse than accepting welfare."

Dennis smiled. His admiration for Kerri had risen several notches. "You're truly unique. Most women I know wouldn't look at the situation quite that way."

"How would they look at it?"

"The old fashioned way. Initially, they would feel abused and damaged. Eventually, consumed with anger and indignation, they would rush off to hire the meanest, nastiest divorce lawyer they can find, the kind who eats raw meat for breakfast. Then together, using the full force of the law, they tap into the husband's jugular vein and open the valve. At the end of the day, they whine and snivel all the way to the bank."

"Well that's not me. I'd feel dirty. I think the best thing for me to do is to go back to Vancouver and start over."

Dennis was troubled. Kerri had become indispensable. He adored her. "I can't let you go, Kerri. You're too valuable to me... If I could make it possible for you to stay in New York, would you consider it?"

"Sure I would. But..."

"Twelve years ago, when our kids were still with us, my wife went back to work. We had an apartment built in the basement and hired an Irish nanny. It was a super arrangement until the kids left home. The nanny moved out and we stopped using the apartment... I would be delighted if you would consider making it your home."

"That's very generous, but it's too much of an imposition. I couldn't."

151

"No imposition at all, but there are strings attached. You have a wonderful future in this business, Kerri. If you accept my offer, you'll have to enroll in the Commodity Trader's Course. If you're successful, you'll become a licensed commodities trader. With your intelligence and my help, you can't miss, and you'll certainly be able to afford to live in New York."

Dennis's unexpected offer was enormously appealing. Suddenly it was possible for her to remain in New York and stay in the business she had grown to love. Even better, she could retain the independence she valued so highly. "Is there a curfew?" she asked, smiling at last.

Dennis shook his head.

"Then I accept." Kerri stood and extended her hand to Dennis.

"Wonderful!" Dennis said, then stood and hugged her instead of accepting her hand. "I promise I'll do everything possible to ensure that you never regret this decision and one day I'm going to refer to you as my colleague."

Surprised by Dennis's uncharacteristic display of emotion, Kerri flinched, then relaxed, happy to feel the strength and warmth of a man's arms.

"You're going to make it through this mess, Kerri, and when you do, it'll be nothing but a bad memory."

"I wish I could share your optimism. I'm really scared, Miles."

"That's understandable. An awful lot's happened to you in a very short period of time. It may not be any consolation to you, but you're not unique. Splits are so common now that surviving first marriages are considered items of curiosity. The game has changed so much that some people think there's something wrong with you if you're still in your first marriage."

"Are you?"

Dennis's face flushed as he nodded. "Andrea and I are a prime example of a prehistoric married couple. We're alone. Not one of our friends is still involved in a first marriage."

"You must have a formula."

152

"I keep telling myself it's love and devotion, but in all honesty, I think there's a bit of inertia involved. Relationships change with the passage of time. When the intense passion subsides, it's replaced by friendship, closer and more precious than any you'll ever experience." Dennis's gray eyes locked on Kerri's. "Let me show you. Have dinner with us tonight." He walked to his telephone and lifted the receiver. "Say yes and I'll call Andrea, right   now."

CHAPTER 48

Brian entered Runway Thirty-eight at seven-thirty and marched to his favorite table at stage side. With a now customary wave of his hand, he ordered a rum and coke. Marsha Ridecki, on bar duty and wearing only tight red silk panties and white cowboy-boots, delivered the drink to his table. "Running a tab tonight, Brian?" she asked, leaning in front of him to advertise her enormous naked breasts.

Brian nodded, his mouth within tongue distance of her breasts. "I'm here for the duration," he said, then leaned back to watch the show.

Nick Bennedetti nursed a beer at the table next to Brian's. He looked every bit the part, built like a bull-dog, dressed in black trousers, black silk shirt, opened at the neck to display a heavy gold chain and generous chest hair. His thick black hair was well oiled and combed straight back. He had begun to enjoy the assignment. Drinking beer and watching girls take their clothes off was substantially more pleasant than cold lonely automobile stakeouts, waiting for something to happen. "Walk in the park," he muttered.

Dinner with Andrea and Miles Dennis exceeded Kerri's expectations. It was served in the high ceilinged dining room of their massive three-story red bricked home in an upscale area of Glen Cove. The warmth with which Andrea had received and welcomed her quickly gave her the assurances she needed. She was glad she had agreed to Miles's proposition. She placed her empty coffee cup in the saucer in front of her and smiled at Andrea. "Thank you for a wonderful dinner, Andrea. This is the first time I've been invited out since I came to New York."

"You're more than welcome," Andrea replied, reaching for Kerri's hand. "May I assume that you'll agree to stay? Before you answer, I want to know that I'll be extremely disappointed if you don't. Now that the kids are gone, Miles is rarely home. You'll be an very welcome addition. I get lonely rattling around in this mausoleum."

Kerri could see why Miles had remained married to Andrea. Vivacious, extremely gregarious and instantly likable, she had retained a youthful figure, and her short auburn hair complemented her freckled smile. Andrea's charm and infectious personality relieved the pressure of her torment. Kerri nodded and grinned. "How can I ever thank you?"

"You just did," Andrea said with a radiant smile. "How soon can you move?"

Kerri was again confronted by her deep sense of responsibility to Brian. Then a frown gradually gave way to a smile. "Guess I don't have to worry about getting anyone's approval."

"Tomorrow?" Andrea asked.

"Tomorrow night, Andrea," Miles answered. He turned to Kerri. "I'll take the car tomorrow. We can leave the office early and go straight to your apartment."

"Do you have much to move?" Andrea asked.

Kerri shook her head. "Not much. Mostly clothes."

"No furniture?"

"It all belongs to Brian."

"That's ridiculous!" Andrea said, raising her voice. "Half of it belongs to you. Just because he paid for it doesn't mean a thing."

"I told Miles I don't want anything from Brian. Taking furniture would be like accepting charity."

Andrea smirked. "Just give me a little time, my dear. I'll change your mind about that."

Miles rolled his eyes skyward, then turned to Kerri. "Andrea's a big city girl from her head to her toes. Don't let her corrupt you, Kerri," he warned.

Andrea glared at him, sticking her tongue out in reaction to her husband's invective. She turned to Kerri again. "I'm having a dinner party on Saturday night. I'd be delighted if you would join us."

CHAPTER 49

Bennedetti watched Brian leaving Runway Thirty-eight with his arm around Tina DeSouza. He glanced at his watch. It was one forty-five. He removed a wad of bills from his right pants pocket, stripped off a fifty and dropped it on the table. He raced to the parking lot and climbed into his 1990 black Dodge Caravan. He drove directly to the building containing his newly rented office space. He took the elevator to the third floor. After fumbling with the keys in near darkness, he finally succeeded in unlocking the door, then hurried to the window facing Tina's apartment. "Damn!" he shouted when he saw no lights on in the apartment. He unfolded his aluminum deck chair and sat to wait, his Exquisito Cuban cigar his only company.

He bolted upright when he saw a light in one of the windows of Tina's apartment. Through the eyepiece of his telescope he saw Brian walking from the bedroom toward the washroom. He smiled. "Just goin' for a whiz, Brian, baby? I want you to get real busy when you get back," he said aloud.

His hopes were quickly dashed when Brian returned to the bedroom less than two minutes later and turned off the light beside his bed. "Too much booze tonight? Maybe you should sleep it off, then wake up, horny as hell." He relaxed in his chair, blowing smoke rings into the darkness.

Bennedetti was awakened at six by the shrill beeping sound of a garbage truck moving in reverse. He looked through his Celestron Omni ZLT telescope. "Wakey, wakey," he said when he saw Tina and Brian still asleep. With the approach of daylight, he could no longer rely on the lights in Tina's apartment to signal him. Now he would have to monitor the telescope almost constantly.

His patience was soon rewarded. Activity began thirty minutes later when Tina moved closer to Brian and kissed his forehead.

Bennedetti smiled and whistled. "Come on Brian, baby! Wake up!" he shouted. His smile broadened when he saw Brian respond to Tina's kiss by wrapping his arms around her and pulling her down on top of him. "Okay kids, it's show time!" he urged, turning to his Nikon and zooming in on the happy couple.

Benedetti's photo-op improved as Tina, naked, hurled the covers from the bed. She stood and straddled Brian's head with her feet. Benedetti cheered while he watched her perform her exotic routine, utilizing the entire surface of the bed. The session culminated in a wild, passionate scene wherein Bennedetti's subjects satisfied each other in a bewildering variety of exciting and provocative positions.

Long before the love making ended, he had accumulated far more photographs than he would ever need to complete Louis Visconti's assignment.

CHAPTER 50

Toronto. Friday, March 23, 1990.

Karen, still in her pink silk nightgown and wearing no makeup, joined Mike for an early breakfast in the penthouse kitchen. She was on a mission. "Let's talk," she said.

Mike lowered his newspaper. "What about?" he asked.

"The trust. I think we've made an enormous mistake."

Mike frowned and rolled his eyes. "Don't do this to me, Karen."

"I have to," she insisted. "We're sitting on over six hundred million dollars of stolen money, and there's no way in God's green earth we'll ever spend it, or do anything with it, other than fret and worry about someone finding out that we have it. I can't get it out of my mind."

"So what do you think we should do?"

"Get rid of it."

"Get rid of it!" Mike protested, then attempted to end the conversation. He stood, loosened his belt, unzipped his fly and lowered his jeans far enough to expose the scars created by the bullet from Servito's gun over ten years earlier. He pointed to the scars. "This is my reminder of what happened in Caracas. The bullet that did this was intended to kill me in a very painful way. Fortunately it didn't, but every day it reminds me of why it happened." He pulled his jeans back to the original position, returned to his chair and glared at Karen, resolve burning in his deep blue eyes. "Don't make me go there," he hissed.

Unimpressed by Mike's theatrics, Karen folded her arms and returned Mike's stare. She persisted. "You're sweeping it under the rug again, King. That history has been every bit as hard for me as it is for you. Besides, your scars aren't the issue and you know it."

159

"I really don't. What is the issue?"

"The money. As long as you insist on keeping it, you'll never be able to forget that part of our past. I don't care how hard you try to hide it, it'll always be there and it'll always be tainted."

"I've been thinking about it a lot lately," Mike conceded, finally accepting the futility of avoiding a forthright discussion about a subject he knew had been tormenting Karen for a very long time.

"So what have you been thinking?"

"I've come to a conclusion. You want to hear it?"

"Not particularly, if it involves keeping even one penny of that money."

"It involves something I said ten years ago, and it's been on my mind ever since. I said we should use the money to do some good in this world. I still think we should. I want to give it anonymously to the World Agricultural Foundation. It's one of the most efficient charities in the world. Instead of feeding hungry people, it teaches them to feed themselves." Mike paused to give Karen time to consider his idea. "If you agree, we'll get started fast, but if you want to give the money back to to the Feds, I'll never agree."

Karen smiled. "That's a beautiful idea. Let's do it."

"Okay, we need to talk to Dan Turner first. We need to find a way of giving the money away without any possibility of anyone tracing the source. I don't want us to go to jail just because we suddenly decided to wash our hands."

Karen reached across the table and grasped Mike's hand. "I can't tell you how happy you've made me," she said, delighted that she would soon be rid of the fruits of her former husband's crimes, a curse that had plagued her for too long,

Phillip, standing out of sight in the hallway, no more than twenty feet away, had overheard the entire conversation, each shocking and disappointing word penetrating his heart like a dagger. His parents had lied to him about his inheritance. Ten years earlier they had told him it was returned to the governments of Canada and the United States. He was excited and stunned to learn that his birthright was still in his parents' hands. He was horrified that they were planning to give it away. "I've got to stop them," he said quietly to himself, then began to dream of a new life with his father's millions.

CHAPTER 51

Glen Cove, Long Island. Saturday, March 24,1990.

"I don't think there's any question Poindexter's guilty as hell," Andrea Dennis postulated, contributing to the conversation at her small but intimate dinner party. "But I'm not sure about Ollie North."

Charles Iacardi, the plump chain smoking partner in Iacardi &Sons, emptied his glass of brandy with one gulp, then turned to face Andrea. "If you listened closely to North's secretary... What the hell was her name?"

"Fawn Hall," Jerry Mara said.

Iacardi nodded. "Yah. Hall admitted she altered documents under orders from North, presumably to remove Poindexter's comments." He winked at Andrea. "Now why would an innocent man order her to do that?"

"North was acting under orders from Poindexter," Miles said.

Andrea smiled. "And maybe Poindexter was acting under orders from McFarlane."

"And Reagan sanctioned the whole scam," Visconti added, chuckling.

Sally Ricci, a twenty-eight year old blonde bimbette from Queens and Charles Iacardi's date for the evening, leaned forward and blinked. "Will somebody tell me what the hell you people are talking about? Who are all these people?"

Iacardi smiled. "Isn't she beautiful? Every time I take her out she shocks me with her knowledge of current events." He gave her a disparaging glare. "If you took time out from all those mind numbing soaps you watch every day, you might actually learn what's happening in this world."

"Don't be nasty, Charles," Visconti said, then turned to Sally. "We're talking about the Iran-Contra Affair. It's been alleged that a number of high-ranking bureaucrats in Washington have secretly diverted funds from the sale of weapons to Iran. The powers that be suspect the money was used to support the Nicaraguan Contras in their civil war with the Sandinistas."

Sally nodded, pretending to understand.

Visconti turned to face Kerri. She was sitting directly opposite him and looking incredibly beautiful in the same formfitting white knitted dress she had worn to her mother's wedding. "Kerri, Miles tells me you're living here now. How do you..."

Andrea interrupted. "Louis, how could you be so insensitive?" she scolded, frowning at him.

"It's okay," Kerri said, then turned to Visconti. "I don't think it would surprise you to know that Brian and I have split. Miles and Andrea have very generously invited me to stay with them."

"Please forgive me," Visconti pleaded. "It really was insensitive of me to mention it."

"Not at all. It's actually therapeutic to talk about it."

After a tense pause in the conversation, Miles stood in response to an overt signal from Andrea. "My wife has asked me to invite you all to join us in the den for Irish coffees." He blew a kiss to Andrea. "That was an outstanding dinner, darling."

After thanking the hostess, the guests followed Dennis toward the den.

Visconti hurried to catch up with Kerri. Before she could enter the den he grasped her arm, causing her to turn and face him. "Can you forgive me for that comment? It really was out of line," he said.

"There's nothing to forgive. What you said wasn't out of line at all. Obviously you didn't know my husband and I had split."

Relieved, he released her arm. "Do you mind waiting here for a second? I have something for you. It's in my briefcase in the hallway. I'll be back in a second."

Puzzled and curious, Kerri nodded and waited.

Visconti returned with his briefcase, then removed the report given to him by Nick Bennedetti earlier in the day. He handed it to her. "Before you open this, I want you to know it's probably going to hurt you. Please understand that I had it done because I care about you, and because I wanted to help."

Kerri opened the report bound in a black folder, then began to scan page after page of photographs of Brian and Tina DeSouza making love in every conceivable position. She closed it and glared at Visconti. "How could you do this?" she asked, her expression contorted by revulsion and anger.

"When I saw that picture of your husband in the Times, I thought of you and what it would do to you. I tried to imagine how totally devastating it must have been for you to find out that way. So I..."

"But why this?" Kerri asked, raising her voice, tears streaming from her eyes. "You had to know how devastating it would be."

"I got mad, Kerri," Visconti said, taking the report from her. He placed it on the dining room table, then turned and took her in his arms. He met no resistance. "Maybe it was wrong of me to interfere, but if I had the choice to do it again, I would. I just couldn't believe your husband could be so blatant about his affair with another woman." He tilted his head backward and looked into her tear filled blue eyes. "If what I did was insensitive, what he did was an atrocity."

"I still don't understand how those photographs could possibly help me."

"My strongest motivation was to let you know what a rat you're married to. A lesser one was to give you some ammunition. You're going to need it."

"You mean something to use against him in court?"

"That's exactly what I mean."

"You're the second man who's made the same erroneous assumption."

"Who was the first?"

"Miles."

"Why was it erroneous?"

"He assumed I wanted something from Brian."

Visconti chuckled. "You will, and when you do, you'll be happy to have that report."

"You're wrong, Louis. I could never stoop to that level. I didn't have any money when I met Brian. All I ever wanted was the man I loved. He no longer exists, so I don't want anything from him."

Visconti was captivated by the passion with which Kerri had spoken. "You're absolutely amazing," he said, the corners of his mouth suggesting a smile. "I had no idea there was a girl left on this planet with your attitude." He startled her by kissing her gently on the lips, then reached for her hand. "Let's go. Andrea's going to wonder where we are."

She squeezed his hand and refused to move. "Thank you, Louis."

"For what?"

"The thought."

"Still friends?"

"Definitely."

"What are we going to do with that?" Visconti asked, pointing to Bennedetti's report.

"You keep it? I'll call you if I ever need it."

Visconti lifted the report and flicked through the pages while continuing to stare at Kerri. "Will you have lunch with me on Monday?"

"Sure."

Their conspicuous delay in joining the guests had been noticed by Andrea. She glared at them as they entered, her curiosity stimulated as she focused on the black folder under Visconti's arm. "I was beginning to think you two had left," she said, then pointed to the coffee table. "Your Irish coffees are waiting for you. I hope you like them cold."

Visconti lifted one of the mugs, then turned to Andrea. "Sorry for the delay. Kerri and I had something important to discuss."

Kerri took the last mug and sat in a well cushioned dark blue chair near the fireplace, close enough to enjoy the heat from the flames. Oblivious to the cacophony of numerous conversations in the room, her eyes were riveted on the fire but her mind focused on the black folder under Visconti's arm. Visions of the graphic photos flashed through her brain. She wondered how a man could transfer physical affections in such a short period of time. She tried to understand how Brian's conscience would allow him to share his body with another woman, while still married to her. Her thoughts surrendered to anger as she thought of Brian's flagrant violation of his marriage vows.

She was startled to see Charles Iacardi and Sally, standing in front of her. "I guess you didn't hear me, Kerri," Iacardi said with a polite smile.

"I'm sorry," Kerri said, blushing. "I was lost in thought."

Iacardi extended his hand. "Unfortunately Sally and I have to leave, but we didn't want to go with out saying good-bye to you... I also wanted to tell you personally how happy we are to have you in the company. Miles has told me nothing but good things about you."

"Thank you, Charles. It was very kind of you to say that," Kerri replied, then turned to Sally. "It was nice to meet you, Sally."

"You bet," Sally said with a plastic smile.

The last guest to leave was Visconti. "Goodnight Kerri," he said, reaching for her hand and wishing he could take her in his arms. "I'll be at your office door at noon on Monday."

Kerri showed a forlorn smile. "I'll see you then."

While Miles accompanied Visconti to the front door, Andrea rushed to sit in the chair adjacent to Kerri's. "Kerri, please forgive me. I have an absolutely insatiable curiosity. I had no idea you knew Louis," she said, leaning against the arm of her chair and focusing on Kerri's eyes.

"Your husband introduced us. He's been doing a lot of business with Iacardi lately."

"Is there something more than a business relationship between you and Louis?"

"What would lead you to believe there is?"

"I noticed the two of you were late for Irish coffees."

Kerri's face flushed as she turned to stare at the fire.

"Kerri, please tell me to shut up if..."

"It had everything to do with the folder Louis was carrying," Kerri admitted. "He decided to try to help me when he saw the picture of Brian and that stripper in the paper. He hired a private detective to follow Brian and take pictures. They were all in that folder."

"It hurt you to see them, didn't it?"

Kerri nodded again, tears flowing. "They were awful. I just can't believe he could jump out of our bed and into someone else's."

Andrea chuckled. "Believe it, dear. A lot of men could, and do. I think they have a switch in their brains. All they have to do is flick it to detach their heads from their dicks... Enough of that crap. I really wanted to talk about Louis. You still haven't answered my question. Is there something more than a business relationship between you and him?"

Kerri shook her head. "I couldn't possibly be interested in another man. I don't think I could even bring myself to trust one again."

Andrea smirked. "You will, and when you do, trust will be a must."

"I wish I could share your optimism."

"You need someone in your life. Spending the rest of it alone is not an option for someone as loving and caring as you obviously are... By the way, Louis Visconti wouldn't be a bad start."

Kerri shook her head, but couldn't hide a blush. "You must be joking. He's almost old enough to be my father."

"So what! He's probably one of the most eligible bachelors in the city. Most women would kill for a man like him. He's incredibly good looking, rich and available. Besides, I saw the way he looked at you tonight. I think he's interested in a lot more than helping you."

Although Andrea had stated what had been apparent to Kerri for some time, Kerri avoided acknowledging it. "Even if he was, I couldn't allow myself to get involved. The last thing I need right now is another relationship."

"Give it time my dear. It's a great healer."

Miles appeared in the doorway to the den. "Goodnight girls. You can stay here and talk your brains out. I'm going to bed." He blew a kiss, then disappeared.

Andrea stood and placed her hand on Kerri's shoulder. "I should go with him. He gets upset when I come to bed and wake him up. Enjoy the fire."

"Thanks again for everything, Andrea."

"My pleasure."

Kerri continued to stare at the flames, pondering her uncertain future.

CHAPTER 52

Toronto. Monday, April 2, 1990

Mike traversed the slush-covered parking lot on his way to the door of his office. He was happy, the warmth of the sunshine and the continued strength of his business and marriage to Karen contributing to his buoyant frame of mind. He whistled as he entered the building and walked down the hallway leading to the open office area. "Hi Margaret," he greeted one of his two secretaries.

She looked up and smiled. "Morning Mike... Chris Lippert's waiting for you in your office. You're not going to like what he has to say."

His smile disappeared. "What is it? Tell me before I go in there?"

"I think I should let him tell you."

Mike hurried to his office, closed the door and faced Terry Lippert, his most experienced representative and responsible for the supervision of Mike's Toronto area retail gasoline outlets. Now thirty-two years of age, Lippert had been hired by Mike as a station manager, eight years earlier. Acknowledging Lippert's commitment to the business and tireless efforts, Mike had rewarded him with generous salary increases and advancing levels of responsibility.

Lippert's worried facial expression spoke volumes. "Did Margaret tell you why I'm here?" he asked.

"No, but she told me I'm not going to like what you're going to tell me."

"She was right about that... I think you should sit down."

"Terry, just do it!" Mike demanded.

"We uncovered a credit card kiting scam... It's an in-house deal." Lippert paused and looked away, wishing he could just stop talking. "Phillip's in on it."

Mike walked slowly behind his desk and sat in his brown velour covered swivel chair. "You sure?" he asked, his eyes locked on Lippert's.

Lippert nodded. "I wish I wasn't. Phillip and Gary Matheson have been doing it for some time. If Phillip hadn't been greedy, we probably wouldn't have known about his involvement. He tried to recruit some of the other managers, but they refused and told me the whole story."

"Were you aware of the scam before they told you?"

Lippert nodded. "It started when one of our customers phoned to complain about an overcharge on his credit card statement. According to his records, he bought twenty dollars worth of gasoline on February twenty-sixth. His statement showed he bought thirty dollars worth. If that was an isolated occurrence, we probably would have told the customer it was impossible to substantiate his claim. It was simply our word against his."

"There were more?"

"A lot more. We audited all the credit card drafts for February and March and found a ton of them."

"How did they do it?"

"Suppose you bought twenty dollars worth of gasoline and used your credit card to pay for it. Now, suppose the attendant takes your signed credit card draft and changes the twenty to a thirty. He puts the thirty dollar draft in his cash drawer and takes out ten dollars, cash. That maneuver balances his cash. Then he puts the ten in his pocket, and you get charged for thirty instead of twenty."

Mike winced and shook his head. "Dammit, Chris, I've heard of a lot of ill-conceived scams in my career, but this is the dumbest. Those kids had to know that eventually some customers would reconcile their purchases with their statements."

170

Lippert chuckled. You'll love this one. "The latest complaint we got was from a woman who got a fifty-six dollar charge on her statement. It bothered her because she said her car won't hold any more than fifty dollars worth."

"How much money are we talking about?"

"So far, we've paid out eight hundred and seventy dollars in claims, but we know there's more. I wonder how many people were ripped off and just blindly paid without checking their statements."

"Has Matheson ever been caught with his hand in the cookie jar before?"

"He's clean. In fact he's a damn good manager... What do you want me to do with them?"

"Haul both of them in here tomorrow morning. I'll talk to them."

CHAPTER 53

New York. Monday, April 2, 1990.

Visconti lifted his left arm to glance at his Rolex. It was exactly twelve noon. Adorned in his new cream colored light suit, he paced in the dour reception area of Iacardi & Sons. A white buttoned-down Polo shirt and navy blue silk tie completed his ensemble. To make the occasion of his first date with Kerri memorable, he had rented a long white Mercedes limousine. He had also made reservations for a table for two, downstairs, along the left wall, at 21, an ultra-expensive chic restaurant on 52nd Street.

Kerri appeared in the doorway seconds later. In spite of her private denials about her interest in Visconti, she too had dressed for the occasion. She wore a pleated white skirt, black blazer and pale pink silk blouse. "Hi," she said with a big smile.

"You look fantastic!" Visconti declared, anxiously looking forward to entering the restaurant with her holding his arm, to experience the rush of having people interrupt their conversations to gaze at him and his incredibly attractive companion. "You still want to do this?" he asked, smiling and reaching for her hand.

"Sure. Where to?"

"It's a surprise. I hope you don't mind."

"Not at all. I like surprises."

"Then let's go. Our chariot awaits."

Visconti put on his sunglasses when he emerged from the building into the warm sunshine. The chauffeur, a sophisticated elderly gentleman, dressed in a tuxedo and standing at attention, opened the rear door. "Good afternoon, Mr. Visconti," he said, continuing to look straight ahead.

Kerri stared at the long white Mercedes, then turned to face Visconti. "I feel like royalty. Is it yours?"

Visconti chuckled. "I rented it for the occasion. It turns into a pumpkin at three."

"Three! I'll be fired if I'm gone that long."

"You've been cleared. I phoned Miles this morning and told him you would be late."

"He agreed?"

"How could he refuse? I'm one of his biggest clients. He even offered to pay for lunch."

"Did you accept?"

"No. I wanted to do this on my own, for more reasons than you could imagine. One of them is to atone for my indiscretion." Visconti winked and extended his left hand in the direction of the limousine. "After you, my dear."

Kerri climbed in and Visconti followed. Kerri, unaccustomed to any form of luxurious transportation, turned to Visconti. "Doesn't it bother you to spend so much money, just to go to lunch?"

"Quite the contrary. It's a pleasant diversion for me. I suppose you wouldn't believe I usually eat cold sandwiches alone in my office. It's also a blast from the past. In the good old days it used to be a big deal to be seen having long extravagant lunches."

"What happened? Why has it changed?"

"No more easy money," Visconti replied with a frown, then turned to stare out his window. "I really miss the eighties. I think we'll all look back on those years as being more roaring than the twenties. Now it's more important not to be seen. People stay in their offices and eat buns on the run."

The white limo glided to a stop at the curb in front of 21. Fashioned from several old townhouses, decorated in antique elegance, and in a class of its own, 21 was the favorite watering hole for the city's movers and shakers, celebrity-watchers and beautiful people.

The chauffeur got out and hurried to open the rear door facing the restaurant.

Visconti stepped out, assisted Kerri, then turned to the chauffeur. "I'll phone you when we're ready to go, George. It should be about two-thirty."

Visconti's expectations were fully realized when the two entered the restaurant and were escorted to their table. He strutted like a conquering bullfighter when he saw the patrons interrupt their conversations to stare at Kerri.

The waiter pulled out a chair for Kerri, then placed menus on the table. "Would you like something to drink before lunch?" he asked.

"A vodka martini. Very dry. Two olives," Visconti ordered, then turned to Kerri. "What would you like, Kerri?"

"I'll have a glass of white wine, please," Kerri said, then leaned forward. "Do you mind if I ask why you asked for two olives?"

"To remind me how many drinks I had. When I get the first martini, I'll eat one of the olives and save the other one for the second martini."

"What if the waiter brings the next one with two olives in it?"

"Off with his head," Visconti replied with a wink. He leaned backward and removed his sunglasses. "Ever since Saturday night I've wanted to call you, but somehow the telephone seemed inadequate. I wanted to apologize to you again for that report. I just wanted to assure you that I had it done with nothing but the best intentions. It was stupid of me. I should have known it would affect you in a negative way."

"Please put it out of your mind. I've already accepted your reasons for doing it, and I'm grateful."

"Any regrets?"

174

"Definitely. I loved Brian. I left my roots to be with him and committed my life to him."

The waiter returned with the drinks and placed them on the table, then turned to Visconti. "Would you care to order now, Mr. Visconti?" he asked.

Visconti shook his head. "I'm at least a drink away from lunch," he said. "How about you, Kerri?"

Kerri glanced at her wine. "At least. I haven't even looked at the menu."

The waiter nodded, then left.

Visconti held his martini above the table and gazed into Kerri's eyes. "May I propose a toast?"

Kerri nodded and reached for her glass.

"To the beginning of the rest of your life... In it, may you find the joy and happiness so mindlessly stolen from you," he said, hoping to be responsible for her future joy and happiness.

Kerri clinked her glass against Visconti's. "Thank you. I'll certainly drink to that."

After taking a sip of his martini, Visconti placed it on the table and leaned forward. "I really envy you... I was reminded of one of the major laments of my life when you answered my question about regrets. You made it obvious how deeply you cared for Brian. I've never felt that way about anyone."

"Not even your wife? Didn't you say you were once married?"

Visconti nodded. "Like most young people, I did it for all the wrong reasons: loneliness, peer-pressure, and sex, not necessarily in that order."

"Then what are the right reasons?"

"I'm pretty sure there's only one."

"What?"

"Love."

Kerri winced. "I married for love. Look where it got me."

"I should never pose as an expert on the subject of love, but I think I've lived long enough to know there's no reasonable substitute."

"Well it was missing from my relationship."

"I don't think it's cast in stone that relationships must survive. There are just too many conflicting external factors these days. In a lot of cases, there's no contest. Love can't compete."

"It sounds like you're saying love is obsolete."

"I'm not saying that at all. I'm simply stating that the fantasy of happy, domestic bliss, 'till death do us part, is being severely tested by the way we live our lives. I don't think we'll ever recapture the simplicity of life as our parents knew it. In retrospect, they were living in a wonderful time. Most of them couldn't have imagined the stress and multiplicity of choices we consider normal today."

"Do you think that's why your marriage failed?" Kerri asked, impressed by Visconti's insight.

The waiter returned to the table. "Forgive me for interrupting," he said. "Would you like to order now?"

Visconti held his empty glass aloft. "Another martini, please. No olives." He turned to Kerri. "Another wine?"

"Not now," Kerri replied, placing her hand over the top of her half empty glass. "Maybe during lunch."

Visconti watched the waiter leave, then turned to Kerri. "My marriage failed because I was selfish. I wanted something more out of life than a simple hand to mouth existence, so I worked night and day to get it. The marriage was a casualty."

"Did you love her?"

Visconti rolled his eyes. "I should have known you would ask that question... I did, but it wasn't the kind of love I dreamed of for years before I got married."

"What kind of love was that?"

176

"A total, all-consuming thing, one that takes hold and never let's go. One that causes every fiber of my body to ache to be with one particular woman... I thought it was happening to me a long time ago. I had an enormous crush on my economics professor during my second year of university. She was beautiful, intelligent, sophisticated, and five years older than me. I really looked forward to her lectures. I rushed to get there early enough to make sure I got a front row seat. Then I lapsed into a mind warp, dreaming of having a physical and intellectual relationship with her. Eventually the dream became so real, I actually believed it was going to happen."

"Did it?"

Visconti grinned and shook his head. "Foolishly, I asked her to go to dinner with me and she made me feel like a fly on her desk. She told me she was madly in love and engaged to be married. The fly swatter had landed, and it hurt. I was devastated, defeated and depressed. I vowed I would never, ever allow myself to be so emotionally vulnerable. I still have scars."

Kerri was fascinated by Visconti's candor and his display of honesty. "So you've been running scared ever since?" she asked.

Visconti nodded. "That's a pretty good way of describing it. I had no right to feel the way I did about her. Foolishly, I did, and suffered the consequences. Since then, I've scrupulously avoided any emotional commitment. The ugly truth is that I'm afraid, terrified of being hurt again. My parachute failed to open and I'm afraid to jump again for fear of the same thing happening."

"Are you suggesting I shouldn't be afraid to jump into another emotional relationship?"

Visconti chuckled. "No. I wouldn't blame you if you locked up your emotions and threw away the key. What I'm trying to say is that you should be aware of your fear. Take command of it. It'll diminish you if you let it control you."

"That's pretty good advice. I'll try to remember it."

The waiter returned to the table. "Would you like to order now?" he asked with a plastic smile, almost suggesting that this was their last chance to do so.

Visconti ordered without looking at the menu. "I'll have the risotto frutti di mare... What's your soup of the day?"

"New England clam chowder."

"Wonderful. I'll have a bowl."

"Yes sir," the waiter said, scribbling the order on his pad, then turning to Kerri. "And for the lady?"

Embarrassed, Kerri looked at Visconti. "What did you order?"

Visconti smiled. "It's a seafood combination of shrimps, scallops and oysters, served on a bed of Italian rice, with carrots onions and celery. You'll love it. Have the clam chowder, too. It'll prepare your palette for the risotto."

Kerri ordered the same.

"Bring two glasses of chilled Rhine Riesling," Visconti ordered, then leaned backward and placed both hands behind his head. "Has Brian made any attempt to contact you since you moved out of the apartment?"

Kerri shook her head.

"Maybe he doesn't know where you went."

"I left a note on the kitchen table before I left. Among other things, it included my new address. I really don't think he want's to. If he did, he'd call my office number."

"So what are you going to do now, aside from getting on with your life?"

"That's about it. I don't think I have any alternative, do you?"

"You could contact Brian and ask him what his plans are."

"No way!" Kerri replied. "Your photographs told me all I need to know about his plans. He can go to hell as far I'm concerned."

"Let me ask you a hypothetical question... If Brian came to you, apologized for everything he's done and pleaded with you to resume the marriage, would you?"

Kerri fidgeted with her napkin, then glared at Visconti, her eyes showing a burning resolve. "I could forgive his excessive drinking, even hitting me, but I could never forgive his adultery. He stole something very important from me, and that theft was premeditated."

"You still haven't answered my question."

"The answer's no. The marriage was built on trust. When Brian violated that trust, he killed it, and the marriage with it."

Delighted with Kerri's answer, Visconti leaned forward and covered her hand with his. "You're tough. It takes a lot of strength to do what you're doing."

Instinctively, Kerri wanted to pull her hand from beneath Visconti's, but his touch was strangely comforting. She smiled. "You give me too much credit. Brian really didn't give me any choice."

"On the contrary. You had choices. You could have packed your bags and gone home, or stayed in the apartment and forced him to keep you in the style. I gave you credit for choosing neither."

The waiter placed the bowls of soup and the glasses of Riesling on the table. "Enjoy," he said. "I'll bring the risotto shortly."

"Don't rush," Visconti said with a sly smile, then turned to face Kerri. "Let's play hooky," he said, again lifting his glass as if in toast.

Kerri looked askance at Visconti. "Are you serious?"

"Sure. It's a beautiful day, far too beautiful for work. We can get George to drive us to Central Park, or down to Pier Eighty-three. We could take a cruise around Manhattan."

Kerri's sense of responsibility overcame a strong urge to agree. "It sounds very appealing, but unfortunately I have to get back to work."

"To hell with work. I'll call Miles and make him an offer he can't refuse. I'll take my business elsewhere if he doesn't agree to give you the rest of the day off."

"I couldn't let you do that, Louis. It's like putting a gun to his head."

Visconti frowned. "Such loyalty. I wish I could find employees like you."

"Miles has been extremely kind to me. I owe him a lot."

"I'll pay him twice whatever you think you owe him if you'll agree to work for me. Then I'll give you the afternoon off."

"No amount of money could ever repay what I owe Miles. I hope you can understand."

"Will you give me a rain-check?"

"Sure."

"Saturday?"

Kerri nodded.

Visconti paid the bill, then frowned at Kerri. "You sure you won't reconsider this afternoon?" he asked, pouting and pretending to be on the brink of tears.

"I'm sure, but not because I don't want to."

"Then back to work it is. If you'll wait here for a minute, I'll call George and tell him to meet us out front."

Five minutes later, the white limousine glided to a stop in front of the restaurant.

Kerri and Visconti climbed into the rear section before George could get out. Kerri sank into the white leather rear seat and turned to face Visconti. "Thank you, Louis. It's been a long time since I've had so much fun."

"You're welcome. It was fun for me, too. I found myself telling you things I've never told anyone," Visconti replied, convinced beyond all doubt that he had at long last found the woman of his dreams.

180

CHAPTER 54

Toronto. Tuesday, April 3, 1990.

Terry Lippert escorted Phillip and Gary Matheson into Mike's office, closed the door, then took a seat on the couch near Mike's desk.

Matheson, a tall gangling red head, fidgeted nervously as Mike glared at him and Phillip from behind his desk.

Phillip, unconcerned, marched to the couch and prepared to sit beside Lippert.

"Don't even think about sitting down!" Mike shouted.

Phillip bristled as he turned to challenge Mike. "What are you going to do, spank me?" he asked, flashing a defiant smirk.

"Go ahead. Sit down and watch what happens," Mike warned.

Phillip resisted the temptation.

Mike leaned forward and placed both forearms on his desk. "In case you two don't know why I asked Terry to bring you here this morning, let me tell you. We've recently received telephone calls from a number of our customers who were anxious to complain about discrepancies in their credit card statements. We initiated an investigation to determine why the discrepancies existed and discovered that someone had fraudulently altered credit card drafts. The alterations were obvious attempts to steal money." Mike's eyes darted back and forth between Phillip and Matheson, searching for reactions. "Would either of you care to comment?"

Matheson shot a nervous glance at Phillip, then the floor. Phillip continued to glare at Mike.

"I'm waiting," Mike said, his voice raised.

"I did it," Matheson admitted, barely loud enough to be heard.

181

"What did you say?" Mike asked.

"I did it," Matheson repeated, his lower lip quivering.

"Was anyone else involved?"

Matheson looked away.

"So you did it all by yourself?"

"Yes sir," Matheson replied, continuing to look away.

Mike turned to face Phillip. "Do you have anything to say?"

"Nope."

Rage and disappointment invaded Mike's mind. The fact the Phillip would steal disappointed him. The fact that he would lie about it and allow Matheson to take the heat enraged him. "Phillip, why do you think we brought you in here?"

"I don't know. Why did you?"

"Because we think you do have something to say... Now I'm going to give you one more chance to answer. Do you know anything about this?"

"Nope," Phillip replied without hesitation, continuing his remorseless stare.

Mike turned to face Matheson. "Gary, since you've admitted your involvement, and it's a first offense for you, I'm going to let you keep your job. I'm also prepared to let this remain a secret between us, so long as there's no repetition of this or any other theft. Of course, all of the stolen money will be deducted from your pay."

Relieved, Matheson exhaled. "Thank you Mister King. I'm very sorry."

Again Mike turned to Phillip. "Still nothing to say?"

"Nope."

Mike pounded the desk with his fist, then sprang to his feet, pushing his chair backward with his legs. "Three times you've denied your participation in this scam! Furthermore, you've allowed your co-conspirator to take full responsibility for the repayment of the money you helped him steal! In my opinion, what you've just done is far worse than stealing the money!"

"There's no way you can prove I was involved," Phillip retorted, stone faced.

"That's probably true, but you and I will always know you were," Mike retorted, fighting the urge to hit his step-son. "Get out!" he shouted. "Get the hell out of here before I do something I'll regret!"

Again Phillip smirked, oozing contempt. "You haven't got the balls." He turned and left the office, slamming the door with force.

CHAPTER 55

Long Island. Friday, April 6, 1990.

"Not again!" Tina groaned when she entered her living room.

Brian was unconscious and spread-eagled on her green leather couch, his mouth opened wide, drool hardened on his right cheek. His loud snoring meshed with the sound of Dan Rather, delivering the CBS Nightly News on the television set in front of him. Newspapers, magazines and numerous empty beer cans littered the coffee table surface and the floor below the couch.

She moved to the kitchen and winced at the sight of the sink, stacked beyond the brim with unclean dishes. The smell of decaying food boosted her Latin temper to critical mass. "What a pig!" she hissed. She reached into the sink and lifted as many dirty dishes as her arms could carry, then marched back to the living room. She stopped in front of Brian and dropped the dishes on the coffee table. Most of the dishes shattered with a loud crash.

"What the hell!" Brian shouted, jerking himself to an upright position, rubbing his eyes and struggling to focus on Tina.

"How can you live this way?" she screamed, lifting her arms above her head in protest. "Don't you ever clean anything?" she shouted, kicking beer cans and broken dishes in all directions. "I go out and work my ass off all day and night, and all you ever do is lie around here and live like a pig!"

Brian reached for the large pitcher of water he had left on the floor beside him. He lifted it, took a long drink, then placed it on the table. He glared at Tina with extreme contempt in his bloodshot eyes. "You broads are all the same," he said hoarsely.

"What's that supposed to mean?"

"It means you're control freaks, telling me how to live my life. It means you're no different than my wife."

Further enraged by the criticism, Tina lifted Brian's pitcher and threw the remaining water in his face. "I'm not telling you how to live your life! I'm telling you how to live in this apartment! It's my place and I like to keep it clean! If you can't live that way, then get the hell out!" she yelled, continuing to kick beer cans and broken dishes in Brian's direction.

"What a bitch," he moaned, still intoxicated by the large quantity of beer he had consumed that afternoon. He hoisted himself from the couch and stepped toward Tina, crunching a beer can under his foot. "I must have been out of my mind to think you were different. What the hell is it about broads that makes them think they can control a man's life? The way I live mine is my business, not yours."

Tina bared her teeth, then slapped Brian's face as hard as she could. "Don't you dare call me a bitch! If this is the way you want to live your life, then do it somewhere else!"

"You may be a bitch, but you're still the best lay I ever had," Brian said with a malicious sneer. "How about one more time before I get out of your life? Would a blow job be out of the question?"

"Not with a pig like you," Tina snorted.

Brian's lips tightened and his eyes closed to a squint. "Thanks for the memories, bitch!" he said, then cocked his right arm and slapped Tina's face as hard as he could, the force of the blow knocking her backward but not off her feet.

With anger suppressing pain, Tina stepped forward and tried to hit Brian with her right fist, but Brian's hand caught her wrist before she could make contact. He squeezed hard. "Go take off your clothes for some other sucker," he hissed, then hurled her to the couch. He raised the middle finger of his right hand, then turned and hurried from the apartment.

CHAPTER 56

Beer was Brian's first priority when he entered his apartment thirty minutes later, hoping to find at least one in the refrigerator. "Disaster!" he groaned, finding nothing but a half-emptied bottle of white wine. He extracted it, pulled the cork and took a long pull. His thirst temporarily satisfied, he wiped his lips and placed the bottle on the counter below the telephone. "Reconciliation time, Brian baby," he declared, then removed Kerri's note from his wallet and dialed the telephone number.

"May I speak to Kerri, please?"

"Who's calling?" Andrea asked, her eyes focused on Kerri, no more than five feet away.

"Brian."

"Please hold for a minute," Andrea said, then cupped her hand over the mouthpiece. "It's your husband," she whispered, frowning and shaking her head, attempting to discourage Kerri from accepting the call.

"I'll take it," Kerri said, reaching for the receiver.

"You want me to leave?" Andrea asked.

Kerri shook her head, then pushed the hair away from her right ear to make room for the receiver. "Hi," she said, already experiencing the shame of being unable to suppress her curiosity.

"Kerri, I need to see you tonight? It's really important."

"Why?"

"There's so much I want to say to you... I want to do it in person."

"Just do it on the telephone."

"I can't. I really want to see you... I miss you."

"Have you been drinking?"

"Not a drop," Brian lied, rolling his eyes. "Please let me see you. I promise I'll behave myself."

"Brian, seeing me won't change a thing. I can't just sweep the past under the..."

"I'm desperate," Brian interrupted. "I'm right on the edge. I don't know what I'll do if I can't see you."

The tone of Brian's voice reminded Kerri of the most romantic time she had ever experienced with him, the night they sat in his car on Mount Seymour, near Vancouver, the loving and incredibly persuasive way he asked her to go to New York with him. The memory softened her resolve. "What do you want to talk about? I can't imagine..."

"Please let me see you, Kerri. I'll tell you when I get there."

Kerri remained silent.

"Please," Brian pleaded. "I can't begin to tell you how important it is to me."

"You can't stay long. I have work to do."

"I'll be there in less than thirty minutes."

"Just ring the doorbell. I'll come out," Kerri said, then hung up and stared forlornly at the telephone.

"I don't believe it," Andrea said, continuing her frown. "You're addicted to pain."

"I won't let him come in," Kerri promised, too embarrassed to make eye contact with Andrea. "We'll talk on the verandah."

"You know that's not what I meant. What I can't understand is why you agreed to see him. I would have told him to screw himself."

Kerri turned to face Andrea. "Would you understand if I told you I feel sorry for him?"

"How could you possibly feel sorry for a bastard like him? What does he have to do to make you realize he's a loser?"

187

"Maybe I'm a slow learner, or maybe there's a part of me that just can't let go."

CHAPTER 57

Kerri opened the door almost an hour later. Conflicting emotions tormented her as she stared at the man she once loved with an intensity she could never forget.

"May I come in?" Brian asked with an awkward smile.

"Let's talk outside," Kerri replied. She stepped onto the verandah, a large wooden structure, painted gray and tastefully decorated with white wooden furniture and numerous hanging plants and flowers. "What did you want to talk about?" she asked, glaring into Brian's puffy and reddened eyes.

"Us," Brian replied, then reached for Kerri's hand.

Kerri withdrew her hand from his reach. "Let's walk," she said.

The two walked in silence along the sidewalk of the brightly lit and well treed avenue.

"How have you been?" Brian asked, attempting only to break the silence.

Kerri's lips tightened. "I'm sure you didn't come all this way just to ask me that. I'm also sure you don't really give a damn how I've been. What do you want, Brian?"

Tears appeared in Brian's bloodshot eyes. "I want us to try again. I miss you and I can't live without you any more."

Kerri caught a whiff of wine mixed with toothpaste. "Are you still drinking?" she asked, offering Brian an opportunity to lie.

"I haven't had a drink for days."

"What happened between you and that stripper?"

"I don't know what you mean. I'm not..."

"Brian, please don't insult my intelligence. The whole world saw the picture of you with her in The Times."

Brian looked away. "She's just a friend. Nothing more."

A deep and growing sense of revulsion enveloped Kerri as visions of the photographs in Visconti's report flashed through her mind. "Did you ever make love to her?" she asked, allowing Brian another opportunity to lie.

"No. I told you we're just friends."

"Where have you been living?" Kerri asked, offering him one further chance to lie.

Brian's eyes darted back and forth. "At Billy Maxwell's, one of my teammates. He's a defensive back. He has a house in Westhampton Beach."

The third lie turned revulsion to anger. "We're both wasting our time," Kerri said, then turned and marched toward Dennis's house.

"What did I say?" Brian asked, hurrying to keep up with her brisk pace.

"Nothing," Kerri hissed, refusing to look at Brian and quickening her pace.

"Bull-shit!" Brian shouted. He raced to catch up, reached around Kerri with both arms and held her against his chest. "What the hell did I say to upset you?"

The vile smell of wine, toothpaste and stale beer sickened Kerri. She struggled to break free. "You're a goddamned liar!" she screamed. "I can forgive you for your drinking, even for hitting me, but never for cheating and lying."

"What!"

Kerri ducked under Brian's grasp, then stood her ground and pointed an accusing finger at him. "There was a time when I worshipped you, Brian Pyper. You were everything to me. I would have given you anything. You abused that commitment, just as much as you abused your God-given talent."

"You mean you imagine that's what I did," Brian retorted.

"How can you stand there and lie about it? That's the worst transgression of all."

"How can you stand there and accuse me of cheating and lying?"

"Your breath smells of booze, you're living with Tina Desouza, and I know she's more than a friend."

"How can you be so sure? Did you have me followed?"

Visions of Brian and Tina in Visconti's photo album swam in her head. She didn't have him followed, Visconti did. "No, I did not have you followed."

"Can't we just forget the past? I love you, Kerri. Doesn't that count for anything?"

"Maybe you can sweep the past under the rug, but I can't." Kerri turned and headed for Dennis's house.

Brian made no further attempt to follow. "I'm never going to stop trying, Kerri," he shouted. "Eventually you're going to realize you belong to me."

Andrea had watched from the bedroom window from the moment Kerri left the house with Brian. She raced to the front door. "What happened?" she asked as Kerri entered.

"He can't accept that it's over. He really scared me. I saw that same look in his eyes."

"Where is he? Is he still out there?"

"He owns that black Jaguar out front."

Andrea opened the curtains no more than an inch and peered through the window. "He's getting into it now."

"Would you please tell me when he's gone?"

The telephone rang, causing Andrea to turn away from the window. "Would you get that, Kerri?" she requested. "I'll keep watching."

Kerri entered the den and lifted the receiver. "Hello," she said, still breathing heavily.

191

"We belong together, Kerri," Brian said in an ominous tone. "I'll follow you forever if I have to."

Kerri slammed the receiver down, then raced to the front door. "It was him," she said, then stepped in front of Andrea and yanked the curtains aside. She saw Brian in the front seat of his car, still holding the receiver of his telephone.

"What did he say?"

Kerri closed the curtains and turned to face Andrea, her face almost devoid of color, tears filling her eyes. "He said he's going to follow me forever. I'm really scared, Andrea. He lied about everything. He wouldn't even admit he's been sleeping with that stripper."

"Did you tell him about Louis's report?"

"No."

"Had he been drinking?"

Kerri nodded.

"Maybe I should call the police."

"No. Let's wait and see what he does. Maybe he'll just leave."

Both looked through the curtains to see the car pull away from the curb, then disappear around the corner.

Andrea turned to face Kerri. "I'm going to tell Miles when he gets home. I'm sure he's going to want you to get a lawyer. The sooner that man's out of your life, the better."

Kerri shook her head. "I can't afford a lawyer."

Andrea chuckled. "Don't worry about that. Brian will pay the bill, one way   or   another."

CHAPTER 58

Andrea kissed her husband's cheek. "How was your day, darling?" she asked, helping to remove his rain soaked coat.

"What do you want, Andrea? You're usually more subtle than this," Miles said.

"I want you to talk to Kerri. She could be in trouble."

Dennis placed his arm around Andrea's shoulders and led her in the direction of the kitchen. "First I need a drink."

Andrea was prepared. "In anticipation of that requirement, I have a jug of chilled martinis waiting for you."

Dennis sat at the counter, took a sip of his first martini, then released a loud gasp. "I feel better already. Now, tell me about Kerri."

Andrea told her husband the story of Brian Pyper's extraordinary visit with Kerri.

Dennis took another sip and shook his head. "She doesn't deserve that. She's too nice a girl... It's really a shame. She was so much in love when I met her. I can't believe that jerk screwed up so badly. Is she okay?"

"Who knows?"

"I'm worried about this weekend. We'll be at the C.B.O.T. Convention, and she'll be alone here until Sunday night."

"Maybe I should stay here. Would you be upset?"

Dennis revealed a sly smirk. "Heartbroken. It's the only time we ever get a chance to go away together. I'll talk to her now."

"You really care about her, don't you?"

Dennis nodded. "I don't want to see her future destroyed by that idiot she married. She's brilliant, Andrea. I've never seen anyone grasp the fundamentals of the business as quickly as she did. She's personable too. I think she's more capable of handling clients that I am." He finished his martini, headed downstairs and knocked on the door to Kerri's apartment.

"It's open," Kerri shouted.

Dennis entered to see Kerri sitting on her bed, reading and dressed in faded blue jeans and an oversized gray sweater. Bare feet.

"Hi boss," she said with a big smile, then placed her book beside her.

"Andrea told me what happened tonight. You okay?"

Kerri nodded, but her smile disappeared.

"Andrea and I are leaving town on Friday morning. We're going to the Chicago Board of Trade Commodities Convention. We'll be there until Sunday night... Now, under the circumstances, I hate like hell to leave you here alone. Brian could be a problem."

"Don't even think about it. I left no doubt in his mind. I told him the marriage was over, and I didn't want anything more to do with him."

"That's great, but he still worries me. Andrea told me he's decided not to give up, and if that's the case, then you shouldn't take it lightly. I've heard all kinds of horror stories about rejected lovers and husbands who let their obsessive possessive fantasies obscure reality."

"Miles, he's a drunk, a liar and a cheat, but I don't think he's crazy."

"I hope you're right, but maybe you're not. Just to be safe, I want you to stay in a hotel for the weekend. I'll pay for it."

"Absolutely not!" Kerri protested. "There's no way I'm going to let you do that. I'm a big girl now and I'll be just fine."

Dennis smiled. "You sure have grown up."

"Thanks for caring, Miles."

Next day. 9:00 A.M.

"Call for Kerri Pyper!" someone shouted.

"I'll take it!" Kerri shouted, rushing from Dennis's office to her desk. She pushed her hair back and lifted her receiver to her ear. "Kerri Pyper," she said.

"How come you're not home yet?" Brian asked, his speech once again slurred, obviously impaired by alcohol. "I've been waiting all afternoon for you. Please come home. I... I need you."

Kerri's heart pounded, but her resolve strengthened. "I'm not coming home, Brian. Not ever! I told you last night it's over, and I meant it. Please don't call me again." She hung up and covered her face with shaking hands.

"What's wrong?" Dennis asked, now standing in the doorway to his office.

Kerri removed her hands from her face, revealing an ashen complexion and a forced smile. "Nothing serious. I just have a bit of a headache. That was Pauline at the Exchange. We got a fill on the platinum offering," she lied.

Dennis stared suspiciously at Kerri for several seconds, then returned to his office.

Brian's determination to be with Kerri had intensified and matured into an obsession. He parked his car a short distance from Dennis's house. He watched in silence for hours, then slept in the front seat until morning. He woke to see Dennis emerging alone at seven-fifteen. After placing his briefcase and two large travel bags on the lawn beside the driveway, Dennis proceeded to the garage. He opened the door, climbed into a burgundy and white Toyota van, and backed it out to a point in the driveway beside the bags. As he placed the bags in the rear section of the van, Andrea emerged from the house with Kerri. The three climbed into the van, then Dennis backed it onto the street and drove away.

Brian followed the van to the train station and watched as Kerri emerged alone. She waved to Miles and Andrea, then turned and ran to the train. Brian waited for two hours, then phoned Kerri's office number from his car. "May I speak to Miles Dennis, please," Brian asked.

"I'm sorry, sir. Mr. Dennis won't be in the office today. May someone else help you?"

"Could you tell me where I could reach him? It's rather important that I talk to him."

"I'm afraid you won't be able to reach him until Monday. He'll be out of town until then. If you would like me to give him a message, I could see that he receives it. Or perhaps you would like me to have him phone you?"

"That won't be necessary. Thank you." Brian smiled as he hung up. "'Tonight you're mine, Kerri," he purred, then rubbed cheeks that hadn't been touched by a razor for two days.

Kerri's office telephone phone rang at four-thirty. She lifted the receiver to her ear. "Kerri Pyper."

"Hi, Kerri. It's Louis. I just called to make sure we're still on for tomorrow."

She smiled, relieved, excited to hear Visconti's voice. "I'm looking forward to it."

"Is ten too early?"

"Ten's fine. I'll have coffee ready for you."

"Great, then would you mind transferring me to Miles's office? I should talk to him."

"He's not here. He and Andrea went to Chicago for the weekend. If it's urgent, I could get him to call you."

"No. It's not urgent, but I'm surprised they left you alone."

"My choice. To exonerate Miles, he offered to get me a hotel room for the weekend."

"He's a good man. Have you heard from your husband?"

"No."

"Would you call me if there's any trouble?" Visconti gave Kerri the number of his home in Connecticut.

CHAPTER 59

Glen Cove. Friday, April 13,1990.

Brian's Jaguar rolled to a stop, no more than a hundred yards from the driveway of Dennis's house. A six-pack of Budweiser rested on the seat beside him. He opened his first can and took a huge gulp. By the time he was half way through his third can, he saw Kerri walking toward him in the distance. Her red spring coat and flowing blond hair convinced him he was minutes away from his date with destiny. He chugged as much beer as he he could, then started his car.

When Kerri turned from the sidewalk to the concrete path leading to Dennis's home he pushed the accelerator to the floor. Kerri froze when she heard the loud squealing of the car's tires against the pavement. She turned to see the black Jaguar racing onto the driveway. She darted toward the verandah, but Brian jumped from the car and caught her before she reached the wooden steps.

"Let me go!" she screamed, struggling frantically to break free of his bear-like hug. Terrifying thoughts raced through her brain. The glazed determination in Brian's eyes was a clear indication of his intentions. The smell of alcohol on his breath was even more ominous.

"I waited and waited for you to come home," Brian said, pulling her against his body. "You're my wife, Kerri. You belong with me."

"It's over, Brian," she said, desperately trying to think of a way to escape. "I told you I'm not coming home. Not ever."

"We belong together," he insisted, the slurring of his words a clear indication that he was intoxicated. "We promised to love each other until death do us part."

"Sure we did, and we also promised to forsake all others."

"Let's go inside," Brian said with a contorted smile. He dragged her up the stairs to the verandah.

"Think about what you're doing, Brian," Kerri warned. "Andrea will call the police as soon as she sees you."

"You and I know they've both gone for the weekend. It'll be just the two of us, and there won't be anyone to bother us. Now open the door like an obedient wife," he demanded.

Shocked that Brian knew she was alone, Kerri feared the worst. "I'm not going to open it," she said defiantly.

"Give me the key!" Brian ordered.

Kerri removed the key from her coat pocket, placed it in Brian's hand, then watched as he turned his body toward the door. The moment he turned to watch the insertion of the key, she bolted from the verandah, leaped down the seven stairs and ran across the the lawn. Her progress slowed as the soles of her leather loafers slipped on the dried grass.

Brian, dressed in jeans and sneakers, caught up with her and tackled her by grasping her shoulders and dragging her to the ground. He cupped his right hand over her mouth, pulled her to her feet and marched her back to the front door of the house. The more she struggled, the tighter he held her. He used his left hand to unlock and open the door, then he pulled her inside. He released her long enough to slam and lock the door. Kerri seized the opportunity to race to the den. She lifted the telephone receiver and began to dial nine-one-one. She heard a loud click before she could complete the dialing. Her heart sank when she looked up to see Brian dangling the telephone plug in front of her eyes.

"Don't try that again," he said with an evil smile. "Show me the kitchen. I could use a cold beer. All this exercise has made me thirsty."

Kerri realized it would be foolish and dangerous to run. She decided to cooperate and wait for an opportunity to escape. She led Brian to the kitchen.

Brian hurried to the refrigerator and removed a can of beer. "Show me where you live," he demanded, then snapped the aluminum lid and guzzled half of its contents. "Maybe there's enough room for both of us."

A loathing hatred gripped Kerri as she watched him wipe his lips with the sleeve of his brown leather jacket. She thought of how unattractive he had become. Gone were the tight physique and sharp features she once adored. The skin on his face had acquired a pale chalky hue, his cheeks and eyes puffy. He had gained a large amount of weight, most of it in the wrong places.

"What's the problem, sweetheart? I hope you're not too embarrassed to show me your little hole in the wall."

Kerri led Brian down the stairs and into her living quarters. He closed and locked the door, then marched directly to the night table beside her bed and jerked the telephone plug from the wall jack. "Any more of these in the house?" he asked, holding the broken wire in his hand.

"Upstairs, in the master bedroom," Kerri confessed, aware of the futility of lying.

Brian flashed a lecherous smirk. "Let's go. The bed up there has to be better than this one."

Kerri's body trembled in fear. She fought to stave off tears. "You're making a big mistake, Brian. Do you have any idea how much trouble you're going to be in when you get caught?"

Tears appeared in Brian's eyes. His smile disappeared. He fell to his knees. "Then come home with me now. We can start over and you won't have to live here any more."

Kerri was astounded by the sudden shift in Brian's tone and attitude. No longer a demanding bully, he appeared to have transformed into a whimpering child. Seconds earlier, he was animalistic, totally unconcerned by the implications of his actions. She had to think. "I'll go home with you on one condition," she said, her heart pounding, her eyes fixed on his.

"Anything," Brian sobbed.

"You have to promise not to touch me until you're completely sober."

Relief and surprise lit up Brian's face. "I'll do anything for you, anything," he said, then watched as Kerri removed a small bag from her closet and filled it with clothing and toiletries.

"Okay, let's go," she said as she zippered the bag and forced a smile.

Brian's smile was replaced with a disappointed frown. "Why don't you take everything? Then you won't have to come back here."

Again Kerri had to think fast. "We can get the rest tomorrow. You should get to bed as soon as possible, and I think you should let me drive."

Brian obediently removed his keys from his jacket pocket and handed them to Kerri. He watched her as she unlocked her apartment door. She was about to open it when she felt the pain of a viselike grip on her left arm. Horrified, she turned to face Brian's evil smile. His blood-shot eyes seemed to penetrate her skin. She trembled in fear.

He jerked her toward him, close enough for her to smell his vile breath. "Thought you had me conned, didn't you? I guess you would've gone home with me. Hell, you might even have stayed until I was asleep. But then you and I both know what you would have done next. You just had to hang a string on it, didn't you? You had to make sex conditional on my sobriety. I told you the way I live my life is my business." He kissed her savagely, thrusting his foul tasting tongue deep into her mouth. When the kiss ended, he snapped his head back and glared at her. "Sex between a husband and wife should be completely unconditional. Now you and I are going upstairs for some unconditional sex."

Kerri closed her eyes and spit at Brian's face, relieving her mouth of the awful taste his tongue has deposited.

"That wasn't very lady like," Brian said, wiping the saliva from his face with his right hand, then using it to slap her face, hard. "We can get it on in the master bedroom or right here on your couch. Your choice."

In an effort to postpone the inevitable, Kerri led Brian to the master bedroom, an immaculately decorated and richly broadloomed area. The sun, now low on the horizon, shone on the outer surface of the translucent pink drapes, causing an erie glow in the room. The decoration focus was the king sized bed, covered with a quilted pale pink spread, and a pile of deep pink silk covered pillows.

"Very nice," Brian observed, then closed the door and approached the bed. He reached for the telephone cord behind the night table and removed the plug, then chuckled as he threw the phone to the floor. "Three phones and you're out! Time to recapture the rapture, sweetheart. Bring your sweet ass over here and let's get it on."

Kerri's time was up. She could think of no more options. Brian's relentless stare sent chills rippling down her spine. She froze, unable to speak or move in any direction. She closed her eyes in terror when she saw him approach her. He grasped her right arm and jerked her toward the bed.

"What you're doing is rape!" she screamed.

"Wrong, darling. It's consensual sex between husband and wife. There isn't a court in the land that would convict me. Now relax and enjoy it."

An explosion of anger and indignation erupted in Kerri when he threw her to the bed. "You bastard! The great Brian Pyper doesn't want anyone to interfere with his life, but he doesn't give a shit how much he interferes with mine. I let you go. You were free to drink yourself into oblivion and screw that stripper silly, but that wasn't enough. You had to have more."

"Sentimental crap!" Brian scoffed.

"It is like hell. Ever since you injured your knee, I've had to put up with a schizophrenic drunk who put his own needs ahead of mine. Then I tried to save his health and his career and he thanked me by wallowing in self pity, hitting me, lying to me, running away and cheating on the marriage."

Brian descended to the bed beside Kerri. He squinted and showed his teeth. The look reminding her of the one he had displayed each time he hit her. He reached behind her head and clutched her hair with his left hand. "I'm going to be in tears if I listen to any more of this bullshit," he said as

202

he started to undo the buttons of her blouse with the fingers of his right hand. Next, he reached beneath her, unzipped her skirt, pulled it down and threw it to the floor.

Kerri struggled to free herself, but Brian restrained her with the strength of his arms and legs. "Damn you!" she shouted when he reached beneath her panties.

CHAPTER 60

Both were startled by the loud thump caused by the bedroom door striking the inside wall. "Don't do it Pyper!" Visconti ordered.

Brian bolted upright and glared at Visconti. "Who the hell are you?" he asked.

"A friend of Kerri's. I think it's time you got the hell out of here."

Brian, four inches taller and forty pounds heavier than Visconti, smirked. "What are you going to do if I don't, hurt me?"

"I'm not going to do anything, but the courts will. I heard enough of what's going on here to qualify as a witness. The choice is yours. You can stay and dig yourself into a deeper hole, or leave now. You don't have much time. The police are on their way as I speak."

Brian stood and approached Visconti with stiffened lips, teeth clenched. Visconti's muscles tightened in anticipation as Brian passed within an inch of his body, avoiding contact, but close enough for Visconti to smell him.

"I won't forget this, asshole!" Brian hissed, then left the room and hurried down the stairs.

Relieved and overjoyed, Kerri leapt from the bed and headed for Visconti. With total disregard for her state of undress, she wept as she threw her arms around him and held him with all of her strength.

Visconti returned the hug, silently wishing the circumstances were different.

"How did you know?" she asked, still clinging tightly to her savior.

"I got lonely, so I decided to drive over here and knock on your door. I saw the black Jaguar in the driveway and assumed you and Brian were making a fast reconciliation, or he was here against your will. "

"How did you know it was him?"

"Easy. He has 'JETS QB' on his plate. I found the front door unlocked, so I just walked in and followed the noise. I can't tell you how happy I was not to hear the sounds of reconciliation."

Kerri lifted her head and looked into Visconti's eyes. "Are the police really coming?"

Visconti shook his head and and placed his index finger against his lips. "Don't tell Brian," he whispered.

"Thank you, Louis. Thank you so very much," Kerri said, strengthening her hold.

"My pleasure... My fondest hope was to find you here alone, bored and receptive to spending a few quality hours with me. Never in my wildest dreams did I expect to have you half naked and in my arms... You should get dressed. Then I want to talk to you about an idea that I have."

"Talk to me now," Kerri demanded. "I'm still not ready to let you go."

Visconti lifted her chin and looked into her eyes. "Your husband might not give up, so I don't think it would be a good idea for you to stay here tonight."

"Where can I go?"

"I own an apartment in Manhattan. There was a time when the company used it a lot for business entertaining, but now that we've established our client base, it's empty most of the time. My partners and I use it only when the weather makes it tough to go home... I'd like you to stay there, at least until Miles and Andrea come home. If you like it, however, you're welcome to stay there as long as you want."

Kerri blushed. "That's an extremely kind offer, but I couldn't."

"You can, and you will, starting right now. You'll be safe there and extremely comfortable. I promise. I also promise to stay there with you until it's safe for you to come back here, if you'll have me."

"Have you! I won't let you out of my sight!" As Kerri spoke she realized that within minutes of being in a terrifying position, she was happy, protected, actually able to smile. "You're very good for me," she said, then kissed his cheek.

"The feeling is mutual, Misses Pyper."

Kerri frowned. "I wish you hadn't mentioned that name. I was just beginning to forget it."

"You should think about getting rid of it forever, but we can talk about that later. Now, we should get out of here. Get yourself dressed, pack a bag, and don't forget to include a track suit. We're going jogging in Central Park tomorrow."

CHAPTER 61

Visconti turned his gray Mercedes onto the Long Island Expressway, then turned to Kerri. "You okay?" he asked.

"Fine," she replied, still trembling. "The further we get from Brian the better I'll be."

"I mentioned earlier that you should seriously consider changing your name forever... Aside from considering it, could you actually divorce him?"

"In a heart-beat. I don't want another thing to do with that man for the rest of my life. Unfortunately, I can't afford to do anything about it."

"Wrong. You can't afford not to do anything about it. It's probably not possible to forget it completely, but you should get rid of it so you're not constantly reminded of it."

"Louis, I can't just wave a magic wand. Divorcing Brian will cost money I don't have."

Visconti reached for Kerri's hand. "I'll make a bet with you."

"On what?"

"I know a lawyer in the city. She's a very good friend. I'm willing to bet you that she can have a comprehensive restraining order slapped on Brian, get you a divorce plus alimony, and have Brian pay for the whole thing. If I lose, I'll pay her fees. If I win, Brian pays. Win or lose, you win. You interested?"

"Sure I'm interested, but I told you I don't want any money from Brian."

Visconti rolled his eyes. "Okay, we'll tell her to forget the alimony. Now, do we have a bet?"

"We have a bet," Kerri agreed, showing a hint of a smile as she shook Visconti's hand.

"Good. Then I'll call her on Monday and set up an appointment. You can walk to her office. She's less than a block away from yours." Visconti glanced at Kerri again and shook his head.

"What?" she asked.

"You continue to amaze me. Your husband has gone out of his way to ruin your life. In addition to drinking excessively, abusing you physically and running off with a stripper, he entered your home tonight and attempted to attack you. In spite of all that, you still insist on taking nothing from him. That's why you amaze me."

"There isn't anything amazing about it. Taking money from him is like descending to his level. That's something I won't do."

"What about the legal fees? Technically you would be accepting money from him if you allowed him to pay them."

"No. I would merely be asking him to return the two things he took from me."

"What things?"

"My freedom and self-respect. I had both before I met him and it's his responsibility to give them back to me. If the process of returning them costs him money, so be it."

Again Visconti was reminded of the elements of Kerri's personality to which he was so attracted. "You're one in a million," he said, placing his arm on her shoulders and drawing her close to him. "Brian's a fool. Maybe one day he'll wake up and realize what he's lost."

CHAPTER 62

Visconti followed Kerri into his apartment on the sixth and top floor of a gray vine-covered building on Fifth Avenue. The residence was thousands of miles and millions of dollars away from her mother's apartment in Vancouver. Brian Pyper had brought her to the suburbs of the crucible of American capitalism, but Louis Visconti had taken her to the nucleus. The aging, almost institutional appearance of the building's exterior gave scarce hint of the effort and treasure spent by some of the city's wealthiest inhabitants on their respective segments of the interior.

Kerri walked gingerly, almost on tiptoes across the polished Florentine marble floor of the foyer. She stopped to gaze around the enormous living room. Its two story high walls were adorned with large and expensive oil paintings. The far wall featured a floor to ceiling, cathedral-like array of windows embracing a massive cut-stone fireplace, and framing a stupendous view of Central Park. The oak floor was covered by a thick and expansive Persian rug. Blue, gray and beige tints of the rug complemented a single large sofa, covered in navy blue velvet and facing the fireplace.

Filled with wonder and amazement, Kerri turned to face Visconti. "This is incredible!" she declared. "It's hard to believe people actually live in places like this. But to own it and not live in it is beyond comprehension."

"You really know how to hurt a guy." Visconti frowned and stared pensively at the fireplace. "In retrospect, I should have sold it two years ago. Like so many other people who had made enormous paper profits on real estate in the eighties, I foolishly assumed the game would continue forever. This place was a shrine to what I thought was my intelligence. If it was worth twice what I paid for it, there seemed to be no reason why it wouldn't double again."

"Would you lose money if you sold it now?"

Visconti nodded. "My glass is always half full, never half empty. I'm confident that if I hold on to it long enough, the market will eventually come back. A lot of people have told me I won't live that long, but I'm absolutely convinced I will."

Kerri regarded Visconti's bold admission as a sign of strength, an ability to understand his mind and to express it without fear of criticism. She was suddenly closer to him, even drawn to him.

"Would you like to take the dollar tour?"

"Lead the way," she replied without hesitation, happy to be where she was, happy to be safe, happy to be with Louis Visconti.

He led her through four thousand square feet of opulent luxury. The tour began in the large high-ceilinged dining room which dwarfed a long polished mahogany table, adorned with gold-plated settings for twelve. The two proceeded to the kitchen which appeared to be the control room for a five star restaurant. Its sparkling white tiled floor was surrounded by expensive stainless steel appliances. A gigantic, black marble-surfaced food preparation island occupied the center of the floor. Beyond the kitchen was the study, expensively furnished and subtly decorated with masculine taste.

The tour ended near the top of a sweeping spiral stairway leading to four lavishly, yet tastefully decorated bedrooms. Visconti stopped and turned to face Kerri at the first door. "This room is yours for as long as you want it," he said, grinning like a Cheshire cat. "I hope you like it."

"Aren't you going to show it to me?"

"I want you to discover it yourself. If I were condemned to be confined to one room for the rest of my life, I couldn't imagine a better place to serve my sentence." Visconti tugged the lapel of his tailored gray pinstriped suit. "While you're exploring this small slice of heaven, I'll be taking a shower and getting out of this monkey-suit."

"I hope you're not planning to leave," Kerri said, insecurity now biting.

Visconti shook his head. "I told you I'm not going to leave this apartment until you do." He pointed to the door of the adjacent bedroom.

"I'll be in there with the shower door closed... Now, go inside and look around. I'll get your bag and leave it right here. If you need me, or anything, shout. I'll be right next door and I'll be there for as long as it takes me to have a shower and change. Then we'll have nightcaps in the kitchen. I'll meet you there in half an hour."

Relieved by Visconti's assurances, Kerri turned and entered the bedroom. She saw immediately why Visconti wanted her to discover it. Her sneakers sank into an ocean of lush deep white broadloom as she walked through the sitting area. Two white velvet covered reclining arm chairs flanked a massive entertainment center, complete with built-in television, state of the art sound system and well stocked bar.

Kerri continued to the bedroom. First to catch her eye was a king-sized bed, covered with a pale green silk spread and perched on a white marble pedestal. She mounted the pedestal and flopped backward onto the bed. After relaxing on the bed for several seconds, she rolled off and continued her discovery. She entered the en suite bathroom, with a floor area exceeding that of her entire apartment at Dennis's house. Excited, she removed her sneakers and stepped into the sunken Jacuzzi, large enough for four people, its rim stacked with large white fluffy towels, its fixtures glittering with gold-plating. Steps from the Jacuzzi was a large shower stall, surrounded by frosted bevel-cut glass. Adjacent to the shower stall was a solid   clear   cedar   door   leading   to   a   large   sauna.

CHAPTER 63

Refreshed, she joined Visconti in the kitchen.

Now dressed in a red velour track suit, no shoes or socks, he was busily engaged in the preparation of a large jug of ice cubes, orange juice and vodka. He waved and smiled, then resumed his focus on the contents of the jug. He poured the entire concoction into a blender, held the cap on top with one hand and plugged the machine in with the other. When he was certain the blender had done its job, he turned it off and filled two crystal wine glasses with the finished product. "I'm sure there's an official name for this," he said as he handed one of the glasses to Kerri. "I call it a vodka slushy. I hope you like it as much as I do."

Kerri took a minuscule sip, then licked her lips. "Delicious. I can't even taste the vodka." She took a larger sip to confirm her initial report.

"Then I've done it right." Visconti pointed to the bar. "Let's sit up there and talk." He helped Kerri climb into one of the white upholstered captain's chairs, then hoisted himself into the one beside her.

"Do you mind answering a personal question?" Kerri asked.

"Hell no. Go ahead."

"How did you get so rich?"

"I don't really know... I guess it was because I hated being poor. Maybe I was just lucky." He gave Kerri a mischievous grin. "How would you define luck?"

"Let me think about it," Kerri said, then drank more of her slushy. "I think luck is a fortuitous event."

"Very good," Visconti said, then poured another drink for himself and refilled Kerri's. "Do you have any idea when luck occurs?"

Kerri giggled, unaware that alcohol had begun to affect her. "That's a tough one. Give me some more time."

"Take all the time you need."

"... I think luck occurs when preparation meets opportunity."

"Brilliant! I couldn't imagine a better way to express it. Do you think it's impossible for luck to occur without a collision of those two factors?"

"I don't really know. I think luck is a subjective thing. One person might think he's lucky to be alive. Another person takes his health for granted and never thinks about it."

Visconti nodded. "Maybe you have to consider the degree of preparation and the size of the opportunity."

"Why?"

"Somewhere along the path of a healthy individual's existence, he must have prepared himself for the opportunity to survive."

Kerri nodded, then took another sip.

"We could carry the argument to the infinite level of resolution, but that's not why I introduced it. I did it because I wanted to give you a better answer to your first question."

"Okay," Kerri said, then took another long sip. "What was my first question?"

"How did I get so rich."

"Right. How did you?"

"For the longest time in my life I considered myself unlucky to have been born to poor parents. Later, I thought I was unlucky not to have married into wealth. When I finally stopped feeling sorry for myself, I realized that the only way I was ever going to be wealthy was to prepare for it. So I did."

"How did you prepare for it?" Kerri asked, fascinated.

"Most people who knew me thought I had the world by the tail, a lovely wife, a good education and a great job with Green-Waltrum, one of the biggest houses on the street. They were wrong. The world had me by the tail. It was confiscating every dime I could make, and I knew it would continue to do so unless I got off the treadmill. I think that was the beginning of my preparation. The opportunity came when Gerry Mara and Allen Greisdorf invited me to fly with them. At that very moment, an opportunity collided with preparation. The rest is history. We started managing other peoples' money at a time when it was like taking candy from a baby." Visconti refilled Kerri's glass. "You could say I was lucky."

"May I ask you another question?" Kerri asked, astounded that she would even consider asking it.

"Sure."

"I'll understand if you'd rather not answer it."

"Don't worry about it. I'll answer any questions you have."

"Miles told me that you lost a half a billion dollars of one client's money in the crash of eighty-seven... Is that true?"

Visconti frowned, clearly indicating that Kerri had introduced a very sensitive subject. "It's true," he said, frown persisting. "Why did you ask that question?"

"I'm sorry. Obviously you don't want to talk about it."

"Sure I do. Why did you ask that question?" Visconti insisted, tightening his lips and facial muscles.

"I had difficulty understanding why you took that big short position on crude oil."

"So what are you getting at?"

Kerri looked away, desperately trying to think of a way out, then took another drink. "I don't even know why I brought it up. Can we change the subject?"

"No," Visconti said with an intense icy gray stare. "We can't change the subject. I want to know why you asked the question, and I'm not going to let it go until you tell me."

"It just seemed to me that you were betting an awful lot on one horse."

"Are you suggesting that I don't know what I'm doing?"

"No. That's not what I'm saying. I have no right to doubt the investment decisions of someone with your experience and track record. I was just curious to know the reasoning behind your decision."

"My track record is no accident. I have it because I wasn't afraid to follow my first instinct. Whenever I did, I won big. Whenever I second-guessed myself, I was almost invariably wrong." Visconti's eyes appeared to burn with resolve. "My decision to short crude oil was a first instinct. I'm absolutely convinced I'm right. If there ever was an immaculate case of preparation colliding with opportunity, that's it." He smiled and raised his glass in the direction of Kerri. "Will you join me in a toast to five dollar crude oil?"

Kerri lifted her glass and clinked it against Visconti's. "To five dollar crude," she said, relieved, then took another gulp of her slushy. "How did you explain the loss to your client?" she asked, unaware of the enormous significance of her question.

"Fortunately, I didn't have to. I pulled out all the stops after the crash. I took some enormous risks and was able to recover most of the loss before I had to send a year-end report to the trustees. They didn't miss what they didn't know."

Visconti's explanation was so convincing that Kerri believed his story without question. She had no idea he was lying through his teeth, or that her question had been tantamount to driving a stake through his heart. To that moment, she had correctly assumed his breathtaking plunge into crude oil futures was a desperate attempt to recover the loss his client had sustained in the crash of eighty-seven. "You can't know how happy I am to hear you say that."

"Why?"

"I was wrong. I thought saving face was your motivation."

Visconti glanced at the empty jug. "My goodness. The slushies are gone. Time to make another batch."

"No," Kerri retorted, her head spinning. "That stuff is delicious but it's lethal. I think I'm smashed. I can't even form my words."

"Then they worked."

"What worked?"

"The slushies. They took your mind off what happened to you tonight."

Visconti was right. Kerri had, for a brief wonderful interval, actually forgotten her ordeal. She raised her empty glass and smiled. "Thanks to you."

"We should get a good night's sleep. Tomorrow's a busy day."

Kerri welcomed the suggestion. She climbed from her stool and watched as Visconti placed the glasses and jug in the sink, then turn and reach for her hand.

"May I walk you to your door?" he asked.

A sudden wave of consternation swept over Kerri. All evening she had assumed Visconti would sleep in a separate bedroom. Perhaps her assumption was wrong. Maybe he was planning to sleep with her. She stiffened as she accepted his hand. He led her up the spiral staircase and stopped at the door to the master bedroom. "I'm serving breakfast in the kitchen at nine. Would you like a wake up call?" he asked.

"No thanks. I'll be there on time."

"Then I'll see you tomorrow. Just knock if you need anything. I'll be right next door. Sleep well. You're safe now." He kissed Kerri's forehead, then turned and walked to the door to the adjacent bedroom.

Within minutes, Kerri had washed, brushed her teeth and removed all of her clothing. Happy and naked, she climbed into the warm comfortable bed. She reached to turn off the final light, one of the two beautiful, cut glass lamps flanking the bed, then flopped her head onto the fluffiest of the many pillows. Sleep was seconds away.

CHAPTER 64

Kerri awoke to a glorious morning. She leaped from the bed, hurried to the windows, pushed aside the drapes and exposed her naked body to the skyline of the Upper East Side and sections of the East River beyond. Sunlight poured onto her and into the most beautiful bedroom she had ever seen. Stretching and breathing deeply, she felt wonderful, revitalized. She was going to see Manhattan today. With her bare feet sinking into the deep soft carpet, she turned and hurried to the lavish bathroom, to pamper herself and prepare for a day she planned to savor against her palate and swallow like a rare wine.

Thirty minutes later, she entered the kitchen, looking radiant in her pink Lizsport. The smell of burning bacon and toast invaded her nostrils. She found Visconti on his knees and attempting to clean up a splattered egg. "Looks like you could use some help," she said with a sympathetic grin.

"Obviously I've got everything under control," Visconti retorted with a pained grin, then continued his cleaning.

Kerri rushed to the stovetop to turn the bacon, seconds before it blackened. Next, she popped the toaster, seconds before its contents burst into flames. She broke the remaining four eggs into a bowl, whipped them with a fork, then heated and stirred them in a pan.

Visconti finished his cleaning, then stood. "Thank you," he said, embarrassed. "Cooking's never been one of my strengths, but if you'll trust me, I think I can manage from here."

Kerri took several steps backward and surveyed Visconti while he leaned over the stove. He looked youthfully svelte in his tight black track suit. She resisted an urge to throw her arms around him, hug him and thank him again for rescuing her, for being there, for making her happy, for everything. "Is there anything I can do?" she asked, feeling redundant.

"You can take a seat at the bar," Visconti offered. "Breakfast is about to be served."

"I'm not going to let you serve me," Kerri snorted. She snatched the spatula from Visconti's hand and moved to the stove. After filling both plates, she placed them on the bar.

Visconti sat on one of the captain's chairs and studied his plate. "Not only is she beautiful and intelligent, she's independent," he said, his voice crackling with sarcasm.

Kerri sat beside him and grinned at her host. "I wasn't going to stand around and let you do all the work."

Visconti placed his hand on top of Kerri's and smiled. "Thank you for your help, and thank you for being here. I can't tell you how delighted I am to have someone to share breakfast with me. It's been too long... Did you sleep well?"

Kerri nodded. "Your slushies put me in a coma."

"Wonderful. Then you should be ready for an action packed day. We're going to jog after we eat all this cholesterol. You still game?"

"Definitely. I can't wait to get outside."

Laughing and joking, Kerri and Visconti jogged in Central Park, then strolled through a melange of fountains, ponds, statues and monuments. They passed numerous park benches lined with old men reflecting on their pasts and speculating on their limited futures. They continued past families and groups of people playing softball, pitching horseshoes, riding the merry-go-round, flying kites or rowing boats, all enjoying the marvelous hiatus from their week long hibernation.

When they arrived at Conservatory Pond, they stood and watched a group of boys racing their model sailboats. A short distance around the shore, a jazz band wailed, while two stilt-walkers, dressed in black top hats, white t-shirts and multi-colored super-long trousers, attempted to dance to the music.

"Are you at all interested in art?" Visconti asked.

"I won a coloring contest in public school," Kerri replied with a modest smile.

"Wanna see some?"

"Sure."

"You could spend a lifetime on either side of this park and never see it all. A lot of it's world class."

"Let's see it all," Kerri urged, excited, and running ahead of Visconti.

After two hours of walking, mingling and pushing with crowds, both agreed they were hungry.

Following a long relaxing lunch at Tavern on the Green, they rented a carriage and took an old-fashioned leisurely turn around the park. After stepping from the carriage, they ran back to Visconti's car and spent the remainder of the afternoon touring Manhattan and shopping.

At five, they delivered their bounty, the prize of which was Kerri's white silk and cashmere pullover and matching skirt, to Visconti's apartment. With breakneck speed, they showered, changed, raced back to the car and drove to Pier 83, at 43rd Street and 12th Avenue. They boarded a Circle Line boat, barely in time for the dinner cruise around Manhattan.

The boat glided from the dock, then headed down the Hudson, passing the enormous Jacob Javits Convention Center, the 14th Street Meat Market, then on to the twin towers of the World Trade Center and Battery Park City. When the boat rounded the southern tip of the island, it was time for dinner, at a table for two on the upper deck, which afforded a wonderful view of the Wall Street skyline and the Statue of Liberty.

The five piece band, set up at the far end of the upper deck, began to play "America the Beautiful", inducing everyone to stand and sing in unison. When they rounded the Statue of Liberty, the band continued with "Pretty Woman."

Kerri was thrilled, exhausted, excited and deliriously happy. Never in her life had she so thoroughly enjoyed a day and the company of one single individual. Never had she been so totally captivated. She reached across the table and held Louis's hand. "Am I dreaming, or am I going to wake up and discover that I'm not really here?" she asked, her mind blissfully detached from her unhappy past.

Visconti smiled. "It's all real, Kerri. Very real."

The boat turned and headed up the East River, passing under the Brooklyn, Manhattan and Williamsburg Bridges, then past the United Nations Headquarters. Visconti was catapulted into a state of melancholy when the boat glided under the Queensboro Bridge. Ugly memories of the crash of eighty-seven invaded his mind.

"Where have you gone, Louis?" Kerri asked, miffed by his failure to respond to her conversation.

Visconti gave Kerri an empty stare with saddened eyes. "I'm sorry. What did you say?"

"Something's wrong. What is it?"

Visconti pointed to the bridge. "That bridge reminded of the dumbest thing I ever did in my life."

"You want to talk about it?"

Visconti slumped forward, covered his face with his hands and exhaled. "You asked me about it last night. I had just returned from spending the weekend in the Bahamas with a woman who meant absolutely nothing to me. I can't even remember her name. I just needed to get away and wanted company," he said, almost apologizing.

"The day the market crashed?" She knew it was, but wanted him to talk about it.

"Yup. In October of eighty-seven. I was right on the edge when I left New York on that Thursday night. I was convinced I had developed a sick dependency on communications. I had to escape. I needed a place with no telephones, no computers, no video ticker-tapes, no newspapers, no television. Nothing but wind, sun and water."

Kerri reached for Visconti's hand. "You don't have to talk about it if you don't want to," she said.

"I want to... We were stuck in traffic up there and the driver mentioned something about people jumping off the bridge, so I asked him to explain." Visconti closed his eyes and shook his head. "In the few seconds it took him to tell me the stock market had fallen further than ever before in history, I saw my whole life flash before my eyes. I thought my heart was going to pound its way out of my chest. Before we got off that bridge, I actually considered jumping."

"What stopped you?" Kerri asked, then realized the incredible insensitivity of her question.

Visconti smirked. "I can't stand cold water. I realized that in the unlikely event I survived the jump, I would be compelled to flounder around before I perished from hypothermia."

"Really?"

"No. It was logic, pure logic. I drew strength from the knowledge that the losses sustained by my clients were not the result of my poor investment decisions. They occurred because I was gone, out of touch, powerless to do anything about them."

A wave of appreciation swept through Kerri. The apparent honesty of Visconti's admission had given her a much deeper insight into his character. He was indeed human, fragile, normal. He had courageously revealed the existence of simple human frailties. She concluded, naively, that it was not greed or avarice that had nearly destroyed his reputation and his life. It was merely human requirements. She felt like a kindred spirit. "We're alike, you and me," she said.

"How so?"

"I was powerless to do anything about my husband's problems, and those problems came very close to destroying me."

221

"What was the source of your strength?"

"You," Kerri replied without hesitation.

"You give me too much credit."

"I don't think I've given you enough. You were there for me when I needed someone. You've taken me from the depths of despair to the point where I realize that there's life after first love. For the first time in at least six months I'm happy. I wouldn't be without you."

"Would you like to dance?"

Kerri nodded.

She immediately submitted to Visconti's arms when they reached the dance floor, oblivious to the sights and sounds around her, aware only of Louis Visconti, and that she was where she wanted to be.

The music stopped when the cruise ship had moved within sight of its point of origin. Disappointed, Kerri lifted her head from Visconti's chest. She stared at the shore, then at him. "Let's go around again. I could dance forever."

He held her tighter and kissed her forehead. "I've got a better idea... Let's go home and dance."

CHAPTER 65

With soft music and chilled pinot grigio the two resumed their dance in the darkened living room of Visconti's apartment. They continued until Kerri's yawn induced Visconti to glance at his watch. "Time for your beauty sleep, young lady."

Kerri nodded, feeling disappointed, yet reckless and impulsive. She placed her hand at the back of Visconti's head and pulled until his lips touched hers. She pressed her body against his. "I'm not going to let you out of my sight tonight," she whispered, then kissed him, with intent.

He led her up the winding staircase, into her bedroom and to the edge of the marble pedestal. He took her in his arms and whispered, "You sure?"

Without a word, she pulled Visconti closer and kissed him hard. While they kissed, they struggled to remove each other's clothing. He lifted her onto the bed, then lowered her head to one of the pillows. She flung her arms around his neck and pulled him down to her. "I can't believe this is happening," she said.

"We've been given a second chance, Kerri. Never forget it," Visconti said, then made slow deliberate love to Kerri, taking her to physical heights she had never before experienced.

Kerri opened her eyes for the first time at eight-thirty. She stared out the window at a dark rainy day and grinned. The weather didn't matter. It could be snowing. She was happy again, a renegade from propriety and responsibility, preposterously, deliriously and utterly happy. Denying that her transformation was the result of a rebound, Louis's wealth and charisma, or the father figure he represented, her happiness was as certain as their proximity at that moment. Naked. No conditions. No representations. Now she was complete. At last she had found what had been missing from her life for so long.

Visconti opened his eyes and placed his hand on Kerri's shoulder. "Hi," he said with a broad grin.

She turned to face her lover, then allowed her head to descend to his chest. "Hi," she groaned. "You were fantastic."

"We were fantastic," Visconti countered, then stroked Kerri's cheek with his index finger. "Making love to you was better than anything I could have imagined. Visconti was contemplating a simple truth: he had, at long last found a woman with whom he wanted to stay after sex. "I don't want to live alone for one more minute. I've been too lonely, too long. I want us to live together, starting right now. I want to spend the rest of my life with you, every delicious minute of it."

"I'm not sure," Kerri replied, feigning a worried frown.

"Why?" Visconti asked, his smile replaced by a pained grimace.

"How can we be sure last night wasn't just preparation colliding with opportunity?"

Visconti smiled, then reached behind Kerri's buttock and pulled her close to his body. "Let's make sure," he said.

Kerri responded, this time more assured. She took time to savor each sensation, to build a crescendo, straining to postpone the ultimate sensation.

When it was over, Visconti nibbled on Kerri's right ear lobe. "You sure now?" he whispered.

"Very."

"Then live with me?"

"On one condition."

"Name it."

"That you take me back to Miles's house on Sunday night."

"Why?"

224

"I want to wake up there on Monday morning and tell Miles and Andrea in person. I couldn't do it any other way. They've been too kind to me."

CHAPTER 66

Toronto. Monday. April 16. Nine, A.M.

The years had been kind to Dan Turner. His hair had whitened, yet the thinning had mercifully stopped. He had retained the same commanding presence, still capable of inspiring confidence with his piercing stare, deep baritone voice and imposing profile. "Welcome," he said, hoisting himself from his chair to greet Mike and Karen King.

"Good to see you again, Dan," Mike said, then shook Turner's hand.

"The pleasure's mine," Turner said, then remained standing and focused on Karen, still every inch a stunning beauty. "It's been a long time, Karen. How have you been?" he asked. "You don't look a day older than the day you were married."

"I feel a lot older, but I appreciate the compliment."

Turner pointed to the windowed corner of his office which faced Lake Ontario, the islands, and the busy Gardiner Expressway. Opposing one another in front of the giant windows were twin sofas, covered in forest green leather and separated by a large and elegant nickel plated coffee table. "Let's sit over there," he suggested.

All three headed for the sofas.

"How has married life been?" Turner asked as he sat facing his clients.

"Wonderful," Mike replied.

"Beyond my wildest expectations," Karen said with a big grin.

"And the children. They are well?"

Karen nodded, then frowned. "We have a problem."

Silence.

"Phillip's part of the problem," Mike said, swallowing hard. "The trust is the other part... Karen and I have decided it's time we did something about it."

Turner leaned backward, hung one leg over the other and glared at his clients. "Obviously something's changed."

"Everything's changed," Mike answered.

"In round numbers, what's the current value of the trust?"

"Around six hundred million."

Turner gave a slow whistle and raised his eyebrows, sharpening the numerous creases in his forehead. "Who's administering it?"

"A man named Louis Visconti. His office is in New York."

"Okay, now I know what we're dealing with. Tell me what's changed."

Mike responded, anxious to give his attorney an accurate answer. Turner had ventured well beyond the call of legal propriety in his efforts to assist him and Karen. "Our attitude toward the Trust. When we first found Servito's money, you know how determined I was to keep it. I'm still not sure why. I guess I just wanted to make a statement. The Feds had treated us like numbers. Karen and I could have spent years in prison, and they wouldn't have given a shit. If I live forever, I'll never forgive them for that... Karen has been very patient with me. I really don't think she ever wanted to keep her husband's money, but she agreed to do it for my benefit. It's taken a long time, but she's finally managed to convince me that we should get rid of it. She thinks that it's never been anything more than a mental ball and chain."

"Am I to assume you want to give it back to the Feds?" Turner asked.

Mike's face reddened. "Over my dead body. I'd rather burn it."

Turner chuckled and rolled his eyes. "It's a very unique problem, one I've never faced in my entire legal career. I suppose under the circumstances you would like it to vanish into thin air, without a trace."

"Not exactly," Mike said, relaxing slightly. "We want to give it anonymously to the World Agricultural Foundation. It's one of the most efficient charities in the world."

"How do you plan to do it?"

"That's what we want to talk to you about."

Turner squinted at Mike. "Okay, it's obvious that you've given this a lot of thought. You'll need an intermediary. It's imperative that you have implicit trust in whoever you chose."

Mike winked at Turner. "There's only one individual who falls into that category."

"I hope you're not referring to me."

"None other."

Turner frowned and shook his head. "I can't. I'm flattered, but I can't do anything that could be construed as complicity in this flagrantly illegal financial adventure of yours. I'm already way over the line with this thing. I do, however, give your latest decision a standing ovation."

"Do you know anyone who would qualify?" Karen asked.

"I know lots of people who would, but you would have to think long and hard about trusting any of them with a six hundred million dollar secret."

Deflated, Mike and Karen exchanged morose expressions. "Isn't this beautiful?" Mike said. "We're sitting on over six hundred million and we can't even give it away."

"I'm sure if you look hard enough you'll find the right person," Turner offered. "The best advice I can give you is to find someone completely removed from the system, someone immune to, or unconstrained by the legal systems of Canada and the United States."

Karen jerked upright, as if bitten by an insect. "I know who we could use," she declared.

"Who?"

"Alfred Schnieder."

Mike smiled and blew her an approving kiss. "If he's still alive, he'd be perfect."

"Do you know where he is," Turner asked.

"He retired and moved to Zurich in nineteen eighty. I hope he's still there."

"Then give him a call, but be careful. You're dealing with an extremely dangerous quantity of money," Turner warned.

CHAPTER 67

The flurry in the kitchen resembled a fast forward video. Breakfast at the Dennis household on a weekday morning, normally a very controlled and civilized event, was vastly different that morning. Kerri, Miles and Andrea, all victims of extraordinary and exhausting weekends, had slept late. Kerri, the first to arrive, proceeded to the refrigerator and removed her beloved orange juice. Andrea, still dressed in her pajamas and nightgown, arrived seconds later. Her eyes showed the affects of consecutive late nights. "Kerri, darling!" she said, delighted to see her. "I'm sorry we missed you last night. How was your weekend?"

Kerri grinned, gulping her juice and measuring ground coffee into a filter. "First tell me about Chicago," she replied.

"I asked you first," Andrea countered.

The kitchen door burst open and Miles rushed in. "Good morning, Kerri," he sang, hugging her with one arm and sticking the other in the sleeve of his blue suit jacket. He took a sip of her orange juice, then grinned at her. "How was your weekend?"

Kerri was about to reply when Miles glanced at his watch. "Sorry. You'll have to tell me later. We're late." He turned to Andrea. "Would you get the car, please, dear?"

Andrea stuck her tongue out at Miles, then reluctantly headed for the garage.

Miles and Kerri filled styrene cups with coffee, then hurried to meet Andrea in the driveway. They climbed into the van while struggling to hold their cups in a perpendicular position.

"Now speak to me, Kerri," Andrea demanded, then placed the gear shift in reverse and turned her head to look out the rear window. "I'm dying to know about your weekend."

"The first part was horrible. The second part was fantastic."

"Tell us about the horrible part," Andrea demanded.

To the horror of both Miles and Andrea, Kerri proceeded to disclose the story of her ugly confrontation with Brian.

Andrea frowned at Miles. "I told you something like that would happen," she scolded.

"Did he hurt you in any way?" Miles asked.

"No, but I'm sure he would have if..." Kerri paused to wipe tears from her eyes.

"If what?" Miles asked, his eyes bulging, his mouth open in anticipation.

"He made me take him to your bedroom. Then he forced off my clothes and..." Again Kerri wiped tears from her eyes. "He grabbed my hair and threw me on the bed... At that point I knew I was going to have to let him rape me."

Andrea slammed the brakes and brought the car to an abrupt stop in the train station parking lot. "My God!" she declared. "What..."

"We've got to run, dear," Miles interrupted. "Kerri will call you the minute she gets to the office. She'll tell you the whole story." He climbed out of the van and started walking toward the station.

"Just tell me fast, Kerri," Andrea insisted. "It'll only take a second."

"It had a happy ending. I'll call you as soon as I get to the office," Kerri promised, then hurried to catch up with Miles.

"I'll kill you if you don't!" Andrea shouted, cursing her decision to remain in pajamas.

"What did happen?" Miles asked as Kerri took a seat on the train beside him.

231

Kerri grinned. "I was rescued."

"By whom?"

"You'll never guess in a million years."

"Give me a clue."

"He's your biggest client."

"Louis Visconti?"

Kerri nodded. "Honestly, Miles, I've never been so happy to see anyone in my life."

"Well I'll be damned! How did Louis know?"

"He said he just decided to come to the house and see how I was. When he saw Brian's car in the driveway, he went in and followed the noise."

"How did he handle Brian?"

"He told him the police were on the way."

"What did Brian do?"

"He left."

"Incredible.! I'm going to thank Louis as soon as I can."

"I've already done that," Kerri said, smiling like the proverbial cat.

"How?"

"We spent the rest of the weekend together, in his apartment."

"Out of gratitude, or did you really want to do it?"

"I resent that, Miles," Kerri said with a scowl of indignation. "I would never do anything I didn't really want to do."

"I'm sorry. I know you wouldn't."

Kerri was now compelled to complete her story. She saw it as necessary to set the stage, or in some way to justify her decision to live with Louis Visconti. Her heart beat faster. She moved forward in her seat, then turned to face Miles. "It was more than gratitude, Miles."

"What are you telling me?"

"I love him."

"You love him! How could you? You barely know him."

"I know him better than I've ever known anyone in my entire life and I love him from the bottom of my heart."

Miles grinned. "I'm shocked, relieved, flabbergasted, and happy as hell for you... I suppose you're going to tell me you want to live with him."

"How could you possibly know?" Kerri asked, feeling an avalanche of relief. The one thing she had thought would be the most difficult had suddenly become a nonevent.

"I didn't have to be a rocket scientist. I brought up three kids in the seventies and eighties."

"Do I have your blessings?"

"You have my blessings, and only one piece of advice."

"I've learned to respect your advice. What is it?"

"However strongly you feel about this relationship, move slowly and keep your eyes wide open. Remember, Louis is a lot older than you and he's lived in the fast lane for a long time."

Kerri kissed Miles on his cheek. "I will, and thank you for being so understanding."

"What are you going to do about your husband?"

"Louis is going to arrange an appointment for me with a lawyer he knows. Hopefully, she'll remove Brian from my life."

As promised, Kerri called Andrea the minute she arrived at her desk and completed the story of her incredible weekend.

"I'm disappointed to lose you and I'm insanely jealous," Andrea declared. "I'm prepared to bless this union on one condition."

"What?"

"I insist that you call me at least once a week and tell me everything that happens in your relationship with that hunk."

"That's the least I can do. I can't thank you enough for all you and Miles have done for me."

CHAPTER 68

Zurich. Monday, April 16.

The tranquillity and serenity of a warm April afternoon on the balcony of Alfred Schnieder's lavish Zurich condominium was broken by the shrill sound of his telephone. Before he could extract himself from the comfort of his chair, his wife appeared in the opened sliding glass doorway. "It's for you, Alfred," she said, frowning to show her displeasure at the intrusion.

"Who is it?"

"He said his name is Mike King. He's calling from Toronto."

"I'll take it in the den," Schnieder said. He hoisted himself to a standing position, then shuffled to the den and lifted his ivory handled, gold trimmed receiver. "It's about time you called," he said with a raspy voice. "One of the simple pleasures an old man holds sacred is to hear from his friends occasionally. An interval of a decade is quite unacceptable."

"How are you, Alfred?"

"My cup runneth over. Were it not for this infernal arthritis, I would be as spry as you remember me... And how did you know where to reach me?"

"I called the Banco International Venezolano. Manuel Blanco gave me your number."

"That little snot could never keep a secret," Schnieder quipped. "He'll never be a successful banker... Manuel is well?"

"I don't know. There was no small talk."

"Tell me about Karen. She is well and has given you many children?"

"She is well and gave me a son, nine years ago."

"Only one. Such a tragedy... And Phillip? He is well?"

"Yes. He's a young man now. He'll be twenty next month," Mike said, rolling his eyes. "Actually, he's the reason I called. As you will no doubt recall, we placed all of the funds in his father's estate in a trust. Simultaneously, we..."

"Yes, I remember it well. We transferred ownership of the trust to an anstalt, to hide it from prying eyes. Did we achieve our objective?"

"The paperwork has stood the test of time."

"The arrangement with Louis Visconti has worked well?"

"It, too has stood the test of time. You might be interested to know the trust's value has grown to over six hundred million."

"A satisfactory performance, but not exactly what I would have expected from a man of his considerable talents."

"In fairness to him, our instructions to Louis were to be conservative and to preserve the capital."

"Good, then what can I do for you?"

"Karen and I have decided to dispose of the money. We need your help, Alfred."

In addition to shocking Schnieder, Mike's announcement succeeded in offending his European and South American banking values. "Please be more specific. Perhaps I misunderstood. Maybe you want the funds moved to another country, or disguised in some more obscure fashion. You might consider moving the money to Switzerland. You should know that tax evasion is not a crime in this country and there is no restriction on currency movements. Banking secrecy here is protected by both civil and criminal law."

"Let me be very specific, Alfred. Karen and I want to give all of the money to charity, and we want to do it anonymously."

"Completely aside from the fact that I think what you are proposing to do is absurd and tantamount to insanity, I fail to understand why are you telling me?"

"We need your help in the disposition. We want you to be an intermediary. We think your role in the creation of the trust and your extensive banking experience makes you uniquely qualified for the job. Most importantly, we don't want anyone else to know we have the money."

"Thank you for the compliment. Is there more to the job than simply acting as an intermediary?"

"No, but the transaction has to clean. It's absolutely imperative that there is no possibility of tracing the source."

"If I were to accomplish your objectives, what compensation did you have in mind?"

"Would one percent be satisfactory?"

Schnieder smiled as he calculated an opportunity to make the easiest six million he had ever made. Still well connected in European banking circles, he could achieve Mike's goal without leaving the comfort of his condominium. "Extremely generous... May I expect your offer in writing?" he asked.

"Nothing in writing, Alfred. Nothing. You do have my word, however. It's as good as a written contract. I've never screwed anyone in my life and I have no intention of starting now."

"Then I will be pleased to accept your assignment. When do you wish to proceed?"

"Very soon. I'll call and let you know."

"Splendid. How may I contact you?"

"You can't. I'll call you."

"As you wish. Please convey my kindest regards to Karen."

"I'll do that," Mike said, then hung up the receiver of his car telephone. He rubbed his face with his hands and smiled. "Yes!" he shouted, clenching his fist, closing his eyes, and experiencing an enormous surge of relief. Soon he would, once and for all time, remove the tainted trust which had tormented his conscience for too long.

CHAPTER 69

New York.

Miles entered Visconti's office and marched to his desk. The menacing scowl he had feigned transformed into a broad smile. "Thank you, Louis," he said, extending his right hand.

Visconti leaned forward and accepted Dennis's hand. "What for?" he asked, puzzled by Dennis's bizarre and uncharacteristic behavior.

"For being there for Kerri. I can't thank you enough."

"I should thank you."

"Why?"

"For not being there. If you and Andrea hadn't been in Chicago last weekend, I would still be a lonely man."

Dennis placed both hands on Visconti's desk and leveled his eyes on Visconti's. "I want to talk to you about that, and I want you to understand how damn serious I am... Kerri's a wonderful trusting naive girl. I care for her a lot. Furthermore, I'm sure you're aware that she's just emerging from a terrible marriage. If you hurt her in any way, I'm going to take it very personally."

Visconti raised his hands in surrender and returned Dennis's stare. "You have nothing to worry about, Miles. Believe it or not, I'm more worried about her hurting me. You can't know how excited I am that she would be interested in an old man like me."

Dennis smirked. "Hurt you? Impossible!" he scoffed, then headed for the door. On his way out, he wheeled and faced Visconti. "I almost forgot. You'll be happy to know that June crude's below seventeen and a half. There's at least another eight million in your margin account."

Visconti flashed a confident smile. "Just the beginning. There's going to be a whole hell of lot more in there, real soon."

Minutes after Dennis left, Visconti's secretary entered with coffee. "There's a call for you on three, Louis," she said, then placed the coffee in front of him. "It's Alfred Schnieder, from Zurich."

"Well I'll be damned! The old fart's still alive!" Visconti declared, reaching for his receiver with one hand and dismissing Sue with the other. He waited until she left, then pressed three. He leaned back and placed his feet on the desk. "Alfred, great to hear from you again. How are you?"

"Less than twenty-four hours ago, I informed Mike King that I am as healthy as a horse. Nothing has changed since then. And you?"

"Mike King!" Visconti exclaimed, agitated by the mere mention of the name. "What could you possibly be talking to him about?"

"... I'm sorry. I thought you knew."

"Knew what?"

"He has been smitten by pangs of conscience. He's asked me to dispose of the money in his trust."

"He what!" Visconti shouted, jerking his feet from his desk and bolting upright, implications blasting through his brain like rockets.

"He wants to wash his hands of the money and give it to charity."

"Jesus! This can't be happening. Did he give you a reason?"

"He expressed fears of being discovered, should word of its disposition be leaked."

"This is a fucking disaster! Did you make him aware of the alternatives?"

"Yes, but he was adamant. He's not prepared to consider any other idea. I have difficulty understanding his position. Given the same set of circumstances, I would behave quite differently."

Visconti's mind was in overdrive. "So what happens now? I hope he plans to inform me at some point."

"I'm sure he does. I don't think he has any problem with you. At least he made no mention of any."

"So he wants you to be his conduit," Visconti mused. "Did he specify how or when he wants it done?"

"No. He simply wants the transaction to be clean."

"That's just terrific," Visconti groaned. "All of a sudden the trustees get philanthropic, and I'm sitting here with a horrendous mess."

"What mess? Please explain."

"It's a very long story. Let's just say there isn't as much money in the trust as King thinks there is."

"How much is there?"

"About four hundred and thirty million, in round numbers."

Schnieder chuckled. "Interesting discrepancy. You have been doing some creative accounting, yes?"

"I won't have to do it much longer. I've just done a deal that's going to do a hell of a lot more than clean up the mess."

"I'm sure you know what you're doing."

"How much is King paying you for the job? Do you mind sharing that information with me?"

"One percent."

"Did he put it in writing?"

"No. He insisted that nothing be written. Normally that would be a problem. But since I am the one who will be arranging the transfer, it will be simple to arrange the removal of my fee."

Visconti was quick to grasp the equation of the situation. "If he doesn't want anything in writing, how can he be assured the transfer was ever made? And if it's not made, what remedies would he have?"

"Your larcenous mind is functioning as well as ever, my friend... King's request can be satisfied in a variety of ways. One is to provide him with a coded recording of a telephone call from an officer of the relevant bank. Perhaps he could receive a call from you at the same time. You could advise him that all of the money has been removed from the trust and transferred to a certain European bank. In my opinion, verification of the ultimate destination is not nearly so important to him as verification that his hands are clean of hot money."

"Alfred, are you still reasonably well connected in European banking circles?"

"I'm not communicating with them every day as I did in the past, but I still go to a lot of parties and other functions. We still speak the same language. Why do you ask?"

"Do you think you could find at least one corruptible banking officer?"

Schnieder chuckled. "It would be more difficult to find one who's not. What is on your mind, my young friend?"

"A fortune for you and me, Alfred. With the cooperation of one corruptible individual banker, we could relieve King of his problem and his money? The three of us, all apparently acting independently, could inform King that the money was dispersed according to his wishes. We could confirm that the transaction was clean, and that there are no traceable records. That should be all the assurance he needs... Is that feasible or am I dreaming in Technicolor?"

"It's not only feasible, it's profoundly exquisite. There's just one aspect of your plan that troubles me. What if our assurances are insufficient to allay the concerns of King?"

"Then I'll scare the shit out of him. I'll give him a Mexican standoff. I'll inform him that I'm fully aware of the original source of the funds, and that I would be pleased to remain silent as long as he was prepared to do the same thing... Now, does the plan still trouble you?"

"No. I'll make some discrete inquiries. As soon as I have something, I'll call you. It should not take long."

241

"Good hunting, Alfred. And thanks for calling." Visconti replaced the receiver, then leaped to his feet. "Fantastic!" he shouted, clenching his teeth and pounding his right fist into the palm of his left hand. The agonizing discipline of managing King's trust would soon be a distant memory. Even better, soon he would rid himself of the relentless telephone calls, the capricious markets and the tedious obligation of managing other peoples' money. Soon he could move to Europe and manage his own money. Lots of it.

Visconti's door opened and Sue appeared at the threshold. "Jackie Crawford's on line four. She's been waiting for a long time."

Visconti nodded, then lifted his receiver and pressed line four. "Sorry to keep you waiting, darling. I was talking to a banker in Zurich."

"You've been keeping me waiting a lot longer than that, you lecherous bastard!"

"Is this the same girl who flew to Aspen with her macho developer friend and left me frustrated and alone in New York?"

"The only reason I did that was because you were too damn busy counting your money... What can I do for you? Sorry I didn't get back to you yesterday. I was in court all day."

"I have a friend who needs your help. She wants out of her marriage."

"Why?"

"She's married to an asshole who's been abusing her both mentally and physically. I'm prepared to testify to that fact. She wants a restraining order and a divorce, in that order. I want this individual put on ice and I want you to nail him for the max. Send me your bills."

"So who is she?"

"Her name is Kerri Pyper. I want it changed to Kerri Visconti at the earliest possible date."

"Don't tell me you're in love again," Jackie snickered.

"Desperately."

"Sure you are, Louis. And you've decided to live happily ever after... So who's the asshole?"

"Brian Pyper."

"The Jets' quarterback?"

"Yup."

"Holy shit! A veritable pot of gold. Let me at him. I'll chew him up and spit him out."

"That's the Jackie Crawford I know and love."

"Money's the only thing you ever loved, Louis. You and I both know that... Can you have her in here at noon tomorrow?"

"Sure, but I want a first class job, Jackie."

"That's the only way I work."

"Then I'll leave it in your very capable hands. See you around."

"Louis, don't hang up."

"Why?"

"There's still time for you and me, you know."

"Forget   it,   Jackie.   You   know   I   can't   ski."

CHAPTER 70

Toronto. Tuesday, April 17.

From the day the adoption papers were signed, Mike had wanted to be a father to Phillip in every sense of the word. High on his priority list was to give the boy a set of values, far different from those he would have received from Jim Servito, his natural father. After almost ten years of frustrating effort, he worried that he had failed, and each day he was brutally reminded of his failure. He cringed at Phillip's shiftless self-indulgent behavior, his flaky lackadaisical approach to his job, and his constant and pathetic scruffy appearance. He was usually dressed in his faded and miserably threadbare jeans, his face perpetually unshaven, his hair too long, his baseball cap almost always on backwards and incredibly, just like his natural father, he had installed a diamond earring in his right ear lobe.

Only the persistent pleadings of Karen had prevented Mike from carrying out his threat to fire Phillip. Out of guilt, maternal instinct, genuine love, or all three, Karen had refused to allow her son thrown to the wolves. Mike was certain she wanted him shielded from the world that had corrupted his natural father.

Mike and Karen entered their den to find the couch had been moved to within five feet of the television set, Hockey Night in Canada near full volume. Phillip's right foot, still clad in his filthy brown boot, was visible above the back of the couch. The remainder of his body occupied the couch, as if it was his private realm.

Mike circled the couch and turned the television set off.

"What did you do that for?" Phillip protested, then propped himself with his elbow.

"Your mother and I would like to talk to you. Surely you could spare the time from your busy schedule."

"Can't you wait until the first period's over?"

Mike shook his head. "What we have to talk about is a little more important than a hockey game, but if the game's really that important to you, watch it later." He turned on the television set, then the VCR, and pressed RECORD. He turned to face Phillip. "Now, let's talk."

"What about?" Phillip asked, glaring angrily at his step father.

"Have you ever taken the time to consider what you're going to do with the rest of your life?"

"Yup."

"Good. What are you going to do?"

"None of your business."

Mike and Karen exchanged pained glances, then Mike turned again to face Phillip. "Your mother and I have something very important to tell you. We think it's something you must know."

"What?"

"It's about the money your natural father left after his death... The truth of it is that we really didn't..."

"I know," Phillip interrupted. "You've been lying to me. You never did give it back to the government, did you?"

"How did you know?" Mike asked, stunned and wondering how Phillip knew.

"I heard you and mom talking. I know you still have it, that it's in a trust, and that you're going to give it to charity... That isn't going to happen. My real father told me the money would be mine if anything happened to him, and that I could use it to become richer than him. That's what I want to do with the rest of my life."

Phillip's revelation introduced a disaster scenario. His attitude, unless adjusted, could ruin everything. "Have you ever considered the implications of that course of action?" Mike asked.

"Sure. I'll be able to watch the hockey game without being interrupted," Phillip replied with a smirk. "I don't care what you say. My real father gave that money to me, and if he was still alive, you and mom wouldn't be here to hassle me about it."

Mike summoned every ounce of patience in his body. "That's probably true, but he's not here and the money's going to charity."

Phillip sprang to his feet, an explosion of disappointment giving way to visceral rage. "Fuck you!" he shouted, pointing an accusing finger at Mike. "You're not my father. You're nothing but my mother's husband. If you so much as even think about giving that money away, I'm going to make your life miserable."

"And how are you going to do that?" Mike asked, fighting an urge to explode.

"I'll go to the Feds and tell them the whole damn story. Then they're gonna ask you where you got the money. What are you gonna tell them?"

Mike shook his head in disgust. "Get out of my sight! Do it fast before I do something I'll regret."

Phillip turned to face his mother. "Don't let him give it away, mom. I don't want to tell the Feds, but I will if..."

Karen slapped her son's face as hard as she could. "You heard what Mike said," she hissed, "Get out!"

Phillip's sneer oozed rage and contempt, his brown eyes displaying an ominous resolve. "If I don't have every dime of that money by my twenty-first birthday, I'm going straight to the government." He turned and marched from the room.

Karen and Mike stared at each other in shocked disbelief. "Do we have any options?" Karen asked, fully aware that there were few, all of which were unpalatable.

Mike took Karen in his arms and exhaled. "I don't know. At least he had the courtesy to give us some time to find one... I feel so guilty. If only I..."

Karen placed her index finger on Mike's lips. "Don't say it. You could second guess yourself all the way to the insane asylum. You've done nothing wrong," she said, failing to mention that Mike's idea to keep her former husband's money was terribly wrong.

"This is absolutely ludicrous!" Mike declared, raising his arms skyward, his face displaying frustration and despair. "That money is cursed! It's giving me the same horrible claustrophobic feeling it did ten years ago. Servito's got to be laughing at me from his grave."

CHAPTER 71

New York.

The heavy mahogany door to the inner office opened and Jackie Crawford appeared. Now thirty-eight, she showed few signs of approaching middle age. Only the hint of crow's feet under her dark brown eyes gave her age away. Her jet black hair was cut short and bounced above her shoulders as she moved. Dressed in a sophisticated gray pinstriped suit and white silk blouse, she exuded professionalism, yet her sassy demeanor belied the image.

"Sorry to keep you waiting," Jackie said, continuing to write feverishly on a pad of yellow foolscap. She lifted her head to glance at her new client. "Hi. Come in and have a seat." She led Kerri to a tan leather upholstered chair in front of her polished teak desk. "Can I get you something? Coffee, tea, cyanide?"

"No thank you," Kerri replied, smiling at Jackie's final offer.

"Then let's get started... Is this your first?"

"You mean my first divorce?"

"Yes."

Kerri nodded.

Jackie smirked. "Before you get your shit in a knot, let me tell you something very important. They're not worth it. No man is. I'm not saying I hate men. Quite the contrary. I'm saying that when it's over, it's over. You want them out of your life, and the process isn't worth getting bent out of shape. I've been through it twice, so you know I'm speaking from experience... How long have you been married?"

Jackie's self-confidence and flamboyant approach made Kerri feel more relaxed. "Almost two years."

248

"Where were you married?"

"Vancouver."

"Are you a Canadian citizen?"

"Yes. Is that a problem?"

"No... In a few sentences, tell me why you want a divorce."

"I could do it in one."

"How?"

"It's no longer a marriage."

Jackie chuckled. "That's good enough for me, my dear, but I think the judge is going to want you to be bit more specific... Louis told me you also want a restraining order. Is that correct?"

Kerri nodded. "My husband's an obsessive drinker. Probably an alcoholic. In either case, I think he needs help. Meanwhile, I'm afraid of him. He's physically abusive."

"Has he ever sought help?"

"No."

"That's good. Please continue. Tell me why it's no longer a marriage."

"He had a sexual affair with another woman and he abused me, both mentally and physically. The physical abuse was the reason I moved out of our apartment."

"I'll want to chronicle those abuses later. Would you be able to give dates and times?"

"Yes."

"Good. Any children?"

"No."

"You're lucky. Next subject... I'll need to know your husband's annual income. Do you know what that is?"

"Yes, but it's irrelevant."

"Why?"

"I thought Louis told you I don't want any money from my husband."

Jackie grinned. "You're right. He did. Forgive me. I was so astounded when he told me, I just had to hear it from you. Besides, I'm incredibly nosy... Are there any assets in the marriage? You know you're entitled to half of those."

"I don't want any assets. All I want is a divorce and for Brian to leave me alone."

"Okay, that's what you shall have. Because of the relative urgency of the restraining order, we should be able to get a hearing fairly soon. The divorce, however... Well, we'll try to move it along as fast as we can."

"How fast?"

"I'll call you and let you know. Where can I reach you?"

"At Iacardi & Sons, in the World Trade Center."

"And at night?"

Kerri gave Jackie the address and telephone number of Visconti's apartment.

Jackie recognized the address and smirked. "So you're living in the palace. I'm insanely jealous."

"Is Louis more than a friend to you?" Kerri asked, disturbed by Jackie's comment.

"Past tense, my dear. It's over between us. Can I offer you a piece of unofficial advice? It's not legal. It's personal."

"Sure."

"Louis is an extremely attractive man, but he's dangerous. Be careful. He could rip your heart out."

"Why do you think he's dangerous?"

"I really wonder if he could ever love a woman, I mean with the kind of love familiar to you and me. I think his only true love is money. If he had a choice of making ten dollars and making mad passionate love to the woman of his dreams, he'd have to think about it."

Jackie's assessment of Louis worried Kerri. "Did he hurt you?" she asked.

Jackie blushed and looked away. "I don't think he knows it."

CHAPTER 72

Visconti used Kerri's first step toward getting Brian Pyper out of her life as an excuse for celebration. He took her to see Jerome Robbin's 'Broadway', a show which had played to near capacity audiences for more than a year and a half. After the show, they went to Paulo's Ristorante, a tiny but intimate eatery nearby, to gorge themselves on spaghetti and meatballs.

The evening was a bitter sweet experience for Kerri. Hours earlier, Jackie Crawford had diminished her marital anxieties, while simultaneously injecting her with new ones. In spite of her concerns for Louis's alleged preference for money, she elected to hold them in abeyance, to enjoy the moment, to savor the euphoria of being with the man she loved. It was, after all, quite conceivable that Jackie's comments were only manifestations of jealousy and bitterness.

"Is it my imagination, or is something bothering you?" Visconti asked as they emerged from the restaurant into a swarming mass of noisy humanity on Broadway.

"It's your imagination," Kerri said, smiling and reaching for Visconti's hand, urging him to walk.

Visconti tugged at Kerri's hand until she stopped and turned to face him. "You can't fool an old dog," he said.

Kerri grinned. "You're very perceptive... I was just thinking about a comment Jackie Crawford made this afternoon. It probably didn't mean a thing."

"About the divorce?"

"No. About you."

Visconti's brows furrowed and his lips tightened. "What did she say?"

"She didn't think you could ever love a woman. She said your only true love is money."

Visconti smiled, then laughed. "Obviously, she allowed the conversation to descend to the personal level."

"Is she jealous?"

Visconti nodded. "I'm sorry. I should have been completely honest with you before I sent you into her den. Jackie's a great gal, but she's incredibly possessive."

"She said your relationship with her is over. Is it?"

"I dated her a number of times this spring. As the relationship progressed, she began to expect more out of it than I did. A couple of weeks ago, she invited me to spend a weekend with her at her ski chalet in Aspen. When I told her I couldn't go because of a business commitment, she tore into me with the vengeance of a scorned tigress."

"Is that what ended it?"

Visconti nodded. "I couldn't believe it. She behaved as though I had cheated on her, or somehow denied her inheritance... So, she invited someone else and that was the end of us."

Relieved, Kerri kissed Visconti's cheek. "Forgive me. Sorry I mentioned it."

"I hope you understand, Kerri. It's extremely important to me. With the exception of my first wife, I have never, ever asked a woman to live with me. You are the only one," Visconti said, his eyes begging for approval.

"I do understand. Let's walk."

Visconti refused to move. "I can't wait until the weekend. Let's take the day off and move you into the apartment."

"I can't."

"Why?"

"I can't just rush out on Andrea and Miles. I'd feel as guilty as hell."

Visconti nodded, accepting her excuse. "I've already waited a lifetime for you. I guess I can wait a few more days... What would you say if I invited you to run away to Europe with me and live in Monte Carlo?"

"You're kidding!"

"I'm very serious." Visconti's somber expression and cold gray stare were clear indications of his sincerity.

"Why would you want to run away? You have everything right here."

"Now that I have you, I have everything but the one thing I've wanted for as long as I can remember."

"What's that?"

"Freedom. I've never really experienced it. I'm trapped here. A slave to telephones, computers, the market, everything. I want to live the rest of my life in a place where everything is a choice, not a decision."

"You're really serious, aren't you?"

"I've never been more serious about anything."

"How would we live? Are you talking about retiring?"

"That's exactly what I'm talking about. I'm close to completing a deal that's going to give me more money than I could spend in several lifetimes."

Kerri was uncomfortable, off balance. Everything had moved too fast and was accelerating. "I don't know what I would say," she replied, desperately trying to think of what her answer would be if Visconti demanded one.

"You don't have to say anything. I just want you to think about it."

CHAPTER 73

Visconti received an urgent call from Zurich at nine the following morning. "Good news. I've found a man who's perfect for our requirements," Schnieder announced.

"Who?" Visconti asked.

"His name is Olaf Leutweiler. He's the president of Weisscredit Bankhaus in Geneva. He has agreed to work with us and to provide Mike King with all the necessary assurances."

"Wonderful. How much is he going to cost us?"

"Five million."

"Ouch! Alfred, that's a ton of money!"

"It is but you must understand that he is a crucial link in the procedure. What we are asking him to do involves great personal risk. It is a serious crime for bankers to behave in a fraudulent manner in this country."

"Can we trust him?"

"Implicitly. He's been a banker in Switzerland for most of his life, and a friend of mine for almost as long. Here, bankers learn quickly that their survival is proportional to their ability to keep secrets and to honor commitments. He has survived for a long time."

"Okay, so we'll give him his pound of flesh," Visconti conceded.

"Has King contacted you?"

"No. Has he called you?"

"No, and it's beginning to concern me. Why do you think he's delaying? He sounded quite anxious when he called and asked me to help him dispose of the money. Perhaps I should call him and tell him how I propose to do it."

"Good idea. While you're at it, ask him if he's called me and let me know how he responds."

Schnieder called Mike at his Toronto office. "Good morning, Mike. It's Alfred Schnieder. I called to inform you that I have developed a plan to achieve all of your objectives, cleanly. I presume you know what I mean. Would you like to hear it?"

"Sure."

"We'll work through a friend of mine. His name is Olaf Leutweiler. He's the president of Weisscredit Bankhaus, a well respected bank in Geneva. He has assured me that the entire exercise can be completed with the utmost secrecy. It will never be necessary for him, or anyone else to know the source of the funds. He suggested that the confirmation can be done by means of a prearranged code into a designated answering machine... How do you like the plan?"

Mike gave no response, his mind far from the conversation.

"Are you still there?"

"Sorry. I was thinking... I like the plan. Thanks for letting me know."

"When would you like to proceed?"

"I'm not sure. I'll let you know."

"Have you made Louis Visconti aware of your plan?"

"Not yet. I just haven't had the time. I've been really busy with a number of other matters," Mike said, reluctant to alarm or trust Schnieder with the knowledge of Phillip's threat.

"I don't mean to impose unwelcome pressure on you, Mike, but Olaf may not be available if we delay too long."

"I understand what you're saying, Alfred. I'll get back to you as soon as I can."

"I'll await your call."

Mike hung up, agonizing over the growing pressure of the vise into which Phillip had placed him. "Damn that kid!" he shouted, thumping his desk with his right fist.

Schnieder again called Visconti. "The good news is that King likes the plan. The bad news is that something is definitely causing him to delay."

"Did he say what it is?" Visconti asked.

"No."

"Can you speculate?"

"I haven't the slightest idea."

"Then call me the minute you hear from him."

"I will, and would be grateful if you did the same."

CHAPTER 74

Glen Cove. Friday, April 20. 7:00 P.M.

With tear-filled hugs and kisses Kerri thanked Miles and Andrea for their kindness and consideration during an extremely trying time of her life. After one last emotional wave, she climbed into the front seat of Visconti's Mercedes, anxious to begin a new life with the man she loved, to share the joy of the intensely physical and passionate phase of a new relationship, to experience the endless fun-filled nights and yawn-filled days.

Dark threatening clouds were gathering beyond the horizon. History had lit the fuse.

In 1922, over three years after the First World War, the British convened a conference in Uquair, a Persian Gulf port. They intended to establish permanent boundaries for Saudi Arabia, Kuwait and Iraq. Significantly, Kuwait was not represented at the conference. Kuwait's boundary with Iraq was moved northward to correspond with a line drawn in 1913 by the Turks and the British. In addition, Iraq was left with a narrow twenty-six mile entrance to the Persian gulf through the shallow Shatt al-Arab waterway. By contrast, Kuwait was given five times as much shoreline, including the enormous natural harbor at Kuwait City, and Bubiyan and Warba Islands, which dominated the approach to Umm Qasr, Iraq's only port. By establishing the new boundaries, the British succeeded in protecting their strategic interests, but had simultaneously planted the seeds of jealousy and hatred. Those seeds, fertilized by a desperate need for money, would bear fruit in the form of Iraq's wrath in 1990, sixty-eight years later.

Iraq's need for money had grown to a critical stage. Crude oil prices were falling and world demand for the precious liquid was declining. Saddam Hussein, Iraq's angry president, claimed the decline was the result of a U.S. induced recession. In desperation, he sent his deputy prime minister, Saadum Hammadi to each of the Persian Gulf states to press them to cut production. Saddam Hussein understood that the only way to increase prices was to curb production. When Hammadi visited Kuwait he also demanded $27 billion as compensation for oil allegedly stolen by the Kuwaitis from the Rumaila oil field, considered an Iraqi possession.

In rejecting the Iraqi claim, the Kuwaitis gave Saddam the excuse he needed to set forces in motion which could only be stopped by extraordinary means. The forces would trigger a chain reaction of events which would dramatically change many lives, including those of Louis Visconti and others close to him.

The arrival of July, 1990, coincided with the invasion of an intense steamy heat wave in the New York area. As temperatures climbed, so too did the price of crude oil. At an O.P.E.C. planning session in Jidda, Saudi Arabia, Kuwait finally agreed to abide by its production quota. News of the agreement sent the spot price of crude oil up two dollars a barrel.

July 16, 1990.

Tariq Aziz, Iraq's foreign minister, wrote to the Arab League accusing Kuwait of overproduction and of stealing oil from the Rumaila oil field. A speech delivered by Saddam Hussein contained a thinly veiled threat of military action if the Kuwaitis continued. The wording alarmed the western world. Unable to decide on an appropriate response to Iraq's threat, the Kuwaiti cabinet made a colossal miscalculation by assuming Saddam was bluffing in an effort to extort money.

July 21, 1990.

The American C.I.A. reported the first Iraqi troop movements near the Kuwait northern border. In an effort to mediate the dispute between Iraq and Kuwait, Egyptian president Hosni Mubarak, King Hussein of Jordan and King Fahd of Saudi Arabia sought and got assurances from Saddam that Iraq would not invade so long as negotiations continued. Not completely appeased by the assurances, investors bid the price of oil up to almost twenty dollars a barrel.

Disturbed and shaken by the unexpected reversal of oil prices, Visconti called Assif Raza at his New York home and quickly dispensed with the pleasantries. "Sorry to bother you, Assif. I need to talk to you about crude oil. Do you mind sparing me a few minutes?" he asked, fidgeting nervously in anticipation of bad news.

"I can give you all the time you need, Louis. Oil is a subject very near and dear to my heart."

"I get a little nervous when I see the price move up four bucks in one week. I can handle movements of a buck or two, but this is beyond my pain threshold. Is this a trend or just an expensive hiccup?"

"I would suggest you relax, Louis," Raza replied. "Even if Kuwait sticks to its production quota, the world will still be swimming in oil. Furthermore, to the extent Kuwait reduces production, Iraq will increase its output to replace it. You must understand that Saddam Hussein is desperate for money. He'll do anything to get it."

"That's what I'm afraid of. What the hell is Saddam doing with his troops on the Kuwaiti border?"

Raza chuckled. "He's a good poker player. He's bluffing. Military action against Kuwait would be lunacy. He knows the United States will protect its interests in the area. They would deal with Iraqi forces like cannon fodder."

"Should I stay short?"

"Most definitely. In fact, you might want to take this opportunity to increase your position."

"Not possible. The FTC is watching me like a hawk. I'm classified as a large trader."

"Then stay where you are and relax. When everyone's finished posturing and all of the hands have been played, you'll be a very wealthy man."

Visconti gazed skyward and breathed a large sigh of relief. "Thanks, Assif. I can't tell you how much I appreciate your advice."

"You're very welcome, Louis. Please call if there's anything else I can do for you."

July 31, 1990, 10:30 A.M.

Miles Dennis's eyes were riveted to the moving electronic tape on the wall outside his office. He read the shocking news with heightened anxiety. "U.S. intelligence sources report a continuing buildup of Iraqi troops on Kuwait's northern border... King Hussein of Jordan visited Sheik Jabir al-Ahmed al-Sabah, the Emir of Kuwait, to warn him that the meeting of the Arab League, scheduled for tomorrow in Jidda, will be critical." He called Andrew Tarquanian, Iacardi's senior oil and gas research analyst.

"Did you see that news flash?" Dennis asked.

"Yup. Why?"

"What do you think Iraq's going to do?"

"Saddam's playing bullshit poker. That's what I think."

"So you think he'll back off?"

"Yup. He'd be out of his mind to invade. He knows the U.S. would kick the shit out of him if he did."

"Is that just your opinion, or is it a consensus?"

"I talked to the boys in Rotterdam this morning. To a man, they agree with me."

"Do we hold our positions?"

"Stay short, and if crude goes to twenty-five, short the hell out of it."

"Thanks, Andrew," Dennis said, then smiled as he hung up. Tarquanian had an uncanny knack of being right, most of the time.

August 1, 1990.

With another miscalculation of horrendous proportions, the Kuwaiti's underestimated Saddam Hussein's intentions and once again rejected his claim for compensation. After an intense two hour negotiation session in Jidda, talks between the two nations collapsed.

World   tensions   heightened.

CHAPTER 75

Kuwait. August 2, 1990.

Kuwaiti border guards were quickly eliminated when Russian made T-72 tanks opened fire on them at short range. Within minutes of the brief but savage engagement, the tanks were racing southward to Kuwait City, while Iraqi Mirages and Migs led the way.

Washington. August 1, 1990, 9:00 P.M.

Brent Scowcroft, George Bush's national security officer, burst into the president's living quarters on the second floor of the White House. He broke the news that Iraqi troops had crossed the Kuwait border and were heading south. While the news was a surprise to Bush, he assumed the Iraqis intended only to plunder the country before withdrawing.

The Iraqis claimed they had been invited into Kuwait to restore order by an "interim free government" of Kuwaiti revolutionaries who had overthrown the Sabah dynasty, rulers of the emirate for two and a half centuries.

In clandestine radio and television broadcasts, Sheik Saad al-Abdallah Al Sabah, crown prince and premier of Kuwait, issued a plea for resistance, "Let them taste the chalice of death," he said. "They have come to kill the sons of Kuwait and its women. We shall fight them everywhere, until we clean up their treachery from our land. The whole world is with us."

Visions of another financial catastrophe raced through Visconti's mind during a nail biting wait for Assif Raza to answer his telephone. Beads of sweat bathed his forehead. "Come on, Assif, answer the phone."

At last Raza picked up.

"Assif, it's Louis. We need to talk."

"Please do it quickly. I have much to do. Most of our holdings in this country have been frozen."

"I'm aware of the freeze. Our office was informed three hour ago. Where do we go from here?"

"I apologize for my oversight in our last conversation, Louis. None of our people had the slightest idea the Iraqis would invade. Believe me, it took all of us by surprise."

"I appreciate that, Assif, but that isn't what I asked you. You have to appreciate that I have a fortune riding on crude oil. I've got to know what's happening. I can't rely on the crap they're feeding us on television."

"One of our investors is extremely close to the Emir. They spoke briefly today. The Emir advised him that once Kuwait accedes to Saddam's outrageous demands, Iraq will withdraw from the country."

"Do you think they will?"

"The Kuwaitis will compromise on money, never on territorial integrity."

"So what do you think? Will Saddam take the money and run?"

"We believe he will, but now that he has had a taste of the land, it's become more a roll of the dice."

"What should I do with my crude position?"

"You could liquidate now and cut your losses. If, however, you have nerves of steel and the patience of Job, you could hold and perhaps make a fortune."

"What would you do if you were in my position?"

"I would never be in your position, Louis. I am an investor, not a speculator."

"So you're really telling me to get out."

"Under the current circumstances, yes."

"That's just lovely," Visconti said, his anxiety exploding into anger. "Last week you told me to short the hell out of crude. Now you're telling me to bail out."

"Unless I misunderstand, Louis, you are being paid to be my financial advisor," Raza countered, clearly irked by Visconti's tirade. "I strongly doubt you could afford the reverse."

"I'm sorry. Assif. This thing is doing funny things to my head."

"You are forgiven. It's affecting all of us in very peculiar ways."

After hanging up, Visconti called Miles Dennis. "Miles, it's Louis. What's happening?"

"I'm damn glad you called. I've been trying to reach you for an hour."

"Why?"

"I want you to listen very carefully. I don't have good news. Are you sitting down?"

"Just give it to me, dammit!"

"Spot crude is going crazy right now. God knows where it'll be at the end of the day. The Merc. is raising margin requirements to fifty percent. That means you'll have to come up with another seventy-five million at the close of business."

"Can you get me out?" Visconti asked, continuing his nail biting in earnest.

"I doubt it. Crude's limit up. I don't think there's a human being on the planet who's willing to sell crude at twenty-five bucks."

"So I've got no choice. Either I come up with seventy-five million, or... What if I don't."

"Don't even think about it. We'll close out your position and you'll blow your brains out."

"That's just beautiful. Now I have to start carving into other investments just to satisfy a margin call."

265

"I thought you had at least two hundred and fifty million in cash in that trust. What happened to it?"

Dennis's comment brutally reminded Visconti of the fraudulent entries he had made in reporting the financial status of the King's trust. "I committed it all to the market," he lied.

"Then tell me what you want me to do with your position."

"What the hell can you do? Didn't you just tell me crude was limit up?"

"I did, but I need your instructions. I don't want to have to wait around for your call if crude comes off the boil."

"What do you think I should do?"

"You're into the spot month on the August contracts... I would put a stop at twenty-six on the August, and ride the September contracts."

"So you're telling me I would be out of the August contracts at twenty-six?"

"Yup, but I think you'll be okay with the September contracts."

Visconti failed to respond for what seemed like an eternity for Dennis.

"I need an answer, Louis," Dennis prodded.

"Screw it, Miles," Visconti said, his teeth clenched. "I stepped up to the table to play the game. I'm not going to chicken out the minute the first deuce is dealt. Don't liquidate a fucking thing!"

Dennis shook his head in disbelief. "Wow! You're either a genius or a masochist.   I'm   not   sure   which."

CHAPTER 76

Despite frenzied trading in the wake of the invasion of Kuwait, West Texas Intermediate ended the day off the boil. Near record stockpiles of petroleum worldwide had tempered the fears of investors and speculators. Visconti's margin call, while still large, was reduced to a mere forty-three million. His determination to play the game had been reinforced. The game had blossomed into a personal crusade.

August 3, 1990.

Iraq said it would withdraw its troops, "As soon as things settle, and when Kuwait's free provisional government asks us to do so. We hope this will be in a few days, or a week at the latest."

Miles Dennis frowned as he watched the latest bad news on the moving electronic tape. "U.S. intelligence have monitored a buildup of one hundred thousand Iraqi troops south of Kuwait City, near the Saudi border."

Fears of an invasion of Saudi Arabia drove the price of crude oil much higher.

August 4, 1990.

More bad news glided across Iacardi's electronic tape. "Iraqi forces have entered the Neutral Zone on the Kuwaiti-Saudi border, a disputed territory from which both countries draw oil."

In spite of Baghdad's denial of the report, fear and tension drove the price of oil still higher.

August 6, 1990.

Turkish president, Turgut Ozal said his country would obey United Nations sanctions and stop unloading Iraq's oil at its pipeline terminus. Until then, Iraq had exported eighty to ninety percent of its oil through two long overland pipelines: one through Turkey to the Mediterranean port of Yamurtauk, the other across the Saudi Arabian desert to the Red Sea port of Yanbu.

The removal of much of Iraqi oil from world markets put further upward pressure on oil prices.

August 8, 1990.

In a stunning announcement, Iraq declared that it had annexed Kuwait as its nineteenth province, calling it Kadhimat and making it clear to the world it had no intention of leaving. With the annexation Saddam declared, "Thank God we are all now one people, one state that will be the pride of all Arabs."

Saddam's intention was to create a regional superpower with enormous economic strength. Together, Iraq and Kuwait had proven reserves of one hundred and ninety-five billion barrels of oil, twenty percent of the world's reserves and second only to Saudi Arabia's two hundred and fifty-five billion barrels.

The spot price shot above twenty-eight dollars per barrel and financial markets were hurled into turmoil.

Kerri watched nervously as the price of oil shot skyward. Her tolerance collapsed when she watched it knife through twenty-eight. Sickened by the sights provided by the moving electronic tape, she jumped to her feet and stormed into Dennis's office. "It's above twenty-eight!" she announced. "We've got to get Louis out!"

"I've given up," Dennis said with a cold stare and a shrug of his shoulders. "I've called every day this week and tried to convince him to get out. I can't believe it. He's absolutely obsessed with this thing."

"Then I'm going to talk to him," Kerri declared. "Somebody's got to stop him."

"That's a noble gesture, but not a good idea."

"Why? I'm sure if I..."

"Every business decision should be made objectively. If Louis's decision is based on your advice, and it turns out to be improvident, he might never forgive you. In other words, the strength of your relationship could work against you. I think it's more important than money, don't you?"

Kerri nodded, reluctantly accepting Dennis's advice.

"I'll call him again," Dennis said, then lifted his receiver and dialed Visconti's number. He used his left hand to beckon Kerri to stay while he waited for his call to be transferred to Visconti.

"I bet you're calling to convince me to liquidate," Visconti said.

"You're farting against a hurricane, Louis. I'm sure you know it's above twenty-eight and climbing."

"Give it another day or two, Miles," Visconti replied, so calmly that Dennis was unable to detect the churning in the pit of his stomach.

Dennis slammed the receiver into its cradle, then lifted his hands above his shoulders and stared at the ceiling. "He's insane, absolutely certifiable!"

"Maybe, but I still love him," Kerri said, then hurried from Dennis's office.

August 9, 1990.

George Bush issued a statement confirming that the U.S. would draw against the six hundred million barrels of oil in its Strategic Petroleum Reserve as a means of easing upward pressure on oil prices. Simultaneously, the International Energy Agency, comprised of twenty-one

269

industrialized nations, urged heightened preparations to meet the need for alternative oil supplies. The two moves, combined with reports that some O.P.E.C. nations planned to boost production, pushed the spot price down to slightly below twenty-six dollars.

Late in the afternoon, Visconti called Dennis and ordered the liquidation of his August contracts. "I'm keeping the September contracts to the death, Miles!" he vowed, well aware that the loss sustained by the King's trust was horrendous.

CHAPTER 77

The deepening crisis in Kuwait raised agonizing doubts in Visconti's mind. The loss of almost eighty-four million from the King's trust had dealt his pride the most severe blow it had received since the crash of 1987. His nightmare had barely begun.

August 22, 1990.

Iraq possessed the fourth largest army in the world. With one million men and fifty-five hundred tanks, the country represented a serious threat to world stability. The massive buildup of troops and armaments on the Saudi Arabian border suggested strongly that Iraq might continue its aggression. It could conceivably capture forty percent of the worlds oil production, or at least knock out a significant portion of Saudi production. The result in either event would force the price of oil much higher and plunge the world into a deep recession. The spot price of oil shot to a seven year high above thirty-one dollars. Gasoline prices headed for the stratosphere.

Now on his own, Phillip was a man of the world. His lifestyle had changed. So had his expenses. Like Saddam Hussein, his need for money had grown to an acute stage. He was tired of waiting until his twenty-first birthday to claim what he considered his birthright.

He marched into Mike's office at eleven A.M. "Morning, chief," he sang, flashing a diabolical smile. He slammed the door behind him, flopped his body onto the couch beside Mike's desk, then placed his hands behind his head and rested his boots on the arm of the couch. "You and I need to talk," he said.

"So talk," Mike said, straining to retain his composure.

"I don't think I should have to wait until my twenty-first birthday to get the money my father left me... I want it now."

"Why?" Mike asked, deeply disturbed.

"Like I said, my father told me I could have it if anything ever happened to him. That means I should have had it ten years ago. I want my money now, and you have no right to play God with it."

Mike glared at Phillip and shook his head. He had to call the bluff. "That isn't going to happen."

The corners of Phillip's mouth turned upward, forming a cocky smirk. "If it doesn't, I'm going straight to the Feds and tell them everything I know."

Mike's stomach churned. "Tell me exactly what you're going to tell them."

"That you kept my father's money and that you know exactly where it is. You know they'll be delighted to hear it."

"Suppose they ask you how much money there is. What will you tell them?"

"Three hundred million," Phillip replied without hesitation. "That's how much my father said I was going to get. That's how much I want, and I'm betting it's worth something to you to keep me quiet."

"How much do you think it's worth to me?"

"About three hundred million," Phillip replied, smirking, aware his answer would enrage Mike.

Mike gripped the arms of his chair to restrain himself from lifting Phillip from the couch and throwing him out of his office. Again he called his bluff. "Obviously I don't want you to go to the Feds, but regardless of what you decide to do, I'm still not going to give you one dime of that money."

272

Phillip's facial expression transformed into one reminding Mike of Jim Servito. Both lips tightened, showing his teeth. "Fuck you!" he shouted, then jumped to his feet and stormed out of the office.

Mike quickly phoned Karen. "We've got big problems. Phillip just marched into my office and told me he wants the money now. He said he's going to the Feds if he doesn't get it... I called his bluff."

"I'm glad you did. I would have done the same thing myself."

Tears gratitude streamed from Mike's eyes. "Do you have any idea how much I love you?"

"Maybe you could show me when you get home tonight."

"That's a promise." Mike hung up, then called Dan Turner. "Maybe all you can do is give me a shoulder to cry on, Dan, but I needed to tell you that Phillip has become a major problem. He just threatened to tell the Feds everything if we don't give him the money now."

"That's kind of a nasty development. What did you say to him?"

"I called his bluff."

"Is it a bluff?"

"I don't know. It's a tough call."

"Then don't make a move until you know. Leave the money where it is for now. If Phillip talks, it won't take the Feds long to contact you. If they do, don't tell them anything. Refer them to me."

"Okay. If it gets that far, what are you going to say to them?"

"Nothing, until they tell me how much they know. When they do, maybe we can do a little horse trading... How much does Phillip know?"

"Too much... What if the Feds are in no mood to trade? Do we run?"

Turner chuckled. "That sounds familiar. I think you're getting ahead of yourself. I know it won't be easy, but try not to think about that for now. Just do nothing and let me know the minute anything significant happens."

Mike hung up, feeling only slightly relieved. He lowered his face into his hands and began to think of the implications of running again. The decision was difficult a decade earlier. This time it would be excruciatingly painful.

CHAPTER 78

Toronto. Friday, August 24, 1990.

Dressed in his bulky faded and torn jeans, wrinkled white sweatshirt and Blue Jays baseball hat, Phillip entered Revenue Canada's regional office on Front Street in the heart of the business district of Toronto. He approached one of five receptionists seated behind the information counter.

"May I help you sir?" she asked, frowning as she examined his sloppy appearance.

"I want to speak to the manager," he demanded.

The receptionist glared at him, turned off by his slovenly appearance. "May I ask what it's about? Is this a tax matter?"

"Yup."

"Your name, please?"

"Phillip Servito."

The receptionist pointed to the waiting area, crowded to the point of standing room only. "Wait over there, please? Someone will be with you as soon as possible."

A tall thin man in his early thirties entered the waiting area twenty minutes later. He had well greased blond hair and wore a dark blue suit, matching tie and glossy black loafers. "Phillip Servito," he bellowed.

Phillip raised his right hand and approached the man.

"Come with me, please." He led Phillip into a small austere conference room, not far from the waiting area. "Please have a seat," he said, pointing to a small round table surrounded by eight wooden chairs.

"Are you the manager?" Phillip asked as he lowered himself onto one of the chairs.

"I'm her assistant. She's in a meeting at this moment." He extended his hand. "My name is David Savage. I understand you want to discuss a tax matter. Is that correct?"

Phillip nodded.

Savage took a seat on the opposite side of the table and dropped a note pad on the table. He glared at Phillip, his pen at the ready. "What specifically did you want to talk about?"

"My father left me a lot of money when he died ten years ago. I never received it."

"And what was your father's name?"

"James Servito."

The name, capable of setting off alarm bells in higher Revenue Canada circles, meant nothing to Savage. "Can you tell me what this has to do with Revenue Canada?"

"My father stole the money from Canada and the United States by evading gasoline taxes."

Savage stopped writing and stared at Phillip in amazement. "Can you tell me how much it was? I mean how much money did your father leave you?"

"Three hundred million."

"How much?" Savage asked, astonished, his attention substantially more focused.

"You heard me. Three hundred million dollars."

A grin broke the veneer of Savage's austere professionalism. He had a very large fish on his line. "Do you know where this money is?"

"I might. Is there a reward? If there is, how much is it?"

Savage frowned. "There's no reward. If you have knowledge of the location of that money, you're legally obliged to disclose it. Furthermore, it's a serious offense to withhold that kind of information from Revenue Canada."

Disappointed with Savage's response and attitude, and confused about the legal implications of his knowledge, Phillip decided to back out. "Listen, I'm really not sure. Like I said, I might know where it is. If I find it, you'll be the first to know. If I don't, then it's still lost."

"You said you might know where the money is. What, exactly did you mean by that?" Savage asked, focusing on Phillip's eyes, certain he knew more.

"That's exactly what I said. I might know where it is. Now I gotta try to find it."

"Is anyone else aware of the existence or location of the money?"

"Yah. My step father also might know."

"Please give me his name and address."

Phillip gave Savage Mike's name, address and telephone number.

"Do you have anything else to say at this time?"

"No."

"If you don't mind, I would like to have someone else talk to you about this. Could you wait here for a minute?"

"No. I gotta get back to work."

"Then please give me your address and telephone number."

Phillip gave him the address and telephone number of Gary Matheson's apartment, then left without uttering another word.

New York.

Visconti's secretary entered his office at two P.M. "Louis, there's a call for you on two," she said, then placed a pile of freshly typed letters on his desk.

"Who is it?"

"Phillip Servito. Would you like me to take a message?"

"No. I'll take it," Visconti said, then lifted the receiver and pressed two. "Visconti."

"Mr. Visconti, my name is Phillip Servito. I'm calling because I want to talk to you about my trust."

"Excuse me. I don't have the slightest idea what you're talking about."

"You know exactly what I'm talking about, so please don't lie to me. I called Alfred Schnieder at the Banco International Venezolano. They told me he wasn't there any more, but a guy named Blanco gave me your number... Can I meet you somewhere? I don't want to talk on the phone."

"First give me some idea what this is about."

"The money. What else?"

"Does Mike know you're talking to me?"

"Nope, and that doesn't matter any more."

"Why?"

"Because the money's mine, and I want it, now."

It was now painfully clear to Visconti that the equation had changed. He had to adjust. "That may be so, but there isn't a thing I can do about it. The money's in a trust, and I work for its trustees. If you have a problem with that, I suggest you talk to them."

"I already have. They told me they're going to give the money to charity. So I told them if they do, I'm going to tell the Feds that they've been hiding it for years."

"I still don't see what that has to do with me," Visconti said, his heart now in his throat.

"I was hoping you could change their minds. Can we talk somewhere?"

Phillip was now a major player and in a position to destroy his plan to steal the money in the trust. Clearly, he was the reason Mike King had delayed the distribution of the trust's funds. "Sure. Where and when?"

"Your office. Friday night."

"Friday night's good, but don't come here. Come to my apartment." Visconti gave Phillip the address and telephone number. "How soon can you get there?"

"I'll call you and let you know."

Phillip called Visconti thirty minutes later. "I have an Eastern Airlines flight from Toronto to Newark. It leaves Toronto at eight-thirty on Friday night. I should be at your apartment by ten-thirty or eleven."

"Good. See you then."

"Wait a minute. This trip's going to cost me. Can you help me pay for it?"

"Just give me your bills when you get here. We'll take it out of the trust's expenses."

Toronto.

Mike received a call from William Dare, now deputy director of Canada's Security Intelligence Service. He immediately remembered Dare, the man who led a team of S.I.S. agents on a search and seizure mission of his office over ten years earlier. "What do you want?" Mike asked, his tone making it clear to Dare that his call was unwelcome.

"Your stepson visited the Toronto regional office of Revenue Canada yesterday. He indicated to one of our people that he might know the location of a lot of money his late father left to him... Would you care to comment on that?"

"No," Mike replied, his heart now racing, his brain processing the implications.

"Does that mean you don't know anything about it or that you don't have anything to add?"

"I don't mean to be rude, Dare, but ten years ago my lawyer advised me to refer any and all inquiries connected with that matter to him. I continue to respect that advice. In case you've forgotten, his name is Dan Turner and his telephone number is the same as it was ten years ago. Do you still have that on file?"

"Yes. Thank you for your time."

Mike hung up, then hurried to call Dan Turner using his car phone. "Dan, I just received a call from William Dare. Remember him?"

"I certainly do. What did he say?"

"He said Phillip went into the Revenue Canada office in Toronto yesterday. He told them he might know the location of a lot of money his father left him."

"Are you in your office?"

"No. I'm in my car."

"Good. Call me from there from now on. If I need to reach you, I'll leave a message... Now, what did you say to Dare?"

"Nothing. I referred him to you."

"Good. I'll take it from here. I'll keep you advised."

Mike hung up, stepped from his car and walked across the parking lot toward his office. A company van raced onto the lot and screeched to a stop beside him. Phillip rolled down his window and leaned out. "Hi boss," he said, flashing an impish smirk. "You having a nice day?"

"What are you doing here? Why aren't you on the road?"

"I won't stay long. I just wanted to find out if you've heard from the Feds yet."

Mike nodded.

Phillip's grin disappeared. "I wanted it to be a warning, to prove I'm serious. Next time I see them I'll give them the rest of the story."

"How much did you tell them?"

"Enough to make them interested."

Mike frowned and gritted his teeth. "You may have started something that can't be stopped."

"Sure it can. All you have to do is give me the money."

"I told you that's not going to happen. The only way you're going to get it is over my dead body. Now get your lazy ass out of my sight!" Mike turned and continued toward his office.

"Have a nice day, boss," Phillip shouted, raising his right hand and pointing its middle finger skyward.

CHAPTER 79

Newark International Airport. 9:35 P.M.

Thirty minutes before Phillip's Air Canada DC-9 touched down, a heavy downpour had drenched the area, bringing welcome relief from the sweltering heat of late August. A spectacular sunset caused the night sky to explode into a pyrotechnical delight.

Phillip's yellow taxi splashed to a stop in front of Visconti's apartment building forty minutes later. The western sky, although almost dark, still glowed with a reddish purple hue. Phillip paid the driver and jumped out. When he reached the front door of the building, he tried to open one of the twin plate glass doors by pulling its gold plated handle. Realizing the door was locked, he pressed polished brass doorbell button on the concrete wall beside the doors.

Seconds later, he heard a man's voice in the stainless steel grating above the button. "Are you visiting, sir?"

"Yes, I'm here to see Louis Visconti. He's expecting me," Phillip replied.

"Your name please?"

"Phillip Servito."

"One moment, sir."

Thirty seconds later, Phillip heard an electronic buzz inside the lock between the doors. "You may open the door now, Mister Servito," the security guard said. "Mister Visconti is on the sixth floor. He'll be waiting for you when you get off the elevator."

"When the doors to the ancient elevator opened on the sixth floor, Phillip stepped out to meet Visconti. "Phillip, good to see you," Visconti said, forcing a smile and attempting to ignore his visitor's scruffy and unshaven appearance. "Welcome to New York and to my home. It's just

282

down the hallway. Follow me." Visconti led his guest to the apartment and to the door of his den. "Take the most comfortable seat you can find in there. I'm going to the kitchen to get myself some tea. Can I get you something?"

"You got any beer?"

"Sure. I'll be right back," Visconti said, then hurried to the kitchen. He found Kerri dressed in her pale pink robe and preparing a small pot of tea. "You look outrageously beautiful," he said, wrapping her in his arms and planting an apologetic kiss on her forehead. "I'm sorry I had to screw up our Friday night."

Kerri smiled and kissed Visconti's cheek. "I really don't mind. I'm going upstairs to have a long hot bath and a good sleep. I need both."

"Stop by the den on your way. I'll introduce you to Phillip. You've got to see this kid. You won't believe him. He looks like a leftover from Woodstock."

"I'll be there in a minute."

Visconti poured himself some tea, removed a can of Heineken from the fridge, then hurried back to the den. He handed the can to Phillip, then took a seat on the couch beside him. "I'm curious to know why you're using your given name. I understand Mike adopted you some time ago."

Phillip snapped the lid of the beer can and chugged several mouthfuls. "I hate Mike King and everything he stands for," he declared, then wiped his mouth with his hand.

Distracted, Visconti shifted his eyes toward the door. "Kerri, come in and meet Phillip," he said, smiling and jumping to his feet.

Phillip turned to face Kerri. His mouth opened involuntarily as he slowly lifted himself from the couch, captivated by her beauty and staring at her as if mesmerized.

Kerri raised her right hand. "Hi," she said, not the slightest bit interested in Visconti's slovenly guest.

"Good to meet you," Phillip said.

"Did you have a pleasant trip?"

"Yah. Pretty fast though."

"Will you be staying here tonight?"

"That's a good idea," Visconti said. "Why don't you stay with us, Phillip? We've got all kinds of room in this place."

"Sure. Thanks."

"Great. Then I'll see you tomorrow morning," Kerri said, then blew Visconti a kiss and left.

"Let's talk about money," Visconti said, anxious to know Phillip's intentions and exactly where he was positioned in an increasingly complex equation. "You mentioned that Mike and your mother are planning to give it to charity."

Phillip sat on the couch and took another large gulp of beer. "Yah. It's all King's idea. I had to do something to stop him. That money's mine. My real father left it to me and I should be the one who decides what to do with it."

"So what do you think Mike's going to do now?"

"I don't know, but I've scared the shit out of him."

Phillip's statement worried Visconti. "Are you bluffing or would you really go to the Feds?"

"No bluff. I've already talked to them."

"Why the hell did you do that?"

"I didn't tell them much. I just told them King and I might know where the money is. I didn't say I knew for sure. I just wanted to scare the hell out of King."

"Did you tell them anything else?"

"Yah. I told them how much money was in the trust."

Visconti winced. "How much did you say there was?"

"Three hundred million, but that's all I said. The Feds can't do a damn thing to him. They don't have enough information."

"Would you like another beer?" Visconti asked, now certain that Phillip had become a major and disruptive factor.

"Sure."

Visconti picked up Phillip's empty can and hurried to the kitchen. He closed the door, rushed to the telephone and dialed Nick Bennedetti's office number. After three rings, he heard a click, then Bennedetti's answering machine tape. "Bennedetti For Hire... Sorry I'm out... Leave a damn short message at the tone, and I'll get back to you, real soon."

Visconti waited for the tone. "Nick, it's Louis. It's Friday night. I need you to do a job, a big one. Call me back. I'll be at the apartment for the weekend." He hung up, raced to the refrigerator, removed a can of beer, then hurried back to the den. "Phillip, what would you say if I told you to go ahead and let Mike give the money to charity?"

"I'd tell you to go fuck yourself."

"What if I told you it would result in you getting your money?"

"How?"

"Mike recently contacted Alfred Schnieder at his home in Switzerland and asked him to be an intermediary in giving your money to charity. Alfred didn't think he was qualified, so he found a banker in Geneva who is. Obviously, Mike has to contact me before he can make this transfer, so Alfred and I have made arrangements with that banker in Geneva to make it appear that the money has gone to Mike's charity. In reality, that charity will never get it."

"Who will?"

"Us."

"How the hell can you do that?" Phillip asked.

"The banker in Geneva will call Mike and confirm that all of the money was transferred to the charity. Then he'll transfer it to us. That's all it takes... You interested?"

"What happens if Mike gets suspicious and checks it out?"

"Come on, think about it," Visconti cajoled. "Do you think he's going to risk being discovered by going to the charity and asking them if they received the money?"

Phillip's skeptical frown graduated to a broad smile. "So you guys are planning to steal stolen money."

"That's too harsh. We're just going to divert it." Visconti's larcenous grin gave way to a cold gray stare. "Of course we'll need to get paid for the service."

"How much?"

"Thirty percent. That'll leave you with seventy percent. You'll get two hundred and ten million."

Phillip's expression saddened. "Sounds great, but I'm not sure I can convince King that I've changed my mind. I don't think he's going to believe me."

"Don't talk like that. He's got to believe you. If he doesn't, our plan washes and we end up with a big zero."

"But how can I do it? I'm going to look like an idiot if I suddenly tell him I don't want the money. I don't think it'll matter what I say to him, he's not going to believe it."

"Tell him you went away for the weekend to think about it. Tell him you're sick with remorse. Tell him the Feds have been bugging you ever since you went to see them. Show some tears and say the whole thing's driving you crazy. Tell him that even though you still want the money, you've decided you can't do anything to hurt your mother. That should do it."

Phillip's frown melted. Visconti was right. His mother would be the convincing factor.

"Do we have a deal?" Visconti asked, extending his hand.

"We have a deal."

"Great! Then we can work out the details tomorrow. We'll get you a flight to Toronto and you can relax here until then. I'll get a cab to drive you to the airport."

"Where am I going to sleep?"

"I'll show you. Follow me." Visconti led him up the winding stairway to the bedroom across the hall from Kerri's, then turned to face him. "I forgot to ask. Do you have a bag?"

"Nope," Phillip said, patting the pocket of his jacket. My toothbrush and paste are right in here. That's all I brought."

"Okay. When you wake up, go to the kitchen. Just keep walking past the den. You'll run right into it. You'll find all kinds of food in the refrigerator... See   you   tomorrow."

CHAPTER 80

Saturday, August 25.

Kerri awoke at nine, showered, put on her pink gown and hurried to the kitchen. She found Phillip sitting at the bar and sipping a glass of orange juice. Same clothes. Blue Jay's cap on backward. His stubble ten hours longer. "Good morning," she said with a warm smile.

Phillip waved his right hand. "Hi," he replied with a lecherous smirk while he examined every inch of Kerri.

"Have you seen Louis?"

"Yah. He told me to tell you he went jogging. He left about fifteen minutes ago. He said he would be back in an hour."

Kerri poured herself a glass of orange juice, then sat on the stool beside Phillip. "Why do you hate Mike King?" she asked, looking straight ahead.

"How do you know I do?" Phillip asked, surprised by Kerri's question.

"I was standing in the doorway to the den last night. I heard you say it just before Louis introduced us."

"Do you know him?"

Kerri shrugged her shoulders, continuing to look straight ahead. "I know a man by that name but he's probably not the same Mike King... How old is he?"

"About fifty."

"What does he do for a living?"

"He owns Reserve Oil. It's a big gasoline company in Canada. Ever heard of it?"

Kerri shook her head. "Tell me what he looks like."

"He's a pretty big guy, about six foot two. He's got blond hair, but it's turning gray now."

"Would you say he's good looking?"

"Yah, probably."

"What color are his eyes?"

"Blue."

The coincidence was utterly preposterous. Even though Phillip had given Kerri all the right answers, she still found it difficult to believe they were talking about the same man, her father. She turned to face him. "Would you mind going upstairs with me? I want to show you something."

"Sure. No problem. Can I take my juice?"

Kerri nodded, then jumped from the stool and led Phillip to the master bedroom. She opened the bottom drawer of her dresser and removed her photograph of her father and mother from beneath her clothing. "Is that him?" she asked, handing the photograph to Phillip.

"Holy shit!" Phillip declared, staring at the photograph in astonishment. "That's him! Where the hell did you get this?"

Kerri was speechless, overcome with joy. She showed a half smile, but her inner jubilation had rendered her incapable of hearing the question. Under the most incredible of circumstances, she had actually found her father.

"Hey, Kerri! You still with me?" Phillip asked, waving the photograph close to her face.

Kerri's eyes focused on Phillip. "What did you say?"

"It's him. The guy in this photograph is my stepfather. He's married to my real mother. How the hell did you get this?"

"You sure?" she asked, still unable to accept the wonderful reality of her discovery.

Phillip glanced at the photograph again, then turned to Kerri. "I'd recognize that asshole from a thousand yards," he declared, scowling as he handed it to her. "Where did you get this?"

"The woman in that photograph is my mother. She dated Mike King a long time ago," Kerri said, unwilling to let Phillip know the truth, at least until she found out why he hated Mike King, and the circumstances under which he became her father's stepson.

Phillip curled his lower lip outward and shook his head. "I really don't give a shit. The only thing I care about is getting my money."

"What money?"

"My real father left me a lot of money when he died." He pointed to the photograph. "And that prick won't let me have it."

"How much did your father leave you?"

"Three hundred million," Phillip answered, exuding pride.

"I don't understand. If he left the money to you, why can't you have it?"

"Oh I'll get it, now that Mr. Visconti's going to help me."

Kerri's curiosity exploded. "What's Louis going to do for you?"

Phillip put his hands in his pockets and looked away. "Hey, I better not say. I don't know you. Maybe you're not supposed to know."

"I'm Louis's girlfriend," Kerri protested, attempting to allay Phillip's concerns. "We don't have any secrets."

"If you're his girlfriend, I'm sure he'll tell you everything he wants you to know." Phillip turned to look at the door. "I'm going back to the kitchen. I'm starved."

Disappointed, Kerri followed him back to the kitchen.

The door to the kitchen burst open and Visconti pranced in, smiling and continuing to run on the spot. "Good morning," he sang. "Both of you should have been out there with me. It's an unbelievably beautiful day." He continued jogging to the refrigerator, poured himself a glass of orange juice, then turned to face Kerri and Phillip. "I'm going upstairs for a quick shower. Then I'll join you guys for breakfast." He chugged his juice, then jogged from the kitchen.

Kerri followed Visconti to the bedroom and found him facing the bathroom mirror. "I missed you this morning," she said, sliding her arms around his waist and hugging him from behind.

"I missed you too," Visconti said. "I want us to go back to bed as soon as I get rid of that kid in the kitchen. Do we have a date?"

"What's he doing here?"

"His parents own a large trust. You and Miles would recognize it as the one with the big short position in crude oil."

Kerri remembered the financial report Visconti had given to Miles to prove the trust's financial capability. It seemed odd to her that the report confirmed the trust had a value of over six hundred million dollars, and Phillip assumed it was worth only three hundred million dollars. "Wow! I can't even comprehend someone having that much money. How did they do it?"

"The woman is Phillip's natural mother. Her first husband died a number of years ago, but acquired the money in the oil business before he did. Her second husband adopted Phillip."

"So Mike King is the woman's second husband?"

Visconti nodded. "How did you know his name?"

"I made an assumption. Just before you introduced me to Phillip last night, I heard him say he hates Mike King. Why does he hate him?"

Visconti smiled. "They're having a big fight over who gets the money, standard procedure for rich families these days."

"Is Phillip here to try to get you to see things his way?"

"Yup."

"Can you do anything for him?"

"Not much. The trustees call all the shots. I'm just a hired gun."

291

There was so much more that Kerri wanted to ask. Now that Louis had injected an inconsistency into the equation, she had become wary, even suspicious. She wondered why Phillip seemed so confident of getting his money with Louis's help, and why Louis had denied it to her. She smiled to hide her suspicion, then kissed his cheek. "I'm going to make breakfast. I'll see you when you get there."

Visconti showered and dressed, then headed for the kitchen. On his way, he was diverted to the den by the loud ring of the telephone. Simultaneously, Kerri lifted the receiver on the kitchen telephone.

"Louis, baby," Nick Benedetti said. "Sorry I didn't get back to you last night. I was up to my ass in alligators. Your message said you had a big job for me."

"I want you to set up a hit, Nick."

"Who's the target?"

"A twenty year old kid. His name's Phillip Servito. He lives in Toronto. I want him to disappear, without a trace."

"How soon?"

"I want him to do a job for me in Toronto before you move on him. I'll let you know when. I want it clean, Nick. Not a trace."

"You know I do clean work, but it's gonna be expensive."

"How expensive?"

"A hundred smackers. Fifty up front, and fifty on delivery of the photograph."

"Not a problem. I'll have fifty delivered and call you when it's time." Visconti chuckled as he hung up, then headed for the kitchen. Phillip's elimination would solve an enormous problem for both himself and Mike King. It amused him that the funeral would be paid out of funds in the trust.

Sickened and horrified, Kerri carefully replaced the receiver. Fear and uncertainty besieged her in undulating waves as she turned to face Phillip.

292

He had been condemned to death by the man she had chosen to love. Suddenly, the unmitigated joy of discovering her father had been shattered by doubt. Questions swirled in her head. Feeling betrayed and cheated, she fought with possible answers. Whatever they were, the ugly truth was that Louis was a dangerous man, substantially more dangerous than Miles had warned.

Struggling to maintain her composure at breakfast, Kerri stared at Phillip, the adopted son of her father, aching to tell him to run away from Louis as fast as he could. She felt a loathing nausea in the pit of her stomach when she looked at Visconti, laughing and joking with Phillip, smugly pretending to be the friend of his naive unsuspecting house guest, within hours of sentencing him to death.

CHAPTER 81

Monday, August 27.

Kerri entered then closed the door to Dennis's office. She stared at her boss, tears streaming from her reddened eyes.

"What's wrong?" Dennis asked.

"Everything," Kerri whimpered, now sobbing into her hands.

Dennis rushed to hold her. "Sit and talk," he ordered, then led her to his own chair. He sat on the desk and faced her. "Talk to me," he demanded.

After more than an hour of emotionally charged, intense discussion, Kerri had managed to tell Dennis the entire story of her incredible weekend.

Dennis frowned and exhaled. "Damn! I'm absolutely delighted that you've found your father, but the news about Louis is awful."

Kerri rubbed her eyes. "What do you think?"

Dennis exhaled again. "Obviously, there's a hell of a lot more to this story."

"Yup, and I'm going to find out what it is."

"Not a good idea. Don't get involved, Kerri. You could find yourself in a world of trouble."

"I'm already involved. It's impossible for me to become uninvolved. The man I'm living with is planning to kill Phillip, and I'm in a position to stop him."

"I think you should talk to your father. May be he can give you some guidance." Dennis grinned. "You might even have a few other things to talk about."

Kerri shook her head. "I don't think I can do it."

"You mean you don't think you can talk to your father, or you don't think you can tell him who you are?"

"I'm definitely going to talk to him, but I'm just not ready to tell him I'm his daughter."

"That's ridiculous! If it were me, I'd run to him, shout the truth to him and hug him as hard as I could. He's your father, Kerri. Aside from anything else you need to tell him, I think your first priority is your relationship. Both of you have a lot of catching up to do."

Privately, Kerri agreed, but fear of rejection troubled her. Her father had stopped seeing her and writing to her. With passing years she had concluded that he had wanted to forget her, have nothing more to do with her, and get on with his life. Her natural mother admitted that her primary motivation for marrying Mike King had been to replace the daughter she had given up for adoption. That, and psychological problems arising from it, ultimately led to the divorce. "I'll think about it," she said.

"You handle it any way you want. I'm sure you'll make the right decision."

The act of sharing her mental burden with Dennis was enormously therapeutic to Kerri. She stood and hugged him. "Thank you, Miles. Thank you for listening. You're always there to catch me when I fall."

"No thanks necessary. You're worth it."

Kerri called Information and was given the telephone number of Reserve Oil in Toronto. Nervous yet excited, she dialed the number and waited, struggling to decide what to say to her father. She asked to speak to Mike King.

"May I ask who's calling?" the receptionist asked.

"My name is Janet Pyper. I'm with Iacardi & Sons, Commodity Brokers in New York."

"One moment, please."

Kerri's heart pounded. The next person she talked to would be her father.

"Hello," Mike barked.

"Mister King, my name is..."

"I know who you are. Is this some kind of sales solicitation?"

"I'm not calling to sell you anything. What I have to tell you is far more important than that," Kerri said, shaken by her father's tone.

"Then please hurry. I'm in the middle of a meeting."

"I'm calling to tell you your stepson's life is in great danger."

"What the hell is this? What did you say your name is?"

"Janet Pyper. I'm Louis Visconti's girlfriend. I'm sure you know him."

"Give me your telephone number. I'll call you right back."

Kerri gave Mike her number, confused as to why he needed to call back.

Minutes later, Mike called Kerri from his car phone. "Sorry for the delay. Now tell me what Louis Visconti's got to do with my stepson, and why his life is in danger."

"Phillip was at our apartment in New York this weekend, to talk to Louis about the money his natural father left him. I assume you know exactly what he was talking about."

"Yes. Please go on," Mike prodded, his tone now softened, his heart pounding.

"Phillip told me he hates you and everything you stand for. When I asked him why, he said it was because you refused to give him his money. He also told me that Louis has agreed to help him get it."

"Did he say how?"

"No. I tried to convince him to tell me, but he refused."

"Did he tell you anything else?"

Kerri ached to tell him Phillip had identified him as her father, but again fear of rejection inhibited her. "I asked Louis why Phillip hates you. He said it was related to a family dispute over who gets the money."

"He was right about that. Please tell me why Phillip's life is in danger."

"I overheard a telephone conversation between Louis and a man called Nick. Louis agreed to pay him a hundred thousand dollars to murder Phillip."

"That's incredible! Why?"

"He didn't say, but he did say he wanted it done as soon as Phillip completes a job for him in Toronto."

"Did he say what the job was?"

"No. I thought you might know."

"I don't, but I'm sure as hell going to find out... I'm curious. If you're Visconti's girlfriend, why are you telling me this?"

"Because I'm... Because I was shocked when I found out what Louis was planning to do.

Whatever my feelings are toward him, I just couldn't let him murder someone."

"How did you find me?" Mike asked.

"Phillip told me the name of your company. I want you to know that I'll be in a lot of trouble if Louis ever finds out where you got this information."

"I'll be extremely careful with it."

"Thank you. If I learn anything more, I'll call you... Would you do the same for me?"

"I will... I can't tell you how much I appreciate your call. It took a lot of courage."

"You're very welcome."

Shaken, yet still skeptical, Mike called Dan Turner and repeated the entire text of his conversation with Janet Pyper.

"Incredible," Turner said. "You're incredible. In fact I think you're addicted to trouble. I think you should find out more about this, Mike. If Visconti's girlfriend is telling the truth, Phillip's in a lot of trouble... By the way, William Dare paid me a visit this morning. He was with a lawyer by the name of Fetterman. They were both breathing fire."

"What did they want?" Mike asked, sickened by the mere mention of Dare's name.

"The money. I asked them how much they wanted, but they refused to tell me. All they said was that Phillip might know where the money is."

"Might?"

"Yes. I questioned them on that. They said he also told them you might know where the money is."

"Ah shit, Dan! Here we go again," Mike said, blood now gushing to his head and creating a throbbing headache.

"Maybe not. All they've got is a smoking gun. As long as nobody tells them anything more, that's all they'll have."

"This thing's out of control. It's ripping me apart. I can't take it any more. Let's just bite the bullet and give them the money. I'm tired of worrying about it."

"We could, but in so doing, you and Karen would risk a lot. By the time you finished paying the fines and the penalties, you would both be broke and relaxing in prison... I urge you, in the strongest possible language, to do nothing to lead the Feds to believe you have ever been aware of the existence or location of that money. I further urge you to do nothing to initiate precipitous action, particularly where Phillip is concerned."

Mike rubbed his eyes with his hand. "Can you see any end?"

"Yes, but I don't think you want to hear it."

"It would appear that I have no alternative but to respect your advice, counselor," Mike conceded, dejected beyond consolation.

CHAPTER 82

Toronto.

Margaret Dupuis, one of Mike's two secretaries, opened his office door and poked her head inside. "Phillip's out here. He's really anxious to see you," she announced.

"Send him in," Mike said, then slumped in his chair.

Phillip entered and walked slowly toward Mike's desk. His eyes were reddened and glazed, the result of hours of rehearsal and anxiety. This was his big chance. His performance would have to be a masterpiece. He had no alternative but to convince Mike he had changed his mind. "Hi," he said, showing no signs of the haughtiness with which he had approached Mike during their previous confrontation.

"What can I do for you?" Mike asked.

"May I have a seat?" Phillip asked, resisting an urge to flop on the couch as he had done in the past.

Mike nodded and pointed.

Phillip lowered himself onto the couch, but sat erect. He gave Mike an expressionless stare. "I've changed my mind about the money. I've had some time to think it and I... I can't do it," he said, sobbing and covering his face with his hands.

"You can't do what?"

"... I can't go through with it. I can't force you and mom to give me the money. No matter how much I want it, I just can't bring myself to hurt mom." He looked up at Mike and blinked. "I know I haven't made it a secret that I don't like you. I probably wouldn't have been sorry to see you go to jail, but I love my mother. I love her too much to do this to her."

Mike leaned forward. "Let me understand this. Are you telling me you're giving up the idea of blackmailing us?"

Phillip removed his hands and stared at Mike, every ounce of concentration focused on appearing sincere. "I can't. I couldn't live with myself if I knew I was responsible for sending mom to prison."

"So you won't object if I give the money to charity?"

Phillip shook his head. "No," he whimpered.

"I'm very proud of you," Mike said, showing a faint smile. "It took a lot of courage to come in here and do this. I'm sure your mother will be proud of you, also."

Phillip's frown slowly give way to a hint of a smile. "Thanks for understanding," he said, then stood and extended his hand. "I'm sorry for all the trouble I've caused you."

"Forget it. Get out of here before I fire you," Mike said with a big wink.

Happy, relieved and triumphant, Phillip wheeled and marched from the office.

Mike hurried to his car and called Dan Turner. "Sorry to bother you again, Dan, but I had to tell you about a very significant development. Phillip just came into my office and told me he doesn't want the money. He said he doesn't want to hurt his mother."

"Do you believe him?"

"I want to, but in all honesty, I don't know what to believe any more. I just wanted you to know what he told me."

"Thanks. I've noted your call."

"Should we do anything?"

"No. Instinct tells me we should do nothing to rock the boat. You've held onto that money for a long time. You can hold onto it a little longer. If there's a plan to get it, eventually it will emerge."

CHAPTER 83

August 29.

The question of the viability of O.P.E.C. hung over intense negotiations among its members, since their meeting in Vienna on August 26. They finally reached an agreement authorizing its members to increase oil production to maintain normal world supplies. The result was to increase O.P.E.C. output by four million barrels a day, almost all of the production lost to the embargo of Iraq and occupied Kuwait. The decision to lift production quotas was supported by ten of the thirteen members. The dissenters were Iraq and Libya, which boycotted the meeting. Iran attended but was a major opponent of the agreement.

To the delight of the industrialized world and Louis Visconti, oil prices dropped sharply on the news to slightly below twenty-six dollars a barrel. To his further delight, he received a call from Phillip, informing him that he had succeeded in convincing his stepfather of his change of heart.

CHAPTER 84

Kerri was on a mission. She entered the luxurious offices of Mara, Griesdorf and Visconti and headed straight for the reception desk.

As with most girls in Visconti's office, Alice Mancowitz, the receptionist, was very much aware of Kerri's relationship with Visconti. "Hi Kerri," she said with a big smile. "What brings you up here? As if I didn't know."

"To pick up the file. Miles wants it yesterday."

"What file?" Alice asked, frantically sorting through the files on her desk.

"It should be right here. Louis told me he would leave it at the reception desk before he left for the airport this morning."

Alice thumbed through the pile of envelopes and files on her desk. "Not here," she said, red faced and shaking her head. "Can you wait for an hour? Sue just left for lunch."

"I can't. Miles is going to have a coronary if I don't get it to him now. Louis promised he would give it to him two days ago... Maybe he left it on Sue's desk."

"I would get it for you, but I'm not supposed to leave this desk."

"Then I'll get it," Kerri offered.

Alice displayed a squeamish smile. "You really shouldn't, Kerri. I'm not supposed to..."

"Come on, Alice," Kerri prodded. "Just close your eyes. I'll be in and out of there in no time."

"Do it fast."

Kerri hurried to the filing cabinets behind Sue's desk and began a frantic search. Her heart pounded wildly as anxious minutes ticked by. She looked through drawer after drawer of files, desperately trying to find Visconti's account files.

Finally, under K, in the sixth drawer, she found the file for the King trust account. She opened it and found copies of quarterly and annual reports dating all the way back to 1980. She looked around to ensure no one was looking, then removed the files for the three years, starting in 1987. She found an empty legal sized envelope and placed her borrowed files in it. She closed the drawer and carried the envelope back to the reception desk. "I found it," she announced, waving the envelope at Alice. "I'll bring it back as soon as Miles is finished with it. Just don't tell Sue I took it."

Alice grinned. "I'm not that stupid."

Kerri returned to the Iacardi office, headed straight for the copying machines and worked feverishly to make a copy of each of the three annual reports. She ran to her desk to drop off the copies, then rushed back to Visconti's office. She returned the original reports to Sue's cabinet, then hurried to the reception area. "Thanks, Alice," she said as she headed for the glass doors. "I owe you one."

Seconds after she stepped into the elevator, Sue emerged from the adjacent one.

Kerri returned to her desk and began to study her numerous unauthorized copies of Visconti's reports. She started with the report for the year ended, December 31, 1987. It showed an enormous decrease in the value of the trust from the previous year end. The decrease verified Visconti's admitted losses from the crash of October,1987.

The reports for the following two years, however, failed to substantiate his claim that he had recovered the losses with astute investments. Of even more interest to her was the absence of any cash in the trust. She distinctly recalled the 1988 year end report which Visconti had given to Miles Dennis in February, 1989, showing a cash reserve of two hundred and fifty million dollars and a net asset value of six hundred and sixty-two million. Her unauthorized copy of the same report showed no cash reserve and a net asset value of only four hundred and twelve million. In addition to the obvious anomaly, she had difficulty understanding why Phillip had said the trust was worth only three hundred million. Finally, none of the 1989 quarterly reports contained any reference to short positions in crude oil. Something was terribly wrong.

She waited for Miles to return from lunch, then gathered her stolen copies, and rushed into his office. "Miles, you've got to see this," she said, handing him her copy of the King trust's 1988 report.

Dennis glanced at the title sheet, then at Kerri. "Where did you get this?" he asked, horrified.

"I borrowed it. Don't worry. No one knows I have it."

"Damn, Kerri! You could go to jail for this!"

"I don't care. Just look at the bottom line."

Dennis lowered his eyes to the report, then turned to the last page. "What am I supposed to see?" he asked, puzzled as he stared at the bottom line.

"Do you still have the copy of the same report Louis gave you in February of eighty-nine?"

"It's in my desk."

"Get it out and compare the two bottom lines. You'll see it immediately."

Dennis opened the lower right drawer of his desk and removed his copy of the 1988 report. He placed it on the desk beside Kerri's copy, then turned to the last page. "Wow!" he said, shaking his head in amazement. "This is weird."

"Weird!" Kerri exclaimed. "It's fraud!

"Maybe not," Miles argued. "Maybe it was just a typographical error."

304

"No way," Kerri challenged, undeterred by Dennis's comments. "The cash reserve doesn't appear in either of the subsequent reports, and there's absolutely no reference to crude shorts."

"It certainly looks odd, but there isn't a damn thing we can do about it. Besides, if Louis knew we had these copies, he'd sue our asses."

"Well I'm going to do something about it. I'm going to take those copies to my father. He'll know if it's a typographical error or not."

"Forget it, Kerri," Miles pleaded. "If your father smells a rat, he'll raise hell with Louis. Then all hell breaks loose. Louis will immediately want to know where your father got the copies."

"That won't happen," Kerri countered. "I can't imagine my father doing anything to hurt someone who's trying to help him."

"So what do you think he'll do?"

"I'm going to tell him to ask Louis for an audited report on the current status of the trust. If the audit reveals no discrepancy, no harm done. If there is a discrepancy, then my father will know Louis has been cooking the books."

"You know Louis is probably going to question your father's motive for the request. He's got to wonder why, after ten years, he suddenly wants audited reports."

"So what if he does? There's no way my father has to disclose his motive, and no way he can link it to me."

Miles looked away momentarily, then nodded slowly. "I know this thing's going to bug you until you get it resolved, and you're going to be no good to me here until you do... Go to him. Show him your copies, and don't forget to tell him you're his daughter."

"What am I going to tell Louis?"

"Don't worry about that. I'll tell him I sent you to Toronto for some good and valid reason."

Kerri hugged Dennis and kissed him on the cheek. "You're the most wonderful, understanding boss I ever had."

"Big deal! I'm the only boss you ever had... Get out of here before I change my mind."

Kerri hurried to her desk and dialed the number for Reserve Oil in Toronto. She asked to speak to Mike King and told her Janet Pyper was calling. Mike called her from his car five minutes later. "Hi. Sorry to bother you, but I needed to tell you that I've discovered something important about your trust. I think you should see it."

Mike was angered and now more worried than ever. A complete stranger had called to tell him something about the trust, a document that he had kept secret for ten years. "How could you possibly know anything about that trust? This is incredible! How the hell can I believe anything you're telling me?"

"I wouldn't blame you if you didn't. Please give me a chance to prove to you that everything I'm telling you is the truth."

"How are you going to do that?"

"I want to meet you. I'm prepared to fly to Toronto to do that."

"So what if we meet? What's that going to prove?"

"Please, just give me a chance."

"When?"

"As soon as I can get a flight. I'll call you and let you know."

"... I'll be waiting for your call."

Kerri called Mike thirty minutes later and Mike returned the call from his car phone. "Did you get a flight?" he asked.

"Yes. Why do you always have to call me back?"

"I'd rather not say. When are you coming?"

"I'll be on American Airlines, flight two twenty-seven. It's scheduled to arrive at Terminal One at Pearson at five-thirty, this afternoon."

"I'll meet you in Terminal One, just outside Arrivals. How will I recognize you?"

"I'll be wearing a red tam, a white silk blouse, a navy blue blazer, and a gray skirt. I'll be carrying a black briefcase, and I'll have a black leather travel bag over my shoulder. I'm twenty-two years of age, and I have blond hair. How will I recognize you?" Kerri asked, curious to know how her father would describe himself.

"I'm fifty years old. I'm six feet tall, and I have blond hair. I'll be wearing beige trousers, a dark green sweater and a white shirt."

"That should be easy. See you soon, Mike."

CHAPTER 85

Toronto.

Kerri stood in one of numerous long lines at Pearson International Airport, waiting impatiently to go through customs. Inching her way toward the Canadian Customs interrogation channels, she could think of nothing but what meeting her father would be like. She had rehearsed numerous ways of telling him who she was, but worried about how he would respond if she actually told him.

When she emerged into the reception area, she was approached by a man wearing a green sweater and beige trousers. She recognized her father immediately. Save and except for the slight graying of his hair, and the perceptible wrinkling under his eyes, he looked identical to the man in her treasured photograph. "Are you Janet Pyper?" he asked, his face expressionless.

"Yes," Kerri replied, smiling and extending her hand to him, fighting an almost overwhelming urge to hug him. Her heart raced as he accepted her hand and shook it.

"Did you book a return flight?" he asked.

"No. I didn't know how long I'd be here."

"Did they feed you on the plane?"

"Peanuts."

"Then you're hungry?"

She nodded.

As Kerri sat facing her father in the Airport Hilton restaurant, she experienced every bit of the thrill and excitement she had so often imagined for the time when she would at last be with him. He was much better looking in person. She was unable to take her eyes from him and was hopelessly speechless.

"Now tell me what was important enough to bring you all the way to Toronto," Mike prodded, leaning forward, his expression exuding suspicion.

Without a word she reached into her briefcase and removed all three copies of the trust's financial reports. "These," she said, placing them in front of him.

Mike glanced at the title sheets, then looked up, astounded. "Where the hell did you get these?"

"I borrowed the originals from Mara, Griesdorf and Visconti and made those copies. Don't worry. No one knows I have them."

"But why did you..."

"I'll tell you how and why, but first look at the reports for the last three years and tell me what you see. Pay particular attention to the bottom lines. Start with the eighty-seven report."

Mike thumbed through the pile, then removed the nineteen eighty-seven report. His face reddened and contorted in obvious anger when he saw the bottom line. He snapped his head upward and glared at Kerri. "There's no cash!" His expression turned quizzical. "How did you know?"

"Louis gave a copy of that report to my boss, Miles Dennis. That's when I..."

"Wait a minute. Why did he do that?"

"He took a large short position in crude oil with our company," Kerri replied, then noticed an expression of surprise and anger in her father's face. "You weren't aware of that?"

"I had no idea. How big was the position?"

"Thirty thousand contracts."

309

"That's an atrocity!" Mike declared, stunned and enraged by Kerri's revelation. He stared at the ceiling to contemplate the enormity of Visconti's transgression. "How long has he been fooling around with crude oil?" he asked, on the verge of exploding.

"On and off for about two years. Mostly on. Right now he's on."

The waiter arrived at the table. "Will you be having drinks before dinner?" he asked.

"Would you like a drink?" Mike asked.

Kerri ordered white wine.

"I'll have Cutty Sark on the rocks. Make it a double, please," Mike ordered, then turned again to Kerri. "How's he doing?"

"I was afraid you'd ask that question. As we speak, he's off over a hundred and fifty million.'

"You've got to be kidding!"

Kerri shook her head.

Mike leaned backward and again looked at the ceiling, his stomach churning as he considered which, if any, courses of action were available to him. "How would you suggest I handle this?" he asked, feeling hopelessly trapped.

"Phone Louis and ask for audited financial statements on the trust."

"I can't."

"Why not?"

"Because of the way in which Phillip's natural father acquired the money. I can't risk having it seen by others."

"How did he acquire it?"

"I'd rather not say."

Kerri showed an understanding smile. "Is it really a risk? You know Louis won't let it go that far. He knows he would be finished if he subjected the trust to an independent audit. He'll delay as much as possible, but

310

ultimately, he'll have to do something. Then I'll be in a position to watch him and tell you what he's doing."

The muscles of Mike's face tightened. He focused on Kerri's eyes, probing for a clue. "Why are you doing this? I have difficulty understanding why, if you really are Visconti's girlfriend, you would fly all the way to Toronto to give me this information. Please don't misunderstand me. It's important and I appreciate it. But why? You don't even know me."

Blood rushed to Kerri's head as she agonized over a proper response. Once again fear of rejection gnawed at her, but gradually surrendered to the overwhelming power of her natural impulses. "I did it because I do know you."

"How?"

"I'm your daughter."

Mike's face blanched. He stared numbly at Kerri, unable to move or speak.

Kerri withdrew her birth certificate from her wallet and handed it to her father.

He stared at it, then her. Kerri's heart pounded as she watched him stand and approach her. He lifted his arms and extended them to her, beckoning her to come to him. Her tears responded to his silent invitation. Excited, she stood and stepped forward into his arms. She closed her eyes as she hugged him and felt the strength of his arms tightening around her.

"Why did you wait so long to tell me?" Mike asked.

"I was so afraid," Kerri cried, tears of joy streaming down her cheeks. "When you stopped seeing me and writing to me, I thought you wanted to forget me."

"I could never forget you. I think of you every day. My heart was ripped from my body when your mother moved away," he said, holding her tighter. "You have nothing to fear any more, Kerri. You are where you belong."

They remained standing, hugging in silence, each drawing strength and comfort from the embrace.

"Excuse me," the waiter said. "Would you like to order dinner now?"

"Just put the drinks on the table," Mike demanded, continuing to hug Kerri. "We'll call you." He glanced over Kerri's shoulder and noticed everyone in the restaurant was staring at them. "It looks like you and I are famous," he said chuckling. "They're probably wondering what an old man like me is doing with you... Let's sit. We have a lot to talk about."

They talked, blissfully oblivious to time and their surroundings, through dinner and afterward in the bar. Kerri told her father about her life with Barbara in San Diego, Los Angeles, and finally Vancouver, her disastrous marriage to Brian Pyper, her wonderful job with Iacardi & Sons, her affair with Louis Visconti, and how Phillip had identified her father from her beloved photograph.

Mike told Kerri about the failure of his marriage to Barbara, about his belated marriage to Karen, the love off his life, the incredible story of Jim Servito, how he acquired his fortune, the dramatic death of Servito in Caracas, and finally, how the fortune ended up in Louis Visconti's hands. "Keeping that money was the dumbest thing I've ever done in my life," Mike admitted. "I kept it because of my stupid pride. I've wanted to wash my hands of it for a long time, but that same stupid pride kept getting in the way."

"Why?"

Mike shrugged his shoulders. "The Feds treated Karen and me like sacrificial lambs. They couldn't get to Servito, so they arrested us, without the slightest concern for what it would do to our lives and the lives of people who depended on us. We were guilty until proven innocent. There was no way I was going to give the money to them. I still won't do it."

"So what now?"

"We're going to give it to charity. To do that and not get caught, we need an intermediary. Our lawyer advised us to use someone who's out of the North American loop. So we made arrangements to have it done by a man in Europe. His name is Alfred Schnieder, Jim Servito's Caracas bank manager until he retired in nineteen eighty and moved to Zurich. He's made arrangements to do the whole transfer through a bank in Geneva. I was planning to ask Visconti to transfer it to Schnieder's numbered account in Switzerland. Then Schnieder was going move it from there. He said it would be done by anonymous deposit... I put the whole thing on hold when Phillip got in the way."

"Did Schnieder tell you the name of the bank?"

Mike nodded. "The Weisscredit Bankhaus. Why do you ask?"

"How well does Louis know Schnieder?"

"Schnieder recommended him to us ten years ago. In fact, he told Karen and me that he would trust Visconti with his life."

"How was Schnieder going to confirm to you that the money actually went where it was supposed to go?"

"He said the manager of Weisscredit Bankhaus would contact me in some discrete way. Why? Where are you going with this?"

"I'm not sure. It might be coincidental... Louis has asked me to run away with him and live happily ever after in Europe. He said he was close to doing a deal that would give him more money than he could ever spend."

Mike rolled his eyes and tightened his lips. "Wow!" he said, raising his hands. "You're very astute. All they needed was my authorization to release the funds, but first Phillip had to convince me he had changed his mind about going to the Feds."

"Then Phillip will have outlived his usefulness," Kerri concluded, grimacing. "We have to stop this. If convincing you was the 'job' Louis needed him to do, and I suspect it was, then Phillip's going to be killed. Also, I don't think you want Louis to live happily ever after in Europe with that money."

"I agree we have to protect Phillip somehow, but I can't just march into Visconti's office and take the money away."

"Why not?"

"As soon as I do, he'll suspect you."

"Don't worry about me. He can suspect me all he wants."

"I couldn't live with myself if I put your life in danger."

Kerri reached for her father's hand and showed a smile radiating unalloyed happiness. "My life is your life. You're my father. I'm so sorry to find you in such a terrible mess."

"Maybe it's not so terrible. It brought us together, and I'm thankful for that. From this moment on I want you to be part of my life, a very large part."

"I want that too."

"I would be honored if you would stay at my home tonight. I want you to meet Karen and Kevin."

"I'd like that very much."

Karen assumed Mike had returned when she heard a noise at the door of the apartment. She hurried to greet him. "Hello," she said, shocked to see her husband with his arm around a young and very beautiful woman.

"Sorry I'm late," Mike apologized. "I had an unexpected surprise tonight... I'd like you to meet my daughter." He smirked as he watched Karen's reaction.

Karen stared at Mike's companion, numbed momentarily by Mike's announcement. "Kerri?" she asked, still disbelieving.

Kerri smiled and nodded.

With a gesture of grace and genuine acceptance, Karen approached Kerri with her arms extended. "Welcome to our home," she said.

Tears flowing, Kerri moved from under Mike's arm into Karen's embrace. "Thank you, Karen. I can't tell you how much I've looked forward to this."

The two hugged in silence for several seconds, then Karen lifted her head and winked at Mike. "Don't just stand there, King. Pour some drinks. You owe me a big explanation."

Mike drove Kerri to Pearson International Airport after breakfast the following morning. They hugged and promised to call each other as often as possible. Kerri broke from the embrace and turned to walk to the terminal. She walked several steps, then turned again and ran back to her father's arms. "I'm so happy," she cried. "I thought it was too late for you and me."

Mike kissed her forehead. "It's never too late. Remember that always."

On his way from the airport to his office, Mike called Dan Turner to tell him the wonderful news of finding his daughter and of the information she had given him.

"You lead an interesting life, Mike King." Turner declared. "Every time I think there can be no more surprises, you manage to come up with another one. Tell me what you've decided to do about the money."

"Nothing. I can't think of a move that wouldn't set up more problems."

"Good. In addition to being very happy for both of you, I applaud your decision. Under the circumstances, it makes infinite sense."

"Thank you. I'm glad you agree."

"Be warned. The delicate balance of this equation will eventually be lost."

"You have a way with words, counselor," Mike said. "So will my sanity."

315

CHAPTER 86

September 2, 1990.

O.P.E.C. announced that it had resolved to lift production quotas, thereby restoring normal supplies of crude oil to world markets. The resolution succeeded in allaying the fears of investors only temporarily.

After an encouraging start, September, 1990 evolved into a terrible ratchet wheel. As the wheel turned, the world's fears and concerns intensified. It became increasingly apparent that Saddam was preparing to invade Saudi Arabia as Iraq's forces and armaments consolidated their positions along the border between Kuwait and Saudi Arabia. It was clear that whatever the outcome of the invasion, the Iraqis would, as a minimum, succeed in knocking out a very significant portion of Saudi oil production. Investors feared the loss of that production could not be replaced by increased production elsewhere in the world and oil prices would skyrocket. Compounding investors concerns were the logistical problems facing the United States and its allies. No matter how quickly they moved to defend Saudi Arabia, it would not be soon enough to stop the Iraqis.

Now desperate, Louis Visconti faced another catastrophic loss with his September crude position, now in the spot month. Like so many investors caught in a loss position, his pride would not allow him to give up. He was in denial and in far too deep. In spite of pleadings from both Kerri and Miles Dennis, he refused to liquidate. Pressure on him mounted as Mike King continued to delay release of the funds in the trust. By the end of the second week of that pressure-filled month, Visconti had begun to receive daily telephone calls from his coconspirators, Phillip and Alfred Schnieder, both anxious to know if Mike had authorized the release the funds.

Kerri found it almost impossible to live with Visconti while simultaneously maintaining the facade of a woman in love. As difficult as it was however, her determination to help her father gave her continued strength. Visconti's betrayal of both Phillip and her father had focused her resolve. It had crystallized it into a personal vendetta.

Strain had also taken its toll on Mike, however he had no choice but to continue into the void of uncertainty. While he worried about thesafety of both Kerri and Phillip, he knew his continued inaction would build pressure on both Visconti and Phillip. It was only a matter of time before one of them reached the breaking point. Like vultures, the Feds were waiting and watching on the sidelines, ready to pounce on the first person who blinked. When it finally happened, Mike prayed he could contain or escape the fallout before it engulfed him.

September 13.

Reports abounded in all forms of the media that an Iraqi invasion of Saudi Arabia was imminent. Investment experts, oil industry analysts and politicians were now making public speculations about the price of oil. They predicted it would reach extraordinary heights, with dire consequences for the world economy. For days, Visconti had digested one after another of the negative developments. Now approaching the breaking point, he called Assif Raza in a desperate attempt to find consolation. To his shock and horror, Raza again advised him to flee the market. His pain threshold had finally been breached. Bitter and confused, he capitulated, his hands shaking, beads of nervous sweat bathing his forehead. "Get me out!" he demanded of Miles Dennis.

"I can't believe it," Dennis quipped. "The great Louis Visconti is finally waving the white flag. You know you're going to take a big hit."

"I don't give a shit! Just do it!" Visconti shouted, then slammed the receiver into its cradle.

Dennis called Visconti forty-five minutes later. "Louis, we got you out. That's the good news. The bad news was the price."

"What was it?"

"Thirty, sixty-five."

"What's the margin call?"

"You sitting down?"

"Never mind the crap! Just tell me what it is."

"Twenty-two million, five hundred and thirty-five thousand."

"Thanks for nothing," Visconti spat. Defeated and emotionally drained, he replaced the receiver, then lowered his face to his hands, condemned to contemplate his grim future in the investment business. After an ill-conceived and protracted experiment with crude oil futures, he had succeeded in losing over two hundred and thirty-six million dollars. His stewardship of the King's trust had been a failure of legendary proportions. After almost exactly ten years on the job, the Crown Prince of Wall Street had succeeded in reducing its value from three hundred and twenty-five million to one hundred and sixty-six million.

If news of his incredibly dismal performance ever became public knowledge, his future as a manager of other peoples' money would be limited, at best. Even if the failure was never made public, his will to continue was gone, his confidence shot. He was finished. Under no circumstances could he risk facing public humiliation. He had to run away as far and as fast as he could. He wiped his face with his hands, lifted the receiver and dialed Kerri's office number. "Hi. It's me," he said, his voice cracking and sullen.

"How are you?" she asked, trying to sound excited, aware he had just liquidated his crude position and was unlikely to be in a good mood.

"I miss you... Can I take you to lunch? Anywhere you want. We need to talk."

"Sounds ominous... Is it?"

"Worst day of my investing life. I'm done, Kerri. I have to get away from this bull-shit life. I just want us to disappear. I want to go so far that no one will ever find us. I want to do it soon, real soon."

Kerri had received an extremely important signal. She was going to have to move fast and think very clearly. "How soon?" she asked.

"Let's talk about it at lunch."

"Louis, I've got to go. I've got two calls waiting. What time?" she asked, anxious to call her father, fast.

"I'll pick you up at your office at twelve-thirty."

"Good. See you then." She hung up using her index finger, then dialed the number for Reserve Oil. She had to wait for Mick to return her call from his car.

"Before you tell me why you called, I want to tell you I love you and I miss you," Mike said.

"I love you and miss you too," Kerri said, thrilled to hear her father's voice again. "It's finally happening, dad. Things are starting to move. Louis liquidated his crude oil position this morning."

"Give me the bad news."

"He lost another hundred and thirty-six million. There's more... He wants me to run away with him as soon as possible."

"How soon? Did he say?"

"No, but he's taking me to lunch today. He told me he wants to talk about it."

Mike gave no response.

"Did you hear me? Dad, are you still there?"

"I can't let him go. I've got to stop him. I'm going to call Dan Turner and tell him what you've just told me. I'll call you back as soon as I've talked to him."

"We're going to lunch at twelve-thirty. If I'm not here, just leave a message. I'll call you when I get back."

Mike called Dan Turner and told him of Kerri's news.

Turner took little time to make a decision. "In spite of the risks involved, I think we're going to have to move. I think you should call Visconti. Tell him you've decided to go ahead with the transfer of funds, but that your Toronto lawyer has insisted on doing the transfer... Do you know of a place where we can park the money? We've got to get it out of Visconti's hands as soon as possible."

"Yes, my daughter works for a company by the name of Iacardi & Sons, in New York. I'm sure we can put it there."

"How much does she know?"

"Everything."

"Good. She has to understand how crucial her cooperation is. Visconti can't know where the money went. I'll need her telephone number. I'm going to have to communicate directly with her."

Mike gave Kerri's business number to Turner.

"For your edification, Mike, I'm stepping way over the line to do this for you. I wouldn't do it if I wasn't so wrapped up in this whole unbelievable mess and if I didn't feel so personally involved."

"I appreciate that, more than you'll ever know, Dan."

"To remove our finger prints, I'm going to arrange to have it done through an unaffiliated law firm in New York. If anyone asks you who moved the money, you can truthfully tell them you don't know. Kerri will know, however, and I'm going to ask her not to tell you. Please don't ask her."

CHAPTER 87

New York. Thursday, September 13.

It was hot for mid September, uncomfortable in the sun for even short exposures.

Visconti took Kerri to lunch at Heinrich's, a tiny restaurant specializing in Bavarian foods and offering pleasant outdoor dining facilities, just off Broadway. They found a table for two, fortunately under a large green umbrella. Both ordered bratwurst on the bun with Bavarian beer. Visconti placed his hands behind his head and leaned backward. He smiled as he closed his eyes and took a deep breath through his nostrils. "This is the way I want us to live the rest of our lives. No more big deals. Just you and me and Europe." He leaned forward, his eyes glazed as he stared into Kerri's, pain and stress obvious. "The thrill of the chase is gone. I'm burned out. I haven't got what it takes any more."

Even though Kerri felt little pity for Visconti, she now knew the enormous losses he had sustained had affected him deeply. "I'm sorry to hear that. How serious are you about getting out?"

"Very. I've never been more serious about anything in my life."

"I hope it's not because you got a bloody nose in crude oil."

"So you know," he said, his face flushing to crimson.

"Of course I know. I was in Miles's office when he got you out."

"It's not just that," Visconti admitted, his eyes twitching. "Burnout isn't the result of one single event. It's a cumulative thing. It's voracious. It eats away at your confidence, and when that's gone, you're finished as an investor."

"When do you intend to go?"

"Tomorrow."

Kerri's internal alarm exploded. Tomorrow was too soon. She had to delay. She knew her father needed more time. "Tomorrow! What am I going to tell Miles?"

"Just tell him we're going to Europe on a short vacation. I'll tell my partners the same thing. That'll be it. We'll be gone."

"What are we going to live on? I don't think we can collect unemployment insurance in Europe."

"We won't have to work another day of our lives. That deal I told you I was working on is about to pay off, big time."

There was now no doubt in Kerri's mind. Visconti intended to scoop the money in the trust and escape to Europe with it. "But what if it doesn't?" she asked.

"Don't worry. It will," Visconti promised.

"How soon?"

Visconti shrugged his shoulders and fidgeted nervously with his fork. "Today or tomorrow."

"Then let me know when your ship comes in. We'll talk then."

"What's the matter? Is it something I said? Are you angry?"

Kerri glared at Visconti with all of the acting skills she could muster. "I can't just pack up and leave. I don't think you understand a damn thing about me, Louis Visconti. Not too long ago, another man lured me all the way to New York with the same kind of promises. I don't think I have to remind you of how many he kept."

"Is it money? Is that what you want?"

"You still don't understand. I don't want money. I want certainty. I want to know I'm not going to be left alone and out of work in some foreign country when you get tired of me."

"Then I'll give you an agreement. I'll sign anything you want. I'll give you fifty percent of everything I own, without conditions. If I die, you can have it all. I love you, Kerri. I'll do anything to prove it to you."

Kerri believed Visconti only so far, but not nearly far enough to let her guard down. Maybe he really did love her, but his love of money ruled him. If he was prepared to kill Phillip for money, he wouldn't hesitate to kill her to release himself from obligations contained in an agreement. She stood and forced a smile. "I have to get back to work, Louis. I've got a million things to do this afternoon."

"Kerri, please give me an answer," he pleaded. "If I give you an agreement, will you come to Europe with me?"

"You're asking me to take a big step, Louis. I need time. You've had a lifetime to think about it."

Again Visconti gave Kerri a cold gray stare. "Don't take long. I have to get out. I'm done."

Visconti's warning sounded more like an ultimatum. It forced her to make a decision. She smiled and reached for his hand. "Get Jackie Crawford to prepare the agreement this afternoon. Now can we get going?"

Within minutes of Visconti's return to his office, he placed orders to sell all of the stocks and bonds in the King's trust. He used the entire cash balance to purchase, for the benefit of the trust, one hundred percent of the shares of Forta Equitas, S.A., a shell company solely owned by Visconti. The proceeds from the sale were placed in his numbered account in the Banco Privata Svissera, in Geneva. He telephoned Jackie Crawford.

"What no good are you up to now, Louis?" Jackie asked.

"Just looking after my interests," Visconti replied with a chuckle. "How are you coming along with Kerri's divorce?"

"At the usual breathtaking pace. Why? You anxious to marry her? You don't deserve her, you know. She's far too young, beautiful and honest for you."

"I probably don't, but I still want to marry her. I also want you to prepare a prenuptial agreement. In it, I want a clause giving her fifty percent of everything I own. No conditions."

"Sounds like she took my advice. Smart girl. What about survivorship? You want her to have all your worldly wealth in the fortunate event of your death?"

"Don't be nasty... Sure. Make it reciprocal."

"How soon do you want it?"

"Courier it to my office before six."

"Wow! You must be in some kind of hurry."

"Just do it, Jackie. See you around."

Kerri received a call from Dan Turner at two-fifteen. "Kerri, my name is Dan Turner. I'm an attorney in Toronto. I act for your father."

"Hi. Yes, my father told me who you are. He spoke very highly of you."

"I advised him that it's time to move the funds in the King's trust out of Louis Visconti's hands. He suggested they could be held by Iacardi & Sons."

"Good. Shortly, you will be contacted by a lawyer in New York. His name is Thomas Hinkin. He'll tell you exactly what he needs and what he wants you to do. Any problems?"

"Sure. I'll have to clear it with my boss. His name is Miles Dennis."

"How much does he know?"

"Everything. I had to tell him to preserve my sanity. Don't worry. I trust him completely. If you don't hear from me within ten minutes, assume it's clear."

"Thank you," Turner said, concerned about the growing list of people who knew everything.

"Don't hang up... Would you please tell my father that Louis is planning to run to Europe tomorrow. I'm going with him."

"Damn! Then we'll have to move fast."

CHAPTER 88

New York. Friday, September 14.

Visconti telephoned Nick Bennedetti at three P.M. "Nick, it's Louis. It's time to move on Phillip Servito."

"Now?"

"Yup. I also want you to do a man who lives in Zurich. His name is Alfred Schnieder. He's..."

"Hold it, Louis. Time out. I don't do European jobs. Too risky. Too many borders. You couldn't pay me enough to get involved. It's going to be tough enough doing this Canadian job."

"You might be wrong about that, Nick. There's a lot of money in it for you."

"Don't even think about it. I'm definitely not interested. Find yourself some people in Europe."

"Okay, but I want a fast clean job on the kid."

"Trust me Louis. He won't know what hit him."

Visconti drove Kerri to his apartment at six-thirty. He smiled proudly as he presented her with two copies of the agreement Jackie Crawford had prepared that afternoon. "This'll prove that I'm a man of my word. It's all there, everything we talked about at lunch today." He removed a gold pen from his jacket and signed both copies in front of her.

Kerri's hands trembled as she attempted to read one of the copies. The words a blurred as too many thoughts raced through her head. She had to delay. She looked up at Louis with pleading eyes. "Would you mind if I talked to Jackie about this tomorrow?" she asked. "I don't doubt your word, but I don't understand all this legal jargon."

Visconti sensed that Kerri had reached the limit of her stress tolerance, and that to hassle her might push her over the top. In spite of his haste to leave the country, he desperately wanted, needed her to go with him. He smiled and nodded. "You do that. You should have legal advice before you sign it."

September 13. Four, P.M.

Mike ran to his car and returned an urgent call from Dan Turner. "Margaret said your call was urgent," he said, struggling to catch his breath.

"It was. I just got a call from Thomas Hinkin. He did not have good news. We were too late. Visconti scooped everything. To punctuate his timing, he told Hinkin to fuck himself."

"That's just wonderful," Mike groaned. "I don't know how much more of this I can take."

"Well I suggest you buckle up. You have no choice. You should also know that Kerri just told me he's leaving for Europe today, and that she's going with him."

"I'll call you right back," Mike said, his mind racing to process the implications of the new equation. He hung up and dialed Visconti's office number, a mixture of rage and anxiety boiling inside him.

"Long time no talk to, Mike," Visconti sang. "How the hell are you?"

"Where's the money?"

"In a very safe place. I used it to make a fabulous investment for the benefit of your trust. I know you're going to like it."

"Why don't you tell me about it?"

"We bought all the outstanding shares of a tremendously promising company. It's called Forta Equitas. I'll send you a prospectus with my next quarterly report."

"No bull-shit, Visconti! Where's the money."

Visconti chuckled. "I'll tell you a little secret. A decade ago Alfred Schnieder told me the whole nasty story about Phillip's natural father. I was amazed when he told me how Jim Servito managed to accumulate a fortune by evading gasoline taxes. Alfred also told me your dirty little secret. He said you had decided to keep the money. You're a bad boy. You really should have turned it over to the Feds, like a good honest citizen. Withholding hundreds of millions of tax dollars is a very serious crime... Now, before I let you go, allow me to give you some friendly advice. If you even think about breathing a word about this to anyone, I'll blow the whistle on you and Karen so fast you won't even have time to take a nervous shit."

"I promise you'll regret this," Mike said, then terminated the call and pressed the redial for Turner's office. He told Turner the story of his conversation with Visconti. "I concede, Dan. Visconti wins. That money's cursed. It's been nothing but misery for anyone who's had anything to do with it. I'm going to wash my hands of it and let it ruin Visconti's life," he said.

"So be it, but I must remind you that the Feds are still breathing fire. What about Phillip?"

"I'm going to tell him everything, including Visconti's plan to kill him. We're probably going to have to hide him somewhere."

"Good luck and stay in touch."

Mike terminated the call, then called Kerri. "Hi... I hope your day's been better than mine."

"What's wrong?"

"Dan Turner just told me Hinkin was too late."

"Damn! Did he find out what Louis did with the money?"

"No. I did. I phoned Louis and he told me he used it to buy the shares of a company called Forta Equitas. He made it obvious that the move was nothing but a scam to scoop the money. I hope he rots in hell."

"I'm going to make sure he does because I'm going to hell with him."

"Kerri, you can't. It's far too dangerous. If he's prepared to kill Phillip, he won't hesitate to kill you, too."

"I don't care how dangerous he is. I'm going to follow him everywhere he goes. If it takes me the rest of my life, I'm going to stop him."

Mike was brutally reminded of his own resolve to stop Jim Servito, a long time ago. No amount of convincing would have changed his mind. "Is there any way I can convince you not to go?"

"No."

"Then be careful and call me collect, as often as you can. And remember that I love you."

"I   will.   I   love   you   too,   dad."

CHAPTER 89

Toronto. Friday, September 14. Nine, A.M.

Phillip entered Mike's office. He had a new mission. "I had to come to the office to pick up my paycheck... So, I thought I would drop in and ask if you gave the money to your charity," he said, his hands in his pockets and squirming uneasily.

Mike looked up, glared at him, then threw his pen to the desk. "It might surprise you to learn that your friend Visconti spent the last ten years losing almost half of your money in senseless investments. To complete the job, he's embezzled what's left of it and fucked off to Europe."

"How do you know?" Phillip asked, stunned, disappointed and astonished that Visconti would do such a thing, and that Mike would know.

"I called him earlier today. He took perverse pleasure in rubbing it in my face." Mike pointed to the couch. "Sit down. I have something far more important to tell you." He waited until Phillip was seated, then leveled his eyes at his step-son. "You should also know that Visconti has a hundred thousand dollar contract on your life. He wants you dead."

Phillip flashed a nervous smile. "I think you're full of shit! There's no way he's gonna kill me. He's gonna..."

"He's going to do what, help you get your money? I know all about your little agreement with Visconti. I also know you had no intention of ever changing your mind about the money... Maybe Visconti would be doing me a favor," he said, shaking his head in disgust.

Tears appeared in Phillip's eyes as he clenched his teeth and fists. "I hate your guts!" he shouted. "You were never a father to me. You were always more interested in messing with my life." He pointed his index finger at Mike. "Now I'm going to mess with yours." He sprang to his feet, ran from the office and headed for his company van. He slammed the door, started the engine and jerked the gearshift into drive. He stomped the accelerator to the floor with his foot, causing the rear wheels to screech as they laid strips of rubber on the parking lot. "I'll show those bastards!" he muttered, his eyes glazed, his fingers applying a death grip on the steering wheel.

Slightly over an hour later, Phillip once again faced David Savage in the regional office of Revenue Canada. Savage had turned on a tape recorder in anticipation of what his visitor was about to say. "Now Mister Servito, you said you had something to tell me," he prompted.

Phillip nodded, his face still crimson with anger. "Yah. You remember I told you I might know where the money my real father left me is? Well all of a sudden I found it." He paused, grinning at Savage and taking sadistic pleasure in the delay.

"You found it! Where?" Savage asked, prompting with his hands, urging Phillip to continue.

"My stepfather's been hiding it all these years. It's in a trust in New York."

"Where in New York?"

"Louis Visconti manages it. He works for a company by the name of Mara, Griesdorf and Visconti. His office is in the World Trade Center."

"How were you able to find it?" Savage asked, continuing to prompt with his hands.

"Doesn't matter. What does matter is that Visconti scooped all of the money and went to Europe with it."

"How do you know that?"

"My stepfather just told me."

"How does he know?"

"Visconti just ruined his day with that news," Phillip hissed, frowning in frustration. "I think it was yesterday."

"How do you know it was yesterday?"

"Because that's what my stepfather just told me."

"Do you or your stepfather know where in Europe Louis Visconti went?"

"I don't, and I don't know if he does or not."

"Do you have anything further to add?" Savage asked, disappointed not to have gleaned any further knowledge.

"Nope. I think that's it."

"Does anyone else know of the existence or location of this money?"

"I don't know."

"Does your stepfather know you're talking to us?"

"Nope."

"Thank you, Mister Servito. You've been most helpful. I'm sure others in this department will want to talk to you about this. Are you still at the same address?"

"Yup."

"You're free to go now."

Phillip climbed into his van and headed west on the Gardiner Expressway. He was startled to hear a hoarse male voice, close to his right ear. "Don't turn around or I'll blow your ear off, kid. I have a gun pointed right at it."

Terrified, Phillip glanced in the rear view mirror to see a man wearing dark sun glasses. His long straight gray hair extended below a light brown fedora. His teeth were crooked and stained. A large dimple punctuated his chin.

"Just keep driving this thing until I tell you to stop."

Phillip's body stiffened. While he focused on the road with his eyes, his mind focused on the gut-wrenching possibility that Mike's warning was valid. He was going to die.

His passenger forced him to continue driving until he entered an auto wrecking yard in the northeast end of Hamilton. Following orders, he drove behind a large corrugated metal building. The adjacent yard was strewn with rusted metal, the ground saturated with an ugly mixture of oil and water. "Stop right here and get out," the man bellowed.

His heart pounding, body shaking, knees close to buckling, Phillip stopped the van and climbed out. His passenger followed him out the same door, then pointed his gun at Phillip's heart and pulled the trigger twice in rapid succession. As the bullets pierced his heart, Phillip's body jerked violently, then slumped to the ground. The man lifted the lifeless body into the van, then drove to the side door of the metal building. Two men hurried from the building, removed the body from the van, and carried it inside. There, the wounds were exposed, the body photographed, then stuffed into a heavy steel drum. The drum was sealed, then hydraulically crushed to a fraction of its original size. The crushed drum was dropped into a second steel drum which was subsequently filled with cement, then sealed.

The drum was driven to a wharf and loaded onto a small fishing vessel. The vessel traversed Burlington Bay and headed under the Burlington Skyway, eastward into Lake Ontario. When it was almost out of sight of land, the drum was committed to the deep.

CHAPTER 90

New York. Friday, September 14, 9:00 A.M.

Six men, three from the F.B.I., and three from the Criminal Investigation Division of the I.R.S., burst into the offices of Mara, Griesdorf and Visconti. After three hours of frantic searching and intensive questioning of all available personnel, they found nothing, no trust, no money, and no Visconti. Sue Franklin, Visconti's secretary, subjected to intensive interrogation, was unable to explain the mysterious disappearance of the money and all of the files related to the trust. She said her boss had told her he was leaving for a short European vacation.

Toronto.

Dan Turner placed an urgent call to Mike at ten-thirty. "I have some extremely bad news," he said, pausing to allow his point to sink in. "William Dare, an attorney and two other heavy hitters from Revenue Canada came in here this morning and made such a stink about wanting to see me, I had to cancel a meeting. They told me Phillip paid them another visit yesterday and sang like a bird. He told them you've known for ten years of the existence and location of Jim Servito's money. Significantly, he didn't mention his mother. He went on to tell them the trust was managed by Louis Visconti, and that Visconti's disappeared to Europe with the money."

Mike closed his eyes and exhaled. "I guess the game's over. Why the hell didn't they just come over here and arrest me?" he asked, his mind in a spiritless state of surrender.

"They said that in view of their past mistakes in this case, they wanted to be absolutely certain... Why did Phillip do that, Mike? Obviously something provoked him."

"I lost it, Dan. He came in here yesterday and asked if I had given his money to charity. I told him everything, including Visconti's plan to kill him."

"How did he respond?"

"He was mad as hell. He said he was going to mess up my life. Then he blew out of here."

"Well Dare and his boys are mad as hell, too. They smell blood, and I don't think they're going to stop until they get it."

"What did you tell them?"

I said I wasn't acting for Phillip and could not account in any way for his behavior, or his claims. When they asked about you, I told them I wasn't prepared to comment until I had an opportunity to consult with you. Needless to say they want to talk to you as soon as possible."

"I can't believe it! That money is a cancer."

"Well you had better believe it, and it's metastasizing, fast."

"What are my options? I really need your advice, Dan"

"Tell the truth. Admit you were aware of the existence and location of the trust from its inception. Then add that you had recently decided to turn the entire amount over to them and the American government. Tell them you asked me to be your intermediary, but you were prevented from proceeding by Louis Visconti. I will certainly corroborate."

"Where does that take me?"

"... They'll prosecute. You'll be fined and assessed with back taxes, possibly do some time. It's difficult to tell at this point. It all depends on how they view your actions. What you've done is very unique. You were not the one who stole the money. In reality, all you did was to follow the wishes of Phillip's natural father, albeit with malicious intent."

"Do I have any other option?"

"Yes... I almost hesitate to suggest it... You could disappear and hope some miracle happens to end this thing. You must understand if you do that, your disappearance is tantamount to admission of guilt. When the Feds realize you've gone, they'll come after you with everything they've got. If they find you, you can kiss your ass goodbye."

"Maybe I should just blow my brains out."

"That's not an option and you know it," Turner admonished. "There is a positive aspect of the second option. Your absence is reversible. In other words, it's the least final of all of your options. If the Feds can't find you or the money, they might tend to be more amenable to negotiation."

"How much time do I have?"

"The meter's running fast. You could look for a subpoena within hours."

"I'll let you know what I've decided." Devastated and deprived of all human consolation, Mike hung up and began to consider his future, all of which was extremely unpalatable. Jim Servito's money had once again become the main focus of his existence. Miserably unhappy, unwilling and unable to continue his work, he picked up his briefcase and left for home and Karen, invariably his emotional salvation.

"It looks like you could use a friend," she whispered, pulling Mike closer."

He held Karen's head close to his chest and wept. "If God had prescribed a worse nightmare, I can't imagine what it would be... It's Phillip. He went to the Feds and told them the whole damn story, and it's my fault... I unloaded on him yesterday... He came into my office and asked if I had given the money away."

"Did you tell him everything?"

Mike nodded. "I couldn't think of any other way."

"You did the right thing."

"I don't think I've ever felt so helpless and guilty in my entire life. Every time I do what I think is the right thing, it gets worse."

"Does Dan know?"

"Yup. The Feds nearly broke his door down this morning. I'm in big trouble. I have two options. You won't like either of them."

Karen gave Mike an understanding smile. "There's only one choice, King. We run."

Mike shook his head. "They want me, Babe. Fortunately, Phillip didn't implicate you."

"Doesn't matter a damn to me. We're in this thing together. We've been there since the beginning."

Again he shook his head. For better or worse, his decision to hide from the Feds had been made. "I love you for your loyalty, but you don't go. I'm going to need you here. I need to hide alone. Somewhere quiet."

"Go to Azimuth Island. There's no one there now. There's enough food in the freezer to last for months. No one would find you there until you decide to be found. I'll have to tell dad you're there. I wouldn't want it to come as a surprise to him."

Mike's frown melted to a grin. "That's a perfect place. Can you stand living without me?"

"No."

He kissed her forehead, then looked into her eyes. "Thank you for being the most incredibly wonderful woman I've ever known, and for putting up with all of my crap."

Karen left Mike's embrace to answer the telephone. "Yes," she said without hesitation, accepting the collect call. She cupped her hand over the mouthpiece and turned to Mike. "It's Kerri. She's in France."

Mike hurried to accept the receiver from Karen. "Kerri, are you all right?" he shouted, his heart pounding.

"I'm okay. I'm..."

"Don't say anything more. Give me one minute to get to my car, then call me again. Do you have the number?"

"Yes. Please hurry. I don't have much time."

Mike hung up, ran from the house to his car and waited. When the phone rang, he jerked it to his ear before the first ring had ended and accepted the charges. "Kerri, now talk your heart out," he demanded.

"I'm at a pay telephone at the airport in Nice. Louis is getting the bags. He's going to rent a car and drive us to Monte Carlo from here. We'll be staying at the Hotel de Paris. I'll call you from there as soon as I get a chance. I'm going to nail him, dad. I'm going to stay with him until I do. I don't care how long it takes... How's Phillip?"

"Right now, I don't know. You should know he went to the Feds and told them the whole story yesterday."

"Oh no! Why? Was it because of Louis?"

"No. It was my fault. I accused him of lying to me and I told him about Visconti's plan to kill him."

"So what's going to happen to you?"

"I don't know. I'm going into hiding for a while to think about it. I'll be at the Taylor's cottage in Muskoka." He gave her the cottage telephone number. "From now on, call me at that number. I'm sure it's not bugged."

"Dad, I've got to go. Louis is coming. Love you." She hung up.

CHAPTER 91

Toronto. Ten minutes later.

Mike and Karen stared at each other, hearts throbbing, trying to decide if their telephone should be answered.

"You get it," Mike said. "If it's the Feds, tell them you don't know where I am."

Karen answered.

"Hello Karen. It's Alfred Schnieder. May I speak to Mike, please?"

"Hold for a second, Alfred," Karen said, then cupped her hand over the mouthpiece and turned to Mike. "Alfred Schnieder," she mouthed.

Mike closed his eyes and shook his head. "I don't want to talk to him," he groaned. "He's a goddamned crook. He told Visconti everything."

"How do you know that?"

"Visconti told me. That knowledge gave him his confidence. Without it, there's no way he would have had the balls to scoop the money."

"Talk to him," Karen demanded. "He might have something very important to tell you."

Mike compressed his lips and nodded slowly.

Karen took Schnieder's number and Mike reluctantly called him from his car phone. "What do you want, Alfred?" he asked, totally disinterested in anything he might want.

"I was anxious to tell you our window of opportunity in the Creditsuisse Bankhaus is about to close. Olaf Leutweiler has advised me that he is about to leave for an extended stay in the Far East."

"As far as I'm concerned Alfred, you can take your window of opportunity and shove it up your ass. Tell Olaf there's no money and there probably never will be."

"There is trouble?"

"There wouldn't be any if you hadn't opened your fat mouth ten years ago. How could you do that? I thought banking secrets were sacred."

"I don't understand what you're talking about. Please explain."

"Visconti just took off for Europe with all the money in our trust. It might interest you to know that our little secret gave him the balls to do it. He said if I tried to stop him, he'd go straight to the Feds and spill his guts. He was laughing at me, Alfred, deliberately trying to humiliate me. He was so certain I wouldn't try to stop him, he even told me what he did with the money."

"And what was that?" Schnieder asked, extremely curious to know why Visconti had not shared the money with him in accordance with their plan.

"He used it to buy shares in some mirage company in Europe. I'll give you three guesses who the seller was. Now he's got the money and I've got the Feds coming at me from all directions."

"He told the Feds?"

"No. Phillip did. Your friend Visconti conned him into believing he was going to help him get his money. In fact, he was planning to have Phillip killed. For all I know, he may have already done that."

"That is not good news. Regrettably, Louis conned me as well. I am ashamed to tell you I was his accomplice. We planned to relieve you of your problem and the trust of its money. Instead of respecting your wish to give the money to charity, we planned to keep it for our own selfish purposes."

"That's beautiful," Mike said, then chuckled at Schnieder's admission. "You know the intriguing reality of the whole thing, Alfred? It's never a question of whether anyone has a price. It's only a matter of how high it is."

"Very true. In addition to preserving clients' secrets, it is a lesson one should learn very quickly in the banking business. After all my years in the business, I am guilty only once. Unfortunately, you are the innocent victim... I only wish there was some way I could make it up to you."

"Only if you could turn back the calendar, Alfred."

"Please accept my sincere apology... If you ever discover where Louis went, please let me know."

"He's staying at the Hotel de Paris, in Monte Carlo. You should go down there and do lunch with him. You deserve each other."

"How did you find him so quickly?"

"It's a secret, Alfred. If I thought you could keep it, I might have been inclined to share it with you."

CHAPTER 92

Muskoka. Tuesday, September 19.

It was dark. No moon. Only a vague silhouette of Azimuth Island could be seen from the shore of Lake Muskoka where Mike stood. After lowering himself into the stern seat of George Taylor's canoe, he pushed off and began to paddle into the blackened serenity, each stroke taking him deeper into his self-imposed exile.

The Hotel de Paris, Monaco.

Prosperity abounds in Monaco, one of the most opulent tax shelters in the world. Unemployment is almost nonexistent, and there is no income tax. Tax evasion is not a criminal offense, so its perpetrators cannot be extradited. Most residents are hiding themselves, their money, or both. Numerous sports celebrities call it their home, attempting to preserve the huge but short term incomes they generate. Squeezed between sea and mountains, Monaco is a place where land is at a premium, measured by the square meter, or centimeter. Grand old villas have been replaced by towering condominiums. Real estate companies have proliferated. Generous sunshine bathes hundreds of ultra expensive cars, the beaches, the beautiful people, the obscenely expensive yachts in the blue harbor.

Kerri was captivated by the scenery and astounded by the people of Monaco. It seemed outrageous to her that while the rest of the world worked and struggled to survive, the wealthy inhabitants of the idyllic sun-drenched paradise frivolously wasted their days and nights in the extravagant pursuit of happiness. After a breakfast of toast and boiled eggs in accommodations befitting Visconti's new found wealth, she relaxed in the warm sunshine on the balcony. Still in her pink silk nightgown, she rested her bare feet on the wrought iron railing and leaned back in her deck chair.

Visconti, looking resplendent in his red and yellow flowered beach clothing, rainbow shades and brown leather sandals, approached her. "How would you like to go for a walk on the beach?" he asked while still grooming his hair with his hands.

"Would you mind if I didn't? I'm exhausted. I really want to put my bathing suit on and just relax in the sun."

Visconti feigned a pout. "Guess I'll have to soldier on without you."

"You poor baby," she said, then stood on her toes and kissed his cheek. "How long will you be gone?"

"An hour, maybe two. See you later," he said, then turned and left.

Kerri waited on the balcony until she saw Visconti leave the hotel, then hurried inside and proceeded to overturn furniture, dump the contents of every drawer on the floor, and overturn rugs and mattresses. When she had finished making the suite appear as if it had been burglarized, she changed into her minuscule peach bikini. She covered herself with sun-glasses, faded jeans, white T-shirt and sneakers, then placed her wallet in a large cotton bag and picked up Visconti's briefcase. She left the door to the suite unlocked.

When the elevator doors opened to the lobby, she stepped out and looked around to ensure no one was looking at her, then hurried to the front doors. She took a taxi to the Banque de Monte Carlo, three blocks from the hotel. She paid the driver, then hurried inside.

"May I be of service?" a young expensively dressed clerk asked, speaking perfect English.

"I would like to rent a safety deposit box," Kerri said as she lifted the briefcase to the counter. "Large enough for this."

"Do you have an account with us?" the clerk asked.

"... No. Can't I just pay cash?"

"Certainly," the clerk said, staring at the dark brown leather briefcase. "Please come this way." He led Kerri to the vault in the rear of the bank, then approached one of the hundreds of safety deposit boxes lining the walls. Using his security key, he unlocked the top lock, then turned the key in the bottom lock. "This should be satisfactory," he said, pulling the box out far enough to show her the size.

Kerri fitted the briefcase into the box. "This is perfect."

"Would you like to be alone for a while? We have some private rooms just outside the vault."

"No. I'll just leave it here for now. Thank you."

"The clerk shoved the box into the opening, then closed and locked the door. He removed the key from the lower lock and handed it to Kerri. "Please come this way." He led her to a small office where he gave her a card. "Here is your identification card. Please do not lose it. It's very important."

Kerri paid in cash for six month's use of the box. "Thank you," she said, extending her hand.

"Thank you very much for your business. Please come and see us often."

Kerri took a taxi back to the hotel and hurried to an empty deck chair on the terrace. She removed her jeans and T-shirt, lifted her sun glasses to the top of her head, closed her eyes and smiled, satisfied that she had finally made something happen.

Visconti inserted his key in the door to the suite, turned it and tried to open the door. When it failed to open, he turned the key the opposite way. "No!" he shouted. He rushed inside and was horrified to see the state of disorder of the suite. He raced to the bedroom, descended to his knees and rooted through the debris like a dog looking for a bone, desperately looking for his briefcase. After fifteen minutes of swearing and unsuccessful search, he snatched the telephone receiver and dialed number of the front desk. "This is Louis Visconti. I want to report a robbery. I want the manager up here immediately," he demanded.

"Is anything missing?"

"Yes. My briefcase."

"Please don't touch a thing, sir. The manager and the house detective will be there very shortly. Would you like me to call the police?"

"Ah, no... The contents of the briefcase are rather sensitive."

"I understand. I must advise you that a claim under the hotel's theft insurance can only be validated by a thorough police investigation and report."

"Forget the police! Just tell the manger to get his ass up here, now!"

The hotel manager and house detective arrived within two minutes. After conducting a survey of the suite and commiserating with Visconti, they promised to interrogate the hotel's staff in the course of completing an exhaustive search for his briefcase. Again Visconti declined an offer to call the police.

As soon as the manager and house detective left, Visconti returned to the bedroom and continued to sort through the debris in search of his briefcase, or some clue as to its disappearance. Instead he found Kerri's photograph of her father and mother. He jumped to his feet and rushed to the window. "Holy shit!" he swore, staring at the photograph in the bright sunlight. He inserted the photograph between the folds of a large white towel, then headed for the hotel's terrace.

Visconti forced a smile as he lowered himself into the deck chair beside Kerri's. "Did you make certain the door was locked when you left for the pool?" he asked, his face almost devoid of color.

Kerri's heart pounded. "Yes. Why?"

"Someone broke into our suite. The place was torn apart."

"Oh, no!" she said, bolting upright, feigning surprise. "Is anything missing?"

Visconti nodded. "My briefcase. My entire life support system is in there."

"Can it be replaced?"

"I don't know. I'm going to have to make some calls to find out."

"Did you call the police?"

"I called the hotel manager. He and the house detective looked around the suite and promised me they would do a complete investigation... Did you bring your wallet with you?"

Kerri gasped as she quickly reached into her bag. "Thank God I did!" she said, removing it for him to see. She stood then sat beside him. "I'm so sorry, Louis. You don't deserve this," she said, forcing herself to hug him, and certain he did.

Visconti reached for his towel and removed the photograph. He held it inches from her face. "I found this while I was looking for my briefcase," he said, glaring at her eyes. "Who are the people in this photograph?"

Kerri stared at the photograph in shock, desperately trying to think of how to respond to Visconti's question. "That's my mother," she said, pointing to Barbara.

"Who's the guy?"

"Mom dated him for a while after she split from my father. She told me his name, but I can't remember."

"So you've never met him?"

"I probably did, but it was a long time ago. I was very young... Do you know him?"

Visconti shook his head. "He looks like someone I used to do business with." Again he looked at Kerri suspiciously. "I never did ask... What's your maiden name?"

Kerri used her mother's maiden name. "Larkin," she lied, holding her breath.

Visconti lowered his eyes to the photograph, then back to Kerri. His frown gradually gave way to a grin. "I think you're better looking than your mother."

Relieved, Kerri swallowed dryly and smiled. "Thank you," she said, releasing her vice-like grip on the arm of Visconti's chair.

"I'll see you later. I've got to go back to the suite and make some calls."

"I'm going with you. I want to see if anything else was stolen."

CHAPTER 93

Deep Bottom Cove, Massachusetts. September 20. 10:00 A.M.

Heavy clouds and a thick morning mist hung over the still water and obscured the view of the trees, less than a hundred yards away from John Hill's sixteen foot aluminum fishing boat. Hill, still head of C.I.D. for the I.R.S., had just cast his line about thirty feet from the boat which floated in a narrow secluded cove on Martha's Vinyard. He turned to his friend, Alex McDowell, now the director of Canada's Security Intelligence Service. For years, the two had annually enjoyed a week of fishing together. They had always alternated between McDowell's summer home in the Gatineau Hills, near Ottawa, and Hill's summer home on Martha's Vinyard. By mutual agreement, both had avoided the razor for three days. "Look's like rain," Hill muttered. "You want to pack it up?"

McDowell secured the handle of his rod under his seat, then scanned the sky. "Let's risk it. I think it's going to clear. Even if it doesn't, I don't mind getting a little wet." He turned to face Hill. "I understand your people struck out at Louis Visconti's office."

"Yup. A big zero," Hill admitted, hiding his disappointment by turning to concentrate on his line. "We couldn't find one shred of evidence, hard or soft. Nothing." He glanced at McDowell. "Have your people talked to King yet?"

McDowell shook his head. "He's disappeared. His wife and his lawyer say they have no idea where he is. We think they're lying through their teeth."

Hill rolled his eyes. "That's nice. So who's got the money, Visconti or King?"

"Good question. Maybe they both have it. Maybe they're in this thing together."

"What does King's stepson say about it?"

Again McDowell shook his head. "He's disappeared also. No one's seen him since he left our office in Toronto last Thursday. The Ontario Provincial Police found his company van on a dirt road about fifty miles west of Toronto. There was absolutely no clue in that vehicle. It was sanitized."

Hill continued to stare at the water and chuckled. "The whole thing is so familiar. As soon as we get close to King and that money, they both disappear."

"We're going to find both," McDowell promised. "What about Visconti? I presume you're looking for him."

Hill nodded.

"John, how much money do you think we're looking for?"

"The only number we have to work with is the one Phillip Servito gave us."

"Three hundred million! That's bull shit. It's got to be more than that after ten years."

"Suppose we recover three hundred million. Would you close the books?"

"Nope, but I'd do it in a heart beat for five. Four would let me sleep at night. We could save the asses of everyone who was even remotely connected to this disastrous investigation"

"And you and I wouldn't have to admit that after ten years of looking, we couldn't find over three hundred million gasoline tax dollars."

CHAPTER 94

Kerri found Visconti seated at the ornate French provincial desk in the living room of their suite. His right hand rested on top of the telephone, his head slumped. He turned to face her. "I have to leave immediately," he said.

Kerri threw her cotton bag onto the couch and hurried to his side. "Why?" she asked, pretending to console him by rubbing his shoulders.

Visconti leaned forward and covered his face with his hands. "I have to drive to Geneva and identify myself in person. It's the only way I can clear up this whole mess."

"Want me to go with you?"

"I'd enjoy the company, but I think you should stay here and try to find out who broke into this place."

Kerri surveyed the mess she had made, then forced herself to hug Visconti. "How long will you be gone?"

"No longer than twenty-four hours." He stood and took her in his arms. "While I'm gone, I want you to buy yourself the most expensive evening dress you can find. When I get back, I'm going to take you to dinner, and then to the European Casino. I think it's time I showed off Monte Carlo's newest and most beautiful resident."

Visconti left almost an hour later, a black leather over-night bag slung over his shoulder.

Kerri returned to the balcony and waited until she saw him leave the hotel and step into a taxi. She raced to the telephone and placed a collect call to her father on Azimuth Island. Her hands trembled as she dialed.

Mike was awakened at four A.M., Toronto time, by the relentless jangle of the rural telephone near his bed.

"I have a collect call for Mike King from Kerri Pyper in Monaco. Will you accept the charges?" the operator asked.

"Yes," Mike said, jerking himself upward in his four poster bed.

"Dad, I'm sorry to call at this time. It's the first chance I've had."

"Are you okay?"

"I'm fine... How are you?"

"Still free and running from the law. I've got all the comforts of home here, but no people. I'm starting to talk to myself. I'm getting more fresh air and exercise than I've had in years. I must have canoed at least a hundred miles since I've been here, I'm sick of reading the same old magazines for the zillionth time, and I'm lonely as hell.

"How's Phillip?"

Mike closed his eyes. "... He's disappeared. No one's seen him since late last week. The police found his van on Friday. It was abandoned on the side of a dirt road... It doesn't look good, Kerri."

Kerri was saddened and angered by the news. "It was Louis. I'm going to get him, dad. I don't care how long it takes, or what I have to do, I'm going to do it."

"He's a dangerous man, Kerri. I think you should come home before you get hurt,or worse."

"No way. I don't care how dangerous he is. It's our last chance to stop that bastard. I'm not going to let it go."

"If anything happened to you, I..."

"Please don't say it, Dad. Just understand that I can't quit now."

"Then be careful. Don't let your emotions take control. Think through every move you make. If you reach a point where you think the risk is too great, run. At least you'll still be alive."

"I stole Louis's briefcase."

351

Thrilled to have heard the first shred of good news in a very long time, Mike's heart rate quickened. "Good girl! What was in it?"

"I don't know yet. It was locked and I'm not sure how to open it. I put it in a safety deposit box in a bank not far from here."

"Does he know it's gone?"

"Yes. I trashed the suite to make it look like a robbery."

"I'd love to have seen his face. Does he believe it was a robbery?"

"I think so. He was really upset. He said he had his life support system in it. Now he's trying to put it all back together. He had to go all the way to Geneva, just to identify himself. He said he'll be back in twenty-four hours. That gives me time to open his briefcase."

"Good. Tell me about the briefcase. Are there three dials under the handle?"

"Yes. I think they're brass."

"Then here's what I want you to do. Buy an electric drill and a quarter inch bit. Ask for one with a cobalt tip. It'll cut through metal like a knife through butter. Make sure you pay cash. Stand the briefcase upright on a hard floor and drill straight down through the dials. If that doesn't work, turn the briefcase over and drill through the hinges. When you get the briefcase open, write down a description of everything you find inside, then put everything back in the safety deposit box, including the drill, the bit, the wrappings, and the briefcase. Call me and let me know what you found."

"I will. I love you, dad."

"Love   you   too."

CHAPTER 95

Kerri stood Visconti's briefcase upright on the white tiled floor of the suite's bathroom. She unpacked the Black & Decker electric drill she had purchased, fastened the cobalt bit in the chuck, then connected the device to an electrical outlet. She descended to her knees and began to drill straight down through the center dial. She had almost finished her third hole when the briefcase opened with a loud snap.

"You should have let me open it for you," Visconti said.

Adrenaline shot through Kerri's body like an electric shock.

He stood in the doorway, his eyes piercing. "I bet you're wondering why I'm not on my way to Geneva," he said, then approached her and closed the briefcase. "I wasn't completely satisfied with your answers when I showed you that photograph. I wasn't sure. It might have been the way you spoke, the color of your face or the fact that you owned a photograph of Mike King. So, while you were in the bedroom cleaning up the mess you created to make this little scam look like a robbery, I decided to verify your story. I pulled your wallet out of your bag and found something very interesting." He reached into the pocket of his shirt and removed Kerri's birth certificate. "I'm confused. Maybe you can explain to me why Kerri Larkin is carrying Kerri King's birth certificate."

Kerri's charade had ended. She knew it was pointless to say anything. All she could think of was how she could escape from the incredible nightmare into which she had maneuvered herself.

"You're King's daughter," he said with a cold penetrating stare. "Aren't you?" he shouted, slapping her face as hard as he could, the force of the blow knocking her sideways to the floor.

"Yes," she sobbed as she covered her face with her hands.

"I underestimated him. All these years I was never quite sure if he trusted me. Never in my wildest dreams did I think he would stoop so low as to ask his own daughter to share my bed with me." His evil smile was replaced by a pained expression. "How could you do this to me, Kerri? We had it made. For the first time in my life I was actually in love."

Kerri refused to speak.

"I asked you a question!" Visconti shouted. "Answer me!" he screamed.

Kerri glared at him defiantly, blood oozing from her mouth. "You're a sick, pathetic excuse for a human being. Jackie Crawford was right about you. You're incapable of loving anything but money."

"I'll show you how to love!" he snarled. He grasped her hair with his right hand and jerked her head upward, then smirked. "Let's do it one last time, just for the record." He pulled her head toward his and kissed her savagely. "Let's do it right here on the floor. I'll show you what's in the briefcase when we're finished. Then you can go for a nice long swim, just like Phillip did." He ripped off her T-shirt and reached for the top of her her jeans. He stopped when he heard a knock on the door to the suite, then stood and hurried to the living room. "Who is it?" he shouted.

Another knock.

"Who the hell's there?"

Again no answer.

"What the fuck is this?" Visconti muttered. He marched to the door of the suite and jerked it open. His mouth opened as he froze in shock at the sight of his visitor. "Jesus! What are you doing here?"

"Hello, Louis. A pleasure to see you again," Alfred Schnieder said with a golden smile. "It would be appreciated if you would invite me in."

Visconti attempted to close the door in Schnieder's face.

"Don't, Louis," Schnieder warned, pointing the muzzle of his Mauser Parabellum at Visconti. "This pistol is almost as old as I am but it is still extremely effective. It is quite capable of putting a bullet through both the door and you. It was given to me in Oberndorf when I was forced to fight for the Nazis. Using it to kill one more American would be no problem for me... Now, may I come in?"

Visconti moved aside and allowed his visitor to enter.

"You may close the door now, Louis. It will be a while before the police get here."

"You've called the police?" Visconti asked, reminded of the night he rescued Kerri and his ruse with Brian Pyper.

"No, but soon I will be inviting them here to investigate your death."

Visconti raised his hands in mock surrender. "Alfred, you wouldn't."

Schnieder nodded, the cold stare of his glazed hazel eyes confirming his resolve. "First I would like to tell you why I am going to kill you." He pointed to the chairs near the glass doors leading to the balcony. "Let's be seated. These old legs need rest."

Visconti focused on the muzzle of Schnieder's gun as he lowered himself into one of the two comfortable French provincial chairs, richly upholstered in light tan Corinthian leather. "Aren't you forgetting we had a deal?" he asked, attempting to postpone his execution.

"Please, no more insults to my intelligence. It is most rude. It is you who has forgotten, my friend. I once told Mike King I would trust you with my life. Now he is extremely displeased with both of us. He placed his trust in us, and we abused it. I am guilty of giving away his secret, and you are guilty of using it to steal his money."

"Forget the sentimental crap, Alfred. We've got the money now. Let's enjoy it. King can go to hell."

"That is an inaccurate statement, Louis," Schnieder said, shaking his head. "You have the money now, and clearly you had no intention of sharing it with me. Now I would appreciate if you would tell me where it is."

"In Switzerland," Visconti disclosed. "But that's all I'm going to tell you."

"Where in Switzerland?"

"Go ahead and shoot me? Then you'll never know where it is."

"That is precisely what I shall do. My primary purpose in coming here was to kill you. I had hoped I might also succeed in returning the money to the custody of Mike King and his wife, but if that is not to be, then there is nothing left to do but pull the trigger." He lifted his gun and pointed it at Visconti's head.

Visconti held up both hands and jerked backward. "Alfred, wait! It's in Geneva. It's in a numbered account in the Banco Privata Svissera. The control and access numbers in my briefcase."

"Where is the briefcase?"

"In the bathroom. I'll get it for you."

"Lead the way. I would like to make sure you get only the briefcase." Schnieder followed Visconti to the bathroom, but stopped at the door when he saw Kerri, leaning against the sink and washing blood from her mouth. "My goodness, Louis! What have we here?" he asked, frowning as he glanced at the briefcase, the drill and droplets of blood on the floor. "Is there no end to your treachery?" Schnieder gave Kerri a golden smile. "Please don't be frightened by the gun, my dear. I intend only to use it on Louis."

"Give it to me," Kerri demanded, glaring with passionate hatred at Visconti. "I'll do it for you."

Gesturing with his hands, Visconti again attempted to delay his execution. "Alfred, this is Kerri... Kerri, this is Alfred Schnieder."

Schnieder shook his head. "It would be a pleasure to watch you kill him, my dear, but it is one that I have reserved for myself." He turned to Visconti. "I see you have alienated her as well, Louis. It would seem you have no friends left in this world." He pointed to the briefcase. "Give me the banking documents, Louis. I would like to make certain they are in order before I kill you."

Visconti lifted the briefcase from the floor, pretended to try to open it, then looked up at Schnieder. "It won't open. The dials are stuck."

"He's lying !" Kerri shouted. "I just broke the lock with the drill!"

Visconti held the briefcase in front of him while continuing to work at moving the shattered dials. He moved closer to Schneider. "I'm not fooling. They really are stuck. Try it yourself."

With cat quickness, he hurled the briefcase at Schnieder's face, distracting him long enough to allow him to lunge and grasp Schnieder's right wrist. He smashed the back of Schnieder's hand against the door jamb repeatedly until his bleeding hand released its grip, allowing the pistol to fall to the tile floor with a loud clatter.

Visconti picked it up and pointed it at Schnieder's forehead. "Now you old fart, the pleasure is mine, but maybe this old Luger makes too much noise." He lowered the gun and placed it in his pocket. "I think we'll do it more quietly." He placed his hands around Schneider's wrinkled neck and squeezed hard. Schnieder's eyes bulged as Visconti's thumbs dug into his Adam's apple. He gasped for air and struggled vainly, his strength no match for Visconti's. When the struggling stopped and Visconti was certain Schnieder was dead, he released his grip, allowing the lifeless body to slump to the floor.

Kerri watched in horror as Visconti dragged the body toward the shower stall. She darted toward the doorway, but Visconti dropped the body and reached the doorway before her. He grabbed both of her arms and pulled her toward him. "You're not going anywhere, sweetheart. We're going to finish what we started before that fat fart interrupted us."

Kerri realized she faced certain death. She fought ferociously, kicking, scratching and screaming until Visconti clenched his fist and hit her mouth as hard as he could. While she covered her face and moaned in pain, he dragged her to the point on the floor where he had begun to attack her, then pulled her down with him. He removed her jeans and panties, then unbuckled his belt, pulled down his zipper and lowered his pants. With a firm grip on both of her wrists, he pinned them to the floor on either side of her head, then separated her legs with both of his knees.

She screamed at the excruciating pain of his entry. The warm saline taste of blood on her tongue nauseated her as she helplessly allowed her body to go limp. A loathing fury grew inside her as she watched him revel in his sadistic pleasure. She turned her head sideways in revulsion when he lowered his body to the point where his lips were within inches of hers. As he approached orgasm, he moved his body faster, thrusting harder and moaning with each stroke.

Kerri slowly moved her right hand to the cord of the electric drill, then pulled it until she could reach the drill. She tightened her grip on the handle and waited until Visconti closed his eyes at the moment of his maximum pleasure. With all of her strength she rammed the cobalt tipped bit into the left side of his head and pulled the trigger. Visconti's eyes and mouth popped open and his body rigidified as the bit ground deeply into his brain. Even though the spinning bit caused blood from the wound to splatter her face and hair, she continued to hold the trigger and press until the chuck hit Visconti's outer skull, preventing further entry.

When his body finally fell limp, she felt its full weight on hers. With almost supernatural strength, born of fright and revulsion, she managed to move from beneath him. She rolled onto her stomach, then tried to lift herself to her knees. Her vision blurred as she slumped to the floor, exhausted. Seconds later, she fell into unconsciousness.

When Kerri's eyes opened thirty minutes later, her pain reminded her of what had happened. She managed to crawl to the sink and hoist herself to a semi erect position. When she looked in the mirror, she was horrified by the sight of heavy bruising and dried blood on her face and hair. She washed off the blood with a warm washcloth, then glanced toward the shower stall through the mirror. The sight of Schnieder's body induced a quick dismissal of her desire to shower. She gagged at the sight of

Visconti's bloodied head, the drill still lodged in its left temporal region. She shifted her focus to the briefcase, its contents strewn on the floor.

Suppressing an overwhelming urge to run, she lowered herself to her knees and crawled to the briefcase and examined the contents. She found a hundred thousand dollars in cash, documents relating to a numbered account in the Banco Privata Svissera, the deeds to Visconti's Manhattan apartment and his Connecticut estate, the corporate seal and share certificates of Forta Equitas, S.A., an itemized list of Visconti's personal investments, and a copy of the agreement he had made with her before leaving for Europe.

She forced herself to wash her finger prints from the drill, and to replace them with those of Visconti. She stuffed the cash, the banking documents and corporate seal and share certificates of Forta Equitas into her bag, then escaped from the bathroom. After dressing in clean clothing, she left the hotel, took a taxi to the Banque de Monte Carlo and returned the stolen items to her safety deposit box. As soon as she returned to the hotel, she called the police.

CHAPTER 96

Horst Ullman, the detective in charge of the investigation, subjected Kerri to an intense interrogation. A tall muscular Arian with deep blue eyes and close cropped blond hair, he spoke reasonably good English, accented with what Kerri thought was a German dialect. He stopped his questioning as soon as she told him of the rape. "You should be taken to the hospital immediately. Please don't worry. Monaco's medical facilities are among the finest in the world. As soon as I finish with my investigation here, I will join you at the hospital. There are a number of questions I would like you to answer." He took her by the arm and led her to the door of the suite, then asked one of his assistants to take her to the Princess Grace Hospital Center.

After a thorough examination, semen samples taken and facial cuts treated, Kerri was allowed to take a shower. She was invited to watch television in the doctors' lounge while she waited for Ullman to join her.

When Ullman arrived an hour and a half later, he led her to a private room to continue the interrogation. "May I call you Kerri?" he asked.

She nodded.

"I have found it necessary to quarantine your hotel suite pending further investigation. I assume you would prefer not to return to that suite in any event. We have made arrangements with the hotel to have you moved to a different suite. The transfer of all of your belongings not critical to the investigation will be completed by the time you return to the hotel. Of course we will provide you with a complete list of everything we confiscate."

"Thank you," she said, attempting to smile.

"Now I must ask you an extremely personal question. I am curious to know why Mister Visconti raped you. It seems a rather odd way to treat a woman who was living with him voluntarily."

"I really wasn't living with him voluntarily," she said, then proceeded to tell Ullman the entire story of her father, Alfred Schnieder, the trust, and finally, her relationship with Visconti. "Shortly after we arrived in Monte Carlo, Louis discovered that I'm Mike King's daughter. It didn't take him long to figure out that I was a serious threat to his retirement plans."

"How did he make this discovery?"

"He found a photograph of my father and mother in my luggage. He wanted to know why I had a picture of Mike King. I told him I had kept the photograph because it was of my mother. When he..."

"Excuse me," Ullman interrupted. "Was it your mother?"

Kerri nodded.

"Please continue."

"When Louis asked me if I knew the man with her, I told him I didn't. There was no way I wanted him to know. I thought he believed me, but evidently he didn't. Then he found my birth certificate and went crazy. He hit me and started to rape me. He said he was going to kill me when he finished. I think it was his idea of sadistic closure." Kerri lowered her head and covered her face with her hands. "You know the rest of the story," she said as tears filled her eyes.

Ullman nodded. "And the electric drill? Perhaps you could explain that."

"The lock on Louis's briefcase was jammed. He used the drill to open it," Kerri lied.

"Were you aware of the contents of the briefcase?"

"No."

"Did you touch any of the items in the briefcase?"

"No," she lied again.

361

"Do you know why Alfred Schnieder was in your suite?"

Kerri proceeded to tell Ullman the story of Schnieder's arrival, of their argument and of the confrontation resulting in Schnieder's murder.

Ullman stood and extended his hand. "Thank you. You've been most helpful. I regret to inform you that you will be detained in Monaco at least until we have completed a full investigation of this matter. We will return your passport once the investigation is completed and you are cleared. I have a car waiting outside. You will be driven back to the hotel. If you think of anything else you should have told me, please do not hesitate to call me." He gave her his card, then locked his eyes on hers. "By the way, did you ever find the money?"

Kerri shook her head. "Believe me, I tried. I searched through every inch of that suite. I couldn't find a single thing to suggest Louis even had it."

Ullman smirked. "Hiding money is our national sport. Please come with me. I'll take you to the car."

Ullman's statement served as a powerful reminder to Kerri of what she still had to do. Even though Louis Visconti no longer stood between her and the money, her father still faced an enormous problem. She now knew where the stolen millions was, but she had to hide it before the police found it. Irrespective of how much remained, it represented the physical evidence the Feds needed to convict her father.

Kerri entered the lobby of the hotel, looked around to make sure no one was watching her, then hurried to a pay telephone and called the operator. "I want to place a collect call to Mike King, in Ontario, Canada. She gave the number to the operator, then her heart pounded as she heard the phone to ring seven times.

"I'm sorry," the operator said. "There's no answer at that number. Do you wish to try a different number?"

"Yes. I'd like to place a collect call to Dan Turner, in Toronto." She gave Turner's number to the operator.

Turner's secretary accepted the charges, then transferred the call to Turner.

"Kerri, I'm so glad you called," Turner said. "I presume you tried to call your father."

"Yes. Is he still on the island?"

"No... Unfortunately, he was arrested early this morning. Someone saw lights on the island last night and called the police. They checked out the lead and found your father. He's been jailed and charged with obstructing justice. I hope to be able to get him out soon, but I'm going to have a little difficulty explaining his behavior. He left his car at Pearson Airport before he went to the island, presumably to make the police believe he had left the country. Of course they found it. That, together with Phillip's latest statement, makes him look very guilty. In that connection, I'm scheduled to meet tomorrow morning with a heavy hitter from Ottawa. Doubtless he'll have a team of lawyers and they'll all be breathing fire. You have to understand that these people are convinced that your father knows exactly where the money is, and that he's been hiding it since Jim Servito died. "

"Damn! So what do you think is going to happen?"

"He's in deep trouble, Kerri, and I'm running out of options. Unfortunately, he's going to spend some time in prison."

"Is there any way I can talk to him privately?"

"Only one. Through me."

"Then please give him a message. Both Louis Visconti and Alfred Schnieder are dead."

"What! How did that happen?"

Kerri told Turner the story of her traumatic experience in the Hotel de Paris, and of her rescue of the cash and banking documents related to Visconti's numbered account at the Banco Privata Svissera in Geneva.

"That's breathtaking!" Turner declared. "You certainly are your father's daughter. I think you're both genetically attracted to excitement. I'll definitely give him your message, and I'm sure he'll be delighted to hear it. When will you be returning to New York?"

"I don't know. The police have my passport. I can't leave until they've completed the investigation."

"Surely they don't suspect you."

"I don't know if they do or not. They didn't say."

"Are you still at the Hotel de Paris?"

"Yes."

"Stay there. I'm going to have a lawyer from our Geneva office contact you. His name is Pierre Lambert. He's one of the best criminal lawyers in Europe. I'm sure I don't have to remind you of the importance of doing exactly as he says and keeping the location of the money a secret. Doing so is your father's only hope. If the Feds find it, he'll have none."

"I understand."

"Good. Keep your chin up, Kerri. We're going to get you out of there."

"Thanks, Dan. There's one more thing I want you to tell my father."

"What's that?"

"Before Louis died, he told me he had Philip killed."

"I'm very sorry to hear that... If you don't mind, I'd like to delay giving your father that message. At this point, I don't think he needs any more bad   news."

CHAPTER 97

Monaco. September 21. 9:00 A.M.

A brief but heavy rain had drenched the principality earlier that morning. The streets were still wet when Pierre Lambert eased his shiny black BMW to a stop in front of the Hotel de Paris. A young valet changed places with Lambert and whisked his car off to the parking area.

Lambert, a sharp featured dark haired man in his early forties, hurried into the hotel and proceeded directly to Kerri's suite. He knocked on the door, then fastened the middle button of the jacket to his dark blue suit and straightened his blue and yellow striped tie. He took a half a step backward when Kerri opened the door. "Hello," he said, offering a polite smile and forcing himself to ignore the swelling and cuts near her mouth. "... Are you Kerri Pyper?"

Kerri gave him a slow expressionless nod.

"I'm Pierre Lambert. Dan Turner has asked me to represent you."

"Hi. Please come in," Kerri said with a big smile, then opened the door wider. "You're early. I wasn't expecting you until noon."

"I'm sorry for that. I didn't expect to finish with the Monaco police so soon."

Kerri poured a black coffee for Lambert, then led him to the living room, anxious to hear what he had to say.

"This is good coffee," he said as he lifted the cup and took a second sip. "May I call you Kerri?"

"Only if I can call you Pierre."

"It's a deal," Lambert said, leaning back and appearing relaxed. "With considerable difficulty, I was able to convince the police to allow me to

365

review the contents of Louis Visconti's briefcase. I want to discuss those with you shortly, but first I want to talk about what wasn't in the briefcase. Dan Turner told me you removed several items."

"Yes. A hundred thousand dollars in cash, some banking documents, share certificates, and a corporate seal."

"Where did you put those items?"

"In a safety deposit box."

"Are you confident the police are unaware that you are in possession of those items?"

"Yes."

"Do you think they suspect you've hidden something?"

"I don't know."

"When did you leave the hotel with them?"

"Between the time I killed Louis and when I contacted the police."

"How much time elapsed between those two events?"

"Less than two hours."

"Can we go to your safety deposit box? I'm not interested in the cash, but I want to see the banking documents as soon as possible. I'm sure you're aware of their potential importance."

Kerri removed the documents from her cotton bag and handed them to Lambert. "I assumed you'd want to see them, so I picked them up earlier this morning."

"Smart girl," Lambert quipped, then put on his spectacles and started to read. After no more than thirty seconds, he peered over the spectacles and smiled. "If the money is in the account specified here, you are an extremely wealthy woman."

"Why?"

"One of the items in the briefcase was an agreement, signed by both you and Louis Visconti. It contains a reciprocal survivorship clause entitling you to one hundred percent of everything he owns, in the event of his death. There were no other conditions." Lambert held up the banking documents. "These documents certify Louis Visconti's ownership of a numbered account in the Banco Privata Svissera."

Kerri's frown blossomed into a broad smile. "Are you telling me that I own all the money in that account?"

Lambert nodded. "Aside from the fact that it makes you an accessory to theft and tax evasion, that's what I'm telling you. Unfortunately, we won't be able to access the account until we can get our hands on that agreement. That won't be until the police have completed their investigation into the deaths of Louis Visconti and Alfred Schnieder. At the earliest, it could be weeks from..."

"I have a duplicate copy."

"You do? Where?"

"In New York. I left it with my lawyer."

"Wonderful. Please arrange to have him fax me a copy of it, I'll get a death certificate for Louis Visconti. Then with that agreement, a directive from you, and a death certificate for Louis Visconti, I can access the account. In the event we find any money, what would you like me to do with it?"

"Wire it to my boss in New York," Kerri said, excited and overjoyed.

"Who's your boss?"

"His name is Miles Dennis. He's with a commodity brokerage company called Iacardi & Sons." Kerri removed Dennis's business card from her wallet and gave it to Lambert. "Here's his address and telephone numbers. I'll call him and tell him what we're going to do."

"Do you trust Miles Dennis? You must understand that what you're doing is extremely dangerous. If the Monaco police discover that you've removed anything from Visconti's briefcase, you'll be in serious trouble. In addition to what I said earlier, they'll have reason to suspect you had a motive for killing Visconti."

"Of course I had a motive. I had to save my own life."

"That's apparent, but I'm sure you understand the need for secrecy... Now, I asked you if you can trust Miles Dennis."

"Absolutely. Miles is completely aware of why I'm here and what my objectives are. There are no secrets between us."

"Okay. Then I'll proceed as soon as I receive the fax from your lawyer."

"My lawyer is a she, Pierre. I'll call her this afternoon. Do you have a business card?"

Lambert gave her his card. "Now, as I said earlier in our discussion, I want to talk about the items in Visconti's briefcase. Who opened it?"

"I did. I used a drill."

"The same one you used to kill Visconti?"

"Yes. Why did you ask?"

"There's an inconsistency in your story. Ullman said you told him it was Visconti who opened the briefcase."

"That's right. I didn't want to implicate myself."

"Did Louis ever use that drill for any purpose, whatsoever?"

"No."

"Then we have a problem."

"What?"

"The police won't find Louis's finger prints on the handle of the drill."

"Yes they will. I cleaned mine and covered the handle with his prints after he raped me."

"You're very clever," Lambert said, obviously relieved. "I'm very impressed by your ability to think clearly in such difficult conditions."

"Thanks."

"Do you know anything about a company called Forta Equitas?"

"Yes. My father told me Visconti used all of the funds in the King's trust to buy the shares of that company from himself. That's why I took the corporate seal and share certificates out of Visconti's briefcase. Why?"

"It now belongs to you. In addition, you now own a house in Connecticut, an apartment in Manhattan, and what appears to be a substantial investment portfolio."

"That interests me, Pierre, because it might be useful in helping my father, but I know I can't do that until I get out of Monaco."

"Getting you out of Monaco is the main reason I'm here. I want you to tell me the entire story of your relationship with Louis Visconti and Alfred Schnieder. Start from the beginning. Take your time and don't leave anything out. I don't care how insignificant or trivial you think it is."

"I don't mind doing that, but why? Aside from hiding the money, and maybe being an accessory to theft and tax evasion, I haven't done anything wrong."

"You know that but no one else does. I suspect the police remain unconvinced of your innocence in the death of two men. Unless I can prove that to them, beyond a reasonable doubt, you could be convicted of murder. To convince them, I must know everything."

Kerri nodded, still shocked that she could in any way be considered responsible for what happened to Visconti and Schnieder. She exhaled, then began her story. She talked for an hour and a half, stopping only to answer Lambert's questions, or to wait while he referred to his notes.

Lambert gave Kerri a pensive stare. "I need to ask you one more question... Did you in any way plan to murder Louis Visconti?"

"No! I'm not the slightest bit sorry he's dead, but I never, ever planned to kill him."

"I believe you," Lambert said with a generous grin. "You gave me the answer I assumed you would give me." He stood, extended his hand, and gave Kerri a confident smile. "Leave the rest to me."

CHAPTER 98

Toronto. Thursday, September 27. 9:00 A.M.

"Give me your take on the confrontation in Monte Carlo last week," John Hill said to his friend, Alex McDowell. Both had spent the night at Toronto's King Edward Hotel and, by mutual agreement, had arrived for breakfast in the hotel's breakfast nook, just off the main lobby.

"Too early to break open the champagne. We still haven't found a dime."

"True, but you've got to believe Mike King knows exactly where the money is."

"You bet your ass we do, and we're going to put pressure on the courts to throw the book at him."

"You have enough to convict him?"

"Yup. We found him hiding out on an island north of Toronto. He left his car at Pearson, an obvious attempt to mislead us. We've also got his stepson's statement on tape. More than enough."

"You'll be happy to know we're pressuring the Monaco authorities to detain Visconti's girlfriend as long as possible. Did you know she's King's daughter?"

"Not until recently. Hell of a coincidence, isn't it?"

"It all fits, Alex. We think King and his daughter were wrapped up in some kind of deal with Visconti and Schnieder."

"How do you explain the fact that all hell broke loose after ten years of silence?"

"I won't even try. King and his daughter have the answer, and the more pressure we put on them, the sooner they're going to talk."

"How long can you keep King's daughter in Monaco?"

"I'll let you know. We're working through the back door on this one. Of course if they manage to convict her of murder, it'll be academic."

"Do they think she's guilty?"

"They don't know what to think. She really must have wanted Visconti dead. She put an electric drill bit through his brain. Maybe Schnieder wanted him dead also. It was his gun the police found at the scene."

"It's absolutely amazing what people will do for money."

"Maybe both of us should take a good look in the mirror," Hill replied.

An hour later, Dan Turner ushered both Hill and McDowell into the ornate boardroom of Turner, Peterson, Greenwell and Worthy on the 65th floor of Toronto's North American Bank Building. Coffee was served and the pleasantries were hurried.

"Would you mind if I taped this meeting, gentlemen?" Turner asked.

"We would," McDowell replied. "This meeting is exploratory. We want it off the record. We're here to negotiate, Mister Turner. As you know, we have your client behind bars, and we have every intention of keeping him there for a very long time. He's clearly demonstrated that he's a flight risk, so bail is out of the question."

"So what's to negotiate?" Turner asked, aware that his guests held all of the cards, and that he held virtually none.

"The money Jim Servito stole from our respective governments," Hill replied. "We suspect your client knows where it is, and that he has access to it. His recent actions have made that quite clear. Furthermore, his step son's statements have strongly supported our suspicion."

Turner decided to plunge with the use of a high risk tactic. He had nothing to lose. His weak bargaining position gave him no choice. "I'm not prepared to confirm nor deny that my client has, or has ever been aware of the location of the money Jim Servito stole from your respective governments, but for the sake of negotiation, suppose he was able to find it. How much would it take to free him, and for all the charges against him to be dropped?" he asked.

Hill and McDowell exchanged barely perceptible glances, then Hill glared at Turner. "Our calculations indicate that Servito stole over three hundred million. Conservatively, that amount would have doubled over the past ten years, so six hundred million gets our attention," he said.

Turner, the consummate professional, struggled to postpone a blink. "That amount closes your files, and all charges dropped?" he asked, aware that his client had no chance of getting his hands on anywhere close to that amount.

Both Hill and McDowell nodded.

"Why not give my client a break and round it out to five hundred million? Do I still have your attention?"

"Show us the money. We'll talk again," Hill replied, showing five fingers

CHAPTER 99

Monaco. Friday, September 28.

"Hi, Pierre," Kerri said, her middle and index fingers of both hands crossed.

Lambert stepped inside her suite and closed the door. He displayed a huge smile. "A numbered Iacardi account just received an injection of slightly more than one hundred and sixty-six million dollars?"

"Yes!" Kerri shouted, her waning confidence having received an enormous boost. "Thank you, Pierre. Thank you from the bottom of my heart."

"Congratulations. It took an enormous amount of courage to do what you've done. You're now my wealthiest client."

"I'll never see or touch that money, Pierre."

Lambert frowned. "On that subject, I just talked to Dan Turner. He regretted to inform me that he tried every trick in the book to get the charges against your father dropped, but couldn't. He said the Feds' influence was obvious. He speculated that they leaned on the court. They did it to put maximum pressure on your father to talk. Now here's the really bad news. He further advised me that if your father can turn over six hundred million to them, they'll drop the charges and close their files. They refused, however, to put it in writing."

Kerri closed her eyes and bit her lip. In spite of all of her efforts, including risking her life, she had nowhere near that amount. "I don't know my father very well, Pierre, but I'm sure even if they gave him a life sentence, he still wouldn't talk."

"Dan was delighted to hear that you had recovered the money. He said he would pass the information along to your father as soon as possible."

"Thank you. What about me? When am I going to be allowed to leave Monaco?'

"I don't know. I'm having a lot of difficulty getting answers from anyone. The police appear to be delaying any formal action on your case. Whenever I press the issue, they just tell me to be patient. I suspect they think you know where the money is."

"Will you call me as soon as you know anything? I'm really scared."

"I will. I suspect the delay is to get you to talk. I'm sure the Monaco police have been informed of the enormous amount of money involved in this case."

"Then I want you to get a message to my father as soon as possible. Tell him that hell will freeze before I breathe a word about that money to anyone."

"I'll certainly do that, but I'm confused. What could you possible hope to achieve by continuing to hide it?"

"I want my father to use it to negotiate with the Feds. Unfortunately, it's not   enough,   not   nearly   enough."

CHAPTER 100

"So what's with the collect call?" Miles jested. "I'm shocked that one of the wealthiest women in Europe can't afford to pay for a telephone call to New York."

Kerri laughed. "So deduct it from my salary."

"Congratulations. You continue to amaze me. You've done exactly what you said you were going to do. I knew you were a winner from the day I met you."

"I haven't done everything yet. I still have to get my dad out of prison. Then I need to get my ass out of this wonderland."

"Why is he in prison, and why can't you just leave?"

"Dad tried to dodge a subpoena by hiding on an island north of Toronto. The Feds found him and convicted him of obstruction of justice. I think I'm being detained here because of the money. Pierre Lambert thinks the Monaco Police are delaying action on my case to put pressure on me to tell them where it is."

"That infernal money! Everyone who touches it rolls snake-eyes."

"Well you're touching it now, Miles."

"What do you want me to do with it?"

"Make it grow."

"And how do you expect me to do that?"

"Short crude oil."

Dennis laughed. "Let me amend my last statement. Everyone who touches that money rolls snake-eyes and goes stark raving mad."

"I'm serious, Miles. I've had nothing to do but watch television for days. I'm convinced that the Kuwait problem is going to come to crashing end and crude oil is going to crash with it."

"You know we could lose it all."

"Yes, but what the hell do we have to lose?"

"Work with me on this. Please explain why a hundred and sixty-six million is nothing to lose."

"My only interest in that money is using it to clear my father. We need at least six hundred million to have any hope of doing that. If you can't pull off a miracle with that money, we might as well give it away to charity."

"How high do you want me to fly?"

"As high as you can. Back up the truck and bet the farm."

"What name do you want to put on the account?"

"Forta Equitas, S.A."

"What's that?"

"Visconti's company."

"Incredible!" Dennis declared. "Now I know you've gone stark raving mad. You've risked your life to give me a ton of money. Then you've told me it's useless unless I almost quadruple its value. Now you're telling me to put into an account for your dead boy friend."

"Forta Equitas is mine now. I inherited it from my dead boy friend... Have fun, Miles."

CHAPTER 101

Monaco. October 14. 11:00 A.M.

"I'll be there in a minute," Kerri shouted, then stepped from the shower. She hurried to put on her pink silk robe and ran to the door, her hair still wet and dripping.

Lambert met her with a frown. "May I come in?"

Her heart pounding, she clutched Lambert's arm and led him to a chair near the balcony. "Tell me what happened," she demanded, taking the seat next to him.

"If there was any doubt that the Monaco police are playing games with us, they put it to rest today. The good news is that Ullman told me that the government of Monaco strongly preferred to avoid the publicity of a murder trial. He also told me that forensics confirmed that Visconti strangled Schnieder, and that the medical evidence confirmed that Visconti raped you... The bad news is that he said they still aren't convinced that you don't know where the money is." Lambert's lips tightened, his eyes fixed on Kerri's. "We have to prove you don't, and I'm powerless to do that."

Lambert's statement hit Kerri like a sledge hammer. She too was powerless to do that, and unless she could, or unless Miles Dennis could perform a miracle, she was condemned to her Monaco prison, alone, scared, bored, and miserably unhappy.

CHAPTER 102

Ottawa. January 16, 1991. Seven P.M.

Alex McDowell, relaxing in the den of his suburban home, was stunned by what he saw and heard on his television set. Live from the window of the Hotel Al-Rasheed in downtown Baghdad, the excited voices of CNN reporters, Bernard Shaw, John Holliman and Peter Arnett described the night sky, ablaze with tracers, and the city, disrupted by the explosions of Tomahawk missiles and smart bombs.

His telephone rang minutes later. He answered, annoyed by the interruption and anxious to return to the unfolding drama in Iraq.

"Alex, It's John Hill. Sorry to bother you. I had to call. I have extremely interesting news."

"Well give it to me fast. I want to get back to the extremely important news on my television set."

"I just got a call from one of our treasury people in Europe. He just came from a meeting with a man by the name of Olaf Leutweiler, the president of the Weisscredit Bankhaus in Geneva. Leutweiler claims his bank just received a deposit of exactly five hundred million dollars. He said a lawyer by the name of Pierre Lambert marched into his office with a bank draft for that amount."

McDowell smirked. "You think King kept any for himself?"

"Wouldn't blame him if he did?"

"Nor would I... Goodnight, John."

"Goodnight,   Alex."

CHAPTER 103

Millhaven, Ontario. January 31. 11:55 A.M.

The air was bitter cold. Nearly a foot of snow had blanketed the ground and fierce north west winds howled across the ice encrusted shores of Lake Ontario. Parked near the imposing gates to Millhaven minimum security prison was Dan Turner's jet black Mercedes 300SE. He had kept the motor running to preserve heat. Karen sat beside Turner in the front seat, Kerri huddled under a blanket in the back. All three strained to focus on the gate.

Sharp at noon, the massive chain link gate began to move. Seconds later, a man wearing jeans, a brown leather jacket and a black baseball cap appeared in the opening. He hung his head to allow the rim of his cap to shield his face from the driving snow, then trudged toward Turner's car.

Kerri tapped Karen's shoulder. "You go."

Karen bolted from car and ran to Mike. She wrapped her arms around him and squeezed. "I missed you, King," she cried, tears flowing from her eyes and nearly freezing on her cheeks.

Mike dropped the small black canvas bag he was carrying and hugged Karen, thrilled to see her and grateful to be free. "I missed you too, Babe, more than you'll ever know."

She smiled. "There's someone in the car who's pretty anxious to see you."

Kingston, Ontario. Thirty minutes later.

The four occupied a small circular table in The Loyalist, a small cozy restaurant near the shore the frozen Lake Ontario.

Mike placed his right arm around Kerri's shoulders. "I can't believe it. How did you do it?"

"Miles did most of it. I just told him to make it grow. He did the rest."

"How?"

"You'll laugh at the irony, dad. He shorted crude oil at forty dollars a barrel in early October. He was within a hair of the top of the market."

Mike smiled, closed his eyes and shook his head.

Turner lifted a champagne bottle and topped up everyone's glass. "So, what are the unpredictable King's going to do with all this money?"

"What money?" Mike asked. "I thought we gave it all to the Feds."

"We sold Visconti's house, his apartment and his portfolio for a little over fifty million," Kerri said, then poked Karen's arm with her finger.

Karen reached for into her purse and removed a check. "You'll love this," she said, then handed it to Mike. "It's a cashier's check for five million dollars, made out to the estate of James Servito. It arrived in the mail in early October with no note or return address. Dan suggested we keep it until you got out of prison."

Mike stared at the check with a puzzled expression, then his quizzical frown transformed into a knowing smile. "Schnieder! The old fox kited five million from the trust!"

"What would you like to do with the shares of Forta Equitas, dad?" Kerri asked, barely able to conceal her excitement.

Mike laughed at the apparent sarcasm of her question. "Put them in an envelope and send them to Mara, Griesdorf and Visconti. Tell them to paper the walls of Visconti's office with them."

"You might not want to do that," Kerri warned.

"Why?"

"I did some horse trading with the Feds," Turner said. "I told them I would arrange an anonymous deposit of five hundred million dollars to credit their account, if they would drop the charges against your father, close the file, and put it in writing. They agreed and that's exactly what we gave them... Miles had a hundred and eighty-six million left over when he covered the short."

Mike rolled his eyes and raised his hands above his shoulders in a gesture of total surrender. "I don't want to know about it and I never want to hear about that money again." He stood and kissed Kerri's forehead. "You keep it," he whispered. "You earned every dime."

Turner refilled all four glasses, then raised his glass to eye level. "To the King family... Survivors, one and all," he declared.

With smiles and loud clinks, all four brought their glasses together. "To the King family," they repeated in unison.

THE END

Be sure to read

KERRI'S WAR

VOLUME THREE OF THE KING TRILOGY

Printed in Poland
by Amazon Fulfillment
Poland Sp. z o.o., Wrocław